SHE'S GOING TO PAY

Books by Alexandra Ivy

Guardians of Eternity
WHEN DARKNESS COMES
EMBRACE THE DARKNESS
DARKNESS EVERLASTING
DARKNESS REVEALED
DARKNESS UNLEASHED
BEYOND THE DARKNESS
DEVOURED BY DARKNESS
BOUND BY DARKNESS
FEAR THE DARKNESS
DARKNESS AVENGED
HUNT THE DARKNESS
WHEN DARKNESS ENDS
DARKNESS RETURNS
BEWARE THE DARKNESS
CONQUER THE DARKNESS
SHADES OF DARKNESS
DARKNESS BETRAYED
BEWITCH THE DARKNESS
STALK THE DARKNESS
SATE THE DARKNESS

The Immortal Rogues
MY LORD VAMPIRE
MY LORD ETERNITY
MY LORD IMMORTALITY

Magic for Hire
WILD MAGIC
ANCIENT MAGIC
ETERNAL MAGIC

Ares Security
KILL WITHOUT MERCY
KILL WITHOUT SHAME

Romantic Suspense
PRETEND YOU'RE SAFE
WHAT ARE YOU AFRAID OF?
YOU WILL SUFFER
THE INTENDED VICTIM
DON'T LOOK
FACELESS
UNSTABLE
DESPERATE ACTS
THE MURDER CLUB
SHE'S GOING TO PAY

Historical Romance
SOME LIKE IT WICKED
SOME LIKE IT SINFUL
SOME LIKE IT BRAZEN

The Sentinels
BORN IN BLOOD
BLOOD ASSASSIN
BLOOD LUST

And don't miss these Guardians of Eternity novellas

TAKEN BY DARKNESS in YOURS FOR ETERNITY
DARKNESS ETERNAL in SUPERNATURAL
WHERE DARKNESS LIVES in THE REAL WEREWIVES
OF VAMPIRE COUNTY
LEVET (ebook only)
A VERY LEVET CHRISTMAS (ebook only)

And don't miss these Sentinel novellas

OUT OF CONTROL
ON THE HUNT

Published by Kensington Publishing Corp.

SHE'S GOING TO PAY

ALEXANDRA IVY

KENSINGTON PUBLISHING CORP.
kensingtonbooks.com

KENSINGTON BOOKS are published by

Kensington Publishing Corp.
900 Third Avenue
New York, NY 10022

Copyright © 2025 by Debbie Raleigh

All rights reserved. No part of this book may be reproduced in any form or by any means without the prior written consent of the Publisher, excepting brief quotes used in reviews.

Without limiting the author's and publisher's exclusive rights, any unauthorized use of this publication to train generative artificial intelligence (AI) technologies is expressly prohibited.

This book is a work of fiction. Names, characters, businesses, organizations, places, events, and incidents either are the product of the author's imagination or are used fictitiously. Any resemblance to actual persons, living or dead, events, or locales is entirely coincidental.

To the extent that the image or images on the cover of this book depict a person or persons, such person or persons are merely models and are not intended to portray any character or characters featured in the book.

All Kensington titles, imprints, and distributed lines are available at special quantity discounts for bulk purchases for sales promotion, premiums, fundraising, educational, or institutional use.

Special book excerpts or customized printings can also be created to fit specific needs. For details, write or phone the office of the Kensington Sales Manager: Kensington Publishing Corp., 900 Third Avenue, New York, NY 10022. Attn. Sales Department. Phone: 1-800-221-2647.

The K with book logo Reg. U.S. Pat. & TM Off

ISBN: 978-1-4967-5547-6

ISBN: 978-1-4967-5548-3 (eBook)

First Kensington Books Trade Paperback Printing: November 2025

10 9 8 7 6 5 4 3 2 1

Printed in the United States of America

The authorized representative in the EU for product safety and compliance is eucomply OU, Parnu mnt 139b-14, Apt 123 Tallinn, Berlin 11317, hello@eucompliancepartner.com.

SHE'S GOING TO PAY

Chapter 1

June 2016
Canton, MO

"Case dismissed."

Bam. The smash of the gavel added an exclamation at the end of the judge's statement.

And that was that.

The nine-month nightmare ended with one resounding thud.

On cue, the avid spectators surged to their feet, their cheers, protests, and gasps of disbelief creating an incoherent babble. Jesse Hudson blocked out the sound as she pushed her way through the crowd that had gathered in tight knots to discuss the abrupt conclusion to the scandal that had rocked Canton, Missouri, a sleepy little college town on the banks of the Mississippi River.

Her neighbors might be packed in the old courthouse, with its layers of dark wood paneling and rows of uncomfortable benches, to enjoy the spectacle of Mac Hudson being charged with the murder of his wife, Victoria Ralston Hudson, and stepdaughter, Tegan Ralston, but for Jesse it had been a matter of life or death. Literally.

"Dad." Leaning across the wooden barrier, she tapped her father on the back of his shoulder to gain his attention.

Mac Hudson slowly turned, and Jesse struggled to hide a dismay. Her dad had always been a large man with a barrel chest and a laugh that could fill the room. He'd never been handsome. His features were too blunt and his jowls too heavy, but there'd been an engaging charm in his ready smile. That charm was one of many reasons that his bar—the Tap Room—had been such a success over the years.

Now he looked worn. Not just because he'd lost weight. Or because his blond hair had receded from his forehead. The months since his second wife and stepdaughter had mysteriously disappeared had drained his very soul, sucking away the joy that once twinkled in his eyes.

"I told you." Her words came out in a fierce burst. "I knew this stupid farce would never go to trial."

His smile didn't reach his eyes. "I'm glad one of us was so certain."

"There was never a doubt. Never."

Mac released a shaky sigh. "What would I do without you?"

"Starve, for one thing. Lucky for you, I have a pot of your favorite chili in the Crock-Pot and a skillet of corn bread waiting to go into the oven."

Her dad groaned. "Oh God, after three months of jail food that sounds like heaven."

Jesse stepped back. "Then let's go."

"I can't. Not yet."

Jesse's heart stopped, instantly assuming the worst. Who could blame her? There'd been one horrible shock after another.

"Why not? Is something wrong?"

"Not wrong, but annoying. My lawyer warned me that there would be a pile of paperwork I would need to read and sign if they let me go today. I assume it's his way of earning his outrageous fee." His gaze drifted to the gathered crowd, a shudder racing through his body that was wrapped in a suit two sizes too large. "Besides, I'd rather wait for the gawkers to drift away before showing my face in public again."

Jesse glanced over her shoulder. The windows of the courtroom were large and arched, but the glass was frosted to mute the late-afternoon sunlight, leaving the dozen or so stragglers in gray shadows. Like black-and-white silhouettes.

One form remained apart from the others, openly glaring in their direction. The short, heavyset man wearing a deputy's uniform stood with his hands planted on his hips, close enough to the handgun holstered at his side to be an unspoken warning.

Adam Tillman was only five years older than Jesse, who'd turned nineteen a month ago, but he looked at least twice her age. His round, pudgy face was twisted into a jaded expression, as if he harbored a general dislike for the world. Plus, there was something sinister about his squinty eyes.

Okay, Jesse might be a tad prejudiced against the deputy. He was the one who'd spent the past months digging up evidence against her father, even though she'd sworn under oath he'd never left the bar that night.

She didn't know if he'd held a personal grudge against Mac Hudson, or if he'd somehow sensed that Jesse wasn't being entirely honest. Whatever the case, he was a total jerk.

She turned back to meet her dad's weary gaze. "Who cares about them?"

"I do." He reached out to tug the end of her silvery-blond ponytail. "And if you're honest, so do you."

"Nothing matters but having you home where you belong," she insisted.

He shook his head. "I'm not so sure about that. Not anymore."

"Not sure about what?"

"Home being where I belong."

She frowned. "What does that mean?"

"Maybe it's time for a change." His voice was suddenly strained. "A new start."

"Dad? Are you okay?"

His jaw clenched before he gave a sharp shake of his head. "Don't mind me. I'm just relieved this is over."

"Really and truly over," she said, as much to reassure herself as her father.

"Go home, Jesse." Leaning forward, Mac brushed a kiss over the top of her head. "I'll see you soon."

She nodded, trying to ignore the darkness in his eyes. "Don't worry. Everything's going to be fine."

But it wasn't.

Not ever again.

August 2025
Chicago, IL

The nightclub reeked of stale cigarette smoke and cheap cologne. Jesse wrinkled her nose as she strolled past the long bar that was reflected in the smoky, mirrored wall behind it. On the other side of the space was a small, sunken dance floor framed by low booths with peeling plastic seats. The walls were hidden behind the crimson wallpaper that was faded to a dull orange. And above the dance floor was a glass booth for the DJ.

The place had been shuttered for months, but it wasn't just neglect that caused the crumbling dust and sagging decay.

Everything about it was fake.

From the vinyl tiles on the floor, to the drop ceiling that was stained from leaks in the roof, to the metal finishings that had been coated with gold spray paint. It was all a sham. Worse, Jesse suspected it was indication that the entire building was dodgy. The electricity, the plumbing, not to mention the actual structure.

"Well?"

The low male voice brushed over her as smooth as velvet. With a tiny shiver, Jesse turned to glance at her companion. It'd been six months since Parker Moreau had taken a job at the club in downtown Chicago where she was currently employed as a bartender.

He'd been a perfect fit for the hipster vibe of the place, with the halo of brown curls that framed his heart-shaped face and tall, slender body. Add in the intense sexuality that smoldered in his mesmerizing black eyes and he'd been a customer favorite within the first week.

Jesse was the opposite of a hipster. Her blond hair was chopped into a short, pixie style when she'd left home years ago, and several tattoos had been added to her slender body as she'd moved from one city to another. The only things that remained of the naïve girl who'd fled her nightmares were the large, hazel eyes and the silver pickup truck that had once belonged to her dad.

Thankfully, her skill as a bartender meant she could get a job at the clubs that were willing to pay a decent wage, along with customers who were generous with their tips.

And even more thankfully, Parker had ignored the hundreds of women who'd done their best to capture his attention. For whatever reason, he'd focused solely on Jesse, as if he'd been as gutted as she'd been at their first meeting. Jesse had never believed in instalove. Sure, she'd been in lust at first glance, but love? Nah. Not until Parker.

One month after he'd arrived in Chicago, Parker had moved into her cramped trailer, which she'd parked at a campground an hour north of the city. Now they were preparing to take the next step in their relationship.

A huge, terrifying step.

Jesse swallowed the sudden lump in her throat. "It's rough."

"A work in progress," he corrected.

She glanced at the ceiling that was sagging beneath the weight of the disco lights.

"More work than progress." She forced a smile as the expression of anticipation on his beautiful face started to dim. "Just like us."

"Which are we? The work or the progress?"

She stepped forward, placing her palms flat on Parker's chest. She could feel the damp perspiration beneath his silk shirt. It was smothering in the building without air-conditioning. Chicago was currently baking in the late August heat, adding layers of humidity to the high temperature.

"Both," she murmured.

Parker bit his lower lip. It was sexy as hell. "You're not as excited as I'd hoped you would be."

"I'm excited. It's just that I'm trying to be practical." She slid her hands over his chest in a soothing gesture. "One of us has to be."

"I thought this was our dream?" Parker wrapped his arms around her waist, tugging her against his body, which was surprisingly hard. Beneath his expensive clothes, he was all toned sinew and muscle. A benefit of his morning runs, which could last a solid three hours. Jesse thought he was crazy to put in so much effort, but then again, she thoroughly appreciated the results. "How many nights have we bitched that we're wasted slaving away for employers who don't have a fraction of our vision or talent?"

"It's what employees do. We go to work and bitch about working."

"Maybe, but why be minimum wage drones making our bosses rich when that money could be in our pockets?"

He wasn't wrong. She was increasingly tired of working for other people. But that didn't mean she wanted to blindly leap into the abyss. Especially an abyss that smelled like sweaty armpits.

"And if it fails?"

"It won't."

"But if it does?"

"Then we pick ourselves up and start over." He brushed his lips over her mouth. "It wouldn't be the first time. For either of us."

She shivered in pleasure. "That's true."

Lifting his head, he studied her with a brooding expression. "What's really bothering you, Jesse?"

She glanced around the room with its tacky décor and abruptly realized exactly why she was reluctant to take the plunge. This place was a sleazy shadow of the business her grandfather and father had built. The Tap Room had never been fancy, but it was solid and cozy, with a welcoming atmosphere to everyone who walked through the front door. It was genuine quality, from top to bottom.

"If our dream is to renovate an old bar and run it together, then I already own one." The words came out in a strange croak. She hadn't considered reopening the Tap Room. Not until this moment. "There's no need to buy anything else."

Parker's brows snapped together. Was he annoyed by her suggestion? "But then it would be your bar and I would always be an intruder."

"You'd never be—"

"Don't, Jesse. In your heart, the Tap Room belongs to your family." He tugged her closer. "You told me a dozen times how your great-great-grandfather cut the lumber that was used to construct the original mercantile shop. And how your great-grandfather changed the store into a bar after he came home at the end of World War II. And how your father asked your mother to marry him by inviting the entire town to the bar to sing her favorite karaoke song when she said yes."

An unexpected longing tugged at her heart. "Is that so bad?"

"No, but eventually you would resent any change I might want to make." He gazed down at her upturned face. "Plus, do you really want to go back to the place you've spent so many years running from?"

She stepped back. She didn't know why she was annoyed. He was right. She didn't want to think about changes to the family bar. Even if they came from the man she loved. And she certainly didn't want to move back to Canton. But he'd been urging her to cut ties with her past for weeks. As if it was as easy as handing a real estate agent the keys to the Tap Room and walking away.

"You're asking me to go back anyway."

"Only for a few days." He ignored her petulant tone, gently wrapping her back in his arms. "Just long enough to get the paperwork started on your inheritance and to put the bar up for sale. Then we can start a new life with a clean slate." He flashed the sexy smile that made her tingle in all the right places. "With a business we can build together. For our future."

With a sigh, Jesse leaned into him, laying her head on his chest. "I like the sound of a future together."

He stiffened, easily sensing her hesitation. "But?"

"But it's hard to think about selling my dad's bar. It's my family legacy."

"You'd rather it sit empty until it rots into oblivion?"

"Of course not."

"Then it's going to have to be taken care of eventually." He hooked a finger beneath her chin, forcing her to meet his steady gaze. "Unless you think your father is coming back?"

Nine years of practice kept her from releasing the howl of agony that she kept trapped in the center of her being.

"No."

"Think of what your father would have wanted, Jesse. You owe it to him to make sure his beloved bar is open to the customers who enjoyed spending time there, not boarded up and abandoned."

Jesse flinched. It felt like a low blow. "And of course it's exactly what you want as well."

He sighed, as if trying not to be offended by her less than subtle accusation. "What I want is a chance to create something special. With you. And that's going to take more money than we can save no matter how many hours we work." His fingers traced the stubborn line of her jaw. "Is that wrong?"

Jesse had never thought she'd be one of those women who'd do anything for love. Men were a dime a dozen. But then Parker had walked into her life.

Now she was convinced she'd lie, cheat, and steal to keep this man.

Or even go back to the one place she'd avoided like the plague.

"No, it's not wrong," she assured him, laying her head back on his chest. "It's what I want too."

"You're sure?"

No. Not at all.

"Very sure." She forced out the words. "I'll go home."

He pressed his lips to the top of her head. "Do it quickly and come back to me. I don't want you gone a second longer than necessary."

She snuggled against him as a sudden chill raced over her. She didn't want to go back to Canton.

"You could come, you know."

He considered her offer before shaking his head. "Tempting, but I think I should stay here and start negotiations on this place." He glanced around the empty nightclub. "We don't want to risk having it snatched away."

"I don't think there's going to be a horde of snatchers." The words were out before she could halt them. It wasn't that she was opposed to starting a future with Parker. She just wasn't convinced this was the place to do it. "And please don't make any commitments until we know that the paperwork on the life insurance policy has been approved."

"Why wouldn't it be?"

"Red tape is always a pain in the ass. And sometimes it can take forever."

"Don't worry. I promise not to spend any money until I have your full approval."

There was an edge in his voice. She tilted back her head to study his delicate features. Was he angry? There was nothing to see, but fear bloomed in the center of her heart.

She'd lost everything. She couldn't lose Parker.

"Are you sure you can't come with me?" she urged.

"One of us needs to keep bringing in a paycheck. We're going to need every penny we can get our hands on."

She grimaced. "I suppose that's true."

He brushed a kiss over her forehead. "Let's go back to our place so we can have a proper goodbye."

A heat that had nothing to do with the sultry weather flowed through her like melted honey.

"What's a proper goodbye?"

"It starts with less clothes and ends with..." His lips pressed against her ear as he whispered exactly what he intended to do with her once she was naked.

Jesse growled in anticipation. "You had me at 'less clothes.'"

Chapter 2

June 2016
Canton, MO

Leaving the courthouse, Jesse returned to the apartment she shared with her father above the Tap Room. She didn't worry when the first hour passed. Her dad had said that he had paperwork to sign. And he no doubt had to collect his belongings from the jail, where he'd been held since his arrest almost three months before.

It was no lie when they claimed the wheels of justice ground slowly. Sometimes if felt as if they were stuck in place.

But as the second hour passed, and then the third, Jesse's patience snapped.

There were a dozen reasons he was late. There could be a snag in the paperwork. Or he might have run into a crowd of friends who insisted on congratulating him on his release. God knew he was outrageously popular around town. Everyone knew and liked Mac Hudson. Or he might have stopped by the cemetery to visit the grave of Jesse's mom. He claimed he always felt better after sharing his problems with love of his life. Even if she couldn't give him the answers he needed.

By the fourth hour, Jesse couldn't pretend that everything was fine.

Her father could be absent-minded, but he wasn't cruel. He knew that she was anxiously waiting for him to come home. He would call if he was going to be this late.

Leaving the bar, she returned to the courthouse, circling each block in case her father was taking a different route. Not that the sleepy college town with tree-lined, cobblestoned streets was large enough for him to stray too far away.

Most of the businesses, including the Tap Room, were built to overlook the mighty Mississippi River. The dozen or so stores and restaurants along Main Street catered mainly to the local citizens, although a few students occasionally ventured down from the college that was sprawled on the high bluff above town.

Ice inched down Jesse's spine as she stopped her hunt to glance toward the dome that gleamed in the late afternoon sunlight. It was the only thing visible of the college, looming over the town with a lofty arrogance.

The rigid separation between town and gown was alive and well in Canton, Missouri.

A lesson that her stepmother had learned too late.

With a shake of her head, Jesse turned toward the center of town, where a pale stone building with a red-tiled roof consumed the bulk of the public square. The courthouse had faded over the past hundred years, but it had the solid bulk of a structure that was going to be around another century.

Climbing the worn cement stairs, Jesse entered the building through the front door. The lobby was eerily empty. Not surprising, she told herself. It was past five o'clock and most of the offices were closed. But that didn't keep her heart from sinking.

A part of her was convinced her father would be sitting in one of the leather chairs, patiently waiting for the judge to finish the paperwork, or surrounded by friends. To accept he wasn't there felt like a physical blow.

"Are you here to gloat?"

Jesse cursed at the sound of the harsh voice. Of course she'd run into the one person she'd hoped to avoid when she came back to the courthouse. Slowly turning, she faced Deputy Adam Tillman.

"Excuse me?"

The pudgy face was hard with anger. "It's your fault a murderer is out there wandering around town instead of behind bars where he belongs."

She took a deliberate backward step. The deputy's habit of invading her personal space went beyond annoying to downright creepy.

"If you're referring to my father, he's free to wander around town because he's innocent." She forced a smile to her stiff lips. "And because your star witness admitted he was too far away and it was too dark for him to see any details of the crash. You know, the one that magically appeared after remaining silent for months, and only decided to testify that he'd seen my dad's truck after you'd charged him with a DUI?"

Adam's face flushed. "Who else would run her off the road? You were the one who testified that your father had argued with his wife. And that you watched your stepmother pack a bag and take off with her daughter in the middle of the night."

"Exactly. She packed up and left. Why would he kill her?"

"Because he didn't want her to go. Some men are like that." His squinty gaze took a slow survey of her slender body. "They think a woman is their property and she should stay in her place."

Jesse resisted the urge to shudder. She wasn't going to give the bastard the satisfaction of knowing he got under her skin.

"Not my dad."

"So you say."

"Yes, so I say. Along with the judge."

Adam sucked air between the gap in his front teeth, the whistling sound grating on Jesse's raw nerves.

Despite the difference in their age, they'd gone to school together. He was the sort of kid who tattled on his classmates, cheated on tests, and tried to peek into the girls' locker room. As far as she knew, no one liked him. Not even the teachers.

"Just as you say that you could swear on a Bible your father never left the bar," he mocked.

Jesse shrugged. "Exactly."

"As if you wouldn't lie your ass off to protect him."

She would. And she had. Not only about what had happened that night, but the reason for it. Just as she would continue to lie until her last dying breath.

"Unlike you, I had no need to manipulate evidence." She reminded the jerk of his attempt to coerce a witness. "My father's innocent, and the case against him was dismissed."

"That doesn't mean this is over. I'm gonna get him. One way or another."

Pasting a fake smile on her lips, Jesse strolled past the deputy, her skin crawling as she felt Adam's glare boring into the center of her back. The deputy was an idiot, but he currently held a position of power. One that came with a weapon and the license to use it.

Only a fool would push him too far.

Heading toward the back of the building where she assumed the judge had his office, Jesse was silently rehashing the unpleasant conversation when her musings were interrupted by the sound of someone clearing their throat.

"Excuse me."

Jesse halted, turning around to discover an older woman in a polyester suit and pearls heading toward her with a click of her low heels. Her silver hair was perfectly curled and sprayed into place like a helmet and her thin face was lined with wrinkles. Jesse had a vague memory of seeing the woman around Canton; what was her name? Rosemary.

Yes, Rosemary Something-or-other. "We're about to lock the building for the evening," Rosemary informed her. "I'm afraid you'll have to come back tomorrow if you need something."

Something that felt like panic flared through Jesse at the thought of the courthouse being locked up for the night. What if her dad was still inside? Maybe he'd passed out. Or had a heart attack from the stress. Or...

Jesse grimly shut down her spiraling fear. There was a perfectly reasonable explanation for why her father was missing.

There had to be.

"I'm looking for Mac Hudson." The words came out steady. Good for her. "He had a pretrial hearing in the courtroom earlier today and—"

"I know Mac," the woman interrupted Jesse's babbling. "He left a couple of hours ago."

"Are you sure?"

"I saw him myself." She pointed toward a nearby hallway. "He went out the side door to the parking lot."

Jesse glanced in the direction the woman indicated as if she expected her father to suddenly appear. It made sense for him to choose to leave by a different exit. There might have been reporters lurking around the front of the building. But what had he been doing for the past couple of hours?

"Was he alone?" she at last demanded.

The pencil-thin brows arched, as if confused by Jesse's questions. "His lawyer walked him to the door, but he went outside alone. Is there a problem?"

"No. No problem."

Jesse clenched her hands and scurried in the direction her father had left.

Where the hell was he?

Returning to the bar, Jesse paced through the public room. It was a long, rectangular space with a hand-carved bar on one side and a dozen round tables in the center of the floor. The ceiling was low and covered with copper tiles that had been salvaged from the original mercantile store, along with the wooden floorboards and red brick walls. At the back of the bar there was just enough space for a dartboard and two pool tables.

Usually by this hour, the place was buzzing with neon lights and country music and the background noise of clinking glasses as her father efficiently served the customers who poured through the doors as soon as their workday ended. The Tap Room was the go-to establishment in Canton for eighty years, and despite the ugly rumors swirling through town, the business had continued to thrive. Jesse wanted to believe that the locals trusted Mac Hudson. Even after his wife and stepdaughter disappeared in the early hours one morning only to have her fancy sports car end up crashed into a tree with splatters of blood on the driver's side seat and no sign of Victoria or Tegan. But it could be they were fascinated by the potential for a lurid scandal.

Whatever the case, they'd never been busier.

That was why Jesse had decided to keep the place closed for the week. As much as the town would want to celebrate Mac's release, she'd known that he needed a few days to recover. Plus, she'd wanted to spend some time alone with her dad. He'd been in jail for months. That was the longest they'd ever been separated. She'd genuinely missed his company.

Her pacing had taken her past the pool table when there was a soft tap on the back door. A heavy weight abruptly lifted from her, allowing her to suck in the first deep breath she'd taken since leaving the courthouse. Shaking off her sense of doom, Jesse hurried through the short hallway. She passed by the stairs that led down to the cellar before entering a cramped foyer. There was another set of stairs. These went up to the private apartment that was spread between the top two floors of the building.

Directly in front of her was a wooden door that opened into the alleyway.

It was for family use only.

"Dad?"

Fully expecting to see her father standing there with a sheepish grin, her heart plummeted at the sight of the short, squat woman with shoulder-length reddish hair that was pulled back with a headband. She had a round face that was streaked with flour that matched the dusting that covered her loose sundress. Her eyes were a warm brown that twinkled with kindness. Beatrice "Bea" Hartman had owned the diner next to the Tap Room since Jesse was just a baby. Over the years, they'd developed a relationship that was closer to family than friendship. Honestly, she didn't know how she or her father would have survived over the years without Bea's steady presence.

"Oh." She forced a smile to her lips. "Hi, Bea."

"Now I don't mean to interrupt your homecoming, but I baked Mac's favorite pie and I wanted to bring it by when it was fresh out of the oven." The older woman pressed her way past Jesse with the casualness of a regular visitor, holding a wicker basket in one hand. "I know he likes to put a dollop of ice cream on top while it's still warm."

Jesse closed the door, the scent of apple pie topped with cinnamon crumb flooding the foyer. Her stomach rumbled. When was the last time she'd eaten? The fact she couldn't remember meant it'd been too long ago.

"You didn't have to do that."

"I know. I wanted to." Bea leaned to the side, peering down the hallway. "Is he already trying to catch up on his chores, or did he have the sense to go upstairs and rest?"

"He's . . ." The words stuck in Jesse's throat. She cleared away the lump. "He's not here."

"He's already taken off?" Bea glanced back in surprise. "Oh. That's a shame. Not that I blame him. Last time I visited him at that awful place, he was complaining that the walls were closing in on him.

I knew he'd be anxious to get out breathing the fresh air. But I'd hoped to catch him first."

"Actually, I'm not sure what he's doing. I haven't seen him since the judge dismissed the charges at the courthouse."

Bea furrowed her brow. "Wait. I saw the two of you talking after the case was dismissed. Didn't he come home with you?"

Jesse shook her head. She hadn't realized that Bea was at the hearing. Of course she hadn't been paying attention to anything except the judge as he'd listened to the lawyers squabbling over her father's fate.

"He told me he had some paperwork to take care of, and that he wanted to wait for the crowd to thin before he walked home. That was hours ago."

"Did you call him?"

"Of course I did. A hundred times. And left a hundred messages."

The furrow deepened. "That's strange."

"It's more than strange." Jesse wrapped her arms around her waist, shivering as a dark fear snaked down her spine. "I'm afraid something's happened to him. Something bad."

Bea clicked her tongue, her mother mode kicking into gear. "Now, let's not get ahead of ourselves, Jesse. Did he seem nervous? Or worried when you spoke to him?"

"No. He was relieved it was over." Jesse abruptly recalled the shadow that'd passed over Mac's face when he'd suggested it was time for a change. "Maybe a little sad."

"Sad?"

"It was more . . ." Jesse struggled for the right word. "Bittersweet. I think he realizes that his life is never going to be the same. But that's expected after what he's been through, right?"

"Of course it is." Bea patted Jesse's arm, her smile reassuring in the shadows of the foyer. "Mac has had more put on his plate than any man should have to endure. The sort of things that would upset anyone. Maybe he just needs some time to decompress and process the fact that the nightmare is over."

It was the same thing Jesse had told herself over and over. So why did the words ring so hollow?

"That's fine, but why wouldn't he call or at least text me?" she protested. "He knows I'm waiting for him."

"I doubt he's thinking clearly. Just give him some space to adjust. In the meantime, have some pie." Bea shoved the basket into Jesse's hand. "Don't forget, it's been tough for you too. You both need time to heal."

Chapter 3

August 2025
Canton, MO

Jesse was busy scribbling a list of to-do items on the back of a cocktail napkin when the knock on the front door disturbed the heavy silence. She wanted to ignore the interruption. After arriving in Canton yesterday, she'd spent her time pulling down the layers of plywood that protected the windows and doors of the Tap Room, followed by a quick inspection that had revealed a growing list of headaches waiting for her. Thankfully, she'd had the smarts to have the electricity and water turned on before she arrived. It not only meant she could run the air conditioner to combat the oppressive heat and enjoy a hot shower this morning, but it'd revealed the less than obvious problems that needed to be fixed. Broken windows, flickering lights, leaking pipes, and a layer of mildew in the cellar that had to be inspected.

Thankfully, she didn't need proof of his death to sell the Tap Room. Unlike her father's savings account and his life insurance policy, the deed to the property had been transferred to her only days after Victoria's disappearance, and Jesse hadn't argued. They both understood there was a chance Mac was going to be arrested no matter how innocent he might be.

At the time, she never dreamed he might have another purpose in handing over his beloved business.

But while there was no legal reason she couldn't put the place up for sale, what was the point? The buyers were going to lowball the offers because it was a mess. Why not put in some hard work and try to get top dollar?

There was another knock. This one more insistent. Dropping the pencil on the bar, Jesse gave into the inevitable. Whoever was out there was clearly determined. And besides, she needed a break before she went to pick up some cleaning supplies, along with a few groceries to tide her over for the next week or so.

Pulling open the door, she frowned at the stranger who was standing there. The woman was wearing a tailored black jacket with a silk shirt and knee-length black skirt. Her shoes were sky-high designer heels and her bleached-blond hair was pulled into an elegant knot at the back of her head. Her makeup was heavy, as if she was covering up a spotty complexion. Or perhaps she was trying to look older than her twenty-odd years. But it was still muted enough not to distract from her image of an elegant, successful businesswoman.

"Jesse Hudson?" she asked with a practiced smile.

"Yes?"

"Hi, I'm Reese Skylar." She paused, as if expecting Jesse to recognize her. "I work for Johnson Real Estate Agency."

"Oh." Jesse tried to place the woman and failed. Not surprising. Reese had probably still been in school when Jesse left Canton. "Did Walter retire?"

"No, but he prefers to stay in the office these days. He hired me to take care of the legwork." She reached into the satchel draped over her shoulder to pull out a glossy brochure and handed it to Jesse. The front flap was dominated by Walter Johnson, posed in front of his office, smiling with smug satisfaction. His silver hair was professionally styled and he was wearing an expensive suit, as if his business was booming. No wonder he could stay in the office.

At the bottom of the brochure was a smaller headshot of Reese Skylar, with the title ASSOCIATE BROKER typed under it. Whatever that meant.

Jesse glanced up, oddly reluctant to let the woman over the threshold. "I know I called the office about selling the Tap Room, but I think I underestimated how much work was going to have to be done before it's ready to be put on the market. I just got the water and electricity turned on. I still need to do several repairs and get it cleaned. It's going to take a while."

"No worries." Reese flashed a smile, revealing teeth that were too perfect and too white to be real. Veneers for sure. For some reason, they reminded Jesse of the Big Bad Wolf. *The better to eat you with, my dear.* "I wanted to stop by and introduce myself. And if you don't mind, I'd like to get a few measurements just to get the ball rolling while I'm here? I'll come back later to take pictures and discuss my ideas on how to get the most for your property."

Jesse squashed her weird hesitation, forcing herself to step back. "Sure. Come in."

"Great. You won't be sorry you put your trust in us."

The woman slid past her, reaching into her satchel to pull out a tape measure and a small notebook. Jesse swallowed a sigh and stepped out of the building, leaving the woman to her task.

She groaned as the heat instantly wrapped around her, as heavy as a wet blanket. The late afternoon sun was obscured behind a layer of gray clouds, but that did nothing to ease the humidity. In fact, it only made things worse. As if the moisture from the clouds was being squeezed into the thick air.

Moving to the center of the cracked sidewalk, Jesse turned back toward the red brick building and glanced up. Long ago, there'd been fancy molding around the windows as well as along the edge of the flat roof, but they'd rotted away. And the letters that spelled out HUDSON MERCANTILE over the door had faded until they were barely visible. Still, there was a sturdy resilience in the structure that couldn't be duplicated by the cheap buildings that were slapped together these days. Not to mention a rich history that had anchored her family to this tiny spot on the vast expanse of the earth.

She was connected to this place in a way that went way beyond the physical.

Was that why she hated the thought of Reese with the too white teeth strolling around the space with her measuring tape? Because this place was in the blood that flowed through her veins. In her very soul?

"Jesse Hudson." A female voice broke into Jesse's unsettling thoughts. "As I live and breathe."

Turning her head, Jesse discovered Bea stepping out the front door of her diner, a smile of pleasure curving her lips.

Happiness flooded through Jesse. Her friend hadn't changed. Oh, there were a few more strands of gray in her reddish hair, and some extra lines on her face, but she was wearing the same headband and the same sundress streaked with flour.

"Hello, Bea."

The older woman spread her arms. "You get your skinny butt over here and give me a hug."

"Yes, ma'am."

Without hesitation, Jesse closed the short distance to be enveloped in Bea's hug. She smelled of fried chicken, lemon pie, and home.

"I've missed you, honey," Bea murmured. "This place hasn't been the same without that face of yours."

Jesse closed her eyes, savoring the feeling of being squeezed tight against the solid form. Bea used to say that she knew God had a sense of humor because he made her look like the cliché of a farmer's wife without her ever stepping foot on a farm or being a wife.

"I've missed you too," Jesse admitted.

"Hmm." Bea leaned back. "Is that why you ignored my calls?"

"Yeah... I know. I'm sorry about that. It wasn't you. I ignored a lot of things. I guess I needed a break from this place."

Bea pressed her lips together. "No, don't mind me. I'm the one who's sorry," she admitted. "It's been a tough time. I understand you wanting to put it all behind you."

"Maybe. But I should have called."

"Well, you're back now." Bea gave her another smothering hug before stepping back. "Everything is right with the world again."

"Actually..." Jesse hesitated, feeling an odd pang of guilt for disappointing the older woman. "I'm not back for long."

"What do you mean?"

"I'm only here to get the Tap Room cleaned up so I can put it on the market."

"On the market? You're selling your dad's bar?"

Jesse flinched at the sharp, accusing edge in Bea's tone. "Technically, it belongs to me."

"Yes, yes. Of course it belongs to you. But it's been in your family from the beginning." Bea knotted her hands together, genuinely distressed. "It won't seem right to have someone else running it."

"I can't leave it boarded up forever, Bea. It's already starting to fall apart. It needs someone who has the commitment—not to mention the money—to get it back to its glory days." Jesse bit her bottom lip, abruptly realizing that her vision for the future of the Tap Room wasn't guaranteed. It was just as likely someone would buy the property to tear down the aging building and put up a laundromat. "At least, that's what I'm hoping for."

"Yes, well... I suppose you're right. Time moves on. Whether we want it to or not." Bea heaved a deep sigh, her expression suddenly somber. "Does this mean you haven't heard from Mac?"

The unexpected question scraped against Jesse's raw nerves. "No. Nothing."

"I was afraid of that. Still." Another sad sigh. "I hoped. I will always hope."

"I can't afford to do that. Not anymore." Jesse caught the glimpse of movement, and she glanced over her shoulder to see Reese stepping out of the Tap Room, pausing to give her a small wave before heading down the sidewalk with a brisk stride. Time to get to the store. "I'll see you later, Bea."

Refusing to dwell on her friend's crestfallen expression at the knowledge the Tap Room would no longer be in the Hudson family, Jesse headed around the corner to where she'd parked her dad's old truck. She'd tried to stay and run the bar after her father disappeared. For six long months she'd gone through the motions of living in a weird limbo as she tried to convince herself that Mac was alive and that he was going to walk through the door any minute.

But eventually she had to concede defeat.

As much as she wanted to cling to the belief that her dad needed time and space to reconcile himself to the strange disappearance of his wife and stepdaughter, there was no way he wouldn't have reached out to contact her.

Which meant he had to be dead.

Either whoever was responsible for making Victoria and Tegan disappear had lured him away from the courthouse and murdered him. Or Victoria had returned and been the one to kill him and dispose of his body.

Why anyone would hurt him was a question she couldn't answer. But she couldn't continue to wallow in the endless guilt and nagging questions. She had to make a clean break or go mad.

Driving the thirty miles to Quincy, the closest town with a big box store, Jesse loaded up on supplies before returning to the Tap Room and throwing herself into a flurry of cleaning. Surely if she kept herself busy, she could block out the memories? Both good and bad.

By nine o'clock she was exhausted. Thankfully, she managed to get rid of the top layer of grime from the public rooms, and for the most part she'd kept herself focused on her task. A major achievement. She wasn't going to dwell on how many layers she still had to go through.

Climbing the back staircase, she headed to the third floor. She'd instinctively chosen her old bedroom when she'd first arrived. The master bedroom would always belong to her father, and she hadn't been in Tegan's room since the girl disappeared. It just felt wrong to invade her privacy. Even if she was dead.

She soaked her sore muscles in a hot bath before pulling on a pair of shorts and a T-shirt. Usually this would be the time she'd be arriving for her shift at the club, preparing for a long night of serving drinks and fending off drunken creepers. Tonight, she hoped her exhaustion would allow her to fall asleep despite the early hour.

Pulling back the covers that she'd washed when she'd first arrived in town, she was about to slide into bed when the sound of three heavy knocks echoed through the silence. Jesse froze, her breath tangled in her throat as she counted to five. Then, on cue, there was another loud knock.

Her breath burst out with a harsh gasp.

Her dad.

That was his knock. The one he used when she was young to let her know it was him if he forgot his keys. Or if he was carrying in supplies and needed a hand. She was never supposed to open the door unless she knew it was him.

No one else knew that knock.

No one.

Not giving herself time to think, Jesse vaulted down the stairs, taking them two at a time as she hit the foyer in less than a minute. Yanking open the back door, she gazed into the darkness that shrouded the alleyway.

What the hell?

There was a part of her that had dared to hope for just a second that her dad would be standing there. Even after all this time. But there was no one.

Not even a stray cat that might have turned over a trash can.

Jesse stepped out, wincing at the gravel that dug into her bare feet.

If she'd been asleep she might have accepted that the knock was a figment of her imagination. But she'd heard it. Loud and clear.

Which meant that someone had been there. Someone real. So where were they?

Glancing from side to side, Jesse searched for any sign of movement. There were no streetlights back here, but she could make out the dumpster behind Bea's restaurant and, closer to her, the Tap Room's rusting air-conditioning unit, which was tilted at a precarious angle. Another problem she needed to deal with, but tonight she only cared about the fact that there was no one around. The downtown was settled in for the night with nothing to see or hear but the proverbial cricket.

Was someone trying to scare her? Not everyone in town was convinced her dad was innocent of his wife's disappearance, and they'd occasionally harassed Jesse when she was running the bar. Word of her return was no doubt circulating through the gossip pipeline. Were they hoping to run her out of town?

Maybe it was just kids messing around.

But how would they know that specific knock?

Shivering despite the heat, Jesse took another step forward. Wait. Was there something . . .

A screech of terror was wrenched from her lips as a harsh, grinding noise exploded behind her. Whirling around in horror, she prepared to fight off a demon. Instead, there was nothing more threatening than the ancient air conditioner that was rattling to life, the motor belching and the blades whirling in a shrill protest.

Shit.

She pressed a hand to the center of her chest.

The stupid thing had nearly given her a heart attack.

Obviously she was too on edge to think clearly. With a curse, she stepped back into the foyer and slammed shut the door, making sure it was locked and bolted.

Tomorrow she'd do a closer investigation of the area.

Someone had been out there.

She'd bet her life on it.

Unfortunately, her plan to inspect the alleyway bright and early was delayed by her restless night. It was almost dawn when she finally fell into a deep sleep, which meant that she'd struggled to drag herself out of bed in time to pull on a pair of clean jeans and a sleeveless yellow sweater that didn't need to be ironed before heading to her meeting with the lawyer.

Jogging the three blocks north, Jesse halted outside the low, gray brick building with a double-glass door painted with WALKER & WALKER LAW OFFICES in bold black letters. Interesting. When her father hired Eric Walker to take his case there had only been one Walker. She assumed that he had a son or daughter who had joined the firm since then.

With a shrug, Jesse pulled open the door and stepped into the hushed lobby, which was decorated in the same muted gray as the outside bricks. There was a white leather couch with matching leather chairs, along with a round table stacked with old magazines.

"Welcome home, Jesse."

Jesse turned toward the reception desk where a young woman with curly brown hair and deeply tanned skin was smiling at her as if they were long-lost friends.

It took a second for Jesse to sift through her memories before she plucked out the image of a young girl running through the cramped apartment above the Tap Room, and tagging along when Jesse was forced to drive her stepsister to the movies. Samantha Yost. Tegan's best friend.

Without warning, a sharp-edged guilt sliced through her. She wasn't proud of the resentment she'd harbored when Victoria and Tegan moved into the apartment. She'd never wanted them there, and during the stormy two years of her dad's marriage, she'd done her best to make the younger girl feel unwelcome.

Not that Tegan had made it easy. The girl was spoiled rotten and jealous of Jesse's tight relationship with her father. She indulged in epic tantrums and demanded constant attention, even making herself sick to gain sympathy.

Honestly, Jesse did her best to avoid being in the same room with her.

Now...

Swallowing a sigh, she forced a smile to her lips. "Hi, Samantha. How are you?"

"Can't complain." The receptionist shrugged. "I mean I do, but I shouldn't."

"Isn't that the truth." Jesse nodded toward the framed picture on the desk that showed Samantha in a white wedding gown with a beaming young man standing next to her. It looked recent. "Congratulations."

"Thanks." The receptionist lifted her hand to flash a modest diamond ring. "I'm now officially Samantha Walker. I married Caleb, Eric's son, after he graduated from law school last year. He always planned to return to Canton so he could work here with his dad and we could settle down together."

"That explains the Walker and Walker on the door."

Samantha looked pleased. "A full partner."

"That's nice," Jesse murmured, not pointing out the fact that they hadn't added an extra Walker on the window for her. Jesse hoped they at least paid the girl a decent salary.

Blissfully unaware of Jesse's jaded concern, Samantha pointed toward the door behind her.

"Mr. Walker is ready for you. Just go on through."

With a small wave, Jesse walked past the desk and opened the door to the main office.

Like most small-town lawyers, Eric Walker was a general practitioner who took care of everything from contracts to personal injury claims. He'd been the first call that Mac Hudson had made after discovering he was the prime suspect in his wife's disappearance. Eric had agreed to represent him, although he'd made it clear that if her father's case went to trial, they would have to hire a seasoned defense attorney.

Thankfully, that hadn't been necessary.

He'd also been Mac Hudson's estate planner. Which was why she was there. Who better to help her navigate the legal maze to get a death certificate?

Entering the large office, she closed the door and crossed the silver carpet to shake the hand of Eric, who leaned across his desk with an outstretched arm.

He was a nice-looking guy closer to sixty than fifty, with brown hair brushed from his narrow face and shrewd green eyes. He was wearing a crisp white shirt that was unbuttoned at the throat and the sleeves rolled up to his elbows and slate gray slacks that matched the jacket tossed around the back of his office chair.

Jesse hadn't decided whether his air of dependability was natural or taught at law school. Either way, he'd kept Jesse from panicking after her father was arrested.

"Jesse." He held on to her hand, his gaze sweeping over her from head to toe. "How are you?"

"Busy," she admitted. "I didn't realize how much work the Tap Room was going to need."

"If you need to reschedule—"

"No." She pulled her hand free of his grasp, surprised by the sharp stab of grief that sliced through her. She'd accepted this moment was inevitable, but that didn't ease the pain. Nine years ago she'd thought Eric Walker was going to be their savior. She'd even bought him a fancy bottle of champagne to celebrate the start of a new life for her father. Giving up that dream felt like she was losing Mac Hudson all over again. "If I don't do this now, I'm not sure I'll have the nerve to come back."

"Understandable. This is never an easy decision." He motioned toward the leather seat in front of the desk, waiting for her to sit down before he settled back into his own chair. He leaned forward, grabbing a pen and a yellow pad. "But if it helps, I think it's the right one. The longer you delay, the harder it becomes to deal with the legal issues."

"Right." She folded her hands in her lap. "So, what happens first?"

He scribbled on the pad as he spoke. "We'll make a legal petition to the courts. I'll get it started today and have you come back in and sign the paperwork." He glanced up, his green eyes as clear as ever despite the deep wrinkles that fanned out from them. "I'll warn you that it could take weeks before we have a formal hearing. Nothing in the justice system works faster than a snail's pace."

She shivered. "I remember. Is there anything else?"

"I have a copy of your father's will, but I'm not sure if there is anyone named in the document that might try to make a claim on your father's estate. You'll need to contact them to let them know you're starting the process to have him declared dead so we can deal with them now. Otherwise they might hold up your inheritance."

"There's no one who is directly related to my dad. He was an only child."

"What about Victoria's family?" he pressed. "I know Mac didn't change his will even after he remarried, but could there be someone who thinks they have a right to his property?"

"Victoria never said anything about her family," she admitted. "I have no idea if she had any siblings or if her parents are still alive. No one ever came to visit while she lived with us, and the police never located anyone after she disappeared. If they're out there they didn't have any contact with her."

He accepted her explanation with a nod of his head. "I'll also need any police reports that you filed after your father went missing."

Jesse's breath hissed through her clenched teeth. "All of them?"

Eric arched a brow. "There's more than one?"

"Are you kidding? I started going into the sheriff's office exactly twenty-four hours after my dad disappeared from the courthouse.

I didn't want to go before then, even though I knew something was wrong, because I didn't want to cause a fuss." Her laugh was sharp. "I shouldn't have worried. Not only was there no fuss, they refused to believe that anything had happened to him. At first the sheriff was certain he'd taken off because he needed time to recover from the stress; then he decided my dad left town to be with Victoria and Tegan, who were remaining in hiding for some mysterious reason. Adam Tillman, of course, was convinced my dad had killed his wife and stepdaughter and was terrified he was going to be arrested again, so he was on the run. Finally, it was concluded that my dad had been driven crazy by the traumatic events, including being arrested, and was out wandering the world without any memory of who he was. Case closed. No one in the sheriff's department was willing to consider the possibility that he'd been hurt. Or worse." She made a sound of disgust. "I filed a dozen reports and they were all ignored."

"I'm sorry they put you through that." Eric sounded genuinely regretful. "And I'm even more sorry to admit that the local law enforcement hasn't improved over the past few years." He shook his head. "Adam Tillman is the sheriff now, and even more willing to cut corners and bend facts when it suits him."

Another shiver raced through her. Of course the bastard was the sheriff. Whoever believed in karma hadn't lived in Canton. It was the jerks who came out on top and the good people who ended up in the gutter. Or dead.

"Thankfully, I'm not going to be in town long enough to care who's sheriff," she muttered.

"Do you have copies of the missing person reports?"

She nodded. "Yeah, I kept them. They're in the safe at the Tap Room."

"Good. It's proof you did your due diligence trying to locate your father."

"Should I include the report from the private detective?" she asked.

Eric blinked in surprise. "You hired a private detective?"

Jesse hunched a shoulder. "Another waste of time. In fact, I'm pretty sure he was a scam. He spent the week sniffing around town, asking questions and pretending to follow clues. Then he demanded his payment and said he couldn't find any trace of Dad. Do you want to know what his final conclusion was?"

A strange expression rippled over the lawyer's face. "What was it?"

"That Dad disappeared into thin air." Jesse snapped her fingers. "Like magic."

"Scam or not, we'll include the report in the petition," Eric decided, scribbling on the pad.

"Is that it?"

"I'll also put an ad in the local paper."

Jesse flinched. The last thing she wanted was publicity that she was in town declaring her father dead. The memory of the knock from last night shattered any hope of a peaceful few days clearing out the bar and saying goodbye to her past.

"Is that necessary?"

"It's more tradition than law these days, but it gives any creditors an opportunity to make a claim against the estate for any outstanding bills. The sooner we wrap up the details, the sooner you can get the death certificate and get on with your life."

"Okay." Jesse rose to her feet. He was right. Time to get on with her life. "Thanks for your help."

"Of course. Mac was a good friend." Something that might have been regret flared through his green eyes. "I've missed him every day for the past nine years."

"Me too."

Turning, Jesse headed toward the door.

"Oh. Wait."

She glanced over her shoulder. "Is there something else?"

"Not for the petition, but I remember you once asked me if your dad said anything that was odd before he left the courthouse the day he disappeared."

"You said he didn't."

Eric tapped a manila folder on the corner of his desk. "It wasn't until I pulled out his old file after you set up this meeting that I recalled our first conversation after he was arrested."

"What about it?"

"I asked him if he wanted me to contact a defense attorney. Someone who specialized in murder investigations, on the off chance his case went to trial. He looked me straight in the eye and said, 'You can't kill a woman who never existed.'"

Chapter 4

Jesse's thoughts whirled round and round, like a hamster on a wheel.

You can't kill a woman who never existed. . . .

What did her father mean?

Was he referring to the way Victoria had changed from a devoted wife who claimed to adore her husband to a nagging harpy who demanded Mac sell his family business and move away from Canton? Certainly she had transformed beyond recognition in their two short years of marriage.

That seemed the most obvious explanation.

But the words continued to nag at her.

It wasn't until she entered the center of town that she realized she'd allowed herself to be dangerously distracted. Something that would never have happened in Chicago. A woman living on her own quickly learned to be on constant guard. But then again, maybe it wasn't distraction that had led her to this precise spot. Maybe it'd been instinct.

Halting in front of the wide cement stairs that led to the courthouse, Jesse studied the building. This was where she'd last seen her dad. It hadn't changed in the past nine years. The bulky sandstones, the red roof that was spotted with tar to cover the leaks, and the faded bushes in dire need of a trim.

Everything the same.

Except for her.

That optimistic young girl who believed in truth and justice had died along with her dreams.

Not sure why she was there, Jesse was on the point of turning away when a shadow dimmed the late morning sunlight. Shivering, she glanced back at the courthouse, realizing that someone had stepped out of the front door and was blatantly staring at her.

Adam Tillman.

His arms were crossed over his chest and his legs were spread in an aggressive stance, while his eyes were hidden behind a pair of reflective sunglasses. He was trying to look like a badass, but he couldn't hide the stomach that now drooped over his belt and the unhealthy flush that stained his square face. Even at a distance, he looked like a walking heart attack.

Jesse turned and darted away. She didn't care if Adam thought that he'd managed to intimidate her. Right now, she felt too raw to deal with the idiot. In fact, she desperately wanted to hop in her truck and drive away from this town.

Scurrying down the sidewalk that was dappled in shadows from the overhanging branches, Jesse strained to hear the sound of footsteps following her. There was nothing. Nothing but the soft lap of water against the bank from the nearby river and the chirp of birds hidden in the leaves.

Jesse tried to untangle the knot in her stomach. Strolling down Main Street should be relaxing. Especially after the bustle and noise of Chicago. But she'd learned her lesson. There was a poison beneath the image of tranquility.

Digging her phone out of her purse, Jesse slowed her pace as she pressed Parker's number. She needed a reminder of why she was there in the first place. A low, static buzz vibrated against her ear as Jesse willed him to answer. A second passed, and then another, before the line connected.

"Hey," she murmured, her voice soft despite the fact there was no one around.

"Hey. What's up?" In contrast, Parker's voice was a harsh rasp.

Jesse glanced at her watch. It was nearly noon. "Were you asleep?"

"Late night."

"That's not what a girl wants to hear when she's out of town."

His low chuckle brushed over her like a caress. "It was a late night because one of the bartenders didn't show up for her shift."

"Ah. That bitch."

"It's okay. I didn't mind covering for her. Although I'd rather be covering her in my bed." His voice was still raspy, but now it was a sensual promise. Heat licked through her veins. No one had ever stirred her lust to such a fever pitch. Honestly, she wasn't sure it was healthy. "When are you coming back?" he demanded.

She stopped to lean against the trunk of a nearby tree. She wanted to concentrate on the sound of Parker's voice, not worry about tripping over the sketchy sidewalk. Plus, her knees felt a little weak. In all the right ways.

"I just got here," she teased.

"And I already miss you."

Her fingers tightened on the phone. "I miss you too."

"Then hurry back."

"That's easier said than done."

There was a pause, as if Parker was surprised by her words. "What does that mean?"

"There are more legal steps to getting my father's death certificate than I expected. And honestly, the bar is a mess. I'm going to have to hire someone to do some repairs before I put it on the market."

"Why waste the money or the time on something you're not going to keep?" he protested.

"Because I'll get more for the property if I take a few days to get it fixed up and polished."

Another pause. It hummed with frustration.

"You said there are steps to getting the death certificate." He abruptly changed the conversation. "Does that mean you don't have a time frame for getting the life insurance money?"

"A few weeks at the shortest, depending on when the hearing is scheduled. And we'll have to wait for the insurance company to send a check," she warned. "I would guess it's going to be the end of the year before the money is in my account. And that's only if there aren't any hiccups along the way."

"Damn." Another pause. "I suppose we could get a loan against the final amount. I'll check into it."

"No." The refusal burst from her lips before she could temper it. Even if she wanted to temper it. And she wasn't sure she did. Parker wasn't a greedy or controlling man, but she didn't understand his fixation on buying the run-down bar. There were thousands of nightclubs that had gone belly-up in the past five years. There was no need to rush into anything. "I don't want to make any commitments until we're sure there aren't going to be any glitches."

He heaved a heavy sigh. "Why do you keep assuming this won't go smoothly? Did someone suggest there was a problem? Is there something you're not telling me?"

"Because there are *always* problems. Especially when you're dealing with the legal system."

Jesse glanced back at the courthouse, where the top of the roof peeked over the treetops. She stiffened. Was that a shadow darting between the trunks of the trees? It was at the end of the block, and far enough away to make it hard to know for sure. But it definitely looked like someone was trying to stay out of sight. Jesse's stomach clenched. Was someone following her? Was it the same person who'd knocked on the door last night? Or was it Adam? He'd certainly looked like he wanted to try to bully her out of town.

"Jesse? What's going on?"

Parker's worried tone jerked her out of her moment of panic. *Get a grip, Jesse.* The shadow could have been a stray dog. Or someone on their morning jog. She was letting her nerves get the best of her.

"Look, Parker, I want to wait on buying another bar until we're sure we have the money, okay?"

"Sure." His tone was soothing. "No worries. I didn't mean to pressure you. I'm just ready to start building our future." He sighed. "And if I'm being honest, I'm even more ready to quit my current job. I'm tired of making money for idiots."

"I haven't finished with the past. Not yet." She pushed away from the tree, suddenly reminded of her long to-do list. "Go back to sleep, Parker. I'll talk to you later."

"Jesse." Her name came out in an urgent plea.

"Yeah?"

"Don't forget."

"Forget what?"

"I love you."

Her tension eased as his low whisper vibrated through her soul. This was why she'd called him. He reminded her why she was ripping open wounds that hadn't healed.

"I love you too."

Ending the call, Jesse dropped the phone into her purse and continued down the sidewalk, refusing to glance over her shoulder. She could jump at shadows or she could concentrate on what needed to be done and get the hell out of there.

Determined to get to work, Jesse had nearly reached the Tap Room when she caught the mouthwatering scent of freshly baked bread and grilled meat. Oh man. Her stomach rumbled and her steps instinctively veered toward the glass front door of Bea's Diner, squished between the Tap Room and a dentist's office.

The loud chatter from the lunch crowd greeted Jesse as she entered the long, narrow space, but thankfully, there was nothing more than mild curiosity as the diners glanced in her direction before returning their attention to their food. No doubt a few of them would eagerly share the information she was back in town, hoping to stir up the past. But that was for later. Right now, they were focused on eating.

Only Bea paused from serving a heavy tray of food to send her a friendly smile, nodding her head toward an empty table in the corner.

Jesse obediently headed in the direction she indicated, mouthing the words "my usual" as she passed the older woman. Bea nodded and bustled to the kitchen, which was separated from the main dining room by a low counter where an old-fashioned cash register stood in a place of honor and two coffee makers were available to anyone who wanted to freshen up their cup.

Settling on one of the hard metal chairs, Jesse leaned back to savor the cool air that blasted from an overhead vent. The diner had been built just a few years after Jesse's family's mercantile store, and it shared a brick wall on one side and a matching copper-tiled ceiling. There'd been a few renovations since the last time that Jesse had been inside the place. The ceramic tiles on the floor were different, and on the opposite wall Bea had replaced the old paneling with a pretty flowered wallpaper. It looked nice, but it wasn't the cozy ambience that made Bea's Diner the go-to place for lunch.

It was the outrageously delicious food.

Twenty minutes later, Jesse was moaning in pleasure as grease from her bacon cheeseburger dripped down her arms. She didn't care. Just as she didn't care what anyone thought when she dipped her hot, salty fries into the thick chocolate shake. She'd been eating this lunch in exactly this way from the time she was three years old.

Parker would be horrified. . . .

She shrugged at the realization, grabbing a wad of napkins as Bea plopped down in the seat across the table and wiped her flushed face with a dish towel. What did it matter? She was in Canton, where people enjoyed tasty food, healthy or not. She'd go back to her organic greens and mixed berry smoothies once she returned to Chicago.

"Good?" Bea nodded toward the empty plate in front of Jesse.

"Orgasmic," Jesse admitted. "I've missed your cooking."

"I'm not going to argue. You're too skinny." Bea dropped the towel in her lap, regarding Jesse with a critical gaze. "And you look tired."

"I'm off my usual schedule," she admitted. "I'm used to working late and sleeping in. I had to get up early to see Eric Walker."

A shadow rippled over Bea's face. "So it's started."

"Yeah."

"Yes, well, I'm not going to lie. I hate the thought of you leaving town and the bar being run by some stranger, but I also know that you need to do what's best for you." She sighed. "It's nothing but selfishness to want you to stay in a place that has so many unhappy memories."

"Not all unhappy," Jesse impulsively denied, glancing around the diner. She'd spent endless hours sitting at this precise table, eating lunch or doing her homework after school if her father was busy. "This will always be home."

With an obvious effort, Bea squashed her personal feelings about the sale of the Tap Room and reached out to pat Jesse's arm.

"I wish I could help make this easier for you."

"Actually, you can."

"Name it."

"I need a good handyman who might have some time in their schedule to help me with a couple of projects before I put the building up for sale." She chuckled as the words left her lips. "I know I'm asking for a miracle. In Chicago, it can take six months to get an estimate, let alone anyone scheduled to get the work done—"

"Actually, I have just the person for you," Bea interrupted.

Jesse blinked, genuinely surprised. "Really?"

Bea leaned back in her chair. "Noah!" she bellowed. "Noah Allen."

On cue, a large, thickly muscled guy with dark hair and a neatly trimmed beard rose from a nearby table. He was wearing a tee stretched tight across his chest with a logo she couldn't read and faded jeans, along with heavy work boots.

Jesse felt a flutter in the pit of her stomach. It wasn't real. Just an echo of excitement that she used to feel every time she caught sight of this man.

Although Noah Allen was two years older, he'd been her school crush from the time she was in kindergarten until he graduated. He'd been the local football star, the homecoming king, and because he worked at his dad's lumberyard, he'd had money to buy a fancy truck when he turned sixteen. The perfect ingredients for childhood adoration.

Of course he wasn't as beautiful or sophisticated as Parker Moreau. His features were carved in blunt lines and his nose was broken and never properly straightened. But there was something solid and resolute about him. Like one of the maple trees that lined the streets.

Jesse watched as her one-time friend strolled across the tiled floor.

"He still works at his dad's lumberyard, but he does odd jobs around town to make some extra money," Bea explained. "He's the best in town."

Noah reached the table. "Hey, Bea. What do you... Jesse." His dark blue eyes widened in surprise as he caught sight of her. "Jesse Hudson. Damn, girl. It's been a minute."

"Noah." Jesse rose to her feet as he stepped toward her, leaning into his friendly hug. His muscles were hard without the layer of fat that often settled on men after they left school. He felt weirdly... real. Probably because Parker was so shockingly beautiful, she sometimes couldn't believe he was more than a figment of her imagination. She pulled back as a stab of guilt pierced her heart. It wasn't Parker's fault he was so gorgeous. "You haven't changed at all," she added.

Noah patted his flat stomach. "A few pounds here." His hand moved to tap his head. "A few less strands there." His gaze swept over her, lingering on the tattoos that decorated her arms. "You look fantastic. I love the artwork."

"Thanks."

"I saw the plywood was pulled off the Tap Room. Are you here to stay?"

"No, I'm putting the bar up for sale."

"Bummer." He looked genuinely disappointed. "I was hoping you were ready to come home."

She shook her head, unable to imagine staying in Canton. "I'm starting a new home in Chicago."

"A big-city gal, eh?"

She hesitated. Was she? That didn't feel right, either. Maybe she didn't fit anywhere. Not until she'd put her past to rest.

"Something like that," she at last murmured.

"You'll be missed."

The sincerity in his words whispered through her, warming a chilled knot in the pit of her stomach. It was all too easy to remember the agonizing disappearance of Victoria and Tegan, followed by the even more agonizing disappearance of her father. She wasn't sure that she'd made the effort to appreciate the friends who'd supported her through those terrible months.

"First I need to get the bar fixed up. Bea said you might be able to help?"

"What does it need?"

"A couple of windows will have to be replaced, and there's some moisture in the cellar. I'm afraid there might be a pipe leaking now that I turned the water back on." She sighed. "And there are probably a few other things I haven't noticed yet. I haven't even started clearing out the place. Who knows what I'll find?"

"I can stop by tomorrow to take a look."

"Oh my God." She smiled in relief. "That would be great. The sooner the better."

He arched a brow. "You're gonna make us feel like you don't enjoy our company."

"Sorry. I'm just so relieved you might be able to help."

"I'd better get back to the yard." He dug in the front pocket of his jeans to pull out his phone, handing it to her. "If you want to put in your number, I'll give you a call before I stop by."

Jesse didn't hesitate. This was Noah Allen. She'd known him her whole life.

"Thanks, Noah." She pulled up his contacts and typed in her information. "You're a lifesaver."

He took back the phone and handed her a business card with the same logo that was printed on his tee.

"This has my number and one to the lumberyard. Let me know if you change your mind on the work." He nodded toward Bea. "Put my lunch on the tab."

With a last smile for Jesse, he turned to head out of the door. Jesse sank back on her seat, tossing the card into her purse despite the fact there was no way in hell she was going to change her mind about hiring him. Not only was he willing to start tomorrow, but she trusted him to do a good job for a reasonable price. An unbeatable combination.

"He's a good guy," Bea said as Noah climbed into a silver truck. It looked like the same one he'd had in high school. "You know, he reminds me of your dad."

Jesse jerked her attention back to her friend. "Seriously?"

"Steady. Loyal," Bea said. "Someone you can depend on when times are tough."

That was certainly true about Mac Hudson. Most of the town had asked him for money or physical labor or a shoulder to cry on over the years.

"Is Noah married?" Jesse blinked. Where had that question come from? Then again, why wouldn't she be interested in an old classmate?

"He was," Bea said. "He and Kelly Durant got married a couple of years after you left town."

"Kelly." Jesse dredged up the memory of a small, brown-haired girl who skimmed along the edges of the school hallways and sat slightly apart in the lunchroom. As if she was there, but not there. "She was that really shy girl who played flute in the band, right? I didn't know her very well, but she seemed nice." Jesse considered the match. Noah wasn't loud or abrasive, but he'd been outgoing. The kind of guy who could lure someone out of their shell. "They would make a good couple," she decided.

Bea clicked her tongue. "That's what I thought until Kelly ran off."

"Ran off? What do you mean?"

"Exactly that. She left town with Noah's best friend, Joe Cochran, three years ago."

"Oh," Jesse breathed. "Poor Noah."

Another click of her tongue. "Lucky escape, if you ask me. She was obviously a nasty piece of work, to cheat on Noah with his best friend. Thankfully, there were no kids. That always complicates things. Now Noah is free to find a decent woman."

"Maybe." Jesse abruptly stood, a haunting dread creeping down her spine. No one would understand the horror of having a loved one simply vanish. Even if Noah knew where his wife was, it would be terrible. "Lunch was delicious."

Bea shook her head as Jesse pulled out her wallet. "This one's on me."

"I can't let you do that—"

"For Mac," Bea sternly insisted.

"Okay. Thanks."

Chapter 5

Leaving the diner, Jesse bypassed the front of the bar and rounded the corner to enter from the back alleyway. She still hadn't checked for any clues that might reveal who'd been knocking on her door last night.

Did she know what she was looking for? Footprints? A half-smoked cigarette? A scrap of clothing? Honestly, she had no idea. It wasn't like she was a trained detective. Without a security camera back here, she had no way of exposing who had been lurking in the dark.

Not that the knowledge kept her from looking around. Whoever had knocked would have had time to flee before she'd come down and opened the door. But they would have to be in the alley watching to see when she switched off the lights to her room. They couldn't see that from the front of the building.

So where had they been waiting?

She moved down the alley. They would no doubt want to stay out of sight in case she glanced out the window. And the most obvious place would be behind Bea's dumpster.

Leaning against the back wall of Bea's Diner, she tried to squeeze behind the heavy metal container. It was impossible. Only a child could fit in the narrow space. So, had the watcher been inside the container?

With a grimace, Jesse grasped the rusty edge and tried to pull herself up far enough to peek inside. If she wasn't careful, she was going to end up in the clinic getting a tetanus shot. Not that she was going to stop. She had to see if someone could stand inside and see her window.

"Dumpster diving?" An unwelcomed male voice scared the crap out of her. "You might do that sort of shit where you live now, but it's illegal in Canton."

Dropping her hands, Jesse kept her back turned as she brushed them together. She needed a minute for her pulse to slow. She wasn't giving the bastard the gratification of knowing he'd scared her.

"Since when did you start caring about what's illegal?" She at last turned to meet Adam Tillman's suspicious glare. "You certainly didn't mind forcing someone to lie under oath."

He sucked air between the gap in his teeth. "Still bitter?" His gaze flicked over her in a dismissive gesture. "No wonder you look like a dried-up raisin."

"Grape."

His gaze jerked back to her face. "What?"

"You mean a grape. A raisin is already dried up. It's redundant."

His face flushed. "I suppose you think you're clever."

"Compared to you?"

He took a step closer, hitching up his utility belt, which was studded with handcuffs, a walkie-talkie, pepper spray, and a small pouch. On one hip was a slender baton and on the other was his service revolver.

He looked like he was hoping for trouble.

"What are you doing, creeping around back here?"

Jesse tilted her chin, refusing to be intimidated. "I'm not creeping around. I'm about to enter my private property. Is that a problem?"

He jerked his thumb to the back door of the Tap Room. "That's your private property. You were snooping into Bea's garbage. Why?"

"I wasn't snooping."

His gaze narrowed. "I know what I saw."

There was no point in arguing, so instead she lied. "I was looking inside because I thought I heard a cat when I came into the alley. I wanted to make sure that there wasn't one stuck in the dumpster." The fib came easily. Jesse had spent the past nine years bouncing around from one place to another, reinventing herself at each location. She'd developed a talent for improvising the truth. "People can be incredibly cruel. Even the ones who are supposed to be the good guys. I found that out when my dad was arrested."

He ignored her deliberate insult. "You expect me to believe that?"

"Actually, I don't care." She shrugged. "Why are you following me?"

"It's my job to keep this town safe."

"Don't let me keep you." She waved toward the opening to the alley. "Go do whatever it is you do. Eating doughnuts. Harassing innocent citizens."

His gaze moved to her exposed tats. "What I do is keep an eye on potential criminals."

"Criminals? Are you referring to me?"

"I might not be as clever as you," Adam sneered. "But I do know that your mother and sister disappeared—"

"Stepmother and stepsister."

The sheriff continued as if she hadn't spoken. "And then, astonishingly, your father vanished. I don't believe in coincidences."

"Wait." She narrowed her eyes. "Are you implying I was somehow involved?"

"You did end up with the family business and are about to come into a tidy fortune once your father's insurance company pays out," he drawled.

Jesse was gutted by his sick accusation. There'd never been a hint that she'd been involved in the nightmare. Hell, she'd still been a senior in high school when Victoria and Tegan disappeared. And everyone in town knew she adored her father. No one with a brain cell would think she could hurt him.

To even think that anyone would . . . no. *Stop it, Jesse.* She forced herself to take a deep breath. He was deliberately provoking her.

Why? The most likely explanation was that he was a jerk. The sort of man who enjoyed kicking puppies and evicting old ladies from their homes. Or he might want revenge. He'd blamed her for getting her dad released from prison, hadn't he? Forget the fact that Mac had disappeared a few hours later. In his twisted little mind, it'd confirmed his belief that Mac had murdered his wife and stepdaughter.

Not that the why mattered. She wasn't going to let him rattle her. Not when there were more important questions nagging in the back of her mind.

"How do you know my dad had a life insurance policy? If you've browbeat my dad's insurance agent into revealing private financial information, I'll sue the sheriff's department."

He flinched, as if caught off guard by her threat. "Everyone has a life insurance policy," he blustered. "Besides, I have the right to gather information in an ongoing investigation."

Jesse shook her head. She was tired of arguing with this idiot. The day was only half over and she was already exhausted.

Time to move on.

Resisting the urge to keep her back against the wall and scoot past Adam's bulk, she stepped forward.

"I would give every penny I have to have my dad back. Every single penny," she hissed. "Now, I have things to do. Go bully someone else."

She swept past him with her head held high, digging into her purse for her keys. Reaching the back door to the Tap Room, she willed her hand not to tremble as she unlocked and shoved it open.

"How long are you going to be in town?"

Jesse shuddered as Adam's hot breath crawled over her nape. "As long as it takes."

"That's not an answer."

"It's the only one you're getting."

"You better watch yourself, Jesse Hudson," he growled. "I'm sheriff now. I enforce the law in this town. And I do it my way."

Grimly, she forced herself to glance over her shoulder, meeting his hot glare. Unease curled through the pit of her stomach. It was daylight, but she was completely alone with this man.

Would Bea hear if she screamed? Would anyone?

She stiffened her spine. "I'm no longer the teenage girl you can frighten with a badge and a gun, Adam Tillman."

He stepped until his pudgy belly pressed against her back. "Is that a threat?"

Her fear transformed into a scalding anger. The creep. How dare he touch her?

"It's a warning from a woman who learned how to protect herself. You try to hurt me and I'll make your life a misery in more ways than you can imagine." She jabbed her elbow into the gut pressed against her. "Screw with me, I'll screw with you. Ten times worse."

He grunted in pain, not sure how to deal with a woman who refused to be browbeaten into submission. Jesse didn't wait for him to figure it out. She slammed the door in his face and locked it.

There was a buzzing sound in her ears as she leaned against the wall, peering out of the back window to keep a watch on the sheriff. He stood, frowning, at the closed door for a full minute. Was he considering the pleasure of forcing it open to punish her? Finally, he turned away with a jerky motion. Expecting him to head out of the alleyway, Jesse frowned as he bent over and shuffled toward the dumpster, moving with slow, deliberate steps.

Was he searching for something? Maybe something he'd dropped last night when he'd been banging on her door?

She pressed her nose against the window, straining to keep him in sight as he got down on to his hands and knees to peer around the rusty container. Whatever he was looking for he didn't find, and he at last shoved himself to his feet and dusted off his hands. He sent one last glare in the direction of the Tap Room before he was marching down the alley and disappearing from view.

What the hell was that?

Jesse forced herself to count to one hundred, making sure the sheriff didn't circle back to spy on her before crossing the foyer.

Then, climbing the stairs to the third floor, she headed to the closed door at the end of the hallway. Without giving herself the opportunity to lose her nerve, she grabbed the knob and shoved open the door.

The smell of stale air and mildew wafted past her, like ghosts being released from their prison. She shivered, her mouth dry as she stepped over the threshold.

The last time she'd been in her dad's private rooms had been a few days after he disappeared. She'd searched for anything that could give her a clue to what might have happened. There'd been nothing to help, and she'd shut the door, refusing to go back in.

Now she glanced around, feeling like an intruder.

For as long as Jesse could remember, the apartment above the bar had been a hodgepodge of shabby, well-loved rooms that were spread over two floors. On this floor there were three bedrooms and a shared bathroom. While the second floor was cut in half for the kitchen and living area, along with a small alcove that her father used as his office.

Victoria, however, had barely unpacked her bags after marrying Jesse's dad before she was demanding that the master bedroom be remodeled and an attached bathroom added. That meant Jesse's bedroom was cut nearly in half to accommodate the addition, while the larger bedroom was given to Tegan. Victoria's reasoning was that Jesse would be turning eighteen in a couple of years and, presumably, moving out. Whether she wanted to or not.

No shocker that Jesse had deeply resented the changes. Just as she resented Victoria throwing out the sturdy furniture her own mother had chosen and replacing it in a pretentious French style. The delicate pieces were cheap knockoffs that looked ridiculous in the rustic surroundings.

Switching on the overhead light, Jesse marched across the Parisian carpet that was layered in dust and yanked open the white armoire with gold trim. The encounter with Adam Tillman had been a sharp reminder to her of why she was in a hurry to leave this godforsaken town. Even more of a reminder than her chat with Parker.

Should that bother her? Probably. Right now she was more concerned with easing the anxiety that hummed through her body. She needed to do something—anything—that made her feel *she* was in control. Otherwise her thoughts would spiral out of control, leading her back to that black hole she'd been in before fleeing Canton.

Aware her breath was too shallow and her heart was racing despite the fact that Adam Tillman was long gone, Jesse grimly concentrated on gathering her father's clothes, which were neatly folded on the wooden shelves to stack them on the bed. Once she had everything in one place, she would sort through what could be donated and what needed to be tossed.

There wasn't a lot. Her dad was never interested in clothes. Not even Victoria's nagging could force him to wear anything but a pair of comfortable jeans and T-shirts with the Tap Room logo. If it was cold, he'd pull on a flannel shirt. Simple.

Next to the stack, she piled his running shoes and boots before covering them with his puffy overcoat. On the other side of the bed, she tossed his underclothes and the toiletries she found in the bathroom. She made another pile for the few personal items that she intended to keep. The wedding ring from her mother, his class ring, and a few trinkets he's saved over the years.

All of his business stuff was in his office on the second floor, or boxed in the cellar.

Once she was done, she stepped back to study the stacks. The meager amount didn't bother her. The Mac Hudson she loved wasn't represented by material belongings.

It was stored in the childhood memories of standing on top of his feet as they danced around the bar on a lazy Sunday morning, and teaching her to drive in an old VW that backfired whenever she took off, and his deep laugh that could make her smile no matter what was happening in her life.

It was in the hours he spent driving her to Chicago to find the perfect prom dress. A prom dress she never wore after her father was arrested...

With a sudden frown, she glanced around the room. Any hint of her real mother had been eradicated by Victoria. The wallpaper was stripped, the drapes changed, and the family pictures relegated to some unspecified location. Then she'd replaced the silver frames with a dozen pictures of Tegan with her "new dad." There wasn't one that included her.

Now the frames were empty. As if someone had gone through the room to erase any memory of them.

Was it her dad? She couldn't remember when she'd come in here after he'd disappeared. Surely she would have noticed if the pictures were gone? Of course she wasn't thinking clearly at the time. In fact, she had no idea what had happened to the stuff Victoria and Tegan had left behind.

Jesse backed toward the open door, her heart once again racing. She suddenly didn't want to be in there. It felt as if the room was closing in on her. As if the bare walls were squeezing together to trap her inside.

Shit.

She needed fresh air.

But the thought of leaving the bar was equally repugnant.

She wasn't in the mood to cross paths with Sheriff Adam Tillman again. Or, frankly, anyone she knew from the past.

She was stuck.

No. Wait. There was one place she could go where she wouldn't have to worry about unwelcome attention. Grabbing the purse she'd dropped on a chair next to the door, Jesse scurried out of the room and back down the stairs. She left through the front door, uneasy at the thought of being alone in the alley. It'd gone from mundane to creepy.

Turning away from Main Street, she zigzagged her way through the quiet neighborhoods. There was a sleepy contentment spread over the tidy rows of homes that she strolled past. It was the end of August, which meant that school was back in session, and at this hour, most people would be at work. She forced herself to slow her quick pace and simply enjoy the silence.

Soon enough she would be back in the hustle and bustle of Chicago. This hushed tranquility was one part of small-town life she truly missed.

Her heartbeat settled to a steady pace and the tension eased from her muscles. She'd been carrying around a foreboding sense of dread from the moment she returned to Canton. No, it'd been longer than that. The dread had started the moment Parker had suggested she come home and declare her father dead.

It was no wonder she'd been jumping at shadows.

For the next couple of hours she didn't want to think about lawyers, or selling the bar, or Adam Tillman. And she certainly didn't want to think about strange knocks and shadows following her.

She just wanted to be Jesse Hudson. A woman enjoying a quiet stroll on a sunny day with nothing on her mind.

Climbing the steps that were dug into the steep hill that led to the top of the bluff, Jesse ignored the paved road that led to the college campus and instead crossed to the line of thick fir trees. She ducked her head and pressed through the branches, the scent of resin thick in the air.

Once on the other side, she paused to brush away the sticky needles, her gaze sweeping over the rolling hill. The Canton Cemetery dated back to the founding of the town in the early eighteen hundreds, with dozens of moss-coated crypts overlooking the river, while the lesser folk made do with simple graves spread along the crest of the bluff. There was a newer cemetery on the outskirts of town, but both Jesse's mother and father came from families who had traveled to this area in covered wagons.

They were born, raised, and buried next to one another, never leaving this remote town. As if clinging to one another would keep away the big, bad world.

Perhaps that was why they'd slowly dwindled to nothing, she acknowledged, strolling along the worn pathway, reading the faded headstones that clustered together. They'd gone from families with a dozen kids until there was no one left but her.

The quiet was even more pronounced as she halted next to a small headstone with small hearts engraved around the name *Clara Hudson*. She had matching hearts tattooed on her shoulder blade.

Bending down, Jesse brushed away the thick layers of dirt and dead leaves that had collected. A pang of guilt tugged at her heart. In the past, her father took care of the grave, making sure the marble was polished and that there were fresh flowers in the copper urn, even when it had infuriated Victoria. It hadn't entered Jesse's mind to return to Canton to visit the burial spot.

Partially because her mother was nothing more than a collection of stories told to her by her dad. She knew that Clara was beautiful, and funny, and that she loved to cook. Her favorite movie was *Moonstruck*, and she'd collected Hummel figurines that were safely packed away in a crate hidden beneath Jesse's bed so Victoria couldn't throw them in the trash. Beyond that, she was nothing more than an aching void in Jesse's life.

Now she kneeled beside the grave and allowed the silence to still her racing thoughts. Her dad had often snuck away to visit this spot when he was feeling overwhelmed. Even before he married Victoria and she'd started her constant bitching. He claimed that just talking out his problems helped him to clear his mind.

Jesse closed her eyes, sucking in deep breaths. She wasn't there to talk out her problems. Honestly, when she'd made the impulsive decision to climb the hill to this spot, she'd simply been in search of fresh air and peace. But now that she was here, she realized a part of her was hoping to connect with the woman who'd given her life.

She was so alone. . . .

Jesse wasn't sure how much time passed. She sensed the sun moving until the branches from the nearby trees cast a welcome shade, but it wasn't until she heard the squeak of rusty iron, as if the main gate to the cemetery was being closed, that she realized it must be five o'clock.

With a groan, she forced herself to rise to her feet, her legs cramping from being in one position for so long. She'd wasted enough time. She needed to get back to the bar and finish packing up her dad's things so she could continue her cleaning.

Besides, there was a whispering breeze beginning to stir the air, as if the dead were urging her to stay.

With a shudder, Jesse left the cemetery the same way she'd entered, heading down the hill and strolling absently in the direction of the Tap Room. She didn't have a particular route in mind, preferring to stroll along the edge of town. Or at least what used to be the edge of town.

Before she'd left Canton, this area was an empty field where the kids played tag and wiffle ball. Now the land had been divided into five large lots, with newly constructed brick homes complete with wide covered porches, circle driveways that led to detached garages, and fenced-in backyards.

They looked as if they'd been constructed at roughly the same time, but they were different enough in style to avoid being cookie-cutter homes. Certainly they were nicer than most of the houses in town.

Absently admiring the neatly trimmed hedges that separated the front lawns, Jesse's attention was captured by the house at the far end of the block. The white, two-storied farmhouse with a wraparound porch and a tin roof wasn't new. In fact, she had a distant memory of an elderly man living there when she was growing up. Watson? Wilson? Something like that. They used to sneak into the field behind his house and swim in the lake, and steal apples from the nearby orchard.

It looked distinctly out of place next to the elegant brick homes. Almost as out of place as the glamorous woman with bleached-blond hair who was currently standing on the porch. She was still some distance away, but it looked like Reese Skylar. Jesse's gaze shifted to the large male who was leaning out of the open front door to talk to the real estate agent. Jesse blinked. Was that Noah Allen?

Her steps slowed, her brows arching as she watched the two share an animated conversation. From a distance, it looked like they were arguing. Not a shouting, threatening-violence sort of fight. But they were each making their point. Forcibly.

Jesse felt a stab of surprise. There was no reason the two wouldn't know each other. It was a small town, and even if Reese was relatively new to the area, it wouldn't take long to become acquainted with the locals. But the sight emphasized just how much had changed in the past nine years.

A new subdivision. Noah living in his own home. Reese Skylar and her bleached-blond hair.

With a shake of her head, she forced herself to continue down the sidewalk. Whatever was happening between the two was none of her business. Even if she was itching with curiosity to know what they were squabbling about.

The cost of small-town living was perpetual interest in other people's private business.

Reaching the end of the block, Jesse realized she'd timed her pace to meet Reese as the woman flounced down Noah's driveway. An accident? Or had she done it on purpose?

She shrugged aside the question. She wanted to know what was going on with Noah. So what? He was an old friend.

"Hello again," she murmured as the woman neared.

Reese jerked up her head, obviously too deep in thought to have noticed Jesse's approach.

"Oh, hi." She flashed her too-white smile. "Jessie, isn't it?"

Jesse nodded, glancing past the woman to watch the front door close with enough force to rattle the large front window.

"Does Noah Allen live there?"

"Yes." Reese looked annoyed. "I've spent the past three months trying to convince him to put his house up for sale. It's really too big for a single man, and he could get a fortune in this market."

Jesse arched a brow, glancing back at the farmhouse. It was sturdy, but the foundation was crumbling in spots, and a few of the boards were beginning to warp. Only the thick layers of paint kept them straight. Not exactly prime real estate.

"A fortune for that house?"

"A fortune for the land. The house would have to come down, of course," Reese clarified. "Walter created this subdivision with the expectation that he could expand it to include this lot, along with the field behind it. Canton desperately needs more decent family homes with plenty of room for children and dogs." She clicked her tongue. "In fact, I have three potential buyers ready to write a check today so they could start building."

"Walter Johnson created this subdivision?"

She nodded. "He was the broker who purchased the land and hired the contractor to build the homes. I think Noah helped with some of the construction. Which is why I don't understand why he's being so stubborn about selling. He has to realize that having his old house on the same block is bringing down the property values."

Ah. Now Jesse understood the younger woman's frustration. Jesse knew Walter Johnson well enough to guess he'd created this fancy subdivision as his personal legacy. There was probably a plaque with his name attached to a post or a tree, proclaiming him as the founding father. The last thing he'd want was a blight in his pretty neighborhood.

Plus, as Reese had pointed out, the land was now worth much more money with the upgrades.

"No luck getting him to sell?"

"Not yet. But I'm nothing if not persistent. Walter wants that property and I intend to get it for him."

With a last, determined glance at the farmhouse, Reese turned to march down the sidewalk, her heels clicking on the cement. Jesse hurried to keep pace. She told herself that she wanted to know more about the agent. It made sense. Reese was young and probably inexperienced. Jesse needed to be confident she was going to get her top dollar for the Tap Room.

But the truth was, she was just being nosy.

A part of her wasn't convinced that the argument between this woman and Noah was nothing more than a request to sell his house.

There had been something intimate in the way they leaned toward each other. And the strain that hummed around their stiff bodies.

They were across the street and angling toward Main Street when Jesse broke the silence.

"What made you move to Canton? Do you have family here?"

"No." She waved toward the bluff behind them. "My boyfriend transferred to the college last year. He decided to transfer again at the end of the semester; I decided to stay."

"Oh." Jesse winced, worried she'd brought up a sore subject. "Sorry about that."

"I'm not. I realized after we moved in together that he didn't have the sort of ambition I'm looking for in a man. Good riddance."

There was a sheer lack of emotion in her voice that Jesse admired. After pretending for years that she was a lone wolf who didn't give a shit about anyone, the myth was shattered the second she'd caught sight of Parker Moreau across the crowded nightclub.

The truth was, she'd been desperate to find someone to love.

"You like it here?" Jesse demanded.

"For now. Unlike my ex, I have plenty of ambition, and Canton is a nice town that gives me an opportunity to get some experience without battling through a ton of competition."

"That's true. There's not much competition for anything around here."

Reese sent her a curious glance. "You don't like Canton?"

"A complicated question," Jesse admitted. "I loved my childhood. I had my dad and a ton of friends. During the summers, we'd zoom our bikes up and down the bluff and eat peanut butter sandwiches next to the river. No one ever went home until it was dark. There's something special about growing up in a small town where you always feel safe." She shook her head, the happy memories fading. "But sometimes bad things do happen in small towns. And it changes everything."

"I'm not going to pretend that I haven't heard the stories."

Jesse wasn't offended by the blunt words. She preferred it to people acting like they weren't obsessed by the nasty rumors.

"I don't doubt that. It's not everyone who has three members of their family disappear."

"You don't have any idea what happened to them?"

"None."

"How odd."

"Yep. Very odd." Realizing she'd gone from questioning the woman to being questioned herself, Jesse came to a sharp halt. She nodded toward the side street. "This is a shortcut for me."

"Of course." Reese stopped to release her blinding smile. "Let me know when you're ready for me to come and take pictures."

"I will."

Jesse walked away, waiting until she reached the corner before she glanced over her shoulder. Reese had disappeared, but a weird feeling crawled down her spine.

Was she being watched?

The suspicion spurred her into motion. Picking up speed, she power walked to the end of the street, once again avoiding the alleyway to enter the bar through the front entrance.

Once inside, she closed the door, relieved there was enough waning sunlight flooding through the windows to chase away the shadows. She hated the sense of emptiness she felt whenever she walked through the door. As if the bar had become a tomb, waiting for someone to once again breathe life into the musty corners.

With a shake of her head, Jesse crossed the wood-planked floor, abruptly halting as she caught a familiar scent.

It was the smell of male cologne. More specifically, it was the smell of her father's cologne.

Her hands clenched, a chill sweeping through her. It wasn't a faded memory. The sharp, citrusy cologne was as pungent as if her dad was standing next to her.

Muttering a curse, Jesse sprinted toward the back foyer and up the stairs. She'd found a bottle of that specific cologne when she was cleaning out her dad's bathroom cabinet. She'd even tossed it on the bed with the rest of his things to be donated. At the time, she hadn't noticed the scent, but there was a possibility that the bottle had broken. Or the top was loose and the cologne had spilled. That would explain why the scent was so fresh.

She slowed her pace as she entered the master bedroom, instinctively glancing around, as if expecting to find someone there waiting for her. There was no one, of course. Not even the ghost of her father.

The room now had the same stale emptiness as the rest of the building.

But the scent of the cologne was even stronger.

Crossing to the bed, Jesse moved aside the various stacks of belongings, searching for the bottle. She remembered pulling it out of the cabinet, along with her dad's shaving kit, but she didn't remember precisely what stack she'd tossed it in.

A couple of minutes later, she'd located the shaving kit, but no cologne.

It was there. It had to be, right?

She sorted through the clothes and shoes and toiletries, then dropped to her knees to peer under the bed, just in case it'd rolled off the mattress. It had to be there. It *had* to be.

Only it wasn't.

It'd vanished. Just like her father.

Chapter 6

After a sleepless night, Jesse rolled out of bed and stood in a hot shower until her skin wrinkled and the fog cleared from her mind. As she pulled on a pair of jean shorts and a Green Day T-shirt, she sternly chided herself for overreacting to the scent of her dad's cologne.

No doubt it'd been a figment of her imagination. Just a faded memory that had seemed painfully real when she'd stepped into the bar. Plus, she couldn't be 100 percent sure she'd seen a bottle of the cologne when she'd cleared out her dad's bathroom. It made more sense that she'd assumed there'd been one, rather than believing the spirit of her father had returned to collect it for his journey through the great beyond.

Downing an entire pot of coffee and munching a piece of toast that was dry enough to choke her because she'd forgotten to buy butter, Jesse was at last ready to face the day.

She jogged down the narrow staircase, heading directly for the large safe that was built into the cellar. Before she'd packed her bags and driven away from Canton, she'd locked away her important papers. She'd fully intended to move from place to place with no permanent home. There was no use taking anything she didn't need on a daily basis.

Wrinkling her nose at the scent of mildew that hit her as she entered the basement, Jesse flicked on the switch that was mounted on the doorframe. A single bulb flared to life. It didn't chase away the shadows, but it gave her enough light to cross the hard-packed dirt floor. More importantly, it allowed her to avoid the electrical cords and metal pipes that crisscrossed the open floor joists just an inch above her head.

The square metal safe was mounted on the brick foundation, protected by an old-fashioned dial lock. It was easier than trying to keep track of a key and, thankfully, Mac had given Jesse the code at the same time he'd transferred the deed.

Spinning the dial from side to side, she heard the low click and pulled open the heavy door. Inside were three deep shelves with stacks of files that were mainly connected to the Tap Room. Taxes, business license, liquor license, and insurance forms. There were also files filled with her dad's personal information. And on the top shelf was the stack of folders that held the police reports and notes from the private investigator.

She pulled them out, cursing when the top file started to slip. Jerking her free hand up to prevent the papers from spilling out, she hit the edge of a shoebox that was perched on a lower shelf. The box tumbled to the ground, the lid popping off to allow the contents to splay across her feet.

Dammit.

Bending down, she dropped her folders on the ground and impatiently shoveled the contents back into the shoebox. It wasn't until she caught sight of the long, thin envelope that she halted. It looked official. Like a legal document. So what was it doing in the shoebox?

Leaning back on her heels, Jesse opened the flap and pulled out a folded piece of paper. It had a fancy logo at the top and a short note below:

Malcom DeWayne Hudson,

As per your request during our telephone conversation, we have completed a second search of our records. There was no marriage certificate issued or registered in your name in Clark County. I assure you that we were quite thorough.

*Sincerely,
Clark County Vital Records Office*

Puzzled, Jesse reread the note. Then realization hit her like a blow to the gut. Clark County. Vegas.

That was where her dad had gone to wed Victoria.

It was a shock to everyone. Not because they'd only been dating a few months when Mac asked Victoria to marry him; it'd been obvious he was besotted with her. But instead of a lavish wedding, which Jesse would have expected from a shallow, annoyingly vain woman like Victoria, she'd instead convinced Mac to run away one weekend to tie the knot in a quickie ceremony in Vegas.

Jesse was convinced the woman must be pregnant. Why else sneak away? But there'd been no baby when they'd come home. Just a marriage that had swiftly crumbled into a war zone.

No, wait. Not a marriage, she reminded herself. At least not a legal one according to the County Clerk of Vital Records.

So what had happened? Had they gone to a shady chapel that had given them a fake certificate? Surely they checked to make sure it was legit? Victoria might have been a shrill, demanding bitch, but she wasn't stupid. When she was making plans for the wedding, there was no way she could have overlooked such an important detail.

Which meant that she deliberately used a fake marriage certificate. And somehow her father had realized he'd been conned.

The question was, when?

Jesse's gaze returned to the top of the page, genuine relief racing through her as she caught sight of the neatly typed date. The letter had come weeks after Victoria had packed her bags and left. In fact, it'd arrived just a couple of days before her dad was arrested. He hadn't known they weren't really married until long after she was gone.

Dropping the letter back into the shoebox, Jesse's thoughts were racing with possibilities as she absently sorted through the other objects that had been hidden by her father.

A couple of faded postcards from Jesse's grandma when she'd traveled to Florida to visit a friend, a few medals from the local high school that her dad had earned playing baseball, her mother's graduation photo, and her great-grandfather's Purple Heart. Nothing that would give her any answers.

Oh, and a yellow sticky note. She leaned forward, trying to make out the scribbled words.

Who are you?

A chill raced through Jesse as she grabbed the note, belatedly realizing it was attached to a photograph. Pulling it off, she studied the picture of Tegan at a birthday party. In the background, Victoria was glaring off to the side, not bothering to pay attention to her daughter. Typical.

Who are you?

A good question.

Dropping the picture on top of her folders, Jesse shoved the shoebox back into the safe and shut the door. A plan was beginning to form in the back of her mind. She shrugged. Not really a plan. More of an avenue of inquiry.

For years, she'd locked away all thoughts of the past. Including the nagging question of what had happened. Now that she was stuck in Canton, she might as well do a little digging. What could it hurt?

Climbing out of the cellar with her folders and the picture, Jesse grabbed her purse and headed out of the bar. She took the time to double-check that the door was firmly locked behind her before she retraced her steps to the lawyer's office. It was another hot, muggy day, but Jesse barely noticed the heat. Or the curious gazes that followed her as she hurried down the sidewalk and into the low brick building.

At her entrance, Samantha lifted her head, her expectant smile fading as she realized who was there.

"Hey, Jesse. I'm sorry the forms aren't ready for you to sign yet. It's probably going to be a few days." Her tone was defensive. "Maybe a week."

"That's fine." Jesse crossed to the desk. "Eric told me it might take some time. I just came by to drop off the police reports and the notes from the private detective I hired to find my dad."

"Oh, right." Relief rippled across the receptionist's face, as if she'd expected Jesse to be angry. "I'll make sure he gets them."

"Thanks." Jesse placed the folders on the desk and turned away. Then, pretending she'd just remembered something, she glanced over her shoulder. "Before I forget, I was cleaning out the apartment and I found a picture I wanted to give your mom. Do your parents still live at the same house?"

"Yes." Samantha rolled her eyes. "Mom refuses to move, despite Dad's insistence that they need to downsize. She won't admit it, but I think she's making plans for grandkids despite the fact that I just got married and my brothers have no intention of settling down."

"It's hard to think about leaving a home with so many memories."

"Yeah, I get that. I'll admit I'd be devastated if they sold the place. It must be extra hard for you."

"Harder than I expected." Jesse forced a tight smile. "See you later."

Jesse left the office and headed toward a sleepy neighborhood in the shadow of the bluff. It had once been the preferred location for the professors who worked at the college, with wide lots shaded by oak trees and solid brick homes that consumed large chunks of space without apology. Over the years, however, it'd lost its status as newer, fancier homes had been built, and the area had faded into obscurity.

Slowing her pace, Jesse studied a two-storied house with brightly painted blue shutters and a wide porch that tilted at one end. It looked old but well-loved, and the yard was a profusion of color from the garden beds that were in full bloom. As she approached, she caught sight of a thin woman with short, dark hair threaded with silver and skin that was tanned from hours in the sun.

Perfect.

"Hello, Lara," she called out, stopping at the end of the cobbled sidewalk.

The older woman lifted her head in surprise, clearly too focused on trimming the already neat bushes that framed the yard to realize that she was no longer alone.

"Hi." She paused, as if unsure why she was being interrupted by a stranger. "I'm sorry, I . . ." Her dark eyes widened as recognition hit. "Jesse. Oh goodness, I didn't even recognize you." Dropping the clippers, she scurried forward to wrap Jesse in her arms. "Welcome home."

Jesse allowed herself to savor the tight hug before she was pulling away. Lara was the sort of motherly figure who treated everyone as her favorite person in the world. A perfect trait, considering her husband was the chaplain at the college and they often hosted students and visiting lecturers.

She was also one of the few people who'd been close to Victoria during her time in Canton. Whether or not Victoria was willing to share her secrets was another matter.

"It's temporary," she murmured.

"Yes, I heard you were in town to sell the bar."

"News travels fast."

Lara clicked her tongue. "Especially in Canton."

Jesse glanced toward the bushes that Lara had been clipping. "Are you busy?"

"Not too busy for you." Tugging off her heavy gloves, Lara wrapped an arm around Jesse's shoulders and urged her up the cobbled path. "Come inside and I'll pour us some iced tea."

Together, they climbed the steps to the porch and into the house. The living room was as tidy as the front yard, with well-worn furniture and framed photos of the family displayed on every surface, including the paneled walls. There was nothing elegant or trendy in the house, but there was a warmth that no money could buy.

Lara disappeared through the opening to the kitchen, returning in less than ten minutes with two glasses of iced tea and a plate of homemade cookies.

"It's sugared," she warned as she handed Jesse a glass that was already beaded with sweat. "I hope you don't mind."

"I'm not a monster." Jesse grabbed two sugar cookies before sinking onto the comfy sofa. "Who drinks tea without sugar?"

"Anyone under the age of thirty." Lara rolled her eyes, sitting next to her. "No sugar. No carbs. No meat. Just raw broccoli and filtered water."

Jesse demolished a cookie in two bites. "Trust me, I work at a nightclub where I meet plenty of young people. They eat total junk, just like I did growing up, only now they have it delivered instead of doing the drive-through."

Lara sipped her tea. "I miss those days. At the time you think your kids will never grow up and you'll be stuck living in a constant mess and running from one endless activity to another with no time to cook a proper dinner. And then they're gone and you're spending your day trimming bushes."

"They are lovely bushes," Jesse assured her.

Lara chuckled. "Yes, yes, they are."

"I did have a reason for stopping by."

"Do you need help with something? As you've discovered, my days are open."

Setting the tea and remaining cookie on the coffee table, Jesse reached into her purse to pull out the photo she'd found in the shoebox. Before leaving the bar, she'd taken several pictures of it with her phone, making it easier to zoom in to study the details. She had no idea why that specific photo was in the safe, when dozens of others had disappeared. It could be that it was her dad's favorite picture of Tegan. Or, she hoped, it might have something in it that could offer a clue.

That was what she was here to discover.

"Actually, I wanted to give you this."

"How sweet." Lara took the photo, a soft smile curving her lips as she recognized the image. "Oh, I remember this day. Tegan and Sam's birthdays were just weeks apart, so we had their party together. This was their twelfth birthday. The last one before . . ."

Her words trailed away, a sadness rippling over her face.

"Yes." Jesse leaned to point at Victoria, who was standing several yards away from the dozen guests and mounds of presents that surrounded Tegan and Sam. Her deep red hair was carefully draped across half her face and her large sunglasses were perched on top of her head as she scowled toward someone to the side of her. She looked more like a petulant fashion model than a devoted mom.

"Victoria doesn't look very happy to be there," she said.

Lara looked embarrassed. "It turned into something of a madhouse. My fault. You can tell by the picture I invited the entire town. I'm afraid Victoria might have felt a little ambushed when she showed up with Tegan and realized what I'd done."

"Looks like fun to me."

"Well, I thought so. I had Bea cater the lunch with hot dogs and hamburgers and mounds of cupcakes. And Kevin came over to set up the dance floor for the kids."

Jesse arched her brows. "Kevin Allen was there? Noah's dad?"

"Yeah, you can just see him in the background." Lara ran her finger along the edge of the photo, where a burly man with a crew cut hairstyle was standing on a ladder as he hammered a board into place. "Noah was there too. He hung all the lights around the yard. It was a princess fairy theme."

Jesse ignored her childish burst of envy. What did it matter that she'd never had a real birthday party growing up? Her father simply hadn't understood it was important to a young girl.

With a small shake of her head, she concentrated on the picture. "Who's that?"

Lara narrowed her eyes as she studied the young man who was standing next to the half-built stage. With his shaggy blond hair and casual pair of board shorts and T-shirt, he didn't fit in with the gathered crowd.

"I'm not sure." There was a short pause as Lara searched her memories. "Oh, wait. He came with Bea to arrange the food tables, and I asked him to help the DJ set up his equipment. I'm sorry, I don't remember his name."

Ah. That explained his bored expression. Every semester Bea reached out to the students who struggled to afford college classes so they could earn a little extra cash. Setting up a children's party clearly hadn't been on his favorite things to do list.

Jesse returned her attention to the fact that there had obviously been more than a few strangers at the party. Bea's staff. The DJ. Whoever had arranged the bouncy castle she could see at the back of the yard. Maybe even someone to deliver and set up the balloons.

"That must have been quite a blowout," she murmured. Lara flushed, as if she thought Jesse was judging her. Reaching out, Jesse gave her arm a gentle squeeze. "Sam is very lucky to have you as a mom."

The flush faded and Lara's smile returned. "Are you sure you don't mind me keeping this?"

"I want you to have it."

"I'll treasure it."

Lara placed the picture on a side table, next to a dozen other pictures of Sam, while Jesse, eating her second cookie, considered her next move. She hadn't figured out why her father would keep the birthday picture, or why he'd scribbled the note, but she would stew over what Lara had shared about the party later. Maybe even ask Noah if he remembered anything about that day. For now, she couldn't waste an opportunity to discover everything possible about Victoria.

"I'm also hoping you can answer a few questions for me," she announced, slowly forming a reasonable lie. "Eventually, I plan to have a small service for my dad." She held up a hand as Lara leaned forward, immediately prepared to start organizing the ceremony. "Not yet. I have too much on my plate over the next few months. But someday."

Lara politely hid her disappointment at the delay. "That would be nice. I've been hoping you would do something when the time was right. We all need the opportunity to mourn his loss."

"Anyway, I have my dad's family history and stories about my parents when they were together, but it wouldn't feel right not to include something about Victoria and Tegan," Jesse plowed on, refusing to feel guilty. Maybe someday she *would* host a ceremony. Stranger things had happened. "I don't want people to think I've forgotten about them."

"No one would think that."

Jesse grimaced. "It was no secret that I wasn't as welcoming to my stepmother as I should have been."

"Blended families are always difficult," Lara sympathized. "Even when everyone is doing their best."

Blended? There'd been nothing blended. More like two armed camps squaring off against each other. Jesse on one side. Victoria and Tegan on the other.

"True." Her hands curled into fists. She couldn't help herself. Victoria's destruction of her family was still an infected wound that refused to heal. "I tried to pretend she didn't exist. And now I realize I really don't know anything about her life before she moved to Canton. I need you to fill in the gaps."

Lara blinked. "Me? We were friends, but truthfully, Victoria didn't really talk about her past. I know she moved to Canton after her husband died. She wanted a fresh start."

"Moved from where?"

"I'm not sure." Lara furrowed her brow. "I think they must have traveled around for a while. When they first arrived in town I asked Tegan if she was settling into school and she said that she was used to making new friends."

Victoria had been equally cagey with Jesse's father. She'd tear up and dab at her eyes whenever anyone asked questions about her past. A perfect way to shut down awkward questions. At the time,

Jesse assumed she enjoyed the drama. She hadn't really considered the possibility she was hiding something.

"Did Victoria ever say why she chose Canton?"

"She always said it was a fluke of fate. Her car broke down outside of town, and she had to stay a few days while it was being fixed. She told me that she woke up on the day she was supposed to leave and decided that she didn't want to. She'd fallen in love with Canton."

Jesse snorted. A pretty story, but she didn't believe it for a second. Not when Victoria had continually bitched about Canton being stuck in the dark ages. She wasn't wrong—Canton *was* stuck in the dark ages—but why pretend she'd been eager to stay there?

Time for a new line of questioning. "I know she didn't have any close family. The police tried to find a relative who could help them locate her after she and Tegan disappeared. As far as I know, they couldn't discover anyone." Jesse felt a stab of frustration. "Not that they tried that hard."

"Yes, they asked me at the time, and I told them that she'd mentioned she'd been orphaned at a young age, and I don't think she was close to her previous husband's family. After he died she told me that they'd cut her off. And not just financially. It was just her and Tegan until she found Mac. And you, of course."

The addition of Jesse was hastily tagged on. No surprise. There'd been no secret about Jesse's relationship with her stepmother.

"Her husband was a doctor, wasn't he?"

"A surgeon, I believe. She said he was rushing to an emergency when he died in a car crash."

"You don't know which hospital he worked at?"

"No, sorry."

Sensing Lara had told her everything she knew about the mysterious dead husband, Jesse shrugged.

"That's okay. I was hoping I might find some pictures on the internet I could display at the service."

"Oh, that would be nice." Lara pursed her lips. "I just can't remember anything that might help. She didn't like to talk about her marriage. It was still a painful subject."

"Understandable. She was young to be a widow."

"Yes, and with a small child. I admired her for starting over."

Jesse didn't bother to point out that Victoria hadn't really started over. She'd just married the first man who asked her.

"I can't remember. Did she have a job when she first moved to Canton?" she asked. "You know, before she married Dad?"

Lara paused. "She volunteered at the church," she said at last. "That's how I met her, but I don't recall her working."

It was what Jesse expected to hear, but it didn't stop her stab of irritation. A local employer would have some background information on Victoria. Even if it was nothing more than a previous address.

"It was such a whirlwind engagement." She smoothly changed to a new topic. She didn't want to give Lara the opportunity to wonder why she had so many questions. "I barely knew they were dating before they were getting married."

"I'll admit I was surprised. I thought . . ." Lara cleared her throat, looking uncomfortable. "Well, it doesn't matter now."

Jesse leaned toward her. "You thought what?"

There was more throat clearing. "When she first came to town she dated Gary Mayfield, and I suspected she was hoping for a future with him."

Jesse struggled to place the name. At last a vague memory of a short, bald-headed man who wore expensive suits to try to hide his thick neck and bulging stomach began to form.

"The owner of the bank?" She waited for Lara's nod. "He had to be twenty years older than her."

"A young widow with a child is looking for security, not wild romance."

As Mac found out, to his sorrow. "What happened between them?"

"I suspect she eventually realized that Gary was a confirmed bachelor. He might have enjoyed her company, but he was never going to marry her."

"Unlike my dad, who couldn't wait to tie the knot."

A sadness rippled over the older woman's face. "He'd been alone a long time, Jesse."

"I know." Jesse shrugged. She didn't want to discuss her father's naïve desire for companionship. "Did Victoria ever show you any pictures from their actual wedding? Dad had a few of them together in Vegas. His favorite was the two of them standing in front of the fountains of the Bellagio. But I was looking through his things and I couldn't find any of the actual wedding ceremony."

"I did see a few pictures from their trip, but I don't recall seeing any from the ceremony. Of course I did see the dress she intended to wear before they left. She came by to model it for me. I'm sure she made a lovely bride."

"Yes, which makes it so strange that I can't find any photos." Looking back, it was easy to notice how camera-shy Victoria was. And how weird it was for such a vain woman to avoid being the center of attention. At the time, however, Jesse simply hadn't been interested enough to care.

"Maybe she took them when she left," Lara suggested.

"That's possible, I suppose. I wonder..."

"What?"

"Would the wedding chapel have copies? I'm sure they must have a photographer on staff who takes at least a few pictures during the ceremony."

"You're right."

"You don't happen to remember the name of the place, do you?"

Lara pursed her lips. "I'm not sure she mentioned...oh, wait. Now that I think about it, I don't think it was a traditional chapel."

"Really?"

"Victoria said she didn't want it to be in one of the tawdry places with Elvis décor. Instead, she rented an outdoor spot with lovely gardens and a gazebo."

"Then who performed the actual ceremony?"

"I'm not sure. Honestly, she didn't give too many details. Only that your father forgot to pack the wedding rings." Lara clicked her tongue. "She wasn't very pleased about that."

"She wasn't pleased about a lot of things after they were married."

"It's never easy. Especially during the first few months together."

"I wish he'd taken more time dating Victoria," Jesse said. "They weren't really compatible after they moved in together."

"I remember that Pete and I had a few battles in our early days. It takes time to smooth out the edges between a couple. They might have worked things out."

"Maybe." Jesse wasn't there to argue. "We'll never know now."

"No." Lara smoothed her hands down her well-worn capris, trying to hide the tears that filled her eyes. "Can I help with the service? You're welcome to hold it here if you want. I have a huge backyard."

Jesse abruptly rose to her feet. She'd abused this woman's kindness enough for one day.

"Thank you, Lara. Right now I'm concentrating on getting the bar ready to sell. Once things are settled I'll give you a call."

"Any time." Lara straightened to give Jesse a tight hug. "Don't be a stranger. I'll expect you to come to visit before you leave town."

"Of course."

Pulling away, Jesse grabbed her purse and headed back to the bar. She kept her head bent to avoid any unwanted interruption to her churning thoughts. Not that it would matter. It wasn't like she'd gotten any answers. Hell, now she had more questions.

Who was Victoria Hudson?

She'd arrived in town with a young daughter and sob story about being recently widowed. From there, she'd added to her woe-is-me vibe by claiming to be an orphan who'd been cut off from her dead husband's family without a penny. And of course it'd all been too painful to discuss.

No one bothered to question her. Why would they? The locals took people at face value. Especially if you happened to be a beautiful woman caring for your young daughter.

But why lie about your identity?

Witness protection was a possibility, but that seemed unlikely. She would surely have a better cover story. And cops would regularly come to check on her. Plus, she wouldn't take off with her daughter without proper safeguards in place.

She could be hiding from something or someone. A woman on the run from her past. That would explain why she refused to discuss anything before she arrived in Canton. But if she was trying to lay low, why would she marry Mac? Why not wait alone in the shadows until the threat passed and she could return to her life?

The most logical answer was that she was a common con artist. Lara had confessed that Victoria tried to get one of the richest men in town to marry her before settling for Mac. And while Jesse's dad was never rich, he owned a thriving business. One that Victoria urged him to sell from the day they got married. She might have planned to drain him dry until she moved on to her next victim. Plus, there was the cash that went missing from the safe the night she disappeared.

That would explain why she'd insisted on a quick Vegas wedding. Not only did it keep Mac from asking too many awkward questions, but she could create a hoax ceremony that would easily fool a man who was blindly devoted. It would also explain her dramatic exit from town.

Victoria Hudson had disappeared, only to be replaced with a new identity in a new town.

Yes. That made sense.

Jesse dismissed the inner voice that warned that she *wanted* to believe that Victoria was the bad guy who was out there conning some other sucker. Granted, it didn't explain what had happened to Mac, but it lightened a burden she'd been carrying for far too long.

Using the front door, Jesse entered the Tap Room and headed upstairs. First she needed something in her gut to ease the pangs of hunger; then she was going to pull out her laptop and do some research. She had no idea how much effort her father had put into discovering the truth about Victoria. Maybe he'd been content with knowing they'd never been officially wed. But even if he had tried to discover who she was and where she'd gone, he wouldn't have had Jesse's skill with a computer, or her access to information.

Grabbing a sandwich and a bag of chips, Jesse settled on her bed and opened her computer. She didn't know how to pull up any legal documents that might reveal Victoria's true identity, and worse was the fact that she had never bothered to spend time online and had flatly refused to allow Tegan to be on social media. A red flag, now that she looked back. It made it almost impossible to follow her digital trail.

Now what?

Munching on her sandwich, she continued to search the internet, looking for stories on surgeons killed in car wrecks around the time that Victoria moved to Canton. Dozens of links popped up. She scanned a few, searching for any mention of a wife or young daughter; then, with a muttered curse, she slammed the laptop shut. It would take her hours to scroll through every news article, with no guarantee that Victoria hadn't made up her dead surgeon husband.

There had to be another way.

Stretching across the mattress, Jesse closed her eyes and tried to dredge up everything she knew about her stepmother. Her lack of interest in the older woman meant she hadn't noticed nearly as much as she should have, but every detail, no matter how small, might help. Like putting together a puzzle to create the real Victoria Hudson.

Who are you?

Chapter 7

After a restless night, Jesse woke before dawn and stepped beneath a cold shower. She'd spent hours racking her brain for the tiniest nugget of a memory that might give her a starting point for her search. Had Victoria mentioned the name of an old friend or a distant family member? Had anyone sent her a Christmas card? When she came up blank she moved to any mention of Victoria's favorite restaurant, or vacation spot, or where she liked to shop before arriving in Canton. Something that might at least give a clue to a general region.

Eventually, she'd conceded defeat.

Victoria was too careful to slip. Or Jesse was too indifferent to care.

Probably a combination of the two.

She was pulling on a pair of jean shorts and crop top when her phone pinged with a text from Noah, asking to swing by the bar before he went to work.

Relief blasted through her as she jogged down the narrow staircase. After hours of brooding on the past, she was in dire need of a distraction. Plus, it meant that the Tap Room would soon be on the market and she could look forward to a future with Parker.

Something that couldn't come soon enough, she grimly assured herself.

Reaching the bottom step, she heard the soft tap on the front door and hurried to pull it open. Morning sunlight tumbled into the room, along with a fresh scent of morning air that cleared the cobwebs from her mind. With a smile, she stepped back, motioning the large man to enter.

"Morning, Noah."

Wearing a blue uniform shirt with Allen Lumberyard stitched on the top pocket and a pair of work pants with a leather tool holster belted around his waist, Noah stepped over the threshold.

"I hope this isn't too early?"

"Nope. I've been up for hours."

Jesse closed the door and reached over to flip on the overhead lights. Noah stood next to her, big and solid and smelling like warm cedar. He glanced down, his brows tugging together.

"Not to be rude, but you look exhausted."

Jesse ran her fingers through the short strands of her damp hair. "I'm not sleeping very well."

"I suppose it must be hard being back here."

"It's more weird than anything."

His frown deepened. "Weird?"

She hesitated. She hated sharing her emotions with anyone, but there was something soothingly familiar about Noah. He reminded her of a time when she didn't keep her heart so carefully guarded. Besides, she was bubbling with curiosity after seeing him with Reese yesterday. If she wanted him to answer her questions, she was going to have to open up. At least a little.

"Since coming back to town I don't know who I am," she confessed. "One minute I feel like I'm an intruder staying in a place I barely recognize, and the next I'm a teenage girl who used to sneak beer from the cooler and meet up with my friends at the old dock."

He studied her upturned face. "I remember that girl."

A wistful regret tugged at her heart. "Honestly, I'd forgotten all about her."

"Maybe you should stay around long enough to find her again."

"No. I can't stay." She glanced around the silent bar. "The emptiness of this place is suffocating me. I still expect to hear my dad's laugh when I walk into a room, or his footsteps walking down the stairs. Even the scent of him lingers. Like his spirit is caught between this world and the next. It's . . . disturbing."

"I'm sorry." He reached to touch her arm. "I can't even imagine."

"No one can."

"True."

Jesse forced her attention back to Noah. "That's why I need to move on."

"I get it," he assured her. "Do you have somewhere to move on to? Or someone?"

"Both. I have a boyfriend. We're going to buy a nightclub in Chicago."

He arched his brows, as if surprised by her answer. "Nice."

Jesse had a flashback to the sleazy nightclub that smelled like defeat. "Not yet. It's going to take a lot of work. But hopefully, it will be a success."

Noah paused, as if he sensed her lack of enthusiasm. "Make sure you have a thorough inspection done before you offer a down payment," he warned. "And double-check any places they recently painted or replastered. They might be trying to hide water damage."

"You sound like a guy who's done a lot of repairs," she teased.

"It's criminal how people will cover up major structural problems. And real estate agents aren't always honest."

There was an edge in his voice that suggested his words were personal. A perfect opening.

"Are you referring to Reese Skylar?"

"Reese?" Heat touched his cheeks. "Not specifically."

"I saw her at your house yesterday." She shrugged when he sent her a startled glance. "I was walking back from the cemetery and happened to notice her on your porch."

His jaw clenched, as if he was gritting his teeth. "She stops by every week or so to harass me about selling the house."

Harass? That was a strong word. "I take it you're not interested?"

"No. And I've told her that. A hundred times."

"I suppose persistence is a necessary quality in a real estate agent," Jesse murmured, wondering if Reese was being paid extra to try to convince Noah to sell. Or if there was something else driving her desire to stay in contact with this man.

"Persistence is one thing. She's—" Noah bit off his insult, heading toward the nearby bar as he reached into his tool holster to pull out some sort of meter. "Never mind."

Jesse followed as he pressed the flashlight app on his phone, his expression grim as he used a meter to test the electricity before turning his attention to the plumbing beneath the sink.

"It sounds personal," she insisted, ignoring his obvious reluctance to discuss the pretty real estate agent.

"Probably." His voice was muffled as he stuck his head in the cabinet. "No one knows better than me that the house is teetering toward the edge of collapse. I keep patching it up, but it's a money pit. It would take a fortune I don't have to get it back in shape."

"So why keep it?"

He sat on the floor, sweeping the flashlight along the baseboards, no doubt searching for mold. Or maybe warps in the floorboards. He paused to make a couple of notes in his phone before shoving himself to his feet.

"At first I wasn't ready to admit defeat," he reluctantly acknowledged.

"With the house?"

"With the dream it represented."

"You mean your marriage?" Jesse demanded.

"Yeah." Noah continued with his inspection, circling the large space with slow steps as he stopped to make occasional notes. "I had this image of a white picket fence and kids playing in the backyard. It never occurred to me that I would be living there alone."

"I'm sorry."

He shrugged. "Shit happens."

Jesse stopped in the center of the floor. Noah had his back to her, but there was no missing the raw regret in his voice. He was still mourning the loss of his marriage.

"I said no one understood how I felt when I stepped into this empty building, but I suppose you do, in a way," she admitted. "You were starting your family and then everything was snatched away. Like a rug being pulled from beneath your feet."

He glanced over his shoulder, his eyes dark with pain. "That's exactly what happened."

She held his gaze. "I probably shouldn't ask, but since we're sharing, is it awkward when your ex comes back to town? I know from painful experience that everyone in Canton is always hoping for some drama."

Noah shook his head. "That's not a problem for Kelly. She never comes back to Canton."

"Never?"

"Not since she left."

Jesse didn't hide her surprise that Kelly would walk away without looking back. Ironic, considering that was exactly what she'd done. Of course she had no reason to stay.

"What about her family?"

"Her parents divorced when she was young. Her father moved to St. Louis and he never bothered to stay in touch with his kids. Kelly reached out a couple of times after we got married, but he ignored her calls. I think being ghosted by her dad hurt Kelly more than she wanted to admit."

"And her mother?"

"She's in the nursing home. Early onset dementia. It was a grueling decline, until she didn't recognize anyone. Including Kelly."

"Tough," Jesse breathed. She didn't know the family, but it was a sharp reminder that everyone had their burdens to bear. "Really tough."

Noah continued with his inspection, heading toward the back of the building. "I'll be honest, I wasn't as sympathetic as I should have been. Kelly was struggling with a dozen upheavals in her life, not only being a new wife and watching her mother slip away. She was fighting with her brothers, who blamed her for forcing them to sell their grandparents' farm to help support their mother's care. I think they expected her to become a personal caregiver so they didn't have to make any sacrifices. In the end, Kelly had to threaten them with a lawyer. After that, they stopped talking to one another. It was all too much for her to bear."

"So she disappeared?"

"Exactly." He glanced back to send her a wry smile. "Perhaps we really do have a lot in common."

Jesse didn't bother to point out that at least he knew where to find his ex-wife. Or at least she assumed he knew how to find her. Jesse abruptly frowned. It was strange that Kelly hadn't been back, even if her mother didn't recognize her. What about her brothers? Or friends? Had they cut her off when she ran off with another man? Or was she just embarrassed to show her face in town?

"Okay." Noah abruptly broke into her churning thoughts. "I've made a list for the main area of the bar. It's mostly minor stuff. Do you want me to head down to the basement?"

She nodded. "It's really more of a cellar, so be careful. My father was constantly whacking his head when he went down there."

"Why don't you turn on some water so I can find the leaks?"

"Got it." She moved to stand in front of the sink, swiveling the faucets until the water was flowing at full strength. If there was a leak, she wanted to make sure that Noah found it before any potential buyer could demand money off the list price.

A few minutes later, she heard Noah climbing back up the stairs, and she switched them off, glancing over her shoulder. "Well?"

Noah crossed the floor to fold his arms on top of the bar. "I need to tack up some loose electrical lines and replace the caulking around the basement window. Minor stuff."

"What about the leak?"

"There's a loose joint. It needs to be replaced ASAP since it's creating a puddle on the dirt floor next to the wall. Eventually, the water will weaken the foundation that's already pretty sketchy."

Jesse's heart started to sink. "Are you saying I need a new foundation?"

"Actually, Bea remodeled her café a couple of years ago, replacing her side of the foundation and the cellar wall. A nice break for you, since it strengthened both buildings. Eventually, the new owner will have to replace the bricks, but I think you'll be able to sell the place without doing a lot of work."

Jesse released a loud sigh. "I'll be sure to thank her."

"There's no need," he assured her. "Bea is always happiest when she's helping someone else."

"That's very true." Jesse stepped forward, leaning on the opposite side of the bar. "I'm going to miss her when I leave."

"I hope she's not the only one."

Even with the width of the bar between them, she had leaned close to Noah. Close enough to fully appreciate the startling blue of his eyes and the chiseled strength of his features. He would never rival Parker in the beauty department, but there was something quietly compelling about him. Hard to believe Kelly could have willingly walked away.

Was she staring? Jesse cleared her throat, battling back a blush. "Of course not. I'll miss a lot of my old friends."

"Me included, I hope," he murmured, reaching out to stroke his fingers over her bare arm. "These are stunning." He lightly traced a tattoo of shattered chains that encircled her wrists. "Do they have a certain meaning?"

Jesse studied the simple designs as if she was seeing them through fresh eyes. To a stranger, they would appear to be a jumble of images that melded together more from the talent of the tattoo artists than any cohesive plan. Kind of like her life, she wryly acknowledged. A bizarre series of events patched together by random fate.

"They're from my dreams," she admitted. "Sometimes I'm obsessed by an image until I can get it out of my mind. The best way to do that is to have it inked onto my skin. I doubt that makes any sense to anyone but me."

"Does it work?"

Jesse shrugged, not willing to admit how many early mornings she'd spent pacing the floor. Or how often she'd waken from a nightmare and impulsively packed her bags, driving to a new place and a new job.

"Not always, but it's cheaper than therapy."

He nodded, almost as if he understood her restless need to outrun her demons.

"I thought about therapy after Kelly left," he said.

"What stopped you?"

"I told myself I didn't have the time. And I most certainly didn't have the money."

She studied his features, which were carved with strong, clean lines. It was a face that suggested a quiet confidence rather than a flashy charm.

"You seem to be doing okay."

"What choice do I have?" He leaned forward, peering deep into her eyes. "We take our blows and move forward, right? Although my moving forward has been stubbornly standing my ground, while you have been traveling around the world."

"Hardly the world," she protested.

"But you've never stopped moving." His gaze lowered to her arm. "Is that what these represent?"

"What do you mean?"

"They're all images of departing." His fingers traced the tattoo on her forearm. "These ravens flying from a tree." He skimmed up to the tattoo she'd gotten during her time in Aspen. "This sun setting over the mountains." He pushed up the sleeve of her shirt. "These footprints walking into the ocean." His eyes darkened as a shiver raced through her, his fingers returning to trace the delicate shackles that encircled her wrist. "These broken chains."

"Freedom," she whispered.

"Ah." There was a long silence; then Noah leaned even closer. Close enough to kiss. "I don't suppose you want to have dinner tonight?"

The invitation came without warning, and Jesse abruptly straightened, putting space between them. Did Noah think she'd been flirting with him? Wait, *had* she been flirting with him?

Maybe.

It was all too easy to slip into old patterns.

"Thanks, but I . . . I really should concentrate on cleaning out this place," she stammered.

"No worries." Noah easily accepted her rejection, stepping back from the bar.

"Maybe some other night. After I get some stuff done."

"Really, it's no problem," he assured her. "I just wanted to catch up on old times." There was an awkward pause. "And I wanted to make sure you knew that I haven't told anyone about seeing Mac that night. And I never will. As far as I'm concerned it's forgotten."

Jesse grunted, as if she'd taken a blow to the gut. "I'm sorry. What night?"

"He didn't tell you?"

"I'm not sure what you're talking about. Tell me what?"

"It doesn't matter." Noah shrugged, casually walking toward the door. As if he hadn't tossed a loaded grenade into the conversation. "I'll make up an inventory of what needs to be fixed and the approximate cost and run it by later."

"No, wait." Jesse scrambled to stop him from leaving. "You have to tell me. Did you see my dad after he disappeared?"

Noah sent her a shocked frown. "Of course not. I would have told you if I'd seen him. I knew how worried you were."

"Then when?"

"The night Victoria and Tegan left town . . ."

His words trailed away as a shrill ring echoed through the air.

Reaching into his pocket, Noah pulled out his phone and answered the call.

"Yeah, I'm on way." Shoving the phone back into his pocket, he headed to the door. "I'm sorry, I'm running late. Dad isn't feeling well and I need to open the lumberyard. I just wanted you to know you didn't have to worry about anything. See you later."

"Noah."

She reached out to grab the back of his shirt but was forced to jerk her hand back when the door snapped shut. Dammit. He couldn't leave without giving her answers.

"Noah, wait!"

Yanking open the door, Jesse stepped into the searing morning sunlight. Momentarily blinded, she narrowed her eyes against the glare, belatedly realizing that Noah was standing directly in front of her. A second later, her eyes adjusted, and she discovered that it was Bea, not Noah, standing there. Noah had already jumped into his truck and switched on the engine.

"He's in a hurry this morning," the older woman complained as Noah stepped on the gas and peeled away.

Jesse ground her teeth, struggling to control the searing blast of frustration. Even if he could have caught Noah, he obviously didn't have time to answer her questions. He was already late because he'd been kind enough to stop by and inspect the bar. It was unreasonable to expect him to ignore his responsibilities.

Later, she silently promised herself. The second he left work.

Releasing a harsh sigh, she forced her coiled muscles to relax. "He said something about being late opening the lumberyard."

Bea clicked her tongue. "I heard his father wasn't feeling well. He had a terrible time with his back since he fell off the roof of his house. Of course he's too stubborn to retire and sell the lumberyard. Not that I'm surprised. When is a man ever reasonable? It's a real shame, since it means more work for poor Noah."

Jesse ducked, pressing against the doorjamb when a loud bang ricocheted down the street. She'd lived in Chicago long enough to fear a drive-by shooting. It took a full minute to realize that it had been nothing more threatening than a backfire.

She pressed a hand over her racing heart, glaring at Noah's silver truck as it turned a corner and disappeared.

"I swear, that pickup looks exactly like the one he had in high school," she muttered. "I thought I was the only one who was driving around an old clunker."

"It probably *is* the same one." Bea sniffed. "Noah isn't the sort of man who tosses things just because they're old or broken. He cares enough to fix them."

Jesse glanced at Bea. She hadn't missed the edge in the older woman's voice.

"Are you talking about Kelly?"

"Among other things."

"Come in." Jesse's frustration was forgotten as she stepped back and waved Bea into the bar, trying to act casual even as her earlier curiosity rushed back with a vengeance. "Noah did mention his ex-wife while he was here this morning," she said as she closed the door behind her friend. "I thought he sounded sad about the end of his marriage, but he wasn't bitter. He said that Kelly was under a lot of pressure before she left."

"That's no excuse for breaking his heart." Bea crossed the wooden planks to place a small basket on top of the bar.

"Have you talked to her since she left town?"

Bea shook her head as she turned back to meet Jesse's curious gaze. "No. I haven't seen her in years, but I heard rumors that people have spotted her in Des Moines off and on. I don't think they ever talked to her."

"It's odd she never comes home."

"You didn't."

Jesse flinched. It was a direct hit. "Touché."

Bea smoothed her hands down her loose sundress, which speckled with flour. "I suppose there's no reason for her to come to Canton. Irene is beyond comfort at this point. Poor thing."

"What about her brothers?"

"They had to sell the family farm a few years ago and moved away. I'm not sure where they went." Bea shrugged. "Maybe they're with Kelly."

Jesse found that hard to believe. Noah made it sound like they'd had an ugly falling out.

"What about the guy she ran off with?" she pressed.

Bea looked confused. "Joe?"

"Has he been back to town?"

Bea snorted. "Last I heard, he'd already ran off with another woman just a year or so after he left town with Kelly. Any man willing to steal his best friend's wife is a man who will dump you the second he gets bored."

"That's true."

"Is there a reason for your interest?"

A good question, Jesse silently acknowledged. Was Noah's relationship with his ex-wife any of her business? Absolutely not. Did she think that Kelly had disappeared like her father? Probably not. Did she think Noah could have anything to do with her avoiding the town of Canton? Perhaps. But not because he'd done anything nefarious.

She was more than likely embarrassed to show her face.

Jesse shook her head. "Not really. It's just that Noah dropped everything to swing by and inspect the bar for me, and it made me wonder what kind of woman would walk away from him and never come back. He's such a nice guy."

Bea heaved a gusty sigh. "Well, they do say that nice guys finish last. Women prefer the bad boys."

Jesse couldn't argue with that. She'd deliberately avoided the hundreds of men she'd met over the years who would have offered her a nice, stable life. And she couldn't deny her initial fascination with Parker had something to do with his bad boy vibe. A psychologist would no doubt claim it had something to do with her messy past.

"What about you?" she asked, not in the mood to delve into her questionable life choices.

"Excuse me?"

"Do you prefer bad boys?"

"Me?" Bea looked shocked. As if she'd never been asked about her love life. "I can't remember. It was all too long ago."

"I don't believe that. There must have been someone special."

"Not really. I was born to be a spinster."

"Bea, there's no such thing as a spinster. Being in a relationship is a choice, not a mandate for women," Jesse chided. "But I can't believe you never thought about marriage."

Bea hesitated before a bittersweet smile curved her lips. "I suppose I did. I was in love once. Long ago."

"What happened?"

"We were in two different places."

Jesse felt a pang of sympathy. If Bea's mystery man lived in another town, that would explain why Jesse had never seen them together.

"Long-distance romances are tough."

"It wouldn't have worked out, anyway," Bea said, waving her hand as if to dismiss the potential relationship. "Truthfully, no one offered me the same sense of satisfaction as watching the café flourish and then going home to a peaceful night on the couch."

"You weren't ever lonely?"

"Better lonely than unhappy." Bea sent her a teasing wink. "I can easily cure loneliness."

Jesse laughed. Bea might be motherly, but she was too practical to let her heart overrule her good sense.

"You have a point."

Bea glanced around the empty bar. "Is Noah going to be able to patch things up for you?"

"Yes, he didn't seem to think there was anything catastrophic, which is a relief. I don't have the money to make major repairs." Jesse abruptly recalled his assessment of the cellar. "And he did mention that I have a partially new foundation thanks to you."

Bea looked confused. Then she snapped her fingers, as if suddenly recalling the renovations. "Right. It was something Mac and

I discussed a dozen times. We were always going to replace the crumbling wall between us, but we never could agree on a mutual date to shut down our businesses. Especially after Mac remarried."

"No doubt." Jesse rolled her eyes. "Dad wanted to take Tegan to St. Louis for a couple of days to enjoy the zoo and a baseball game and Victoria threw a fit. She informed him that if he wanted to do something special for Tegan, he could take on an extra job so she could have some decent clothes."

Bea's features pinched at the mention of Victoria. Had she sensed the beautiful woman wasn't who she claimed to be? It was doubtful. If Bea had discovered there was something off about Victoria, she would have outed her immediately. Bea was many things, but she wasn't subtle.

"The work is done now," Bea murmured. "Best for both of us to keep those memories in the past." Jesse didn't know if the older woman was talking to her or herself. Maybe both. "Now, I have muffins that are fresh from the oven." She patted the top of the basket, her smile returning. "Eat them while they're warm."

Jesse's stomach rumbled in anticipation. "They smell delicious, but please don't feel like you have to fuss over me, Bea. I know the café is always slammed this time of morning."

"It's no fuss," Bea protested, moving to pat Jesse's hand. "I have a couple of college students working today. Both of them are a lot of help, which is not always the case."

"Wait, I almost forgot."

Jesse reached into her back pocket to pull out her phone. Bea's mention of college students reminded her that she wanted to ask her about the mystery guy at Tegan's birthday party. It was a long shot that he would have an information to help. But right now she had zero leads to follow.

"Forgot what?"

"I'm thinking about doing a small memorial for my dad once everything is settled." Jesse used the same story she'd given Lara. It was too small a town to have more than one lie circulating.

"That's nice." Bea offered a sympathetic smile. "We could all use the closure."

"I agree." Once again, Jesse felt a pang of guilt. Maybe she *should* have a memorial.

"What do you need from me? I could do the catering, if you want."

"I wouldn't have anyone else," Jesse assured her. "But until the plans are finalized, I was wondering if you could tell me who this is?"

Swiping up the picture, Jesse zoomed in until the guy's face dominated the screen and turned it toward Bea.

The older woman leaned forward, studying the image for a long moment before shaking her head.

"I don't have a clue. Why do you ask?"

Jesse ground her teeth again. It felt like another dead end, but she refused to give up.

"I only have a couple of pictures of Victoria and Tegan." She zoomed out so Bea could see the whole image. "I wanted to include this one in a video slideshow to run at the ceremony, but I didn't recognize the guy in the background. It seems weird to put up his picture without asking his permission."

"I can't imagine he would care. You can barely see his face."

"Maybe not, but you never know. I'd rather ask," Jesse insisted, although she knew it sounded stupid. "He worked for you around the time this picture was taken. Just before Victoria left town."

"He worked for me? Really? I don't remember him."

"Lara said that he came to help you set up for the party."

"Hmm. It's possible, I suppose. I don't think he worked at the diner, but over the years I've hired lots of students to help with my catering. They're all just temporary. Too many to remember, I'm afraid."

"Would you have any record of him?"

"I suppose I could look back at my old tax returns to see if I can track him down," Bea offered, although she didn't sound enthusiastic. "First I'll have to find the forms from that year. I don't think I'd started to computerize my taxes back then. They're probably in my storage shed."

Jesse resisted the urge to tell her not to bother. She wanted the name.

"Thanks, Bea. I appreciate that."

"I would do anything for you, Jesse." Bea patted her arm. "You only have to ask."

Chapter 8

Jesse spent the day cleaning the bar like a woman possessed. It was the only way to keep herself from marching down to the lumberyard and demanding that Noah tell her what he'd seen and how Mac Hudson was involved.

Why was she even worrying? It had to be some sort of mix-up. Noah probably remembered the wrong night. Or the wrong time. Or maybe it was a simple case of mistaken identity. Something would prove that Noah hadn't seen her dad the night that Victoria and Tegan left town.

Until then, there was no use in driving herself crazy.

She managed to stay busy until the clock hit five o'clock, but even then she didn't rush over to Noah's. Instead, she took a long hot shower and changed into a pair of Bermuda shorts and a sleeveless sweater before walking to the Canton Bait Shop. The small convenience store sold more alcohol and cigarettes than bait, but they'd never bothered to change the name. Grabbing a six-pack of the locally brewed IPA, she slowly strolled along the riverbank, ignoring the muggy air and swarms of mosquitoes as she took a few minutes to simply appreciate the view.

Since returning to Canton, she'd been distracted by one thing after another. Not just dealing with the bar and her father's death certificate, but the unexpected suspicion that Victoria was a fraud. She'd spent very little time appreciating her return to the place she'd called home for nineteen years.

What if she never came back?

It would be nice to have a few good memories to take with her.

It was close to six thirty when she knocked on Noah's door. She judged that was plenty of time to lock up the lumberyard and drive the few blocks home. Her suspicion proved right as Noah pulled open the door, his hair damp from his shower and his work clothes replaced by a casual pair of khaki shorts and a camo T-shirt stretched tight over his broad chest.

The scent of warm male skin and soap rushed over her as he motioned her to enter the house.

"Hey Jesse."

"Are you busy?" she asked even as she stepped over the threshold. She wasn't going to give him the chance to change his mind.

"Nope."

"Good." She raised her arm. "I brought the beer."

He arched his brows. "My favorite. Lucky guess?"

"It's my secret talent as a bartender," she told him. "I can predict what a customer is going to order as soon as they walk up to the bar."

Jesse didn't add that she'd spent enough time in the Tap Room to know that all the guys in town drank the same IPA when her father had it in stock. It hadn't taken much talent to assume that it was still a favorite.

He grabbed the six-pack from her and turned to lead her down a short hallway.

"I'll get us glasses. I should have a couple in the freezer."

They entered a narrow kitchen that looked as if it'd been remodeled in the fifties with white painted cabinets and linoleum floors. It was also small enough to feel uncomfortably cramped. Or maybe it was just that Noah consumed more than his fair share of space.

Noah pulled out two tall glasses and filled them with a quick tilt of his wrist that kept the foam to a thin layer.

"Impressive," Jesse murmured as he handed her a frosty glass. "If you ever decide to change careers, give me a call."

"I'll keep that in mind." Taking a deep drink, Noah watched her over the rim. Then, lowering his glass, he asked the question that had no doubt been on the tip of his tongue since she'd knocked on his door. "Is there a reason for your visit?"

Jesse leaned against the counter, taking a small sip. She wanted a clear head for this conversation.

"First, it's a thank-you for agreeing to fix up the bar on such short notice. You're a lifesaver."

Noah grunted. "Hardly a lifesaver."

"You are to me," she insisted. "And secondly, I want to apologize for not agreeing to get together for a beer when you asked. That was rude."

"Not rude." He polished off his beer and poured a second one. Had it been a long day for him? In the dim light that crept through the small kitchen window, she could see shadows beneath his eyes. "I get it. You're not here to socialize."

Guilt stabbed through her. God, he was such a nice guy, and she was a bitch for taking advantage of his kindness. But she was going to do it.

She had to know.

"Getting the bar sold is my first priority, along with figuring out the paperwork to get my dad's death certificate," she agreed. "But I'm also hoping to close the door on my past."

His eyes narrowed. "Your father's disappearance?"

She nodded. "That's part of it."

"Let's go outside."

With a jerky motion, Noah turned to pull open the back door and stepped out of the kitchen. Jesse followed him onto the wooden deck. Was he angry? Disappointed?

Stepping onto the worn planks, Jesse's heavy discomfort was thankfully forgotten as she caught sight of the view.

"Okay. Wow. Now I get it," she murmured as her gaze swept over the manicured lawn stretching toward the distant lake that sparkled in the sunlight. Flagstones carved a path from the deck toward the lake, framed by ancient trees that spread their limbs to offer a perfect tunnel of shade. Best of all, there was a high fence that gave the property a sense of privacy from the neighbors.

It looked like something you would find in a fancy mansion, not an old farmhouse.

"Get what?" Noah demanded.

"Why you refuse to sell this place." She set down her glass on the picnic table to move toward the edge of the deck. "This view is amazing."

"Yeah." The planks squeaked in protest as Noah joined her. "It was one of the reasons I chose the house. The backyard is over three acres. It goes all the way past the lake and over the hill to an access road that no one uses."

"No wonder Reese Skylar is itching to get her hands on it."

Noah downed the rest of his beer in one gulp before setting the empty glass on the railing. He wiped the foam from his lips with the back of his hand.

"That woman puts a price tag on everything she sees."

"Including you?"

He hesitated. Not because he didn't understand what she was asking, but because he was deciding whether to confirm her suspicions.

"We had a brief relationship," he abruptly admitted. "With the emphasis on 'brief.'"

Jesse turned to face him. "Since she's still appearing on your doorstep, I assume she wasn't ready for it to be over?"

"Who knows what she wanted." Noah made a sound of disgust. "I thought at first it was me, but while we were dating she was always too busy to go out, and when we did manage to spend some time together she wandered around this property, pointing out hidden assets that would give me the most bang for the buck when I decided to sell. Seriously, I wasn't sure she was dating me or my house."

Hard to believe any woman could think of anything but Noah when she was in his company, but then again, Reese had struck her as someone who knew exactly where she was going, and if you got in her way, there was a good chance you'd be bulldozed.

"When people are crazy focused on their career they can forget there are things that are more important than money."

"I admire ambition, but it's not great for the old ego to be in bed with your lover and have them spend more time whispering in your ear about return on investment than how much they desire you."

Against her will, the memory of lying in Parker's arms the night before she'd left Chicago seared through her mind. She'd still been trembling from the aftermath of their lovemaking and wallowing in a glow of happiness when it'd been destroyed by Parker's whispered words.

At last. It's finally our turn, babe. No more waiting. We're gonna have it all.

It wasn't so much what he'd said, but the fierce anticipation in his voice. As if their current situation was unbearable. Not the most pleasant insinuation when they were snuggled in bed together.

"Yeah, ambition can spiral out of control," she muttered.

Noah regarded her with a steady gaze. "That sounds personal. Are you talking about yourself?"

"No. I have a job I can take or leave. It's a paycheck, not a career." she admitted. "I suppose I was thinking about Parker. My boyfriend."

"The one who wants you to buy him a nightclub?"

Had she said it like that? "Technically, it would be *our* nightclub."

"Technically, it would be *your* nightclub, unless the boyfriend is ponying up some cash," Noah insisted.

"He's bringing the expertise."

"I would say you have all the expertise you need and more. Mac was training you to take over the family business from the day you were born."

"That's true." Everyone in town knew that Mac expected her to continue the family legacy.

"Is there a reason you don't want to reopen the Tap Room?" he asked the obvious question. "That seems like the simplest solution."

"I did consider the possibility."

"But?"

"Parker convinced me that I would see him as an intruder. It's been in my family for so long, I would resent him making any changes."

Noah looked annoyed. "And you agreed?"

She had. At least at the time. Now the thought of selling the place was becoming painfully real. The ghosts had driven her away—ghosts that still lingered after all these years—but were they any more frightening than handing the keys to a stranger? Would she instead be haunted by regret?

She shook her head. It was too late for second thoughts. She'd made her decision.

"I'm ready to settle down with the man I love," she forced herself to say.

"What about these?" He reached out to stroke a finger down her bare arm, lingering on the broken chains tattooed around her wrists. "I thought you wanted your freedom?"

Goose bumps tightened her skin at his light touch. "Dreams can change."

"That's your dream? To settle down?"

She frowned at the accusation in his tone. "I know it sounds boring—"

"I'm not saying that," he interrupted. "Settling down with the person you love and who brings you happiness sounds beautiful. I only hope the dream is worth the sacrifice." He clicked his tongue. "Sorry. I know that it's none of my business. It's just that I've learned that relationships ebb and change over the years, and not always for the better."

Jesse glanced away, refusing to acknowledge the unease that sat like a lump in the pit of her stomach. She'd spent too long avoiding relationships out of fear. It was time to start living.

And that included a future with Parker.

But for that to happen, she had to close the door on her past.

"Before you left the Tap Room earlier, you mentioned you'd seen my dad the night Victoria left Canton."

Noah looked like he wanted to continue his warnings, but with a visible effort, he allowed her to change the direction of the conversation. No doubt her stubborn expression had convinced him that she wasn't going to listen.

"Actually, it was closer to the next morning," he admitted.

It wasn't the answer she wanted to hear. "What time?"

Noah leaned his hip against the railing, his brow furrowed. "I don't recall an exact time. It was still dark, but it was close to dawn. Probably around six thirty."

"Where?"

"I'd spent the night down by the river—"

"Is that a joke?" she interrupted with a frown.

"What?"

She waved a hand. "You know . . . that skit about living down by the river?"

"Oh no." He chuckled. "Back then, Kelly and I were dating, but we were both living at home. It made it hard to have private time together, so we would meet at night in the boathouse next to the old ferry."

Jesse remembered the place. It was warped and rotting and in danger of collapse, but it was a perfect spot to hide from prying eyes. She'd shared more than one kiss in the damp, moldy darkness.

"Ah, I get it. Desperate times," she teased.

He heaved a deep sigh. "It felt like it. Probably one of the reasons we rushed into marriage."

"So you spent the night out there?" she asked, refusing to be distracted. This was too important.

"I did. Kelly left around midnight, but I fell asleep. It wasn't until a barge blasted its horn that I woke up and headed home."

"And that's when you saw my dad?"

"Yes." He studied her tense expression, clearly sensing his answer was important. "I was walking down Main Street when Mac swerved around the corner and onto the sidewalk. If I hadn't jumped into the alley, he would have taken me out."

Her mouth was so dry it was hard to form the words. "He was driving?"

"Not very well." Noah sent her a rueful smile. "Honestly, I think he was drunk."

Jesse knew beyond a shadow of a doubt he was thoroughly blasted. She'd seen the empty bottle of whiskey. But she'd sworn on a Bible in court that he'd never left the bar.

"Then what happened?"

"He slammed on the brakes and rolled down his window to apologize."

She sucked in a slow breath as the hope she'd been clinging to was abruptly shattered. Noah hadn't made a mistake. A rural town like Canton had a hundred pickups that all looked the same. It would be easy to think you recognized who was driving when it was someone else. But not if they spoke to each other.

"Was he alone?"

"As far as I could tell. I stayed at the edge of the alley as he backed up and pulled the truck next to the curb before switching off the engine. I assumed he realized he shouldn't be behind the wheel and was going inside. I didn't want to embarrass him, so I went on my way, and I didn't really think about it again until Mac was arrested."

"Why didn't you say something to the sheriff?"

Noah blinked, as if confused by the question. "Because I knew Mac my entire life. There was no way he could have hurt his family. Why give those assholes a reason to lock him up?"

"Not everyone believed that."

"Then they're idiots." Noah's voice was harsh with disgust. "The man owned a bar. He had to deal with obnoxious drunks on a nightly basis. I never once heard anyone complain about him losing his temper or becoming violent. Even when he was breaking up a fight."

A sad smile curled her lips. Most people had shared Noah's unwavering belief in Mac, but there were a few ugly rumors that swirled through town. They'd wounded Jesse more than she wanted to admit.

"He was the most gentle man I've ever known," she murmured.

"And the most patient. You know, I once saw him at the homecoming bonfire protecting Coach Matthews from an angry dad who was furious his son had been cut from the team. Mac stood between them, dodging the man's punches without ever lifting a hand. He didn't even raise his voice. Eventually, the dude realized he was making a fool of himself and let Mac drive him home. That's not the sort of guy who's going to snap just because his wife decides to leave town."

Jesse reached out to lay her hand on Noah's arm. "Thanks."

"For what?"

"For believing in Dad." She shrugged. "And for not saying anything after he was arrested. I know Dad didn't do anything to Victoria, but..."

"Yeah, I get it."

Jesse turned back to admire the view, willing her muscles to relax as she shoved aside Noah's disturbing revelation. She would grapple with the implications later. Right now she had to make sure that Noah didn't realize just how unnerved she was by his confession.

"I hope you don't sell," she said in low tones. "It's so peaceful here. It would be a shame to have the property chopped up to build another boring brick house. It's like you're a rebel."

He snorted, thankfully distracted by her words. "A rebel who is deadass broke. Right now my pride and the money I received from a small inheritance a few years ago is the only thing keeping a roof over my head."

Jesse sent him a startled glance. Before she'd left Canton the Allen family hadn't been rich, but they certainly hadn't been poor.

"Really?"

"Unfortunately." He shrugged, but she didn't miss his clenched teeth. The stress was bothering him more than he wanted anyone to realize. "The lumberyard has been struggling for years, and my dad can't really afford to give me a steady salary. Hell, there are months when we lose money. If it wasn't for the odd jobs I do around town, I wouldn't be bringing in enough to cover the bare minimum."

"Why doesn't your father sell the place?"

"Would your dad have sold the Tap Room?"

"Okay." She smiled wryly. "Point made."

He returned her smile. "Eventually, I'll have to get a full-time job. But for now I do what I can to keep the bills paid."

"I'm sorry." She covered his hand that was resting on the railing.

"No use crying over spilt milk, as my mom would say." He flipped over his hand and threaded their fingers together. His touch was warm and intimate, and a dangerous awareness hummed through her. Noah's eyes darkened, but before the moment could become awkward—at least for Jesse—the ring of an old-fashioned landline blasted from the open kitchen door. "Damn." Noah looked genuinely annoyed. "I should see who's calling."

Jesse tugged her fingers free, assuring herself it was relief, not frustration, that tingled through her.

"Go ahead."

"I won't be long."

With a lingering glance, he turned to hurry into the house, and Jesse climbed off the deck. It was the easiest way to give Noah privacy for his call; plus, she'd wanted to stroll down the flagstone path from the moment she'd caught sight of it. Who knew if she'd ever have another chance?

Clearing away the troubling thoughts that stewed like poison in the back of her mind, Jesse concentrated on the beauty of the branches interlocked above her head and the sweet scent of freshly mowed grass. She felt as if she was surrounded by a vibrant green tunnel, safely hidden from the world, and just for a moment she wanted to enjoy the sensation.

This was what she missed when she was in the chaotic bustle of Chicago. As much as she enjoyed the crowds and the boisterous excitement when she worked at the nightclub, there were days when the incessant noise wore on her nerves. And the traffic...

Jesse shuddered. She'd forgotten how nice it was to be able to drive from point A to point B without open warfare. There were even parking spots in front of the places she wanted to visit. Nothing short of a miracle.

Strolling toward the lake, Jesse rounded a small curve, her gaze following the erratic dance of a butterfly as it disappeared between an opening in the trees. Her steps slowed as the butterfly zigzagged its way toward a patch of weeds that looked completely out of place. Why would Noah mow his lawn until it was a smooth carpet of green and then ruin it with that ugly spot?

Curious to know what was hidden in the weeds, Jesse squeezed between the tree trunks and angled toward the edge of the yard. She sensed that the ground was dipping down, the soil beneath her feet feeling oddly spongy.

"Jesse! Stop."

The sharp urgency in Noah's voice forced her to an abrupt halt. She stiffened as he rushed to stand next to her, his hand wrapping around her arm as if he intended to physically hold her in place.

"What's wrong?" she demanded, barely resisting the urge to pull away from his firm grip.

He used his free hand to point toward the center of the overgrown area. "There's an old well hidden in the grass. This house used to get its water from the lake until I had new lines laid to connect to the city system. Eventually, I'll get around to having it filled in, but right now it's a death trap. I should have warned you."

Jesse leaned forward, catching a glimpse of a round grate dug into the ground. It was crusted with mud, but it looked as if it'd rusted through in several spots. She wrinkled her nose as she belatedly realized there was a foul odor wafting from the shadowed depths.

"No worries," she forced herself to say, even as a dark unease spread through her. It wasn't a reaction to Noah. Or at least she didn't think it was. But there was something unnerving about the smelly, overgrown area. A dark stain on an otherwise picturesque scene. "I shouldn't have been wandering around."

He tugged her away from the well. "Maybe we should go back to the house. It's starting to get dark."

Jesse glanced up, realizing that the sun was dipping over the trees, leaving them shrouded in shadow.

"Actually, I need to get home."

"So soon? There's more beer."

She shook her head. "I'm still trying to scrub off the layers of dirt that accumulated in the bar. It's going to take longer than I expected."

With an effort, she kept a casual pace as she crossed the yard toward the gate that led out of the backyard. She didn't want Noah to sense her urgent need to be away from his house. He'd done nothing but try to help her since she'd come back to Canton.

As they reached the edge of the house, Noah reached past her to grab the top of the gate, trapping her between the fence and his towering form.

"I'm glad you stopped by."

Jesse swallowed the lump trying to form in her throat, tilting back her head to meet his steady gaze. He was standing too close, but it wasn't threatening.

"Me too." She kept her tone light. "Let me know when you have the quote for the work I need done."

There was a long, not quite comfortable silence before Noah gave a nod of his head, pulling open the gate.

"I'll run it by tomorrow."

"Sounds good." Stretching her lips into a smile, she darted through the opening. "See ya."

Keeping her head lowered, Jesse scurried back to the Tap Room, sensing the stares as she hurried past the crowd milling through the farmers market at the nearby intersection. She wasn't in the mood for chitchat. In fact, she wasn't in the mood for anything but a sleeping pill and an early night, she decided, as she slammed the door shut behind her and slid the bolt into place.

She did take the time to walk around the bar area before heading upstairs. She was still creeped out from the abandoned well in Noah's backyard, which made absolutely no sense, but she had to reassure herself there was no one hiding in the shadows before she headed to her room and locking that door as well.

By eight thirty she was tucked into bed with a bowl of cereal and a glass of milk she used to wash down the sleeping pills. At some point she was going to have to deal with the revelation that Mac had lied to her about leaving the bar that night. As well as her suspicions that Victoria was playing an ugly game with all of them from the moment she arrived in Canton.

But not tonight.

She desperately needed a few hours' sleep to clear the dread that was clouding her mind. Right now, everything felt ominous. As if an unseen threat was looming just out of sight. Even poor Noah, who'd done nothing more than be a good friend, had set off her alarms.

It was a waste of time searching for the truth when she was jumping at shadows.

She'd start again tomorrow.

Setting aside her empty bowl, Jesse snuggled beneath the covers and allowed the drowsiness to suck her into the void.

Chapter 9

At first Jesse floated in the welcome darkness, her muscles slowly relaxing and her pulse slowing to a steady pace. It was like being wrapped in a cocoon. Exactly what she needed.

Then the dreams intruded.

She was seventeen years old again, snuggled in her bed. As usual, she'd stayed up too late the night before chatting online with her friends, and she groaned in annoyance when the sound of raised voices intruded into her deep sleep.

It wasn't the first time she'd been awakened by a fight between her dad and stepmother, but usually it was Victoria's shrill voice that shattered the peace, while Mac tried to keep his tone low enough to avoid disturbing Jesse and Tegan. This time it was her father's voice that was raised in anger. Throwing back the covers and crawling out of bed, she crossed to the door and pulled it open an inch. Just far enough to witness the latest family drama.

Her dad was standing in the middle of the hallway wearing a pair of sweatpants and a T-shirt with his hair sticking up, as if he'd just jumped out of bed. Victoria, on the other hand, was fully dressed and wrapped in her expensive Burberry trench coat. She was holding a suitcase as well as a matching overnight bag. Tegan was also dressed and wearing a coat, her expression oddly stoic as she watched Mac grab her mother by the arm. As if this was a scene she'd seen before.

"Victoria, please," Mac pleaded.

Victoria tried to tug free of his grasp. "Leave me alone."

"We need to talk."

Victoria glanced toward her daughter. "Get your bags and wait for me in the car." With that same stoic expression, Tegan turned and headed down the stairs. Victoria waited for her daughter to disappear before glaring at her husband. "Remove your hand."

Mac jerked back as if he'd been burned. "Why are you leaving? I don't understand."

"Of course you don't understand, you stupid ass," Victoria drawled, her voice edged with pure pleasure. As if she'd waited a long time to share the cruel taunt. "You never get it, do you?"

"Did I do something wrong?"

"Everything."

"It can't be everything," Mac protested.

"Really? Do you want a detailed list?"

"You have a list?"

"A long list. Let's start with the way you talk."

"The way I talk? Are you serious?"

"You bellow like everyone around you is deaf. I swear, I can't get away from the noise. Even when I'm up here and you're in the bar I can hear you. And that laugh. God, you sound like a braying donkey." Victoria wasn't done as she ran a slow gaze down Mac's sturdy body. "And then there's the way you look."

Mac glanced down, his round face filled with a heartbreaking confusion. "What's wrong with the way I look?"

"You have an entire closet stuffed with flannel shirts and old jeans. The only time you bother to put on a decent shirt and shave your face is when you go to church. And only because I insist you clean up."

Mac shook his head. "That's why you're leaving? Because of flannel shirts?"

"Because you're a slob," Victoria snapped. "And you snore." She leaned forward, spitting the words directly into her husband's face. "And you suck in bed."

Jesse flinched, her stomach clenching with pity as her father slowly stepped back, his face flushed with shame at the ugly accusation.

"Anything else?" he asked stiffly.

"Yes. You're cheap." Victoria waved a hand around the cramped hall with its faded paneling. "We live in a dump, and the pittance you give me barely pays for the bare essentials, let alone the comforts that Tegan and I deserve. I haven't had a decent manicure in months."

Mac folded his arms over his chest, as if trying to ward off invisible blows. "I give you what I can."

"That's a lie," Victoria abruptly snarled. "I've seen your accounts. I know you're hiding money. You're stealing my fair share."

Jesse clenched her hands into fists, longing to rush out and punch the bitch in the face. How dare she accuse the man who kept a roof over her head and food on the table of stealing? She sat around doing nothing all day, expecting to be treated like a princess. She was lucky she got anything.

Mac's expression hardened. "You knew I wasn't rich when you married me."

"I assumed you would have the decency to sell this place and get a real job." Victoria pursed her lips as she visibly shuddered. Like a bad actress in a cheesy melodrama. "Instead, I've been stuck in this hellhole with my young, impressionable daughter, smelling like beer and cigarettes. Even worse, you keep me trapped in poverty."

"Trapped in poverty?" Mac's sharp laugh echoed down the hallway. "Were you trapped in poverty when I bought you the new sports car you said you couldn't live without? It's an obscene waste of money in this area. Or maybe you mean you were trapped when you insisted on ordering brand-new furniture from Chicago because it's obviously better to get crap that's pumped out of a factory rather than hand-carved local pieces that have lasted a hundred years? Or when you made your secret trip to St. Louis for a little snip and tuck to keep your shit from sagging?"

Victoria's spine was rigid, genuine hatred flaring over her face. "Mac Hudson," she spit out. "Always with the joke. I suppose you think you're funny?"

Mac's brief amusement faded like dew beneath a scorching sun. "There's nothing funny about this situation. It's tragic. How did you go from ordering new curtains for the bedroom last week to deciding you can't stay here another second?" He reached out a hand. "Something must have happened. Talk to me. Please."

She ignored his plea. "The only thing that happened was that I realized I can't pretend anymore. The pathetic crumbs I have to beg for aren't worth the effort."

"If this is about money—"

"Would you listen to me?" Victoria interrupted. "I don't love you. I never loved you. If you want the blunt truth, I don't even like you."

Mac jerked. Of all the hateful things that Victoria had thrown at him, that seemed to hurt the most.

"Then why did you marry me?"

"I needed someone to take care of me and Tegan. You were the only one to offer."

He shook his head in pained bewilderment. "Our entire marriage was a lie?"

She snorted, turning to head toward the stairs. "You have no idea," she muttered, the words barely loud enough for Jesse to hear them.

"Where are you going?" Mac called out.

"Someplace you'll never find us." She glanced over her shoulder. "If you care for me at all, don't bother looking."

Mac squared his shoulders. "Why would I look? Good riddance."

With a toss of her head, Victoria headed down the stairs with her suitcases clutched tightly in her hands. The minutes ticked past—Jesse wasn't sure how many, but it felt like an eternity—before she at last heard the sound of a door being slammed shut.

Victoria had left the building.

Another minute passed before Mac slowly dropped to his knees, burying his face in his hands.

Yanking the door fully open, Jesse rushed out of her bedroom to kneel beside the broken man.

"Dad." She wrapped an arm around his slumped shoulders.

Lowering his hands, her dad lifted his head to meet her worried gaze. "Jesse. I suppose it was too much to hope you didn't have to hear all that?"

"It doesn't matter. Are you okay?"

He groaned, forcing himself back to his feet. He was clearly uncomfortable at her witnessing him in such a vulnerable position.

"Of course I'm okay. It's just . . ." He visibly tried to pull himself together. "Honestly, I don't know what it is, but everything is going to be fine."

She grabbed his hand, giving it a squeeze. She was too young to fully understand how devastated her father must be to not only lose his wife, but the stepdaughter that he loved.

"It will be. I promise. We have each other and that's all that matters."

He managed a weary smile. "Go back to bed, Jesse. We'll talk about this later."

"What about you?" She bit her lip, frowning at her father.

She was worried that he might try to follow Victoria and continue his pleas for her to stay. It didn't matter that the bitch had trampled his pride and brutally confirmed Jesse's suspicion that she'd never loved him. Mac was stubborn enough to try to work through their problems if he could convince his wife to give him a second chance.

"I'm going downstairs to make sure everything is locked up. I'll be back up in a few minutes," he reassured her.

Jesse reluctantly returned to her room, but she didn't make the mistake of climbing back into bed. It was past five thirty, which meant her alarm would be going off in an hour. What was the point in trying to go back to sleep?

Besides, she was too wound up to relax. The arguments between her dad and Victoria always filled the apartment with a sour atmosphere that lingered for days. And this one was more heated than most.

Of course if she was being honest, the fight wasn't the only reason her pulse was racing and her nerves on edge.

Victoria had packed her bags and left. Could it be a stunt to force her dad to sell the bar? Maybe. That seemed in character. And even if the witch had decided to leave, there was no guarantee that she wouldn't return. Victoria wasn't the sort of woman to suffer, even for a day. If she didn't have a better option already lined up, then she would soon scurry back. Like a rat burrowing in the dark corners of Jesse's existence.

But what if she didn't come back?

A tentative hope bloomed in the center of Jesse's heart. *Very* tentative. More than once, Jesse had dared to anticipate the end of her dad's stormy marriage only to be disappointed. The only thing different this time was that Victoria had actually walked out. It might mean something, right?

Hopping in the shower, Jesse stayed beneath the scalding water until her skin was red and puckered. For the first time since Victoria moved in, Jesse didn't have to worry about the older woman bitching because she'd used all the hot water or that the steam from the shower was ruining her new wallpaper. She even left her bedroom door open as she dried her hair, savoring the knowledge that there were no intrusive gazes monitoring her every movement.

Once she was ready for the day, she paused to stare in the mirror, smoothing her expression to hide the satisfaction that lurked just below the surface. Her father was hurting. She wouldn't let him see how happy she was that she might never have to see Victoria again.

Convinced she looked properly sympathetic, Jesse left her room and headed to the kitchen. She was still in the hallway when she heard a loud slam from downstairs. Was that the door? Shit, was Victoria back?

Thoroughly disgusted, Jesse raced toward the steps and vaulted down them two at a time. Victoria had treated her dad like he was trash. Not only taunting him for his lack of sophistication, but bluntly confessing she'd never, ever loved him. Jesse would be damned if she waltzed in and pretended that nothing had happened.

It didn't matter if she pissed off her father or not, she was going to tell the witch exactly what she thought of her.

Her righteous anger was bubbling through her as she entered the main bar, but there was no Victoria there to vent it on. Just her dad, who was stumbling to the bar to grab a nearly empty bottle of whiskey.

Cautiously moving forward, Jesse took in the sight of the barstool that looked as if it'd been tossed across the room, and the broken glass on the floor. Had there been a fight? Was that what she'd heard?

"Dad?" She slowly walked forward, her gaze searching the shadowed room. "What happened?"

"Exactly what I should have expected to happen." Without warning Mac slapped his open palm on the top of the bar. "Christ, Victoria was right. I'm an idiot."

Jesse hurried to wrap an arm around her father's shoulders, guilt slicing through her like a dagger. While she'd been upstairs gloating at the thought of Victoria leaving, her dad had been tortured with loss. He'd truly loved the woman, for whatever mysterious reason, and she'd broken his heart.

"Don't say that," she murmured.

"It's true." A choked sob was ripped from his throat. "How stupid did I have to be to believe a woman like Victoria would be interested in a man like me? I bet the whole town was laughing behind my back."

"No one was laughing," she insisted. "In fact, I don't know how many times one of our neighbors said that Victoria hit the jackpot when you asked her to be your wife. They all knew she was lucky to ever have you."

"They had to say that because I'm your dad."

"No, because they know you're a loyal, hardworking man who genuinely cares about people." Her arm tightened around him, determined to make him realize how much he was loved by everyone in town. "You're decent in a way a woman like Victoria could never appreciate."

He snorted, but Jesse didn't miss the gratitude that glowed in his weary eyes. "I'm just a glorified bartender who's well past his prime. Victoria's beautiful enough to have any man she wants."

"If that was true, then why wasn't she with one of those other men?"

"I'm sure she will be soon enough."

"Good. I'm glad she's gone."

Mac flinched, bowing his head as if a heavy weight was settling over him. "You won't be so happy when you learn what she's done."

Jesse frowned. "What do you mean?"

"She took everything. I'm sorry, Jesse." She felt him shudder, as if he was battling against an intense surge of emotion. "I tried to stop her but couldn't even do that right."

She laid her head on top of his. "Don't worry, Dad. I know it hurts now, but eventually, you'll realize it's for the best. She never truly appreciated you."

"No. I mean it's all gone. She took it," he rasped.

"Took what?"

"The money."

"What money?"

"Your money."

Jesse tried to remember where she'd left her purse. Probably the living room. It would be just like Victoria to steal from her own stepdaughter.

"It doesn't matter. I only had twenty bucks or so. It's worth every penny to get rid of Victoria."

"No." Mac slammed his hand on the bar again, his smoldering anger abruptly flaring. "Your college fund."

Jesse lifted her head. Her dad had obviously been drinking since he came downstairs—the whiskey bottle hadn't emptied itself—and he wasn't thinking clearly.

"Are you feeling okay?" she demanded. For as long as she could remember, the bar had barely scraped by. Any extra money was used for the constant repairs on the old building. "I don't have a college fund."

He glanced up, his bleary eyes filled with tears. "Your mother made me promise before she died that I would set aside money from the till every night for you to use for college, or just getting started in your own home."

Jesse took a moment to absorb his words. "Are you serious?"

"It tore her apart to know she wouldn't be there for your big moments in life. And she knew me well enough to realize I wouldn't think of the future until too late."

A savage combination of regret and bittersweet joy swept over her, nearly sending her to her knees.

"I had no idea."

Mac reached up to place his hand over her fingers, resting on his shoulder. "It wasn't a huge amount every night, but it added up to be a nice surprise for your eighteenth birthday."

Jesse remembered the earlier argument and her stepmother's accusation. Now she understood.

"That's why Victoria claimed there was money missing."

"Yeah."

"How much?"

"Close to twenty thousand dollars. Not a huge amount."

Jesse nearly choked. That was ten times more than she could ever have expected.

"Not a huge amount? That's a fortune."

Mac flinched, as if he'd taken a blow. "You're right. It is a fortune. And now it's gone."

Jesse abruptly straightened, glaring down at her father as fury seared through her. It didn't matter that she'd never expected money for college. Honestly, she'd assumed she would stay in Canton and work in the Tap Room. Just like her dad and her granddad. But the knowledge that the beautiful legacy from her mother was stolen by a worthless cow made her want to punch something. Or someone.

"Victoria should be in jail." Jesse could barely form the words, she was so angry. Then she was struck by a sudden realization. "Wait. When did she take the money?"

"Right before she left."

Jesse glanced at the neon beer sign above the bar that doubled as a clock. A quarter to seven. Hope surged through her. The banks wouldn't have opened yet.

"If she transferred it out of the account, then we should go to the bank as soon as it opens. There's a good chance we can get it stopped. Or even if it's gone through, we can try to have it reversed."

Mac hunched his shoulders, grabbing the bottle of whiskey to drain the last dregs. He shuddered as the fiery liquid slid down his throat.

"It wasn't in the bank," he managed to croak. "I kept the money in the downstairs safe."

Jesse blinked. She loved her father, but who kept twenty thousand dollars in cash in the cellar of an old building? It was insane. Even if was in a safe, there could be a fire or a flood.

Or a thief.

"Why would you have that much money laying around?" She glared at him as he polished off the last of the whiskey. "Dad?"

"I took a few dollars out before counting the till for the night," he grudgingly confessed. "That way I didn't have to add it to the total income. It was a college fund; why should I have to pay taxes on it? I just wanted to make sure you would have what you needed for your future."

Jesse didn't judge her dad for concealing a few dollars out of the till. It wasn't like he was a billionaire hiding his money in offshore accounts. She did, however, blame him for letting her stepmother get her greedy hands on it.

If he hadn't been so blinded by Victoria's pretty face and soft curves, he might have considered whether or not she was a trustworthy partner. And maybe he wouldn't be blind drunk at seven in the morning.

With a shake of her head, she squashed her frustration. She couldn't change the past. She had to concentrate on salvaging something for the future.

But how? If Victoria had taken the cash from the safe . . .

"Oh my God," she breathed as she realized that the older woman hadn't simply stumbled across the cash. "Victoria knew it was there."

Mac looked grim. "You're right. She must have been spying on me. Otherwise she wouldn't have known the combination to the lock." He glanced over his shoulder. "When I came down to lock up I saw the door to the cellar was open. When I went downstairs I realized that she'd cleaned out every penny. I didn't even think about how she knew that it was there."

"We need to call the sheriff." She reached into her back pocket, annoyed when she realized she'd left her phone upstairs. The sooner they caught up to Victoria the less chance she had of disappearing with the cash.

"No."

Jesse scowled. "He can get our money back."

"I don't care. She's gone. Just . . ." With a muttered curse, Mac grabbed the empty bottle and threw it against the wall behind the bar. It shattered, leaving behind a deafening silence. Jesse stared at her father in shock. The explosion of emotion was completely out of character. "Just let it be, Jesse. I'll get you the money some other way. I promise."

Jesse clenched her hands. "It's not about the money. At least not entirely. She shouldn't get away with stealing."

Mac turned his head, his face frighteningly pale. "Please, Jesse. I told you. She's gone."

Jesse refused to concede defeat. Her father didn't understand. Her need to get back the money had nothing to do with what it could buy. It was what it represented. A connection to her mother.

"Maybe not. I should go look for her," Jesse insisted, mentally running through the various places Victoria could go at such an early hour. "Maybe she went to stay with a local friend."

"I told you, she's gone," her dad rasped.

"How do you know?" Jesse stilled, belatedly remembering the sound of a slam that brought her downstairs in the first place. "You didn't go after her, did you?"

"Of course not. I can barely walk, let alone drive." With a scowl that warned he was done discussing the subject, her dad pointed toward the back of the bar. "Go eat some breakfast and get to school. We'll discuss this later."

Chapter 10

Jesse slept in late, still feeling sluggish when she finally forced herself out of bed and into the shower. It wasn't until she'd consumed the muffins that Bea had delivered the day before and caffeinated herself with several cups of coffee that she could clear the fuzz from her brain and consider the implications of Noah's confession.

Sitting at the kitchen table, Jesse massaged her temples, trying to hold back a looming headache.

It shouldn't matter that her father had left the bar the night Victoria disappeared. What did it change? Okay, he'd lied to her. Probably because he hoped to avoid a lecture on drinking and driving. But it wasn't like she would ever believe that her father would hurt Victoria. As Noah had pointed out, Mac Hudson didn't have a violent bone in his body.

Unfortunately, she couldn't dismiss the niggling itch in the back of her mind.

What if everything had been a terrible accident? Maybe he'd chased after Victoria and she'd run off the road. And if the worst had happened, her dad might have panicked. He'd been drinking. Drinking heavily. He wouldn't have been thinking clearly.

Was it possible?

Jesse dug her fingers into her temples, as if she could crush the awful thought.

Nothing that happened that night could ever destroy her love for her dad. Mac Hudson was the anchor in her life no matter what was happening. Nothing could change that. But if he had accidentally hurt Victoria and Tegan, and then committed suicide out of guilt, she couldn't blame anyone but herself.

Her father had devoted his life to raising her, ignoring his own needs to make sure she never felt as if she was being pushed into second place. He hadn't even dated, instead working day and night to keep a roof over their head.

And, in return, she'd been a selfish brat. Had she been happy for him when he'd considered her mature enough for him to seek out a partner and fall in love? No. She'd been a jealous cat who refused to listen to his pleas for understanding. Even if she told herself that she'd suspected that Victoria was a bitch and destined to betray her father, the truth was that she would have resented anyone who wanted to share his attention.

Maybe if she'd tried to accept the marriage and been supportive instead of doing everything in her power to cause trouble, the two of them might have worked through their problems. Jesse clicked her tongue. That seemed a stretch. Her dad and Victoria were tragically incompatible. Still, there might have been a less explosive end to their marriage.

One that didn't include Victoria stealing her college fund and her father pouring a bottle of whiskey down his throat.

With an abrupt shake of her head, Jesse pushed herself to her feet. She was punishing herself for something that probably never happened. At this point, it was nothing more than a wild conjecture.

What she needed to do was find out if it was even possible before she indulged in an epic pity party.

Grabbing her purse, Jesse jogged downstairs and out of the bar. She hissed as the heat hit her like the blast from an oven. It felt like the scalding air and thick humidity were tag teaming to melt her into a puddle of sweat. She hurried around the corner to climb into her truck, blasting on the air-conditioner in an effort to unglue the crop top and cutoff jeans from her damp skin.

She pulled her phone out of her purse, glancing at the exact time before she put the truck in gear and pulled away from the curb, driving down Main Street until she was out of town. Once away from the city limits, she punched on the gas, rattling down the road at top speed. Victoria had been in a huff when she'd left the bar, and if she'd feared that she was being followed, she would have done whatever was necessary to disappear through the maze of backroads.

Obviously Jesse's old clunker couldn't reach the speed of a sports car, but once she turned onto the deeply rutted side road, she knew that Victoria would have had to slow down to keep from bottoming out. Her sports car sat too low to travel easily over the gravel lanes.

Keeping to a reasonable speed, Jesse rounded the sharp curve in the road where Victoria had lost control of her car and rammed into a tree. Only then did she pull to the side and put the truck in Park. Grabbing her phone, she looked at the time. It'd taken her twenty-two minutes to get to this spot. And even if she was off by a minute or two, it would have been next to impossible for her dad to have anything to do with Victoria's disappearance. Not unless he managed to follow them, watch them crash into the tree, determine they were dead, load the bodies in his truck, figure out some place to dump them where they wouldn't be found in less than ten minutes so he could make the twenty-two-minute drive back to town and be inside the bar before she came downstairs to find him.

Was it doable? Maybe for a man half his age and stone-cold sober. But not her dad, who suffered from back problems and was so drunk he could barely stand.

Undeniable relief raced through her.

For now, she was convinced that her father didn't have anything to do with what happened.

Shutting off the engine, Jesse jumped out of the truck and waded through the thick grass that surrounded the tree. She didn't know what was compelling her forward, but now that she was out there, she wasn't leaving until she had a look around.

She'd reached the tree and was bent down to examine the scars that were still visible on the thick trunk when she heard an approaching vehicle. Turning toward the road, she furrowed her brow when she couldn't see anyone. Where was the sound coming from? It wasn't until a tractor appeared from the far side of the open field that she noticed the cattle gathered around a fresh bale of hay.

She stepped away from the tree as the tractor rolled to a halt a few feet away and a thin, wiry man jumped down.

He was wearing jeans that were coated in dirt and a work shirt that was unbuttoned to reveal the lean muscles of someone who spends their days hauling, lifting, and tossing around heavy objects. As he neared, Jesse could make out the narrow face, which was deeply tanned by hours in the sun despite the seed cap he had pulled low on his head. There were a few new wrinkles around the brown eyes and an attempt at a patchy mustache, but Jesse easily recognized Clint Frazer, the witness who'd supposedly seen her dad in this precise spot.

"This is private property," he was calling out as he stomped his way toward the tree.

"Sorry. I was just leaving."

Jesse grimaced, wondering if there were people who came to gawk at the spot where Victoria Hudson had disappeared, along with her daughter. Probably. There were all sorts of podcasts that concentrated on unsolved mysteries these days. It wouldn't be surprising if one or more had mentioned this strange case.

"Jesse?" The man moved to stand directly in front of her, planting his hands on his hips. A genuine smile curved his lips. "Sorry, I didn't recognize you at first."

Jesse forced herself to return the smile. She wasn't really in the mood to chat. She was still processing her earlier unease that her dad might somehow have been involved in Victoria's disappearance. Then again, she had a dozen questions that only this man could answer, she sternly reminded herself.

She would be an idiot to waste this golden opportunity.

"Hi, Clint. How are you?"

"Good." He pushed back his cap an inch, allowing her to see a glimpse of his ginger hair, which was cut short. "I heard you were back."

"I'm pretty sure everyone in the tristate area knows," she said wryly.

"Yeah, not much happens around here. Any news is big news."

"I remember," she assured him. "Like when Jessica Sutton got stuck on her roof trying to rescue her cat, and half the town showed up to watch the firemen try to get her down."

"Yup. And when someone claimed that they'd seen Bigfoot in the woods near Deer Ridge. The whole place was flooded with campers trying to get a picture." They chuckled at the shared memory, his expression curious as he studied her. "Is it true that you're selling the bar?"

"I am. Or at least I intend to put it on the market as soon as I get it patched up. Right now it's a mess."

"It's been sitting empty for a while. How long has it been?"

"Nine years. Too long," Jesse admitted. While she'd been bopping from one place to another, time had lost all meaning. One month blended into the next as she tried to outrun her memories. It wasn't until she stopped long enough to look around that she realized how much time had passed. "The town needs the Tap Room back in business."

"Won't be the same without Mac."

"I know." The familiar sense of loss gripped her heart. "But life moves on. Or at least it's supposed to move on."

He tilted his head to the side, his expression suddenly wary. "Is that why you're out here?"

"I'm not sure what I'm doing." She glanced toward the tree. It'd haunted her dreams for years, the barren branches stark against a stormy night sky. What she'd never been able to figure out was if it symbolized the beginning or the ending of her nightmares. "I suppose I'm hoping for some sort of closure."

"Closure would be nice, but it's not easy to forget what happened." His face flushed with a distressed combination of guilt and shame. "I still feel terrible about what I said. I'm never going to forgive myself."

"Don't," Jesse commanded. "That's in the past."

"Mac might have gone to jail."

"My dad never blamed you, Clint." Jesse didn't add that she'd wanted to throttle him at the time. "He understood the pressure Adam used to get you to say what you did, and that you were as much a victim as he was."

Clint shook his head. "None of it would have happened if I hadn't been stupid enough to get the DUI in the first place."

Jesse hesitated. She didn't want him to feel worse about what had happened, but she wasn't above using his guilt for her own ends. As far as she knew, he was the only witness to the crash.

"If you don't mind, could you walk me through what happened that night?"

His jaw clenched. "The night Victoria crashed?"

"Yeah."

"Why?"

"I don't have a good answer." She lifted her hands in a helpless gesture. "I suppose I'm trying to wrap my head around what happened before I walk away and put it all behind me."

There was a strained silence before Clint heaved a resigned sigh. "Yeah. Okay. There's not that much to tell. I heard a crash—"

"What time?" she interrupted.

He took a moment to search through his memories. "I'm not sure of an exact time, but it was starting to get light."

"What were you doing out so early?"

"Starting my chores." He shook his head. "And it wasn't early. I remember that I'd overslept and was in a hurry to get them done."

"Right." She sent him a wry smile. "I forget most farmers start before the crack of dawn, just about the time I'm headed to bed."

Clint shuddered. Jesse assumed he was a morning person. "You work the night shift?"

"Something like that. I'm a bartender."

"Just like your dad."

It was Jesse's turn to shudder. Her dad would hate the fancy nightclub where she was working. In his mind, a bar was a comfortable place for the community to gather, where old and new friends could enjoy a few hours together. It wasn't a trendy spot where the music was too loud, the drinks obscenely expensive, and people spent more time staring at their phones than talking to one another.

"So you heard a crash?" She directed the conversation back to the night Victoria disappeared.

"I didn't know what it was at first. The sound came from over the hill and far enough away to muffle it." He waved a hand toward the steep slope that rose toward the massive red barn and, beyond that, a brick, two-storied farmhouse with an attached garage. "I didn't want to drive down to see what happened, so I climbed into the hayloft. That's when I saw a car had run off the road and hit a tree."

"Did you recognize it?"

Clint snorted. "Hard not to. As far as I know, your stepmother was the only one in town to drive a fancy sports car."

Jesse glanced toward the tree. "This is the spot it crashed?"

"Yes. I don't know if she took the corner too fast, or if the gravel was slick with dew."

It was a question that Jesse hadn't considered until that morning. Now it felt excruciatingly important to know if Victoria was forced off the road because she was running from someone. Or had it been a random accident? And what did it have to do with her disappearance?

"My dad warned her that the car was a death trap on the roads around here."

"Not very practical, that's for sure."

Understatement of the decade.

"Was there anyone else around?"

He glanced toward the road, his jaw clenched as if the memories bothered him more than he wanted her to realize.

"I didn't see anyone at first, but before I could climb out of the loft to go see if anyone was hurt, a pickup came around the curve."

It was the same story he'd told the judge. Almost word for word.

"The one you said was my dad's truck."

His gaze jerked back toward her, as if she'd physically slapped him. "Not in the beginning," he protested. "When I talked to Adam the first time I told him that it was still too dark for me to make out the actual color of the truck. I said it was light. Maybe white, or it could have been silver or a light gray."

"There are dozens of people in Canton that drive a light-colored pickup."

He blinked at the sharp rebuke, and Jesse silently cursed her raw nerves. Dammit. She wasn't there to harass the poor man. Not when he still felt guilty for what had happened to her dad.

"I said that too. It was only because it appeared just minutes after Victoria's crash that I assumed it was Mac." His expression was defensive. "It made sense they were headed somewhere together but decided to take separate vehicles."

Jesse forced herself to take a deep, calming breath. "Did you see him get out of the truck?"

Clint shook his head. "The crash didn't look that serious. Besides, I really and truly thought it was your dad who'd stopped to help Victoria. I jumped out of the loft and got on with my business."

"Before you jumped down, did you notice if the person in the truck was alone?"

"I couldn't see." Clint pointed toward the opposite field. "The truck had pulled over to side of the road and left its headlights on. They were pointed directly at me. Even from the loft, I couldn't see much more than a glare of light."

Jesse glanced from the road to the barn on top of the hill, her brows pulling together at the distance. She hadn't realized it was so far.

"I'm not sure it would have mattered if the headlights were off. It would have been hard to make out any details in the early morning shadows."

Clint nodded. "That's true. The only reason I recognized Victoria's car was because of the shape. I couldn't have told you the exact color or who was inside the vehicle."

Frustration sliced through Jesse. Why hadn't the sheriff come out here to see for himself if the surprise witness was credible? It was an obscene injustice that her father ever had been charged with a crime. With an effort, she kept her dark thoughts to herself.

"You didn't hear anything?" she asked. "No screams or gunshot?"

"Nothing."

So, did that mean Victoria had known the person in the truck and wasn't afraid? Or had she been unconscious? There was blood found in the car.

"Did you look back down there when you finished your chores?"

Clint nodded. "The car was still there, but the truck was gone."

"I don't suppose you know which way it went?"

"It had to have turned around and headed back toward town."

She arched her brows at his confident response. "Why do you say that?"

"The dogs would have gone bonkers if it went past the house. We had a dozen beagles back then. Noisy bastards."

She glanced toward the empty pens built behind the farmhouse. Obviously, Clint didn't use dogs to hunt, although there were a couple of large mutts who were patiently waiting for his return at the top of the hill.

"You didn't notice anything else?" she asked, returning her attention to the man standing in front of her.

"Not really. A wrecker came a day or so later and hauled away the car." He hunched his shoulders. "I was a selfish jerk back then. I didn't really care what had happened or who cleaned up the mess. I was too busy with my own stuff."

"We were all selfish. Me especially."

Clint looked pained. "Not Mac Hudson. He was always good to

me. He even offered me a job and a place to sleep when my dad kicked me out of the house when I was sixteen."

She blinked. "Your dad seriously kicked you out of the house?"

"He told me to pack my bags after I left a gate open and our cattle disappeared. It took two weeks to locate them all." He shoved his hands in his front pockets. "I walked into town, pissed and hoping I never had to see my parents again, but I was only at the bar a couple of hours when my mom came after me."

Jesse hadn't heard her dad talk about the incident, but it wouldn't have been the first time he offered the bar as a place of refuge. Until he'd married Victoria, he'd had an open-door policy.

"If you cared so much, how did Adam convince you to say that you'd seen my dad at the crash?" She was careful to keep any hint of accusation out of her voice.

"He came by after the wreck to ask questions. I told him exactly what I just said."

"Including the fact that you never saw who was driving the truck?"

"Yes, although I probably shouldn't have mentioned that I'd thought it was Mac." His features tightened into an expression of disgust. "The moment I mentioned your dad, the deputy was convinced he had something to do with Victoria's disappearance. It was like he was obsessed. He tried to bully me into saying I'd seen him, but I refused."

Obsessed? Yes, that was the perfect word for Adam's desire to frame her father.

"You didn't change your mind until you were stopped for drinking and driving?"

A dark flush stained his cheeks. "When he pulled me over I knew I was screwed. I'd been partying all night and there was no way I should have gotten behind the wheel. I hoped if I took the back roads I wouldn't get caught."

"But you did."

"I sometimes wonder if Adam was following me around, waiting for a chance to get me in trouble. It was no secret I enjoyed the beer back in those days. I know it sounds psycho, but..." His words trailed away with a shrug.

Jesse had zero trouble imagining Adam Tillman lurking in the shadows, waiting for a chance to pounce. Like a bloated spider eager to trap his victim.

"It's not psycho. One of my friends swore Adam was peeking through her bedroom window when we were in high school. No one ever caught him, but she swore she saw him more than once." Jesse ground her teeth. "I assume he threatened you?"

"Not exactly a physical threat, but he pointed out how much I had to lose if he arrested me. Not only my license, but having to tell my parents." A dark expression tightened Clint's features. "At the time, I'd rather have faced a firing squad."

"Were you afraid of your father?" Jesse hadn't known Norris Frazer very well, but she'd seen him in the Tap Room. He'd been an aggressive drunk who was always trying to start a fight.

"He was a hard man. And he was never slow to use a belt when I disappointed him. Which was ninety percent of the time." The very lack of emotion in Clint's voice revealed how painful the relationship was with his dad. "But I was more worried about my mother. I didn't want to see the disappointment in her eyes."

"I get that."

Clint shuffled his feet, his shame hanging heavy in the humid air. "Adam promised all I had to do was sign a piece of paper saying that I saw Mac Hudson at the crash that night. He never said anything about using my statement to arrest your dad, or getting up in court and swearing on a Bible. Not that it matters what he promised." He clenched his hands into tight fists. "I was a coward to agree."

Jesse laid her hand on his arm. There was a time when she'd hated this man. She'd been so horrified her dad would go to jail that she didn't consider how frightened he must be. Now she understood why her dad had refused to be angry.

"That's not true," she insisted. "You were scared, and Adam took advantage of his position of authority to bully you into lying. And in the end you did the right thing."

"I couldn't let your dad go to jail."

Jesse lowered her hand, glancing back to the tree. If only Clint had climbed down from the loft to check on Victoria that night. Or if he'd stayed up there to watch what happened after the truck arrived. Or if he'd called 911 as soon as he'd heard the crash.

So many if onlys.

She heaved a sigh, the scars on the tree matching her wounded heart.

"Are you okay?" Clint asked.

"No." It was an honest answer. She glanced back at the man studying her with a worried gaze. "I'll never understand why Adam was so determined to blame my dad for murder when there was no proof that Victoria or Tegan were even dead. Maybe it was weird that they'd disappeared, but there was nothing to suggest that they'd been hurt beyond the original crash. Especially considering Victoria had just stolen a large chunk of money from my dad and she had every reason to cover her trail." Clint looked surprised at the mention of Victoria taking off with Jesse's college fund. It wasn't information Mac had wanted to share. "And even if they had died, why did Adam insist on pointing the finger at my dad? As far as I know, he'd never done anything to make Adam his enemy. He obeyed the law, paid his taxes, went about his business without bothering anyone."

She expected Clint to shrug aside her question. Trying to decipher what made Adam Tillman tick was a creepy proposition. But her companion slowly nodded, as if he'd given Adam's motivation some thought over the years.

"At first I thought he wanted to be the center of attention," he said. "You know how he liked to strut around."

Jesse made a sound of disgust. "Jerk."

"What better way to show off than by solving the only murder ever to happen in this boring town?"

"There's no proof there was a murder."

"It wouldn't matter to Adam."

"That's true." Jesse considered the possibility. She wouldn't put it past Adam to use a tragedy for his own gain, but putting an innocent man in jail seemed like a stretch. "You said 'at first.' Was there another reason you thought he might have accused my dad?"

He nodded. "My mom was friends with Rosemary Jacobs."

"Who?"

"She worked at the courthouse up until she died last year."

The memory of an older woman in her polyester suit and pearls assuring her that her dad had left the courthouse seared through Jesse's mind. "I know who she is. I'm sorry for your loss."

Clint shrugged. "I didn't really know her, but she told my mom she'd seen Victoria arguing with Adam. And she insisted that it was more than a mild disagreement. She said they were yelling at each other."

Jesse jerked in shock. Victoria had never mentioned Adam or an argument. Which was weird. She loved complaining about the locals, and anyone who had the misfortune to piss her off was the center of her conversation for endless days.

"When was the argument?"

"Two nights before Victoria disappeared."

"What were they arguing about?"

"She didn't know. Rosemary said that she'd been to her daughter's house for dinner and was walking through the park on her way home when she overheard raised voices. I guess she was worried, so she went to check out what was happening. That's when she saw Victoria standing in the small gazebo near the back parking lot with a man she thought was Adam."

"Wait." Jesse grudgingly reined in her imagination. She was ready, willing, and eager to jump to conclusions, but what was the point if they led her in the wrong direction? "Rosemary *thought* it was Adam? She didn't see him?"

"Apparently, he had his back to her, and before she could get close enough to the gazebo to get a good look, Victoria called out for her to mind her own business," Clint explained.

"That sounds like Victoria," Jesse muttered. "Did Rosemary hear anything before Victoria sent her away?"

"She told my mom that she overheard the man telling Victoria that she had twenty-four hours to get out of town or he was taking matters into his own hands."

"Seriously?" Jesse blinked. "Twenty-four hours to get out of town? That sounds like a line from a cheesy movie."

Clint shrugged. "That's what she heard. She also believed it was a real threat, since he was grabbing her arm in a super tight grip. That's why she remembered seeing them together."

"Why would Adam tell her to leave town?"

The question was more for herself than Clint as she inwardly debated the potential explanations.

Was it possible Adam had discovered Victoria was an imposter? But if he had, why not expose her? Maybe he'd blackmailed her? She knew where to get her hands on some ready cash. But if she'd paid to keep him quiet, why leave town?

"I have no idea," Clint interrupted her futile attempts to make sense out of the latest twist.

"Did Rosemary tell anyone besides your mom about the meeting?"

"After Victoria disappeared she went to the sheriff."

A sour frustration curled through the pit of her stomach. "Of course he did nothing."

"Actually, I think he did check into her story," Clint surprised her by insisting. Her opinion of the previous sheriff wasn't much better than of the current one. He wasn't dishonest, just lazy and incompetent. "Adam claimed he'd spent that particular evening with some buddies playing poker, and they backed him up," Clint continued. "Plus, the morning of the crash he was on duty at the sheriff's station. Eventually, Rosemary had to admit she didn't get a good enough look to swear it was Adam in the park."

Jesse snorted. She didn't doubt that Adam had the sort of friends who would lie to cover for him, but it was also possible the older woman had made a mistake.

"Who else could it have been arguing with Victoria in the park?" She forced herself to ask. "Not my father."

"No, there's no way to mistake those two. Your dad was half a foot taller than Adam."

"And twenty years older."

"There's that."

Jesse tried to imagine who else had the same shape as Adam only to give a shake of her head. She'd try to make a list later. Right now, she was still wrapping her brain around the fact that Rosemary had accused Adam Tillman of conducting a public argument with a woman who went missing only days later.

"You know, even if Adam wasn't in the park, he wouldn't want rumors getting around that he was involved in Victoria's disappearance," she pointed out, determined to find some way to blame the deputy for what he'd done to her father. "Not when he was obviously desperate to become the next sheriff. What better way to squash any suspicions than by having my dad arrested for the crime? I don't doubt for a second he'd throw an innocent man in jail just to protect his own reputation."

"I suppose he could have used Mac to take away attention from himself, but we don't know anything for sure." Clint abruptly looked uncomfortable, as if he was remembering the last time he'd been pressured into accusing someone without evidence. "Sorry, but I should be getting on with my chores. Good to see you again, Jesse."

"Thanks, Clint."

With long strides, he was climbing back onto the tractor and heading up the hill. Jesse watched him disappear before she returned to her truck to make a U-turn.

On her trip out to this spot she'd been concentrating on whether there would be adequate time for her father to have followed Victoria, dispose of the bodies, and be back at the bar before she came downstairs.

Although she hadn't eliminated the possibility, it seemed highly unlikely.

And while she wanted to believe that Adam was the one who'd followed Victoria out of town and caused the crash that morning, she'd never seen him driving a pickup, and he'd supposedly been working that morning.

If neither were responsible for following Victoria, then how had she disappeared with her young daughter?

Crawling at a snail's pace, Jesse concentrated on the narrow access roads that split off to cut through the fields and pastures that surrounded Canton. They were secluded enough they could have been used to hide a couple of bodies, but it was hard to believe that they wouldn't have been discovered in the past nine years. After all, the land was owned by local farmers. Most acres were planted with crops, and others were used for pastureland and paddocks for livestock. Even the wooded areas were used to collect firewood or rented out to hunters and fishermen. Not to mention the wildlife and stray dogs that dug up everything in the area.

It would be hard to keep two graves from being discovered.

But there would be a handy way for someone to leave the area without being spotted, she abruptly realized, rolling to a stop as she allowed the random thought to fully form.

From the beginning she'd tried to hold on to the belief that Victoria and Tegan were still alive. Even after the sports car was found wrecked, with blood in the driver's seat, she'd grimly tried to cling to hope. Not just because it would be horrible to think they were dead, but she couldn't bear for her father to live with the whispers he was involved in their tragic end.

Now, she forced herself to think through the necessary steps it would take to genuinely disappear forever.

She started with the thought that Victoria had been threatened. Either by Adam or a stranger? What would she have done? Panicked? No. Victoria was many things, but she wasn't a coward.

If she'd been threatened by someone, then she was cunning enough to have considered a way to eliminate that threat. First by putting a knife in their back. If that didn't work, she would have plotted the best means to escape.

There wouldn't have been any fleeing in the early hours of the morning without a destination in mind. And she would have made sure she wasn't being followed by her enemy. What was the point of leaving the comfort and safety of her home—along with a husband who would do anything to protect her—unless she was confident she had an equally safe place to go where no one could find her once she vanished?

So there must have been a plan.

Tapping her fingers on the steering wheel, Jesse shuffled through her memories. She didn't recall what Victoria was doing the night before she disappeared. Jesse had tried to avoid the woman whenever possible. But there'd been no missing the dramatic exit the next morning.

No missing it . . . no missing it . . .

The words whirled through her mind. At the time, it'd seemed like just another argument, only this one had ended with Victoria storming away. But why argue at all? If she was determined to leave Mac and steal his money, why not sneak away? She could easily have packed a few bags and had them stored in her car before she went to bed. Her dad always worked until late into the night; he wouldn't have noticed anything missing. And then she could have snuck away, along with the money, before Mac or Jesse woke.

Instead, she'd created a huge scene.

Which meant she'd wanted everyone to know she was leaving.

Why?

One option was that she wanted to make sure that she hurt Mac Hudson so deeply he didn't come looking for her. He wasn't the sort of man who would just let his wife take off with his stepdaughter without making sure they were okay. But why crash her car? She could have just vanished. Unless she wanted him to think she was dead?

It wasn't a bad theory, but it didn't fully answer all her questions.

Like what happened to her father. It was too much of a coincidence for him to disappear for it not to be connected to Victoria.

Jesse's fingers suddenly tightened on the wheel until her knuckles turned white. Wait. What if the scene hadn't been for her dad's benefit, but for her?

What if Victoria was threatened and returned home to tell her husband what happened? They didn't have a perfect marriage, but she knew that Mac Hudson would give his life to keep her and Tegan safe.

He might have staged the fight for her to overhear. Certainly it would make it all much more believable if she truly assumed that Victoria had left in a huff. Everyone knew that Jesse was a terrible liar. It would be obvious whether she was genuinely upset by the disappearance of her stepmother and stepsister or faking it.

It would even explain why Noah had seen her father out that morning. If Victoria had staged the fight and then staged the crash, she would need a getaway car hidden somewhere close by. Maybe her father had arranged the crash, and planted the blood, before driving Victoria and Tegan to a vehicle hidden along one of the numerous access roads.

Then, returning to the bar, he'd realized he'd been seen by Noah and pretended to be drunk so the younger man wouldn't ask awkward questions.

It was obviously one of endless possibilities, like Schrödinger's cat, but it did fit most of the facts. Or at least the facts she currently possessed.

The problem now was how to prove whether it was true or not.

With a burst of determination, Jesse hit the gas pedal and rattled her way back to town. She had new information and a new hypothesis to what happened, but in some ways she was back to where she'd started.

She had to expose the real Victoria. How else could she discover who'd terrified the older woman into hiding if she didn't know her identity or who might be a threat? Once she had a name and her previous location, she would be able to backtrack to talk to her friends and family.

She might even find Victoria.

Of course she'd already discovered that learning the truth was easier said than done. How did you discover information on a person without knowing their real name?

Jesse pulled the truck to a halt in front of the Tap Room and switched off the engine with a vague sense of defeat. She'd already searched through social media and questioned Victoria's one friend in town. She couldn't even use Victoria's marriage certificate because it was obviously bogus. All she had was an old picture from a birthday party nine years ago.

Jesse sucked in a sharp breath. A picture. Maybe that was all she needed. One of the waitresses at the nightclub had been griping a few months ago about being catfished by a guy who was pretending to be the son of a Saudi oil sheik. She said that she'd used a reverse image search to pull up his real identity. He was really an out-of-work actor who was living in his mother's basement.

She should at least give it a try.

Jesse slid out of the truck and headed toward the front door. She was pulling out her keys when she caught a movement out of the corner of her eye, as if someone had started around the edge of the building only to turn back when they realized she was there.

Unable to squash her curiosity, Jesse jogged to the end of the block and glanced down the street. Nothing. She looked both ways before scurrying forward to enter the alley that ran behind the Tap Room. It seemed impossible that anyone could have vanished so quickly. Had she imagined the shadow?

Taking a quick peek behind the dumpsters, Jesse turned back toward the Tap Room. It was only then that she caught sight of the spray-painted words on the back door.

Leave now or else.

She clenched her teeth. Not very original. But at least she knew that she wasn't losing her mind. She'd seen whoever had done this a second before they'd disappeared.

Unfortunately, that didn't help identify the jerk.

Jamming her key into the lock, she shoved open the door and stepped into the small foyer. Then, closing the door behind her, she made sure it was tightly bolted before she slumped against the wall.

Who the hell would spray-paint her door? And why threaten her? It wasn't like she had a lot of enemies in Canton. She hadn't been around for years. And now that she was back, it was just to get the paperwork for her dad's death certificate so she could sell the bar. Something that should make the whole town happy.

Unless someone realized that she was investigating the past? She *was* asking a lot of questions.

It made sense that there was someone in town who was afraid of having the truth exposed.

So what should she do? She wasn't stupid enough to try to chase down whoever had vandalized her door. For one thing, they were long gone by now. And for another, they might be dangerous. And she wasn't going to report the crime. Not when the current sheriff might easily be the one responsible. He could lose everything if he was involved in Victoria's disappearance.

Mired in her inability to decide how best to deal with the threat, Jesse nearly jumped out of her skin when a knock shattered the thick silence.

Now what?

Straightening her spine, she forced herself to march through the main area of the bar to yank open the front door.

"Leave me the hell alone," she snapped, blinking against the morning light. It was blinding, in contrast to the gloom of the bar. A second later, her eyes adjusted, and she could make out the details of the tall man with neatly trimmed brown hair.

Her lawyer, Eric Walker.

Her gaze lowered, to take in his khaki slacks and polo shirt. It was the first time she'd seem him without a suit.

"Sorry," she murmured, stepping back. "Come in."

His expression was concerned. "Is something wrong, Jesse?"

She shook her head, forcing a stiff smile. "I'm just on edge. I didn't realize it would be so stressful staying in this place."

He continued to study her, clearly not believing her lame excuse. For a tense moment, she feared he might demand to know why her cheeks were flushed and her hand was pressed over her racing heart. At last, he lifted a manila folder clutched in his fingers.

"Then you'll be happy to know that these are the papers you need to sign to get things moving. I know it's Sunday, and if you want a few days to read them over—"

"There's no need. I trust you," she interrupted, plucking the file from his fingers. The air in the bar was hot and stuffy despite the air-conditioning, but suddenly she felt chilled to the bone. She couldn't give herself time to consider what the papers represented. Not when it felt as if she was losing her dad all over again. "If you have a minute I'll sign them now."

"Sure." Eric stepped into the bar as she crossed toward the closest table to spread out the official-looking papers. "They're marked where I need your signature," he assured her.

"Great." She reached into the purse that was still slung over her shoulder and dug out a pen. A second later, she'd scribbled her name next to the yellow sticky arrows. "Done."

She scooped the papers into the folder and handed it back to Eric.

"Hopefully, we'll hear something within a few weeks," he murmured, turning to leave. "I'll give you a call as soon as I have a firm date."

Caught between the desire for the man to go away so she could concentrate on her search into Victoria's mysterious past and a vague sense of anxiety at being alone after the threat left scrawled on her back door, Jesse suddenly realized that the lawyer could answer at least one question that was nagging at her.

"Before you go."

Eric turned back. "Yes?"

"Did you know that my dad had requested a copy of his marriage certificate, and that he'd received a letter saying that there was nothing on record?"

"What do you mean, nothing on record?"

"No official marriage certificate ever was filed in Vegas."

The green eyes narrowed. "They weren't legally married?"

"Not according to the Clark County Vital Records Office. Whatever ceremony they went through was evidently a sham. Although my dad obviously didn't know it at the time. He thought they were married."

Eric pinched his lips in annoyance, as if he was personally offended by the information. "Why didn't Mac tell me?"

"Maybe he was afraid it would make him look guilty," Jesse suggested. "Victoria went to a lot of effort to make him believe they were legally man and wife. Anyone would be furious to learn they'd been deceived."

"That's ridiculous," Eric snapped. "It would have been a powerful defense if his case had gone to trial. Anyone who would lie about a marriage ceremony would certainly fake their own death. Not to mention the fact that one of Victoria's relations might have tried to claim a portion of his inheritance." There was a short silence as Eric visibly regained command of his composure. "When did he discover the truth?"

"A few weeks after she disappeared."

"He didn't say anything to you?"

"No." The denial was sharper than she'd intended, revealing her simmering sense of guilt. It stung that her dad hadn't told her about the faux wedding. It meant that he didn't trust her with the information, or he couldn't bear to hear her say "I told you so." Either way, it proved Victoria had managed to damage their relationship in a way that was never fully repaired. "I knew that he was worried. Who wouldn't be after they found Victoria's sports car smashed into a tree but no sign of her or Tegan? And I watched him trying to do everything humanly possible to locate them. He followed up on every single lead, no matter how silly, even driving to Little Rock, Arkansas, because someone swore they saw Victoria working as a waitress in a truck stop." She shook her head. "But in hindsight, I think I suspected he was hiding something from me in the last days before he was arrested. But I would never have guessed it had anything to do with his quickie Vegas marriage. I mean, why did Victoria go through the ceremony at all if it wasn't going to be legal? And why lie to Dad about it? I doubt he would have cared if she simply wanted to live together without the formalities."

"It is odd," Eric agreed, his annoyance fading as he considered the implications of Victoria's deceit. "I wonder why he requested the marriage certificate in the first place."

A good question, Jesse silently acknowledged. "I don't know. Maybe he discovered something during his search for Victoria that made him suspicious."

"Suspicious of what?"

Jesse pretended to consider the question. "Maybe she wasn't Victoria," she said slowly, as if she'd just now been struck by the possibility. "Maybe when she came to Canton she invented the name."

He frowned. "Like an alias?"

"Yes."

"Why would she do that?"

Jesse shrugged. "There could be a dozen reasons. Maybe she's in witness protection. Or maybe she's running from someone, like an abusive lover. Or maybe she was hiding Tegan from her biological dad. Some women don't want to share custody of their kids after a divorce, and she was overly protective of her daughter."

Eric didn't look convinced. "If she wasn't Victoria, then who would she be?"

"Anybody. Nobody." Jesse sent him an impatient glare. "But it feels important to find out. Don't you think?"

She'd hoped Eric would be equally inspired to discover why Victoria had duped her father into a fake ceremony. With his legal connections, he might be able to track down whether she'd lied about her real identity. Instead, he stepped forward and grabbed her hand.

"Jesse. I don't know what happened in the past, but it caused three people to disappear and a lot of heartbreak. Especially for you." He squeezed her fingers tight enough to send a tiny jolt of pain up her arm. "I think it's best that you wrap up your business here and get on with your future."

She jerked her hand free. "I seem to hear that a lot lately."

He frowned. "There's an old saying about letting sleeping dogs lie. You should—" His warning was cut short as a sharp knock on the doorframe echoed through the room. "Busy place for a Sunday."

"You have no idea," Jesse muttered, turning to watch the pretty blonde wearing white capris and a sleeveless shirt stroll through the open door. "Reese," she said, loud enough for the intruder to hear.

The woman halted, blinking until her eyes adjusted to the gloom. Then, with a blinding smile, she waved a folder in Jesse's direction.

"Good, you're here."

"I am."

Reese moved in her direction, her heels clicking on the floorboards. "Now, I know you haven't officially put the place on the market, but word has spread you're intending to sell the Tap Room. No surprise; this is a prime piece of property." She gave another wave of the folder. "I've already had some interest."

Jesse took an instinctive step back. She was struggling to deal with signing the paperwork that made her dad's death painfully real. She wasn't prepared to lose the only home she'd ever known. Not today.

"I haven't had time for the repairs," she protested.

Reese never slowed. "That's what's so great about these offers. They're 'as is.' You wouldn't have to lift a finger. Just sign the deed and hand over the keys."

"I don't think I'm ready to look at offers." Jesse took another step back. The woman was a steamroller, running over anything in her path.

"That's fine." Reese veered to the right, dropping the folder on the table. "I'll just leave these here in case you change your mind."

"She said she's not ready," Eric said, as if Reese hadn't heard Jesse's protest.

Reese kept her gaze locked on Jesse. "Doesn't hurt to look, does it? No pressure, of course. We'll chat later. 'Bye."

With a finger wave, she turned to click her way across the floor and out the door. Jesse shook her head, wondering if Reese ever stopped moving long enough to relax.

Probably not. Didn't sharks have to perpetually swim so they didn't drown?

"She's very persistent."

Eric clicked his tongue. "I don't think she fully understands that this isn't Chicago or St. Louis. Around here, good manners and decency are more important than money." He snapped his lips together, a hint of red staining his cheeks as he recalled that Jesse had been living in Chicago and intended to return as soon as she sold the bar. "I'm not saying the people here are better or worse, just that we don't have the same rat race mentality. There are plenty of folks who love the excitement and competition of the big city. Nothing wrong with that. Just . . ." He lifted his hands in a vague gesture. "Different."

"True enough."

Clearing his throat, Eric headed toward the door. "I'll let you know as soon as we have an official declaration of death." He paused, glancing back with an expression that was impossible to read. "Until then, my suggestion is to try to concentrate on where you're going, not where you've been."

Chapter 11

Waiting for Eric to disappear around the corner, Jesse slammed shut the door and shoved home the heavy bolt. She was starting to worry that she'd have to hide under her bed to get a few hours of peace.

It'd been a long time since she'd lived in a small town where neighbors dropped by without warning. Plus, she now had a paint-spraying vandal who was lurking in the shadows and an overly zealous Realtor who were both trying to drive her out of town.

Ignoring the folder Reese had left on the table, Jesse headed to the back of the building and climbed the stairs to the private apartment. She wasn't sure if it was lunchtime or not, but her stomach was rumbling. She needed food in her gut, but that didn't mean she couldn't multitask.

Jesse stepped into her bedroom to grab her laptop before entering the kitchen. Then, she threw a frozen pizza into the oven and placed the computer on the table, pulling up the various websites offering a reverse image search. She chose the free one and downloaded the photo of the birthday party she'd saved on her phone.

It was a long shot, but a long shot was better than no shot, right?

Letting the program do its thing, she gathered a paper plate and a bottle of water before pulling the pizza out of the oven and cutting it into small slices. She was starving, but she'd discovered over the past few weeks that it didn't take much to satisfy her hunger.

A reaction to Parker insisting that she finally confront her past.

Once this was all over, she had full confidence her appetite would return.

Tossing a couple of slices on her plate, she carried it with her water to the table and settled in a chair in front of the computer.

There were several results that'd already popped up, but none looked promising. With a sigh, Jesse concentrated on her lunch before returning her attention to the computer and the dozen links that looked like advertisements or travel sites. What did that have to do with the people in the photo?

More annoyed than curious, Jesse at last clicked on the first link, not surprised when it took her to the website of a local gym.

"A waste of time," she muttered, about to click out when her attention was captured by the image of a man with bleached blond hair and a square face that had the orangish hue of a fake tan. Beneath the photo was a banner:

Dixon Hooper, certified personal trainer. Call today to start living your best life! Walk-ins welcome.

At first she wasn't sure why the photo had captured her attention, not until she looked back at the picture she'd uploaded and realized there was a remarkable resemblance between Dixon Hooper and the mystery boy.

Was this the dude who'd helped Bea during the birthday party? The one Victoria was glaring at as if he'd shit on her Louboutins?

It sure looked like the same person.

Certainly it was worth investigating.

Checking the gym hours, Jesse covered her pizza with a napkin and shoved it in the fridge before washing her hands and grabbing her purse. Jesse was in high school when the gym first opened, but she'd never been there. Probably because she'd never been a health nut. More of a work-until-she-dropped-and-eat-junk-food kind of nut.

Half an hour later, she was across the bridge that spanned the Mississippi River and in Quincy, driving down Broadway. She weaved her way through traffic before pulling into the parking lot of the shopping mall. Angling through the marked spaces that looked depressingly deserted, she circled to the back. There were a few more cars in the shaded area, but Jesse could remember when this place would be packed on a Sunday afternoon. Either enjoying a movie or hanging out with friends at the food court.

Feeling weirdly old, Jesse entered the mall and headed toward the far end of the building. Her shoes squeaked on the tiled floor, echoing eerily against the shuttered storefronts. At last reaching the double glass doors, she pushed one open and stepped inside.

Long ago, this place was a roller rink, followed by a BBQ joint, and then a video game arcade. Now it was a sleek, open facility with a surprising number of weight machines, ellipticals, and treadmills. At the moment, there were only a handful of customers spotted around the gym, but she suspected it would quickly fill up once people started getting out of church or finishing lunch.

At her entrance, the blond-haired man she'd been hoping to find straightened from stacking the free weights in a corner and sauntered toward her with a smile he'd no doubt practiced in front of a mirror.

He was predictably buff, with a tee stretched tight over his broad chest and biker shorts that emphasized his bulging thighs. He only topped her by an inch, but he held his spine stiff, as if trying to appear taller.

"Welcome," he murmured with a faint Southern accent, his gaze boldly sweeping down her body before returning to her bare arms. "Nice ink. That's not local."

"No." She studied his features, which were handsome in a Neanderthal kind of way, trying to determine if this was the man in the picture. "Dixon Hooper?"

"You can call me Dix."

"Hi, I'm Jesse Hudson. I was wondering if you have a minute for a couple of questions?"

He glanced toward the front desk, which was empty. She assumed there was a surveillance camera currently watching them.

"Sorry, but if it's about exercise or training, you'll have to book a session. Gym rules."

"It's not about training," she assured him. "It's personal."

"Nice." He stepped closer. "What's up?"

Jesse ignored his flirtatious tone. He no doubt spent the bulk of his time hitting on the women who came to the gym.

"I was cleaning out my father's bar and I found a picture of you."

He looked perplexed. "A picture?"

Jesse suddenly realized how weird her words had sounded. "I thought you might want to see it. And since I was in the area..."

"Okay." He shrugged. "I've been in a lot of bars. You're going to have to be more specific."

"The Tap Room. In Canton."

Something that might be bitterness darkened his pale eyes. "Ah. My less-than-glorious college days. Blew out my knee a week into my sophomore year and lost my baseball scholarship. I ended up working here." He glanced down at his leg, which was marred by two long scars. "Been here ever since."

"That sucks."

"Not really." He lifted his head, his bitterness replaced with resignation. "I spent more time partying than going to class. I was only there for baseball, and when that was gone I was ready to bail. Although I don't remember doing much partying at the Tap Room. That was the place they always carded the students, right?"

"Yeah, my dad was pretty strict."

"So what's the picture?"

Jesse pulled her phone out of her purse and tapped on the photo, zooming in on the mystery guy's face.

"Is this you?"

Taking the phone, Dix's brows lifted in surprise. "Yeah, that's me. But I don't remember this." He glanced up with a puzzled expression. "Where was it taken?"

Excitement sizzled through Jesse. This was the dude from the picture, which meant this wasn't a wild-goose chase. Of course it could still fizzle into a mire of unanswered questions. That seemed to be a depressing theme lately.

"It's Lara Yost's backyard," she said. "Her husband is the chaplain at the college. This picture was taken during a birthday party for her daughter, Samantha, as well as my stepsister, Tegan."

He shook his head. "I'm still clueless."

"I think you were there to help Bea Hartman."

Another shake of his head. "Who?"

"She owns the local diner."

"Oh yeah." His confusion cleared, as if he'd managed to dig up a distant memory. "I was short of money that summer." He snorted. "Hell, I was always short of money. Still am. Anyway, my coach suggested I ask the old woman at the diner for a job that didn't interfere with my training. She was pretty cool about it. I mostly worked in the kitchen washing dishes, but she also asked me to do a few catering gigs. This must have been one of them."

"But you don't remember that day?" Jesse pressed.

"I don't remember much from *any* of those days. I was probably stoned the whole time I was working. Sorry."

She forced a fake smile, reaching to take her phone. "No worries."

He held the phone out of reach, a smile that was supposed to be sexy plastered to his lips.

"I hope you didn't come here just to show me this picture. I mean, I'm happy for any excuse to meet you, Jessica—"

"Jesse."

"Close enough."

"Not even." She snatched the phone from his hand, rolling her eyes. Typical gym rat. She tapped the screen to zoom in on the image, framing Victoria's face in the center. "I'm here because I was hoping you could tell me about this woman."

He leaned forward as she turned the phone toward him. "Tell you what about her?"

"It looks like she's glaring at you. As if the two of you had an argument."

"Really?" He shook his head. "I have no idea. Like I said, I was probably toasted." He straightened, looking bored. "Now, unless you're interested in some up close and personal training, I need to get back to work."

"That's it."

"A shame," he murmured, about to turn away. Then, without warning, his brows snapped together, and he grabbed her wrist to prevent her from lowering the phone. "Wait."

She forced herself to endure his touch.

"What is it?"

"I remember something from that day." He nodded toward the phone. "This woman."

"What about her?"

"I thought I recognized her."

Jesse was confused. "You recognize her or you don't?"

"I mean, when I saw her in Canton, she reminded me of someone I knew back home."

Jesse's breath tangled in her throat as a tiny seed of hope began to bloom. Had his caveman brain managed to dig up a nugget of information that might be helpful?

"Where's back home?" She struggled to keep her tone casual.

"Little Rock, Arkansas."

That explained the accent, but Jesse couldn't deny a stab of surprise. Little Rock was an eight-hour drive from Canton. It wasn't that unusual for students to come from all over the world, especially if they were athletes, but they rarely stayed in the area after they left school. There wasn't much around to tempt them to linger.

"And you thought this woman lived there?" She nodded toward the phone.

"Her hair was red instead of brown like I remembered, but she was the spitting image of my next-door neighbor when I was growing up. Sylvie . . ." His brow furrowed as he searched for the name. "Sylvie Fulton. Yeah, that was it. I could have sworn it was her."

Sylvie Fulton. Jesse silently repeated the name until she was certain she wouldn't forget.

"She didn't recognize you?"

"Naw. She said I made a mistake. Claimed that she'd never been to Little Rock, and then she threatened to call the cops if I didn't stay away from her."

"She threatened to call the cops?" Jesse blinked. Even for Victoria, that was dramatic. Unless she had something to hide.

Like the fact that she was actually Sylvie Fulton from Little Rock.

"Yup. Acted as if I'd insulted her." He glared at the image on her phone. "Whatever. Seemed like a stuck-up bitch."

"She was." Jesse gently tugged her wrist out of his grip. She was getting a cramp in her shoulder. "You said Sylvie was your neighbor?"

"If she really was Sylvie, then yeah. She lived next to me for five or six years."

"What do you remember about her?"

He hesitated, as if realizing her questions weren't just casual interest in an old picture she'd found.

"What does it matter? I told you, it wasn't the same woman."

"Maybe it was," she insisted. "I think you were right and she was your neighbor. I also think the reason she went full Karen on you was because she didn't want anyone else to know."

"Why not?"

"Because she was going by the name of Victoria Ralston when she moved to Canton."

"Seriously?"

"Seriously."

"Weird. Why change her name?"

"That's what I'm trying to figure out," Jesse confessed.

Dix frowned. "Are you a cop?"

"No. This woman was married to my father, but she left town years ago. I have some paperwork I need her to sign, but I can't locate her. I'm trying everything to track her down." Jesse lied easily. "What do you remember about her?"

"Nothing much." He hunched a shoulder, seemingly satisfied with her explanation. "She lived next door in a crappy trailer that matched our crappy trailer in a crappy trailer park."

There was an edge in his voice, as if he didn't have the fondest memories of his time in Little Rock. Was that why he'd stayed in this area instead of heading home when he dropped out?

"Did she live alone?"

"There was some dude there. I don't know if they were married or not. He sold weed and pills when he could get a supply. Everyone called him Buzz, for obvious reasons."

Jesse hesitated, doubt pricking her bubble of hope. She was ready and willing to believe that Victoria had arrived in Canton with a fake name and the hope of landing a husband to take care of her and her daughter. But it wasn't as easy to believe that Victoria had once been a woman named Sylvie who lived in a trailer park with a drug-dealing lover called Buzz.

"Did she have any kids?"

"I don't think so, but it's hard to say." His sharp laugh echoed through the room. "There were a dozen kids running around the trailer park. Like a pack of wolves. No one knew who they belonged to. Most of the time, no one cared. Especially the parents." There was a whoosh of air as the door was pulled open and a large man in gray sweats entered the gym and headed straight to the counter. Without waiting to see if anyone would appear to help him, he mashed his fist on the silver bell with the built-up angst of a teenage girl. The dude was obviously tweaking on testosterone and steroids. Dix rolled his eyes. "I gotta go."

"No shit."

Jesse left the gym, her thoughts buzzing with the possibility that Victoria wasn't Victoria, but instead a woman named Sylvie Fulton from a trailer park in Little Rock, Arkansas. She did force herself to take the time to swing by the grocery store, only because she was sick of toast without butter, before returning to Canton at a speed that had the old truck rattling. Although in fairness, any speed over fifty miles an hour made the truck rattle.

Once back at the Tap Room, she put away the groceries before settling at the kitchen table and opening her laptop. Then, barely daring to breathe, she typed in the name Sylvie Fulton.

A second later she had a dozen hits. She clicked on the first link, her heart racing as she read the headline from a local Little Rock paper dated January 2003.

Sylvie Fulton weds Larry Maitland in private ceremony

There was a short paragraph that focused on Larry Maitland, who was a local entrepreneur with several rental properties and apartment complexes spread around Little Rock, and at the end a brief mention of Sylvie Fulton, who wore a white Vera Wang pantsuit during the courthouse wedding. There wasn't even a photo.

Jesse rolled her eyes. Trust the paper to focus on the man, who obviously had some money, while reducing the bride to a pantsuit.

Not that it mattered. She was more interested in the fact that there was no picture or mention of a reception. If Larry was so successful, why not flaunt his wealth?

Was it possible that Victoria had arranged a fake wedding? Jesse pursed her lips. That didn't seem likely. Not at the courthouse. So maybe they'd been in a hurry. But why?

Jesse abruptly clicked her tongue, mentally subtracting Tegan's age from the date of the article. Yes. That was it. Sylvie Fulton was pregnant with Larry Maitland's baby. That could explain the quiet wedding.

Clicking out of the article, she pulled up the next link, her brows arching as a large image filled the screen. Jesse could see a faded brick building in the background with a wide, sweeping staircase that was lined with a crowd of people, along with the professional cameras used by television stations. At the top of the steps was a podium, where a dark-haired woman with large sunglasses was speaking into a clump of microphones. She was holding a small child who had a tangle of brown curls and her thumb stuck in her mouth.

Jesse leaned toward the computer, as if it would help her make out the fuzzy features of the woman behind the microphones. Was it Victoria? It was possible. The shape of the face was the same, along with a similar body type, although in the photo the woman was wrapped in an expensive fur coat.

Her attention moved to the story beneath the image.

> *Sylvie Maitland, widow of Lawrence "Larry" Maitland, holding daughter Brooke as she addresses questions from the press outside the Little Rock Courthouse.*

> *According to police reports, fifty-five-year-old Larry Maitland was discovered deceased last week in one of his rental properties with a gunshot wound to the head. The property was empty at the time, and there was no evidence of foul play. The police haven't offered an official cause of death, although they stated that suicide isn't*

being ruled out. According to his widow, Sylvie Maitland, her husband was being investigated for tax evasion, money laundering, and conspiracy to commit fraud. She also admitted that they were on the verge of bankruptcy.

Sylvie ended the press conference with a request for privacy for her and her daughter as they try to cope during this difficult time.

Jesse reached the end of the article and clicked out, eagerly moving to the next link. It was a similar news article about Larry Maitland, only this one emphasized his shady dealings, and the fact that there was a large amount of money missing from his accounts that couldn't be traced. She rolled her eyes at the swift transformation from hometown success story to being labeled a slum lord, a tax evader, and even hinting at laundering cash for drug dealers. It didn't take long after his suicide for the vultures to start circling.

She shook her head, refusing to be distracted. She finally had what felt like a genuine lead. If this was Victoria—still a big if—she now knew that her stepmother had gone from living with a low-level thug in a trailer park to a high-level thug who'd ended up with a bullet in his head. She also knew that there was a lot of missing cash that could keep a woman and her daughter in comfort for a few years.

Unfortunately, the links led to similar articles that focused on the dead husband, barely mentioning Sylvie except to say she'd left town without further comment. And one that mentioned the property and bank accounts had been seized by the government.

Jesse turned her attention to social media, using both Sylvie Fulton and Sylvie Maitland, and even Brooke Maitland. There were a dozen matches, but none of them could be Victoria. She tried Victoria Maitland and Vickie Fulton and every other combo she could think of, only to draw a blank.

Dammit.

It was like the woman could appear and disappear out of thin air.

How? And why? And did that mean she was out there somewhere with a new name and a new husband, as Jesse had always hoped? More importantly, if she was out there, would she have had reason to return and kill her former husband? Her *fake* former husband, Jesse silently added.

Shoving away from the table, Jesse stretched her back and wandered toward the sink to get a drink of water. It was only late afternoon, but it felt as if it'd been a long day. She could use something stronger than water.

Debating whether to grab a beer out of the fridge, she was distracted by a faint sound. What was that? She turned toward the open door, cocking her head as if it would help her hear. A second later, the same sound echoed through the building.

The rap, rap, rap followed by a five-second silence before another rap.

Her father's knock. A breath hissed through her clenched teeth as Jesse grabbed a butcher knife off the counter and headed downstairs. Enough was enough. She was done screwing around with whoever was tormenting her.

Jogging down the stairs, she crossed the foyer and glanced out the back window. No one. She unlocked the door, pulling it open to look up and down the empty alley. Swearing in frustration, she slammed the door shut and locked it. Whoever was knocking had disappeared. Again.

She turned back, intending to head upstairs, when the unmistakable scent of her father's cologne wafted through the air. She froze, her heart squeezing as fear trickled down her spine. Was the intruder in the bar? How? The doors were locked.

Cautiously, she glanced around, her gaze at last lingering on the door to the cellar, which wasn't fully latched. As if someone had tried to sneak down there without making a sound. Jesse hesitated before she moved forward, pulling open the door and staring down at the darkness.

It was stupid, so stupid, but she had to know.

Pulling out her phone from her back pocket, she switched on the camera, holding it in front of her as she inched her way down the steep steps.

"Hello? I know you're down there," she called out, wrinkling her nose as the smell of cologne hit her. It was like someone had dumped an entire bottle nearby. "I've called the sheriff, plus, I'm recording this. It's going out live to the world," she lied, reaching the bottom step. "Show yourself."

Silence greeted her demands. A thick, heavy silence that revealed she was alone in the cellar. Turning in a slow circle, she used the light from her phone to scan the cramped space. Nothing. She started to lower her hand when she noticed that the safe in the wall was wide open. And that everything inside was gone.

Was that why the intruder had snuck into the bar? To steal the contents of the safe?

But why? There really wasn't anything worth taking. No money or jewels or gold coins. And why alert her to their presence with the knock? And why the cologne? Did they think she was stupid enough to believe her father's ghost had returned to take a few legal papers?

Jesse shuddered, hating the feeling that there was some master puppeteer out there, pulling her strings and laughing at her blind stupidity. Why couldn't she guess who was behind this? There were so many clues. Why couldn't she put them together?

Shutting the safe, she climbed the stairs. She wasn't going to solve anything in the dusty cellar. Besides, the shadowy darkness with the choking stench of cologne was giving her the heebie-jeebies. She wanted out in the fresh air to clear her mind.

She was at the top of the steps when she felt a rush of air. As if there was a sudden breeze swirling through the bar. Then, without warning, the door to the cellar was abruptly slammed shut, nearly smacking her in the face. With a shriek of shock, Jesse spun away, knocked off-balance. Pressing her back against the wall, she hissed as the bricks scraped her skin and the knife clattered down the stairs, but she at least saved herself from a broken neck.

That was the only good thing, she discovered, as she reached out to grab the knob, her heart racing as it refused to budge.

"Dammit," she rasped, pounding her fist against the wooden door. "This isn't funny. Let me out. Do you hear? Let me out!"

She continued to pound until her knuckles were bruised and her arm ached, despite the fact she knew it was a wasted effort. Someone had gone to a lot of effort to lure her into this trap. She had no idea why, or what they hoped to achieve. Or even if it was the same person who stole her father's belongings from the safe. But she did know whoever had locked her in wasn't letting her out.

Chapter 12

Pain was radiating up her arm when Jesse at last forced herself to drop her hand and take a deep, calming breath. Around her, the silence settled with a smothering weight. Not the aching silence that Jesse felt whenever she walked through the empty bar. This was a menacing hush. As if the evil that had driven her from this place had been waiting for her return. Only this time, it wasn't going to let her escape.

"For God's sake, get a grip," she muttered, lifting her phone to punch the top number.

A second later, Noah answered. "Hi, Jesse, what's up?"

Relief flooded through her, nearly sending her to her knees. Until that moment she hadn't realized how terrified she was that she might be trapped in the musty cellar forever. That she would perish alone in the dark with no idea of who wanted her dead.

Forced to clear the lump from her throat, Jesse at last managed to respond. "Hey, Noah, sorry to bother you, but I could use your help."

"Sure, what's up?"

"I've somehow managed to lock myself in the cellar of the Tap Room."

There was a silence, as if Noah just noticed the raspy fear in her voice. "Are you okay?"

"Yeah, I'm fine. The door swung shut and now it won't open. I don't suppose you could come over and let me out?" She grunted as she remembered that she'd locked the doors. "I think you'll have to break out the window in the back door to get in. I'll pay you, of course—"

"I'll be right there," he interrupted, ending the call before she could say thank you.

Jesse released a slow breath as she slid down the brick wall, perching on the top step. She felt better knowing that the cavalry was on the way. Or if not the cavalry, at least Noah, who was big enough to deal with whoever had locked her in.

Not that she expected the intruder to linger. She assumed that they discovered she didn't have anything of value after they'd cleaned out the safe. Unless they'd lured her into the cellar to lock her in and continue with their search? If that was the case, they were going to be severely disappointed. She didn't have anything of value. A little cash, a maxed-out credit card, and clothes you could buy at a thrift shop.

Right now she was more interested in *how* they got in as opposed to *why* they'd gotten in.

The doors were locked, which meant they had a key. But who? She had her key, along with the master key that had belonged to her dad. As far as she knew, no one else had one.

No, wait. That wasn't true. An icy chill crawled over her skin. There was one other person with a key. A person who also knew the combination to the safe. And her father's secret knock. And his favorite cologne.

Victoria.

But why would she be sneaking around? Even if she didn't want to reveal she was alive, she could easily have snuck in and out of the bar during the past nine years. Why wait until Jesse was there?

The answer whispered in the back of her mind...

To stop her from looking into the past.

Yes. That seemed the most likely hypothesis, right? It wasn't just that Victoria didn't want anyone to question why she'd disappeared from Canton; she didn't want anyone poking into who she'd been before she ever arrived.

Especially if she'd disappeared with money from her dead husband, Larry Maitland, who'd stolen from a bunch of mob guys. They seemed the sort who would want it back, no matter how long ago it went missing.

So how far would Victoria go to keep her secrets?

It was a question that gnawed at Jesse until the sound of her name being called out thankfully broke into her broodings.

"Jesse?"

The heavy tread of footsteps vibrated the stairs before the door was pulled open to reveal Noah's welcome silhouette.

Without giving herself time to consider the impulse, Jesse jumped up and flung herself against the hard male body, wrapping her arms around his waist.

"Oh, thank God," she breathed. "You're a lifesaver, Noah Allen. Again."

Noah froze, clearly caught off guard by her dramatic gesture of gratitude; then he lifted his hands to smooth them down her back in a comforting gesture.

"What happened?"

"I..." She paused to lick her lips, not sure how much she wanted to share. She was still shaken by the thought of someone creeping through the bar. She wanted time to clear her mind before she revealed anything. "I'm not sure," she hedged. "I'd gone down to the cellar and a gust of wind must have slammed shut the door. When I tried to open it I realized it was jammed. Thankfully, I'd taken my phone with me, so

I could give you a call." She tilted back her head, forcing a smile. "And here you are."

He didn't return her smile. In fact, his expression was grim. "It wasn't jammed; it was locked."

"Was it? The . . . um . . . lock must have tripped when the door slammed shut."

"Doubtful. Plus, the back door was left wide open."

Open? She stepped back, breaking away from his embrace as she glanced toward the back door. Whoever had locked her in must have gone out that way.

She shoved her phone in her back pocket, trying to disguise the tremor of her hands. She didn't have an answer for that.

"Sorry to bother you. I know you're crazy busy without having to add rescuing damsels in distress to your to-do list. If you tell me how much I owe you, then you can get back to work."

He frowned at her rambling. "Jesse. What's going on?"

"Going on? Nothing."

"Jesse."

"I told you, the door slammed shut and—"

"Horseshit. There's no wind today. Which means no gust slammed that door shut, and even if it did, it couldn't lock itself."

Her gaze lowered to the tips of his worn work boots. "I don't know what to tell you."

"How about the truth?"

"I . . ." The lie wouldn't form.

"Jesse?" He stepped forward, slipping a finger beneath her chin to tilt back her head.

With a sigh, she forced herself to meet his searching gaze. "I don't know the truth. That's the problem."

"Talk to me."

His touch was warm and soft, as if he sensed she was too fragile to be pressured into confessing. It was that gentleness that undermined her instinctive barriers. A part of her needed to tell someone her fears. As if saying the words out loud would ease the looming cloud of dread.

"Since I've been back home, it feels like I'm being haunted."

She winced. She sounded like a lunatic. Thankfully, Noah merely glanced around the bar, as if searching for an unseen presence.

"You think the Tap Room has a ghost?"

"No," she firmly denied. "I think someone wants me to *believe* there's a ghost. More specifically, my father's ghost."

His gaze jerked back to her face, his expression tightening. "What makes you say that?"

"It's going to sound stupid."

His thumb stroked the stubborn line of her jaw. "Nothing you say is going to sound stupid. Trust me."

Jesse hesitated. Did she trust him? Maybe. At least as much as she trusted anyone right now.

She cleared her throat. "A couple of nights ago I was in bed, and I could swear that I heard my dad knocking on the back door."

"You didn't see him?"

"No."

He looked confused. "Then why did you assume it was Mac? It could have been anyone knocking."

"No, my dad had a very specific knock," she insisted. "He created it so I would always know it was him outside. Otherwise I wasn't allowed to open the door if he was gone."

"And you're sure you heard that knock?"

"One hundred percent. But when I went downstairs there was no one there." Jesse abruptly glanced toward the back door. "Wait, that's not true." She spoke slowly as the memory formed. "Adam was there."

"Adam Tillman?"

"That's the one."

"Do you think it was him?"

"If I'm being honest, I *want* to believe it was him. And after talking to Clint Frazer this morning I have legit reason to suspect him. You know, a reason beyond the fact I think he's a total jackass."

"What reason?"

"Clint said that Rosemary Jacobs claimed that she saw Adam and

Victoria having a public argument in the park shortly before Victoria and Tegan disappeared."

"Right." Noah slowly nodded. "I have a vague memory of hearing a rumor about that." He took a moment to dredge up the old gossip. "But didn't he have some friends who swore he was with him the night Rosemary supposedly saw him?"

Jesse nodded. "And he was on duty at the sheriff's office when Victoria crashed her car."

"So how is he involved as a ghost?"

"I don't know if he is or not. I just remember he was lurking in the alley." Jesse shrugged. "Anyway, it wasn't just the knocking. I've also walked into the bar and smelled my dad's cologne. As if he was in the room."

Noah didn't look convinced. "This is an old building. I'm sure there are lots of lingering scents."

"It was too strong to be from nine years ago," she protested. "And when I went upstairs I realized the bottle of my dad's cologne was missing. I'd just placed it on the bed with his other belongings to give away. I left the room and came back, and it had just disappeared."

Noah studied her in confusion. "You think someone snuck in and stole it?"

It sounded far-fetched when he said it. "I suppose it's possible I misplaced it, but I don't think so." Her tone was defensive. "And I smelled it again today."

"Where?"

"First I heard the knock. I was upstairs—" She bit off her words. She didn't want to discuss Victoria or her mysterious past until she had more information. "Working when I heard it. I came down to see if there was someone here, and that's when I noticed the door to the cellar was unlatched. When I got near the steps I could distinctly smell my dad's cologne again. That's why I went downstairs."

His brows lowered, as if he was angered by her explanation. "Are you serious right now?"

She stiffened her spine. Did he think she was lying? "What?"

"You suspect that someone is deliberately trying to make you believe you're being haunted and you let yourself be lured into a creepy cellar with no way to escape?"

"I had a knife," she retorted, not about to admit that she'd been acutely aware she was acting like an idiot. "I had to know."

His jaw tightened. "A knife? You think that's going to protect you?"

"I wasn't going to cower under my bed while some jerk tried to gaslight me."

"Fine, don't cower. But also, don't go down into creepy cellars alone," he protested. "All you had to do was lock the door and wait until someone could go down there with you."

For whatever ridiculous reason, his rational suggestion scraped against her raw nerves and she glared at him in frustration. "Who? Who would go with me? The sheriff?"

"Me."

The word was soft, but it slammed into her with shocking force. With a blink, she stared into his dark blue eyes, knowing she should step back even as she swayed forward.

"You have enough on your plate without worrying about me," she said in a husky voice.

His gaze lowered to her parted lips. "You're the only thing that I'd actually enjoy having on my plate right now."

The sound of something heavy thumping against the wood-planked floor sounded as loud as a gunshot, shattering the dangerous sense of intimacy.

"Am I interrupting?"

With a gasp, Jesse jumped back, her gaze swinging toward the open door where a man was standing.

"Parker," she breathed, for a second wondering if he were an illusion.

Caught in a shaft of late afternoon sunlight that emphasized his delicate features and glowed in his satiny halo of curls, he appeared more ethereal than usual. As if he were a fantasy, not a flesh-and-blood man.

The black eyes, however, were all too real as they swept from Jesse to Noah with a searing intensity.

"So you do remember me," he said in a tight voice.

"Don't be silly." Jesse felt a heat stain her cheeks, immediately followed by a pang of annoyance. She hadn't been doing anything wrong. Besides, she was too damned old to be blushing. She squared her shoulders. "What are you doing here?"

"I thought my girlfriend might be missing me." Parker stepped over the backpack at his feet. She assumed the canvas bag hitting the floor was what had caused the loud thump. "Now I'm not so sure."

"Of course I've missed you." With a click of her tongue she moved to meet him, as much to keep him away from Noah as to make sure he realized that he had nothing to worry about. Once she was close enough, she wrapped her arms around his waist and kissed him. "Desperately," she whispered against his lips.

He returned her hug, but his gaze remained locked on the man standing near the cellar door. "Desperately?"

Jesse heaved a sigh. Parker had never been irrationally jealous, but there was no doubt he was protective. She'd assumed it was because they worked in an environment where men were constantly hitting on her.

Swiveling until she was facing Noah with her back pressed against Parker's chest, she made the introductions.

"Parker, this is an old friend of mine, Noah. Noah, Parker Moreau."

Noah casually ignored Parker, clearly blatantly indifferent to Parker's jealousy.

"I should be getting back to the lumberyard." There was a deliberate pause, his gaze locked on Jesse's face. "If you're sure that everything's okay?"

"Yep, it's all better now, thanks." Her tone was ridiculously chirpy, but she just wanted the tense atmosphere to go away.

"No problem."

Noah walked past them with a slow stroll, as if emphasizing the fact that he was several inches taller than Parker. Jesse rolled her eyes. Men.

Waiting until she heard the back door snap shut, Jesse turned to meet Parker's smoldering glare.

"An old friend, eh?" he demanded.

Jesse tilted her chin. She was willing to make allowances for Parker's mood. He'd walked in to find her standing suspiciously close to an attractive man. But she hadn't done anything wrong and she wasn't going to apologize.

"I do have a few," she informed him.

"What was he doing here?"

"He owns the local lumberyard and I hired him to take care of some repairs on the bar before I put it up for sale."

Her explanation did nothing to ease Parker's annoyance. In fact, his brows lowered and his eyes narrowed. "Repairs? Why are you paying for repairs if you're going to sell the place?"

"Because I want to get top dollar."

He swept a disbelieving glance around the shadowed bar. "Top dollar?"

Jesse forced a smile to her lips even as she squashed the stab of betrayal. Of course Parker wouldn't feel her intense loyalty for this place. To him, it was just another run-down building. For her... well, it'd always been home.

"Hey, this is prime real estate. Or at least that's what my real estate agent keeps telling me. All it needs is some TLC."

Her tone was teasing, but Parker must have sensed he'd stepped over a line. With a visible effort, he relaxed his tense expression.

"What about me? Do I get some of that TLC?"

She met his smoldering gaze, a spark of desire igniting in the pit of her stomach. She arched until she was pressed against his slender form.

"Do you want some?"

He lowered his head, his lips finding the spot behind her ear that made her toes curl in anticipation.

"Desperately."

Chapter 13

Jesse gasped for air as they tumbled onto the bed. Her body felt oddly numb after being pressed against the wall as Parker had pounded into her with a ruthless force. She wasn't sure if he was punishing her for being alone with another man in the bar or reminding her of the passion that exploded between them whenever they touched.

Probably both.

Whatever the reason, she was drenched in sweat and her muscles were as limp as noodles. Exactly what she needed to remind herself why she was selling the bar and moving on. This was her future. Right?

Turning on her side, she rubbed her hands over Parker's smooth chest. He kept it shaved and tanned to impress the ladies at the club when he went shirtless, but Jesse preferred some fur. Like Noah . . .

No, no, no. She squashed the thought before it could form, grimly concentrating on the exquisite man lying next to her. And he was exquisite, she sternly reminded herself. There wasn't a woman around who wouldn't be eager to attract his attention.

She pressed a kiss directly over his heart. "Confess, is this why you're here?" she teased. "To get me naked?"

He stroked his hand down the curve of her back. "It's not a bad reason, is it?"

"Not bad at all."

"Did you miss me?"

"Of course I missed you."

"You're sure?"

She tilted back her head to meet his brooding gaze. "Why would you even ask?"

There was a sullen silence. Not the comfortable silence that descended when both people were breathless from sex, but one that held a prickle of tension.

"Noah," Parker growled.

She stiffened. "An old friend, nothing more."

"He wasn't looking at you like an old friend. Is he the reason it's taking you so long to get stuff finished up here?"

With a sharp burst of fury, Jesse shoved her hands against his chest before climbing off the bed and crossing to the nearby chair. She grabbed an oversize T-shirt she slept in and jerked it on.

She didn't know why she was so angry. Maybe because of guilt? She couldn't deny her treacherous mind was secretly comparing the two men. Or maybe she didn't like the knowledge that Parker was more obsessed with Noah than the woman he supposedly loved, despite the fact that he hadn't seen her in days.

"I told you it was going to take time. You don't snap your fingers and get a man declared dead," she bit out. "And you don't sell a building that's been abandoned for over nine years without a few repairs."

"I didn't come here to argue." Parker shoved himself to a sitting position, looking like a disheveled angel with his tousled curls and delicate features.

"You could have fooled me," she muttered.

"All I'm saying is that you've obviously hired a handyman to deal with the bar and I assume you've done the paperwork to get your dad's death certificate."

"And?"

"And there's no reason for you to still be here." He glanced around her childhood bedroom. When she'd first returned to the Tap Room a musty emptiness had permeated every inch of the building. Now it was messy with dirty clothes, personal items, and forgotten dishes she'd left sitting around like she was seventeen and confident someone else would clean it up. It felt lived in. "Not unless you want to be here."

She refused to consider the question. "And what about my father's belongings that have to be packed up and taken to the thrift shop?" she instead demanded, pacing the floor with short, angry stomps. "And closing out his bank accounts and dealing with the life insurance policy? Plus, there are a few people I'd like to say goodbye to before I pack up and leave forever. I know all you care about is the money that I'm going to inherit, but—"

"Stop." With a swift movement he was blocking her path to wrap his arms around her. "I'm sorry. It's just that I've missed you."

She remained stiff in his embrace. "How much time did you get off?"

"I'll have to be back in Chicago before my shift tomorrow night."

Jesse considered his words. It was Sunday, which meant the club was closed tonight. She didn't know if she was disappointed or relieved he hadn't been willing to ask for actual time off to stay with her.

"So soon?" she forced herself to ask. "We'll have to make the most of your flying visit."

"I heartily agree." He lowered his head to find the tender spot behind her ear. "Come back to bed."

Jesse pulled away, heading toward the door. "I'll meet you in the shower."

A wicked smile curved his lips. "That works."

An hour later they were back in the bedroom as Jesse pulled on a pair of cutoff shorts and a purple T-shirt that clung to her slender curves. Parker stood in all his naked glory in the center of the floor, his arms folded over his chest as he glared at her.

"Tell me again why you're getting dressed."

She slid her feet into a pair of leather sandals. "First off, I'm starving."

"We can order in."

Jesse snorted. "This is Canton, not Chicago. And second, I want to show you around. I spent nineteen years of my life here."

His jaw clenched. "It's important to you?"

She moved to stand in front of him, placing her palm over the steady beat of his heart. "Yeah, it's important to me."

"Fine." He brushed a kiss over her lips. "Then it's important to me."

Less than an hour later, Jesse and Parker were standing in front of a narrow brick building that was half-buried into the banks of the Mississippi River.

"The Ice House?" Parker read the gold letters painted on the large front window. "What is this place?"

Jesse headed down the short flight of cement steps and pushed open the glass door. "A combination gift shop, butcher shop, and ice cream parlor. They have sandwiches and chips, along with orgasmic root beer floats."

They entered the brightly lit restaurant, with a high ceiling where industrial lights dangled from the open beams and a stone floor that was worn until it dipped in the center of the room. A dozen tables were haphazardly set around the space and glass coolers at the back where you could buy anything from deli meat and sliced cheese to a gallon of butterscotch ice cream.

To say the Ice House was retro was an understatement. It looked like it was a couple of centuries old, mainly because it *was* a couple of centuries old. And huddled so deep in the banks of the Mississippi River that time had simply passed it by.

She led him to a small square table pushed against the brick wall that was covered with framed photographs and settled on one of the chrome and fake, red-plastic-cushioned chairs. You didn't wait to be seated in the local restaurants. It was first come, first served. Which was why the place was already half empty. The locals showed up at five o'clock on the dot and were back home by six.

Jesse grabbed a laminated menu that rested between the silver napkin holder and the salt and pepper shakers, handing it to Parker. She already knew what she was eating.

A BLT with fries and a root beer float. The nectar of the gods.

Parker held the menu with the edges of his fingers, as if afraid it might be sticky, and ordered a house salad with water when the waitress appeared. Jesse managed not to sigh, reminding herself that Parker was accustomed to the big city. He no doubt felt like a fish out of water. She should just appreciate the fact he'd driven hours on his day off to be with her.

With a determination to avoid any arguments, Jesse encouraged Parker to tell her what had been happening at the nightclub while she'd been gone, and even listened to his latest ideas on how they could use what they'd learned working at the successful club for their own business without reminding him they didn't own anything yet.

Once they were done eating, Parker rose to his feet as she left money on the table and glanced at the wall of pictures. They started at one end of the building with black-and-white prints of Canton during the days of horses and buggies and ended near the door with current photos.

"Looks like this place has been here a while," Parker said, slowly moving down the wall.

"It started off as an actual icehouse," she explained. "That's why it's built half underground. There was also a creamery where the gift shop is now." She pointed toward a door across the room, where stairs led up to the connected building. "Eventually, people started buying refrigerators, so they turned this part into a butcher shop and started selling sandwiches to the passengers getting off the ferry, along with ice cream from the creamery."

Parker sent her a puzzled glance. "How did the gift shop get included?"

"The creamery closed down and the ice cream shop moved into this area, so the connected building was empty. The story is that the grandfather of the current owner went to St. Louis, where he met a pretty artist who he invited to stay at the shop and use the empty space as her studio and a place to sell her paintings."

Parker chuckled. "Bold. I assume they fell in love and lived happily ever after?"

"Nope. His wife marched in one day with a shotgun and blew a hole in the ceiling and then turned around and walked out of the place." She pointed toward the soaring ceiling, where it was possible to see the contrast of newer boards. "You can tell where it's patched, although it was probably just a leak in the roof that caused the damage. Anyway, the next day the artist was packed up and on her way back to St. Louis and the wife was using the empty space to sell the dollies and pot holders she crocheted. The merchandise has improved over the years." She sent him a wry glance. "If country crafty is your thing."

"I'm not sure if that story is romantic or horrifying."

"You gotta admire the wife. She wasn't going to sit around being humiliated by another woman. Although I don't understand why she bothered. Her husband was obviously a jerk. She should have packed her bags and moved on."

Parker sent her a curious glance. "Is that what you would do?"

"Without hesitation. Life is too short to waste on losers."

He arched a brow. "What about fighting for the one you love?"

A shiver raced through Jesse. She'd watched her dad struggle to earn Victoria's affection. It'd been a losing battle that had destroyed his pride, along with his belief that he was worthy of love. In the process, Jesse had lost her father's carefree spirit and ready smile.

"Is it love if you have to fight for it?"

"People make mistakes," Parker reminded her. "Surely you have some forgiveness in your heart?"

"Not for betrayal." There was an edge to her voice. An unspoken warning. "Never for that."

With a shrug, Parker resumed his stroll along the wall, his attention returning to the framed photos. They were nearing the door when he abruptly stopped to point at one of the photos. It was a picture of four teenage girls who looked remarkably alike, with their hair pulled into high ponytails and wearing matching softball uniforms.

A bittersweet nostalgia settled in the center of Jesse's heart as she thought back to those uncomplicated days. There'd been nothing but friends and fun and secret crushes. Certainly she'd never dreamed her life was on the brink of falling apart.

"Is that you?" Parker demanded.

"Yeah." She determinedly headed toward the door. That innocent child was gone. Destroyed by Victoria. Or rather, Sylvie Fulton Maitland. The bitch. "We all used to stop by here after a game for a root beer float, back when I could eat anything I wanted without worrying it might give me diabetes."

Parker made a sound of disgust as they climbed out of the building and strolled along the banks of the river.

"You still eat whatever you want. I've seen you survive for a week on a bag of gummy worms."

Jesse chuckled. He wasn't exaggerating. "I think I mixed a few of those gummy worms into yogurt. That's healthy, right?"

He shuddered. "Disgusting."

Grabbing his hand, she threaded their fingers together. Evening had descended, leaving them shrouded in darkness, with only the soft brush of water against the rocks to break the silence. It was deliciously serene, and for the first time since Parker had made his unexpected appearance, Jesse felt her tension begin to ease.

Next to her, Parker pinched his lips in disgust, obviously not as happy with the sensation that they were alone in the world.

"It's so quiet. Does everything in town shut down at five?"

"Most places," she conceded. "Especially on Sunday."

"You must have been bored out of your mind living here."

If Parker had asked her that question a week ago, she would have agreed. After traveling from one major city to another, there was no denying that Canton, Missouri, was the pinnacle of dullness. But the past few days had reminded her that there was more to life than bright lights and making money.

"There were times when I felt smothered, but there was also a sense of being part of a family that I miss." She glanced toward the slumbering buildings that lined Main Street. "This will always be home."

Parker's hand tightened around hers as he tugged her close to his side. "You have me now."

"True."

"And once we get our new business up and running, we can start looking for a real house to move into."

Jesse kept her gaze averted. "Eventually," she murmured.

She sensed his sharp glance, as if he was annoyed at her vague response. She didn't bother to elaborate. They'd reached the Tap Room, giving her the perfect excuse to concentrate on finding the key and shoving it into the lock. A second later, she was stepping into the bar and switching on the lights.

She waited for Parker to enter before she closed the door and led him toward the back of the building. He was right when he said the town closed down at five o'clock. There wasn't much entertainment to offer beyond a glass of wine and watching a movie on the couch.

They were near the opening to the foyer when Jesse felt it. She reached out to grab Parker's arm, her sense of peace shattered.

"Stop," she rasped.

He sent her a baffled frown. "What's wrong?"

"Don't you feel the breeze?"

"So what? You probably left a window open."

Her stomach clenched. Having Parker with her had allowed her to let down her guard. As if nothing bad could happen as long as she wasn't alone. Now the terror she'd felt when she was locked in the cellar came crashing back.

"No, everything was locked up before we left."

Refusing to give into her unease, Jesse calmly circled behind the bar to grab the baseball bat that her dad had kept on a bottom shelf. It wasn't often he had to resort to violence, but she'd witnessed him knock a three-hundred-pound football player through the window.

Clenching the bat in a death grip, she cautiously made her way toward the foyer.

"Why are you so worried? You said yourself this is Canton, not Chicago." Parker walked beside her, clearly amused by her attempt to be a weapon-toting badass. "Surely there's not a lot of crime around here?"

"You'd be surprised," she muttered, grimly forcing herself to step into the dark foyer and flip the switch. Light from the bare bulb dangling from the ceiling immediately flooded the small area.

The first thing she noticed was that she hadn't been imagining things. The back door was wide open, allowing the night breeze to swirl into the building. The second thing was the motionless form stretched across the wooden planks. Lowering the bat, Jesse stepped forward. The person had their back to her, but there was no mistaking the reddish hair and well-worn sundress.

"Oh no. Bea."

Dropping the bat, Jesse rushed forward, kneeling next to the older woman. Then, gently turning her onto her back, she studied the round face that was pale in the harsh light and the swelling bump just above her right eye.

Jesse shoved her hand into her purse, pulling out her phone and dialing 911. In clipped tones, she reported finding a woman unconscious and gave the address even as the older woman began to stir, a groan wrenching from lips as she lifted her lashes to stare at Jesse in confusion.

"Bea, don't move," Jesse commanded, dropping the phone back into her purse. "You've been hurt."

"What?" Bea blinked. "No, I'm fine."

Jesse pressed a gentle hand against the woman's chest as she tried to lift herself off the floor. "You're not fine. You were knocked out. Or you passed out."

Bea winced, lifting her hand to touch the knot that was turning a dark shade of purple.

"Ouch. I think it was the knocked-out option," she muttered.

"What happened?"

"I must have tripped and fallen." Bea's voice trailed away, her expression confused, as if she was struggling to remember how she'd ended up on the floor. "Wait. No. I was hit."

Jesse ground her teeth. She wasn't surprised. It would be too much of a coincidence for the older woman simply to have tripped. Not when Jesse had been stalked and terrorized since her return to Canton.

She could only hope that poor Bea didn't have a concussion or, worse, a fractured skull.

"Do you know who hit you?" she asked.

Bea started to shake her head, only to flinch in pain. "No, I'm sorry. I didn't get a good look."

There was the sound of footsteps as Parker belatedly moved to join her, staring down at Bea with a frown.

"Should you be questioning her right now? I doubt she can think clearly after getting whacked on the head."

"I can think just fine, young man," Bea snapped, glaring up at Parker. "Who are you?"

Jesse tried not to be angered by Parker's lack of sympathy. Bea was a stranger to him, after all. Still, he was acting as if he was more annoyed than worried to find the older woman knocked out.

"This is Parker Moreau," she said.

"The boyfriend?"

"Yes." Jesse gently brushed a strand of hair off Bea's face. "Can you tell me what happened?"

Bea reluctantly returned her attention to Jesse. "I was upstairs watching television when I remembered that the garbageman comes by in the morning. I came down to throw a few bags into the dumpster when I saw someone going into your building." She waved a hand weakly at the open door. "I just caught a glimpse, so I assumed it was you. I followed to make sure that you'd eaten dinner. Then . . ." Her hand moved to touch her swollen forehead. "Everything went dark."

"There was someone inside the bar?" Jesse shivered. She'd assumed that someone had been lurking in the alley when Bea caught them. Which was stupid. The only reason the back door would be wide open was if an intruder had managed to break in.

"I'll take a look around," Parker said, as if eager to get away from the injured woman.

Bea sent Jesse a strange glance. "So that's Parker."

Jesse grimaced. She didn't want to discuss Parker with Bea. One was a part of her future and the other was her past. The two things had always been separated in her mind. She wanted them to stay that way.

No doubt that was why she'd been so uncomfortable since Parker arrived in Canton.

Jesse shook her head, forcing herself to concentrate on Bea as the older woman started to sit up.

"Stay still. I've called for an ambulance. They should be here any minute."

"Oh, Jesse, I wish you hadn't done that." Bea's face flushed, although she obediently lay back down. "I don't want any fuss."

"Having EMTs doing their job isn't a fuss."

"It's just a bump."

Jesse pinched her lips together. She prayed it *was* just a bump and nothing more serious. She already felt awful that the poor woman was injured. If Bea had some sort of permanent damage, she would never forgive herself.

"When you receive your medical degree you can give me advice on your condition. Until then, I'll leave it to the professionals."

Bea parted her lips, but before she could insist that she was fine, there was movement near the back door. Jesse turned her head to discover the short, stocky form of Sheriff Adam Tillman.

"What's going on?" he demanded, his gaze narrowing at the sight of Bea on the floor.

Straightening, Jesse placed herself in front of the injured woman. She didn't trust this man. "Why are you here?"

"You called 911."

Jesse grimaced. If she'd known that hitting 911 would summon the devil, she would have driven Bea to the hospital personally.

"I called for an ambulance, not the sheriff."

"I'm here to find out what happened."

"Bea isn't in any condition to be questioned."

Adam scowled, and Jesse felt Bea shove herself into a seating position. "It's okay, Jesse." Bea interrupted the looming battle, giving the sheriff a condensed version of how she ended up on the floor.

When she was done Adam turned his scowl back to Jesse. "You weren't here when she was attacked?"

"No. We were at the Ice House for dinner. When we came back we found Bea lying in the doorway."

"We? Who was with you?"

Jesse resisted the urge to tell him to mind his own damned business. "Parker Moreau. He's a friend from Chicago."

Adam glanced over her shoulder, trying to peer into the main bar. "Where is he now? No one should leave the scene of the crime until I've interviewed them."

"He didn't leave. He's searching the building in case the intruder is hiding inside."

"That's my job."

"Obviously you weren't here."

"You should have called me."

Jesse folded her arms over her chest, meeting him glare for glare. "And be attacked by some crazed intruder while we waited?"

Frustrated he couldn't arrest Jesse or her boyfriend, Adam glanced back at Bea. "You're sure you didn't see who hit you?"

"Absolutely sure. It was dark in here and I wasn't paying attention. I thought it was Jesse."

The shrill sound of sirens brought a thankful end to Adam's interrogation, and Jesse shoved past him to direct the ambulance into the alleyway. They were fortunate enough in Canton to have local EMTs because the nearest hospital was over a half hour away. Leading them to Bea, she watched as the older woman was loaded onto a gurney.

"This is so unnecessary," Bea muttered, fidgeting in embarrassment.

Jesse grabbed Bea's hand, giving it a squeeze. "Go with them and get checked out. I'll be right behind you."

"Absolutely not. You stay here with your boyfriend."

"No arguments."

Bea clicked her tongue. "As stubborn as Mac."

With reassuring efficiency, Bea was loaded into the ambulance and the doors slammed shut. A few minutes later, it was pulling away with the lights flashing, although the sirens had been turned off. They obviously didn't feel as if Bea was in a life-threatening situation.

Thank God.

"What's this?"

Jesse's momentary sense of relief was destroyed as she turned back to face Adam. He was standing near the back door, which he'd pushed closed to reveal the spray-painted warning.

"Obviously someone doesn't want me to be in Canton," she said.

He rubbed a pudgy finger against the paint as if trying to determine if it was a recent addition.

"Did this happen tonight?"

"No."

He stared at her, as if waiting for her to elaborate. She didn't. He planted his fists on his hips, his chin tilted to an aggressive angle.

"Why didn't you report it?"

"To you?"

"Yeah, to me."

Jesse's humorless laugh echoed through the alley. "You can't be serious?"

His jaws bulged, as if he was gritting his teeth, but he wasn't stupid enough to pretend he cared. Instead, he lowered his hand to pull open the door, bending down as if he was inspecting the knob.

"Was this door locked when you left?"

"Of course."

"Doesn't look like it was forced." He straightened to glance in Jesse's direction. "Who has a key?"

"Just me."

"Interesting."

"What's interesting?"

"The door wasn't forced, and only you have the key." Adam sucked air between his teeth, rocking back on his heels as if he thought he'd scored a point.

Jesse rolled her eyes, but before she could say something that would get her locked in a cell, Parker jogged down the stairs and stepped into the open doorway. His expression tightened at the sight of the stranger.

"Who's this?" he demanded.

Adam flicked a glance over Parker, inspecting the hard, leanly muscled body before taking in the younger man's exquisite beauty. Like most men, he puffed out his chest, instantly intimidated by the knowledge he could never compare.

"This is Adam Tillman." Jesse moved to stand next to Parker, not bothering to hide her amusement.

"Sheriff Tillman," Adam snapped, his jaw jutting out even further. "And you are?"

"Parker Moreau." Parker turned his attention to Jesse, ignoring the sheriff's prickly attitude. "There's no one here. Whoever hit your friend must have taken off before we got back."

Adam stepped forward. "I should take a look around."

Parker shifted to the side, as if he intended to block the lawman. "I just did."

"There was a crime committed. There might be evidence I need to collect."

Jesse shook her head. She didn't have the time or energy to deal with the bubbling testosterone.

"Collect whatever you want," she told Adam. "I'm going to the hospital to check on Bea."

"Wait." Parker turned toward her, grabbing her shoulders in a tight grip. "You're leaving?"

"I have to make sure Bea is okay."

"Why you? Doesn't she have a husband? Or kids?"

"No. And even if she did, I would go." Jesse was annoyed by the defensive edge in her voice. She didn't have to explain her choices. Not even to Parker. "She was hurt on my property."

"That's not your fault."

Jesse cast a quick glance toward Adam. It was her fault, of course. If it wasn't for her return to Canton, there wouldn't be a stalker hanging around the Tap Room whacking unsuspecting people on the head. But she wasn't going to admit that in front of the sheriff.

"I'm not saying it is, but I do feel responsible," she finally muttered.

Parker's fingers dug into her flesh, threatening to leave bruises. "Jesse, I know you're worried, but I'm leaving in the morning. I'd like to spend some time together."

She pulled away from his painful grasp. "I know. I'm sorry, but I'll be back in a couple of hours. I promise."

"Jesse."

He reached out a hand, but with a sudden need to be far from the bar and the two men glaring at her in frustration, she turned to rush down the alleyway. She would circle around the building, where she'd parked the truck.

Once she was sure that Bea wasn't seriously injured, she would return and apologize to Parker in a more tangible way. One that included lots of bare, sweaty skin and tangled sheets.

Chapter 14

It was well past midnight when Jesse quietly pushed open the front door of the Tap Room. It'd taken longer than expected for Bea to get settled in a hospital room, and for the doctor to arrive to assure her that she was going to be fine. And if she was being completely honest, she'd lingered beyond what was necessary, waiting until the older woman had fallen into a deep sleep before slipping out of the hospital room.

It wasn't just that she felt guilty. Or that she was worried. It was a reluctance to return and confront Parker's petulant resentment.

She didn't understand what had happened between them. Just a few months ago she'd been bubbling with anticipation when Parker discussed opening a business. She was wildly in love with the man and there was nothing she wanted more than to create a future together.

But then he'd started pressing her to cash out her father's life insurance policy and to sell the bar. It made sense, of course. How else could they put a down payment on a new nightclub? Unfortunately, she hadn't anticipated how the need for money would alter their relationship. Or how she would start to resent the pressure to cut the last ties to her past.

Obviously they needed a conversation to clear the air. Otherwise the tension would turn into a toxic brew, corroding their relationship.

But not tonight, she cowardly decided. She'd been through a meat grinder of a day that included being locked in her cellar and discovering her friend lying unconscious on the floor of her bar. She wasn't prepared for yet another confrontation.

Lost in her thoughts, Jesse had closed and locked the door before she realized that she wasn't alone. Abruptly freezing in place, she slowly glanced around the shadowed room.

"Hello?"

"I'm here."

There was a loud click as one of the neon signs that promoted a local beer was switched on. She jerked around to discover Parker standing next to a table near the front window.

He was wearing the same clothes as when she'd left, and his jaw was darkened by his unshaved whiskers. He looked like he'd been standing there for hours, waiting for her to return.

Jesse blinked in confusion. She assumed he would be in bed. Or at least upstairs in the apartment.

"What are you doing down here?"

"Waiting for you."

"Oh." She glanced around. "Is Adam gone?"

"Finally." Parker made a sound of disgust. "I started to think he was searching for the Holy Grail. He's either the most meticulous cop I've ever encountered or he was searching for something specific."

Jesse shuddered, hating the thought of Adam poking through her personal space.

"He probably assumed I had a horde of drugs stashed somewhere," she muttered.

"Drugs? You?" Parker arched his brows.

Jesse worked at bars and nightclubs, but she rarely drank more than the occasional beer and never indulged in drugs. She had an obsessive need to stay in control.

"It's the tats." Jesse held out her arms. "Around here, only military vets and drug dealers have ink that isn't rainbows and butterflies."

Parker shrugged. "I finally told him to go get a warrant. I didn't want him here when you came back."

Jesse grimaced. "Me either."

"How's your friend?"

Jesse blinked at the abrupt shift in conversation. "No concussion, but they want to keep her overnight for observation. She wasn't happy, but she agreed to stay. I'm sorry I left you all alone."

"Are you?"

Cautiously moving forward, Jesse studied Parker's grim expression. He looked different in the greenish glow of the neon sign. More like a stranger than the man who'd shared her bed for months.

"Parker, what's wrong?"

He ignored her question. "What happened to your back door?"

"What happened . . ." It took a second to realize what he meant. "You mean the spray paint?"

"I mean the threat for you to get out of town," he growled. "Why didn't you tell me about it?"

"Because there wasn't anything to tell. I'm sure it was just some local kids."

"Why would they threaten you?"

"They weren't. They were just being idiots. That's what kids do."

"And if it wasn't kids?"

"It has to be," she stubbornly insisted. She had enough to worry about without adding to the list. "What sort of pathetic loser would use spray paint to threaten me?"

"Possibly a dangerous one." He shook his head, as if he couldn't believe she was really that stupid. "You should have told me. Just like you should have told me about these."

Jesse jerked back as Parker stretched out his arm to wave a manila folder in her face.

"What is it?"

"Offers to buy the Tap Room."

Jesse grabbed the folder Reese had dropped by. She'd left them on the table because she wasn't interested. Now she wished she'd tossed them in the trash. "Honestly, I forgot all about them."

Parker studied her with an expression that was impossible to read. "You came back here to sell this place, but you forgot about the offers you've already gotten?"

"They weren't official offers. I told my real estate agent that I want to fix the place up before I put it on the market. She's . . . an overachiever."

"Why would you waste money?" He pointed to the folder. "More than one of those offers would make a significant down payment on the nightclub. We could be ready to open the doors within a couple of months."

Jesse felt her muscles clenching. This was the conversation she didn't want to have tonight. Hell, she didn't *ever* want to have it. But maybe Parker was right. It was better to clear the air.

How else could they have a fresh start?

"I don't feel like it's wasting money," she said in a reasonable tone. "Not when it gives us the best chance for selling the Tap Room for top dollar. That way we can put down an even larger deposit and still have money to make it the place of our dreams."

"*Our* dreams? Are you sure about that?"

"What are you asking?"

"I'm not convinced that we still share the same dream."

"Of course we do," she insisted, more out of habit than conviction.

Parker shook his head, stepping toward her. "You were giddy with excitement when we first started talking about opening a club together. But then I found the perfect place and you started acting like you were too good to be stuck in that sort of dump."

"That's not true—"

"And it's only gotten worse since you came back here. Over the past few days, you've found a dozen excuses to drag your feet so you could stay," he overrode her protest.

Jesse swallowed the urge to apologize. Honestly, the nightclub he wanted to buy *was* a dump. And she wasn't dragging her feet. She had real responsibilities that she could no longer ignore.

"They're not excuses."

His dark eyes smoldered with frustration. "We both know you could go back to Chicago with me tomorrow." He grabbed the folder out of her hand, once again waving it in her face. "Everything you need to do could be finished up in a few hours and we could be on the road. If you decide to remain, it's because you want to be here."

"It's not that simple."

"Yeah, it is."

She glared at him, suddenly deciding his face was too pretty. Like a sweet treat that became sickly when she overindulged.

"You were the one who wanted me to come in the first place," she reminded him in sharp tones. "Now you're complaining because I . . ."

Her words trailed away as Parker dropped the folder on the floor, sending the papers skidding over the worn planks. Then, spinning on his heel, he returned to the table where he'd been standing and reached beneath it to grab his backpack.

"Wait. Are you leaving?" she asked in shock.

He slung the backpack over his shoulder, strolling toward the door with an expression she'd never seen on his face before.

Indifference.

"Unlike you, I have a life and a future outside this backwater dump of dreariness," he drawled. "You can come if you want or stay here. I'm not going to beg."

"Parker—"

Without glancing back, he unlocked the door and pulled it open. A moment later, he'd disappeared into the darkness.

Jesse wasn't surprised that she managed to fall asleep after Parker's dramatic exit. It was more shocking she'd managed to make it all the way to her bed before she collapsed in exhaustion.

She was still tired when she woke with the midmorning sunlight streaming into her room, but she managed to zombie walk into the shower before pulling on a pair of shorts and a scoop-necked tee. She was going to have to do laundry, she wryly concluded. Parker was right when he said that she'd stayed longer than either of them had intended. But first she had more important things on her mind.

Two hours later, she had Bea safely returned to her small apartment. Like Mac and Jesse, she'd chosen to live above her business to save on a separate mortgage. Although the older woman refused to be tucked into bed. She even threatened Jesse with a wooden spoon when she promised to return in a couple of hours to check on her. Bea claimed that Jesse was making her feel like a decrepit old lady.

Forced to leave her neighbor to rest in peace, Jesse returned to her own apartment and threw in a load of laundry before she headed into the kitchen. She wasn't going to waste her day brooding on her argument with Parker. Eventually, she would return to Chicago and patch things up. Or at least *try* to patch things up.

For now, she had a dozen other things to occupy her attention. Starting with her father's personal belongings that she wanted to donate to the local charity shop. It was the sort of task she could complete without having to concentrate. Plus, she could check it off her to-do list.

Grabbing a garbage bag from under the sink, Jesse made her way to her father's bedroom and crossed the floor to pull open the curtains. She needed sunlight to banish the ghosts that lingered in the room. Especially after yesterday, when the haunting had been terrifyingly real.

Grabbing the heavy fabric, she shoved the curtains aside to allow the sunlight to spill in. It also gave her a perfect view of the alley below. Her breath lodged in her throat. Was there someone leaning against the dumpster?

For a crazed moment, she thought it was her father. The sense of him was so painfully tangible, it felt inevitable that he would appear from the shadows. Then she leaned forward and tilted her head, getting a better look.

Her breath hissed between her clenched teeth. Of course it was

Adam Pain-in-her-ass Tillman. God forbid she go a day without him ruining it.

With clenched fists, she marched down the stairs and yanked open the back door. "What are you doing here?"

Adam remained propped against the nasty dumpster, his arms folded over his chest. "My job."

"Spying on me is your job?"

"This is a crime scene. I was waiting to see if the perp came back." A taunting smile curved his lips. "You should be thanking me."

"Don't hold your breath."

"Where's the boyfriend?"

Jesse frowned at the abrupt question. "Why?"

"Just curious." He cleared a lump of phlegm from his throat. "Seems odd that he would come to town and the next thing you know, Bea is being hit over the head."

"What are you implying?"

"Stranger in town. Who knows what he might do?"

"Oh for God's sakes," she muttered. "We were having dinner at the Ice House when Bea was attacked. You can check."

"I did."

"And?"

"And you ate there, but no one noticed the exact time you left. And we only have your word that you didn't return until after Bea was knocked unconscious." He nodded toward the back door. "She did say she was following you into the building."

Jesse was more resigned than annoyed. Of course the lazy jerk would try to pin the blame on her. It was a family tradition.

"Why would we hurt Bea?"

"Maybe you had something you didn't want her to see."

"Like what?"

He shrugged. "Could be drugs. Who knows what else? People from the big city are in to all sorts of weird stuff."

She shook her head. She'd been right last night. Adam was searching for something he could use against her. It was obviously time she gave him a taste of his own medicine.

"I get it." She stepped toward him, proving that she wasn't going to be bullied. Not by Adam Tillman or anyone else. "You haven't changed a bit, have you?"

"What are you talking about?"

"Ten years ago you did everything possible, including bullying poor Clint into committing perjury, just to throw an innocent man in jail. At the time, I didn't understand why. Now, I know."

"Know what?"

"That you were trying to deflect attention from the fact that you were seen having a very public argument with my stepmother right before she mysteriously disappeared. If anyone should have been a suspect, it was you."

Adam abruptly shoved away from the dumpster, his face flushed and his nostrils flared. "That's a lie."

She pretended not to hear his protest. "And now, when Bea almost catches whoever has been sneaking onto my property, she gets bashed on the head, and miraculously, you show up to once again point fingers. Only this time, it's at me."

"I'm doing my job," he ground out.

She smiled. It was deliciously easy to provoke Adam's temper. Like all bullies, he crumbled when someone stood up to him.

"You know what I think?"

"I don't care." He sounded like a sulky child.

"I think you were breaking into the bar and Bea caught you. How else could you have arrived so quickly?"

"I already told you. I answered the 911 call."

"In less than five minutes?" She deliberately glanced at his protruding stomach. "You're not that fast."

"I was just around the corner."

"Well, wasn't that convenient?" She took another step closer, ignoring the fact that they were alone in the alley and that he was carrying a weapon. She wanted to believe it was sheer courage that allowed her to stand up to the man who'd tried to destroy her dad's life. Honestly, it was more than likely a combination of anger, stress, and brain fog. "Too convenient."

On cue, Adam slammed his hands onto his hips, just inches from his handgun.

"Why would I break in?"

"Someone's been snooping around here. There's not only the spray paint on my door, but there's stuff missing from my dad's safe."

Adam managed to look genuinely surprised. "If that's true, then why didn't you report the theft?"

"To you? No thanks. You already used every excuse possible to creep around the bar." She paused, struck by a sudden suspicion. She'd leaped to the assumption that Adam was trying to frighten her out of town. But what if he had another reason to be hanging around? "And it wasn't just last night you've been lurking in this alley. What are you looking for?"

"I'm looking for evidence."

"Evidence you left behind last night when you attacked Bea? Or evidence of the crimes you committed a decade ago?" she demanded. "Did my dad find out what you did to Victoria and Tegan? Is that why you accused him of murder and then when he was released, you had to get rid of him another way?"

Adam's flush deepened until it was a dangerous shade of burgundy. Like he was on the verge of an apoplectic fit.

"Your dad disappeared because he was a pervert and everyone in town knew it. Everyone but you." Spittle formed in the corners of his mouth, his pudgy finger stabbing the air as if he wished it was a gun. Jesse had never seen anyone so angry. "If you really want to know why Mac Hudson is missing, why don't you ask the husband of whoever's wife he was sleeping with? I hope he's burning in hell."

Jesse's mouth dropped open as Adam stalked away, sheer disbelief blasting through her. Okay, Mac Hudson hadn't been perfect, but he most certainly hadn't been a pervert.

"How dare you!" she rasped as Adam stalked past her, heading for the opening of the alleyway. She went after him. "My father would never—"

Her words were cut off as a firm hand grabbed her arm. "Jesse. Let him go."

Her first instinct was to jerk away so she could chase after the sheriff. There was no way she was going to let him slander her dad without a fight.

It was only because she recognized her voice that she forced herself to turn and face the woman who was standing behind her.

"Bea, I'm sorry." Jesse grimaced as she caught sight of the older woman's tousled hair and the lump on her forehead that had grown to the size of an egg. She was supposed to be resting, not breaking up a squabble between supposed adults. "Did we disturb you?"

Bea sighed, glancing at the door to her building, which she'd left open. "Honestly, it was the quiet that disturbed me. I hate when the diner is closed."

"It's just for a couple of days. You need to rest."

Bea pursed her lips, as if debating whether to push her argument that her staff could do most of the work while she supervised from the kitchen. One glance into Jesse's stern expression had her heaving a sigh of resignation.

"What was Adam doing here?" she asked instead.

Jesse forced herself to take a deep breath. The mere mention of Adam was enough to send her blood pressure soaring. She was going to give herself a stroke if she didn't calm down.

"He claimed he was looking for evidence."

"You don't believe him?"

"Why would I? Didn't you hear what he said about my dad? The bastard is a dirty, rotten liar."

Bea bit her lower lip, staring at Jesse with a strange expression. "Why don't you come in and we'll have some iced tea?"

Jesse started to shake her head. She wasn't in the mood for a nice chat over a glass of tea. She was in the mood to punch something.

Which was why she should go have a glass of tea instead of brooding on Adam Tillman and his seething hatred toward her father, a voice whispered in the back of her mind. Nothing good ever came from punching things. Especially if those things wore a badge and carried a gun.

"Okay."

Chapter 15

Bea led Jesse through the open door to the large kitchen, which was brightly illuminated by the industrial lights hanging from the ceiling. The glow bounced off the polished stainless-steel appliances that framed the space. Walk-in coolers, cabinets, and stoves. Even the countertops were stainless steel. It was blinding.

Bea motioned her toward a small table set beneath the window as she moved to the fridge and pulled out a pitcher of freshly brewed iced tea. Then, grabbing two glasses, she joined Jesse.

Jesse remained silent as the older woman took a seat and poured out the tea. She'd assumed that Bea was trying to distract her, but there was something troubling about the way the older woman sat stiffly on the edge of her seat.

"Is something wrong?" she asked.

Bea delicately cleared her throat. "You know how much I admired your dad."

"Of course." She reached out to grasp Bea's hand. "And he felt the same about you. As far as he was concerned, you were a part of our family."

"Nothing made me happier. Truly." A wistful expression settled on her round face. "I understood that no one could ever replace your mother, and I would never have tried. But I hoped both of you knew that I would be there whenever you needed me."

Jesse squeezed Bea's fingers. She wasn't sure what she would have done without Bea's steady presence in her life. Obviously she couldn't replace Jesse's mother, but she'd been like a favorite aunt.

"Why do I sense there's a 'but' coming?" she demanded.

"But Mac was . . ." There was an awkward pause, as if Bea was struggling to come up with the right word. "Restless after your mother passed."

"What does 'restless' mean?"

"He missed having a woman in his life, but I think he worried about dating."

Jesse was caught off guard. It was true that her father rarely went out, but she'd assumed it was because he was so busy with the bar, not to mention raising a daughter on his own.

"Why would he be worried?"

"Because he didn't want you to think that he was going to replace you in his heart with another woman. You'd already lost your mother. He didn't want you to fear you were losing your dad as well."

Jesse's heart twisted with regret. He'd been right to worry. She'd felt vulnerable growing up without her mother, and acutely aware that he was all the family she had in the world. That made her depend on him more than was healthy. And even though she'd been sixteen when he'd married Victoria, she'd resented having to share him with someone else.

"He sacrificed everything for me," she muttered.

"Yes, well . . ." Bea took a drink of tea, glancing away as if embarrassed. "A man in his prime has needs, and since Mac wasn't interested in traditional dating, he sought out relationships that were temporary."

It didn't take a genius to guess what the older woman was implying. "You mean one-night stands?"

"Sometimes."

The air was slowly squeezed from Jesse's lungs. "And affairs with married women?"

"Yes."

"Women in town?" Bea nodded, keeping her gaze averted. Jesse swallowed the sudden lump in her throat. "A lot of them?"

"More than a few."

"And people knew about this?"

"It wasn't much of a secret. Especially after he was caught by Virgil Tillman in bed with his wife."

Jesse didn't recognize the name. "Who?"

"Adam's dad."

"Oh my God." The truth stabbed into her heart like a dagger. Adam hadn't been making wild accusations. He had intimate knowledge of her dad's indiscretions. "What happened?"

"They divorced when Adam was around seven or eight years old and Virgil moved away. I think he got married again and has a new family."

"That's why Adam hates my dad," she breathed.

"He's certainly held a grudge over the years."

Jesse swore in frustration. It was petty, but she'd wanted to believe that Adam had tried to frame her father because he was guilty. Instead he was just a petulant victim. And worse, she couldn't deny a disappointment in her father. Not that he'd sought out someone to ease his loneliness. He wasn't a monk. But that he'd been willing to betray his morals.

He'd destroyed families. The thought made her sick to her stomach. "I had no idea."

Bea at last met Jesse's disappointed gaze. "We all loved you, Jesse. Everyone in town. We'd do anything to protect you."

Jesse abruptly rose to her feet. She didn't doubt her friends had truly intended to protect her, but right now she felt like a blind fool. How often had people whispered behind her back? Or laughed when she naïvely claimed her dad was happy with just the two of them.

Was anything from her past what it seemed? Her dad. Victoria...

Had everything been a lie?

Ignoring Bea's worried frown, Jesse hurried out of the kitchen and returned to the Tap Room. Parker hadn't been wrong to bitch about her procrastination. She'd been deliberately dragging her feet. Partially to give herself time to discover the truth about Victoria's mysterious past. And partially to reconcile herself to the knowledge that her father was never coming home.

But she couldn't dawdle in Canton forever. She needed to take care of the tasks that she'd been putting off. That didn't mean she couldn't continue with her investigation. Or have the repairs she wanted done on the bar before she put it up for sale. But she needed to feel as if she was moving forward, not forever stuck in the past.

Returning to her dad's room, Jesse grabbed the garbage bag and started stuffing it with the clothes that she intended to take to the charity shop. First, she dumped in the shoes and coats before grabbing the stack of jeans, doing her best not to think about the last time her dad had been in this room getting dressed for the day.

She was moving forward, right?

It was only when a small metal object slid out of the jeans and onto the floor with a loud ping that she realized she should have checked the pockets. With a frown, Jesse finished pushing the clothes into the bag and then leaned down to pick up the object.

A key.

But to what?

It was too small for any of the doors. It was more like something for a drawer. Or a small safe.

Curious, Jesse moved around the bedroom, searching for the matching keyhole. When she came up empty, she circled through the rest of the apartment, eventually expanding her search through the rest of the building. She even went down to the cellar to see if there was another safe she'd somehow overlooked.

At last forced to admit there was nothing in the building that the key could unlock, Jesse told herself to forget about it. If the key was important, her dad would have put it in the safe, right? Then again, he might have had it in his pocket and forgotten about it.

Jesse muttered an expletive. The key was going to gnaw at her until she figured out where it went. The last thing she needed was another mystery.

Refusing to consider whether she was using this as yet another excuse to avoid dealing with the task she'd set for herself, Jesse grabbed her purse and power walked her way to WALKER & WALKER and pushed open the door.

She blinked as she stepped into the lobby, briefly blinded. It was a shock to go from the searing sunlight to the dark shadows. A second later, her eyes adjusted enough for her to see that the reception desk was empty. Sam was nowhere to be seen and the blinds had been lowered over the large front windows. Which explained the gloom.

Jesse hovered next to the door, belatedly realizing it must be close to lunchtime. Was the office closed?

It was the creak of a chair followed by the soft tread of footsteps that warned Jesse that she wasn't alone in the office. Instinctively, she prepared to flee as a tall form appeared in the connecting doorway. Right now she didn't trust anyone or anything. If anything felt weird, she was going to run first and ask questions later.

Thankfully, she could easily make out the older man's handsome features and tailored suit despite the shadows. He halted as he caught sight of her, deliberately glancing at the expensive watch strapped around his wrist.

"Hello, Jesse," he murmured. "Do we have an appointment?"

"No." Jesse cleared a lump from her throat. During her impetuous dash to the office, she hadn't considered the fact that she was intruding into Eric's busy schedule, not to mention interrupting his lunch. "I'm sorry I keep bothering you, but I have a quick question."

"Okay." It was obvious he was struggling to remain polite. Understandable. His lunch was no doubt getting cold.

Jesse held up her hand. "I found this key in my dad's stuff, but I have no idea what it unlocks."

"Can I see?"

"Of course." Jesse forced herself to move forward. Her feet felt heavy, and she stopped well out of arm's reach. As if her subconscious was warning her to be careful. "I thought it might be for a safe-deposit box?"

Eric flipped on the overhead light and leaned forward to study the key. "Your father didn't have a safe-deposit box. At least as far as I know."

"It doesn't fit anything in the bar."

Eric wrinkled his brow, as if he was considering the various possibilities. "It must go to his storage unit," he at last said.

"My dad had a storage unit?"

"He still does." Eric stared at her in confusion. "You should have seen the monthly bill on the statement I emailed to you. It's listed in the itemized section."

Jesse knew about the statement. It came the tenth of every month, without fail. And she had a vague idea that it listed the lawyer's retainer fee, plus the expenses from her father's estate. Taxes, insurance . . . the sort of stuff that bored her silly. It was all automatically deducted from her dad's savings account.

"Sorry, I barely glance at it," she admitted.

"Seriously?" Eric clicked his tongue in disappointment. "There's important information in the statement."

"I know. I told myself that I needed to pay more attention, but it was easier to ignore it. A part of me just didn't want to take responsibility for the Tap Room. Once I did, it would mean my dad was really gone and never coming back. Stupid, but that's the truth."

Eric's expression softened, and a stab of guilt pierced Jesse's heart.

She was using that excuse with depressing regularity. Did she truly believe she should have a free pass for every poor decision she'd made over the past decade?

"I forget how difficult this must be for you," Eric said in apologetic tones.

Jesse shook her head. "No. I've let things slide for too long. It's time to step up and be an adult. Do you know where the storage unit is?"

"Crawdaddy's Storage. It's in the lot behind the lumberyard."

Jesse nodded. She remembered when they started construction. It was a huge disappointment to discover they weren't building a new restaurant or a tanning salon.

"Thanks. I'll try not to bother you again."

"No bother." Eric smiled, but once again it failed to reach his eyes.

Making a mental note to avoid rushing to the lawyer without making an appointment that could be properly billed, Jesse left the office and crossed the street, keeping her pace steady as she headed to the lumberyard. She'd attracted enough attention racing around like a madwoman since her return to Canton.

Whatever was in the unit had been there for years. It would be there ten minutes from now.

Futilely trying to imagine what her father considered so important he was willing to pay for it to be held in storage, Jesse rounded the corner and crossed directly through the back of the lumberyard, weaving her way through the bricks and paving stones that were neatly stacked to create a barrier between the adjoining lot. Once through the building supplies, Jesse was able to study the rectangular cement structure painted a bright blue with metal roll-up doors. A wooden sign strapped to a tall pole assured her this was indeed Crawdaddy's Storage. Unfortunately, there was no one around to tell her which unit belonged to her father.

She stopped, glancing around in the vain hope someone might appear. When she accepted she was on her own she strolled past the doors, relieved to discover that most of them had combination locks or heavy-duty padlocks that were too large for her key. Rounding the end of the building, she started down the other side, stopping when she reached the second unit. It was the only one so far that had a small padlock and a thick layer of dust on the door that indicated it hadn't been opened in a long time.

This had to be it.

Inserting the key, Jess smiled when there was a soft click and the padlock easily fell open. She twisted it off and shoved it into her pocket before bending down to grab the handle at the bottom of the door. With a grunt, she lifted the heavy steel that hadn't been opened in years. It was a struggle, but with grim determination, she at last had it fully open to allow the searing sunlight to banish the darkness.

She stood in front of the unit for a minute, taking a visual inventory of the items piled inside. The majority of the space was consumed by a large object covered by a heavy tarp. Along the back wall were stacks of plastic tubs with garment bags thrown on top.

Once she was convinced that nothing was going to jump out or fall on her head, Jesse cautiously entered the unit. She squeezed past the covered object to unzip one of the garment bags, revealing a beaded cocktail dress and matching shawl. She easily recognized it. It had belonged to Victoria. The older woman had been forced to abandon a ton of stuff when she packed her bags and left. Sports cars weren't famous for large trunks. She'd left behind more belongings than she'd been able to take. Now Jesse knew what'd happened to them.

A quick peek into the plastic tubs revealed more of Victoria's things, along with a few that belonged to Tegan.

At last, she slowly turned to face the large object in the center of the unit, her heart sinking as she realized what it had to be.

Reaching out, she grabbed the tarp and slowly began to pull it to the side, coughing as a cloud of dust swirled through the air, aiming directly for her face. She turned her head to the side as she continued to yank off the heavy canvas, her attention suddenly captured by something on the ground next to her feet. Continuing to pull the tarp, she bent down to grab what turned out to be a business card.

Allen Lumberyard
Lumber and Hardware Supplies
Noah Allen

Jesse frowned. Noah's business card? What was it doing in her dad's storage unit? She turned it over, noticing the dirt that had been ground into the heavy paper. The card had been there a while, but how long?

With a shake of her head, she shoved the card into her back pocket along with the lock. It was a worry for later. Now she turned back to the car, wincing at the sight of the smashed front.

She hadn't seen the vehicle since Victoria drove away from the Tap Room. After her wreck the sheriff had it towed to an impoundment lot, presumably to be searched for clues. Jesse hadn't even known that her father had gotten it back.

Yet another thing he'd kept hidden from her, she acknowledged with a pang of bitterness.

With an impatient hiss, Jesse squashed the surge of self-pity. Her dad no doubt had his reasons. Maybe to protect her. Or just because he needed to lock away his painful memories. God knew she'd made more than a few sketchy decisions she wouldn't want to explain to anyone.

It was all a part of being human.

Squaring her shoulders, she moved toward the side of the car, grabbing the handle to pull the passenger door. She was a little surprised when it opened easily. She'd expected it to be locked.

Lowering herself onto the soft leather seat, Jesse glanced around. The air inside was musty, but a lingering scent of perfume made Jesse shudder. She remembered that cloying scent. With an effort, she forced herself to remain in the car. She didn't know what she was searching for; the sheriff had stated during the preliminary hearings that nothing had been found in the car. No bags or personal items; but then again, he'd never suspected there was foul play. Unlike Adam Tillman, the older man was convinced that Victoria had taken her daughter and disappeared.

There was a chance he hadn't done a thorough investigation.

Gathering her courage, Jesse opened the glove compartment and shuffled through the junk crammed inside. There was nothing but the usual insurance cards and car manual that no one ever looked at, along with a pair of sunglasses and extra napkins. She bent down, feeling under the seats, before lifting the floor mats. Nothing. The same when she pulled down the sunshades and felt inside the cupholders. On the point of conceding defeat, Jesse impulsively shoved her hand between the seat and the center console. Anything she'd ever lost in a car had ended up in that awkward space. Keys, her phone, lip balm . . .

Her breath caught as the tips of her fingers brushed against something. A piece of paper? She struggled to twist her hand to get a grip on the damned thing.

At last she managed to slip the paper between her first and middle fingers, squeezing tight as she wiggled her hand out. Jesse sucked in a sharp breath as she realized she hadn't dug out a piece of paper. It was a photograph.

Climbing out of the car, Jesse moved toward the door, tilting the photo until it was bathed in sunlight. It was slightly faded and bent in a couple of places, but the image of two young girls standing in front of the St. Louis Arch was unmistakable.

A flare of excitement raced through Jesse. She didn't know if the snapshot was deliberately hidden or if it had fallen accidentally between the seats, but she was certain that one of the girls was Tegan. She was only five or six in the picture, but she hadn't changed much by the time she moved to Canton. And it was obvious she was in St. Louis. Even better, she was wearing a short plaid skirt and a dark blue sweater with a badge sewn on the upper right chest.

It looked like a private school uniform.

Pulling out her phone, Jesse tapped on the magnifying app and hovered it above the photograph. It took a second to focus before she could make out the stitching on the badge.

"'Saint Mary's Elementary School,'" she read out loud. Her mouth went dry as she silently repeated the name. "Saint Mary's Elementary School."

It was a clue. A genuine clue to Tegan's past. And, hopefully, Victoria.

Barely daring to hope for more, Jesse slowly turned the picture over, her breath catching as she studied the faded ink strokes on the back. Was it a name? She studied the scribbles, at last using her phone to magnify the marks.

It wasn't a name, she accepted with a pang of disappointment, but it looked like initials.

K-LA? Yes, that was it. K-LA.

"Jesse?"

The sound of her name had her twisting around with a shrill squeak to discover Noah standing a few feet away. Instinctively, she shoved the picture in her back pocket, a tingle of alarm inching down her spine.

Noah wasn't blocking her exit, but that didn't keep her heart from slamming against her ribs. He appeared disturbingly large as she tilted back her head to meet his brooding gaze.

"Noah. I didn't hear you coming."

He shoved his hands into the pockets of his work khakis. "I'm sorry. I didn't mean to startle you."

"Not your fault." She managed a weak smile. "I'm a little on edge."

His gaze lifted over her shoulder, as if searching the unit for something. *Maybe the business card he'd left behind*, a voice whispered in the back of her mind.

"I don't blame you." He returned his attention to her. "Your homecoming hasn't been the best. Are you okay?"

She cleared the lump from her throat, squashing her bout of nerves. She wasn't going to leap to conclusions because she found a business card.

"Actually, I'm confused," she confessed. "I had no idea that my dad rented this storage unit. I don't even know how long he had it."

"He rented it a few weeks after Victoria and Tegan disappeared."

"Really?" Jesse arched her brow. "Dad never said a word about it to me."

"Mac said that he wanted someplace to store Victoria's belongings so they weren't a constant reminder that she was missing." His jaw tightened. "And I think that Adam made it clear that Victoria's car was still evidence, even if the sheriff had released it from the impound. That was back when Adam was trying his best to find a reason to arrest your dad. Mac felt like he had to store it somewhere."

Jesse turned so she was standing next to Noah, easily imagining her dad's emotions as he hauled the shattered remnants of his marriage to this block of cement. He would have been heartbroken, and scared, and maybe even furious. The fact that he hadn't been able to share his feelings with her was a wound that would never heal.

She cleared a sudden lump from her throat. "How did you know about this place?" she asked.

Noah nodded toward the less than impressive sign. "My cousin was the one to build it; unfortunately, back in those days, he liked to drink. I was covering for him when your dad called to rent one of the units. I showed up to give him a key, and since he had a lot of stuff to unload, I gave him a hand."

Ah. That explained the business card, she silently acknowledged, feeling a pang of guilt. Poor Noah had done nothing more sinister than assist her dad when he needed someone.

"Is there anyone in this town you don't give a helping hand?"

Noah jerked, as if he was insulted by her teasing. "Just being a good neighbor."

She studied his grim profile, worried that he thought she was mocking his kind heart.

"I'm sorry. That came out wrong." She reached to touch his arm. "Over the years I've been bouncing from place to place. I forgot what it means to be part of a small town," she admitted. "You're a good guy, Noah Allen."

Her words did nothing to ease his tension. In fact, his lips twisted into a bitter smile.

"A good guy? Great. You wanna rub some salt into the wound?"

Jesse shook her head. It didn't take a genius to guess that Noah's ex-wife was responsible for that raw nerve. No doubt she told Noah that he was boring and predictable and every other insult, to gaslight him into thinking it was his fault she'd cheated. It was a tactic used by many abusers. Kelly could run off with the man she wanted and, at the same time, paint herself the victim.

A win-win for her, while leaving behind a husband who was still nursing the injuries she'd inflicted.

"Not this time." She squeezed his arm. "Bad boys are highly overrated."

He slowly shook his head. Not in rejection, but in a visible effort to dismiss his dark memories. Then he deliberately glanced around the storage lot baking in the sun, as if emphasizing that they were all alone.

"Speaking of bad boys," he murmured. "Where's yours?"

Jesse stiffened. "He left town last night."

"Any certain reason?"

Jesse silently cataloged the endless list of reasons. The sight of Noah standing so close to her when he'd first arrived in town. The fact that she was taking too long to put the bar on the market. Her refusal to return to Chicago. And her lack of enthusiasm for the nightclub he wanted to buy and restore with her inheritance.

She at last offered the reason that had given her a glimpse into Parker's personality. A glimpse that had made her question their future together.

"He wasn't happy I left him last night to make sure Bea was comfortably settled at the hospital."

Noah's expression darkened, but he didn't share his opinion of her choice in men. Instead, he concentrated on Bea's unfortunate incident.

"I heard that she'd been hit over the head. How is she?"

"I brought her home this morning. She claims she's fine, but the doctor ordered her to rest for a few days, which means shutting down the diner. She's not happy."

"I bet not. I swear, that woman is as tough as an old boot."

"True."

"The rumors said she was hit by someone who was sneaking into the Tap Room."

Jesse ground her teeth. Of course the gossips were out in full force. The attack on Bea would be the prime topic of conversation. That didn't make it any easier to realize they were no doubt blaming her for the older woman's injuries.

"I found her lying near the back door. We're not sure exactly what happened, but I suspect that she startled a trespasser who attacked her so they could get away."

Noah gazed down at her, but she didn't see the censure she'd expected. Instead he looked worried.

"Jesse, it's not safe for you to stay at the bar. I don't know what's going on, but whoever is sneaking around the Tap Room is obviously growing desperate. Next time they might not be satisfied with locking you in the cellar or knocking an old woman over the head."

Jesse wrapped her arms around her waist. A part of her knew he was right. If this was a movie, she would be yelling at the stupid woman who stubbornly remained alone in the creepy haunted building where strange things kept happening. Another part of her found it impossible to think of the Tap Room as anything but home. A place where she would always be safe.

She heaved a resigned sigh. "I have too much to do to leave now."

Noah paused, as if considering how to knock some sense into her. Literally, if not figuratively.

"Look, I'm going to come by tomorrow and get started on the repairs," he said at last. "Things are going to be a mess for a while. Why don't you stay at my house until I'm done?"

Caught off guard by the offer, Jesse stumbled back a step before she could halt the impulsive retreat.

"I . . . don't . . ."

"No strings attached," he interrupted her stammering, holding up his hand and wiggling his little finger. "Pinkie promise."

Embarrassed at having overreacted once again, Jesse forced a smile. "Well, if it's a pinkie promise."

"At least think about it," he urged.

"I will."

With brisk movements, Jesse turned to enter the unit. She didn't want to be rude, but she finally had a clue and she didn't want to waste any more time. Closing the car door, she didn't bother with the tarp. She was going to have to empty the unit at some point. Yet another task to put on her list.

Heading out of the unit, she pulled the lock out of her pocket, not surprised when Noah reached up to pull down the rolling door so she could snap the padlock into place. He might hate being called a nice guy, but that was who he was.

Of course, being nice didn't mean he couldn't have a dark side.

With a shiver, Jesse straightened and took a step away. She hated the feeling she couldn't trust anyone, not even a great guy like Noah Allen. But what choice did she have?

Better safe than dead.

"I'll see you later, Noah."

"Be careful, Jesse," he urged. "Whoever is messing with you is obviously unhinged. I don't want you to be hurt."

"I don't want me to be hurt, either. I'll be careful."

With a wave of her hand, Jesse turned and headed away from the storage facility, refusing to glance over her shoulder to see if Noah was watching her. She would drive herself nuts trying to decide who could or couldn't be trusted. The best way to protect herself was to discover who was creeping around the Tap Room and why.

Chapter 16

It was only a few blocks back to the bar, but Jesse was coated in a fine layer of sweat by the time she was pushing open the front door and entering the welcome shadows. Her job as a bartender had made her a creature of the night, like a vampire. She wasn't used to being out in the afternoon heat.

Heading up the stairs, Jesse hopped in the shower, washing off the sweat and grime from the storage unit before she dressed in fresh shorts and a T-shirt. Then, entering the kitchen, she made herself a sandwich and a bowl of fruit before taking a seat at the table.

She opened her laptop, but she didn't immediately start her search. Her stomach was rumbling, reminding her that she hadn't bothered with breakfast. She needed to be better about eating regular meals or she was going to make herself sick. Besides, she wanted to properly study the picture she'd discovered in Victoria's car before she did anything else.

Smoothing out the photograph, which hadn't been improved after being stuffed into her pocket, Jesse nibbled at her sandwich. The image wasn't perfect. The background was blurry and it was too far away to make out the exact expressions on the girls' faces. But she was able to determine they were standing in front of the silver Gateway, and they had their arms entwined, as if they were clinging to each other. They even had their heads leaning together in a gesture of intimate friendship.

Jesse finished her lunch, dredging up her memories of Tegan. She didn't have that many. They were too far apart in age to attend the same school, and Jesse had made it clear she didn't want Tegan bothering her when they were in the apartment.

Not that the younger girl ever made an effort, Jesse recalled, refusing to take all the blame. Tegan was as cold and standoffish as her mother, preferring to stay in her room or spend time with her friend, Samantha Yost. She hadn't been physically affectionate with anyone, not even her mother.

It was like she'd built a wall around herself, keeping everyone at a distance.

Did it have something to do with the reason they'd come to Canton?

Only one way to find out.

Shoving aside her empty plate, Jesse wiped her hands on a napkin before pulling the laptop in front of her. Then, sending up a silent prayer to whatever deity might be listening, she typed in the name *Saint Mary Elementary School* in St. Louis, Missouri.

A few links popped up, and Jesse clicked on the top one. The header of the front page was a picture of the solid brick school, surrounded by manicured grounds and a group of girls in uniforms. Jesse zoomed in, her heart thundering. They were wearing the same uniform as the one that Tegan and the mystery girl was wearing in the picture. She zoomed in closer, filling the screen with the image of the badge sewn onto their sweaters.

Yep. That was the same.

She'd found the school where Tegan was . . . what? Sixteen or seventeen years ago? It was exciting, but she wasn't sure how to translate this knowledge into an actual lead.

She glanced toward the picture, suddenly remembering the scribbled initials on the back.

It was worth a try.

She typed in K-LA, followed by the name of the school and the physical address of the campus. Nothing.

K-LA. Could it be a place? A favorite song?

No. Wait. A nickname.

Once again, Jess typed in the name of the school and the physical address of the campus, along with the name *Kayla*.

This time a dozen links popped up, and Jesse scrolled down, searching for one that might be helpful. At last, she clicked on a link to a newsletter from the school to alumni and donors. At the end of the document was a congratulations to Kayla Lasky for her recent marriage to a Kenneth Murphy II. They'd included a picture of a smiling dark-haired woman and a large man who had to be twenty years her senior.

Jesse enlarged the picture. It was impossible to know for sure if it was the girl in the photo, but she looked the right age. It was worth a try.

Clicking out of the newsletter, Jesse typed in Kayla Lansky Murphy, her heart jumping when she was taken to a website for a business in Lake Saint Louis.

THE REVOLVING CLOSET
Curated fashion rentals. High-end designer pieces professionally chosen for the most fastidious shoppers.
Owner Kayla Murphy
Call for an appointment

Anticipation sizzled through her despite the fact that she didn't know if Kayla Murphy was connected to her stepsister or, even if she was, that she remembered anything about Tegan. It felt like forward progress. And right now, she was ready to grasp any straw.

Jesse grabbed her phone to pull up the address of The Revolving Closet before shutting the laptop and jumping to her feet. She didn't consider calling to make sure that Kayla was at the shop, or if she was willing to talk to her. The drive to Lake Saint Louis was only a couple of hours, and she didn't want to waste a second. Not if this woman had information that could help her discover the truth about Tegan and her treacherous mother.

Besides, she could use some time and distance away from Canton, she acknowledged as she headed out of the bar. Maybe the space would allow her to clear her mind and put things into perspective. Right now, she couldn't distinguish between what was real or what was a figment of her imagination.

If nothing else, perhaps she could escape the sense of impending doom.

It was nearing three o'clock when Jesse pulled into the parking lot next to the elegant row of brick buildings. There were a dozen shops and restaurants perched along the wide sidewalk with large front windows and striped awnings that catered to the locals, who lived in clusters around the nearby lake.

Parking her old truck near the far side of the lot, Jesse strolled past the hipster barbershop, a tea emporium, and a bistro before she stopped in front of a glass door with the name painted in gold.

The Revolving Closet
by appointment only

With a shrug, Jesse shoved open the door and entered the boutique. Not that it looked like a boutique. Or any other clothing shop she'd ever been in. Honestly, she felt as if she was in a fancy bedroom, with several large armoires arranged strategically next to the powder-blue walls. There were floor-to-ceiling mirrors placed in between them, and overhead, a chandelier glittered with a silver light, reflecting off the polished marble floor.

An older woman appeared from a hidden doorway, her dark hair smoothed into a tight knot and the sharp angles of her face settling into an expression of aversion as she took in Jesse's casual shorts and the tattoos that covered her bare arms.

"Can I help you?" Her tone suggested that the only assistance she wanted to offer was herding Jesse out of the elegant shop and back into the gutter she'd crawled out of.

A smile curled Jesse's lips. She'd spent a lot of years dealing with snotty bitches who thought they were better than her.

"I need to speak with Ms. Murphy."

"Do you have an appointment?"

"No."

"Then I'm afraid you've had a wasted journey. Next time call the number listed on our website and speak with Ms. Murphy before coming. She doesn't take walk-in clients."

"Is she here?"

"She is, but as I said, you have to have an appointment."

"I don't want an appointment."

The woman stepped forward. She was closer to fifty than forty, but she carried herself with the confidence of a pampered woman who knew she looked fantastic in her black sheath dress and designer heels.

"This isn't a clothing store. Ms. Murphy is a fashion consultant, not a saleslady."

"Then it's a good thing I'm not here for clothes."

"Then what do you want?"

"It's personal."

"Then I suggest you contact Ms. Murphy at home. The boutique closes at five."

Jesse shrugged. "This can't wait."

The woman clicked her tongue. "It will have to wait. She has a client in ten minutes."

"Okay." Jesse folded her arms over her chest. "The quicker I talk to her, the quicker I can leave."

"I've told you—"

"I'm not leaving until I've spoken to her. So unless you intend to physically drag me out of here kicking and screaming, I suggest you go get her."

Jesse jutted her chin to a stubborn angle. It wasn't exactly a threat, but it was a warning she wasn't afraid to make a scene.

The woman's lips pinched, something that might be frustration flashing through her dark eyes. She wasn't used to anyone calling her bluff.

"Fine. I'll see if she can be disturbed. Your name?"

"Jesse Hudson. Tell her that I have something she'll be interested to see. A blast from her past."

With a sniff, the woman turned to disappear through a hidden panel in the wall. Jesse heaved a sigh. Maybe she should have handled that better. It was quite possible the condescending witch was right now urging her employer to call the cops. But Jesse's bullshit tolerance was at an all-time low and she wasn't in the mood to play nice.

Thankfully, there was no sound of approaching sirens, and within five minutes, the woman was back to wave Jesse forward with a sour expression.

"You can go in."

Jesse didn't bother to gloat as she passed the woman and stepped into a private office. She was here to get information, not bicker with the employees. No matter how condescending they might be.

She managed a quick glance around the narrow space, which was decorated in the same powder blue and silver as the main boutique, before the woman seated at the rolltop desk rose to her feet. Like her employee, she was wearing a simple sheath dress and high heels, although her curves added an extra layer of sensuality, and she was at least twenty-five years younger.

"Jesse?" She smiled, a pair of dimples appearing next to her full lips.

Jesse's defensive antagonism abruptly shattered. There was no patronizing stiffness about this woman. Her round face and dark eyes held curiosity, but she didn't act like Jesse was something that needed to be scraped off her Jimmy Choos.

"Sorry about showing up without an appointment."

Kayla waved aside the apology. "Carol said that you have something of interest for me?"

"Yes." Reaching into her purse, Jesse pulled out the picture and handed it to her. "This is how I managed to track you down."

Kayla tilted the picture to catch the light from the chandelier, which was a smaller version of the one in the main room.

"Oh my God. You weren't lying. This really is a blast from the past."

Relief raced through Jesse, making her knees oddly weak. This was her. The girl from the photo. She'd found her.

It felt like a miracle.

Jesse cleared her throat, struggling to keep her tone casual. She didn't want to frighten the woman.

"Do you recognize the girl standing next to you?"

"Of course." Kayla glanced up, as if surprised by the question. "It's Sierra Lowe. I even remember this day." She waved the picture. "It was our first week at Saint Mary's, and neither of us had attended one of the fancy preschools that the other girls went to, so we didn't know anyone. We were only five, but our classmates quickly let us know we were going to be the designated outcasts. We clung together out of desperation."

Sierra Lowe. Jesse tucked away the name, even as satisfaction surged through her. She was inching closer to the truth. She felt it in her very soul.

"Did the two of you become friends?" she asked.

"Best friends." Kayla smoothed a finger over the picture, as if savoring her childhood memories. "We did everything together. We sat next to each other during lunch and played together at recess. She even spent the night a few times. Until . . . you know . . ."

Her words trailed away, and Jesse frowned. "Until what?"

"The accident."

Jesse licked her dry lips, taking a moment to organize her thoughts. She'd rushed to question this woman with no firm plan of action. Now she had to scramble for a reasonable excuse to be prying into Sierra's past.

"Sierra was a part of our family, but we lost track of her when she moved to St. Louis." She nodded toward the picture in Kayla's hand. "I came here to see if I could discover what happened."

"I'm not sure I can add anything that wasn't in the papers."

There was something in the younger woman's tone that warned that she was reluctant to discuss the mysterious accident.

"I wouldn't ask, but my grandmother's growing older and she's determined to write down the family history. It would mean a lot to her to hear the story from someone who knew Sierra."

Kayla slowly nodded. "I suppose that's understandable. My grandma is in her reminiscing stage too. Last week she insisted we all come over and help her sort through her boxes of pictures to put them in her scrapbook. It took us hours."

Jesse ignored the tiny pang of envy. Most people had no idea what it was like to be alone in the world. Not just independent, or estranged from their family. But really and truly alone.

She managed to keep her encouraging smile intact. "Anything you can remember about the accident would be awesome."

"Okay." Tapping the picture against her chin, Kayla leaned against the edge of the desk. "Well, it was our second year at Saint Mary's. I remember we'd just come back from our winter break, and when I arrived at school I was taken into an office. At first I was afraid I'd done something wrong. I wasn't as sneaky as Sierra, and more than once we'd pulled a prank and I was the one who ended up in trouble." She hesitated, the smile fading from her lips. "It wasn't until a nun came in to tell me that Sierra, along with her mother and stepfather, had died in a house fire the night before that I knew she was dead. I remember crying. And then my mother came to pick me up."

Jesse coughed to cover her gasp of surprise. The girl in the picture was killed in a house fire? Then it couldn't be Tegan. Not unless she'd come back from the dead.

So why had the picture been hidden in Victoria's car, next to where Tegan would have been sitting? And why did she look like Tegan?

No, wait. It was too much of a coincidence.

That had to be Tegan. And there had to be some explanation for how she'd escaped, along with Victoria.

"Did you know Sierra's parents?" she pressed.

"I met her mother when she came to school events, but she didn't really mingle with the students," Kayla said. "Or even with the other mothers, or the staff. And I never went to her house."

"Any certain reason?"

"Sierra's stepfather, Liam Tanner."

"What about him?"

Kayla looked confused. "You don't know his reputation?"

"I'm afraid I've never heard the name."

"He was pretty notorious in St. Louis."

Jesse narrowed her eyes. "Notorious? I'm assuming you don't mean famous. Like a singer or an actor?"

Kayla shook her head. "It's terrible to speak ill of the dead, but it was common knowledge around here that his dozen or so car dealerships were used to transport drugs and launder money." She waved a hand toward the window that offered a view of the nearby town. "He had a huge mansion on the lake with a couple of pools and a tennis court, but none of the mothers would let their kids go near the place."

"He was a criminal?" It was a question, but Jesse already knew the answer.

If Victoria really was married to Liam Tanner, then he was just another villain in her collection. She'd started with a petty drug dealer, then moved up to a midlevel slumlord, before landing a mansion-owning drug trafficker. How she ended up with Mac Hudson remained a mystery. But everything else fit a pattern.

"I don't think he was ever arrested," Kayla conceded. "He had the sort of money and connections to avoid that. But several of his employees ended up in jail later."

Jesse didn't have much experience with traffickers, but her job had taken her to some shady bars where the drug trade was openly discussed.

"Is it possible the house fire wasn't an accident?" she asked, not sure why it would matter.

"It was never proven, but everyone suspected it was arson," Kayla confirmed Jesse's suspicion.

"The cartel?"

"Actually, I heard rumors that the cops suspected Liam started the fire himself."

"A murder-suicide?"

"More of a pretend murder-suicide."

"I don't understand." Jesse felt as if her entire body was vibrating with anticipation. She was getting closer. "Was there a question about who died in the fire?"

"No, not that. Liam's body was found near the door, like he was trying to get out of the house."

"And? That seems like a reasonable reaction to a fire."

"Yeah, but the bodies of Sierra and her mother were never found. Which meant they had to be in the basement when the house exploded."

"Wait." Grim satisfaction blasted through her. There it was. No bodies. She hadn't been crazy to cling to her belief that it was Tegan in the picture. She didn't know how Victoria had pulled it off, but there was no doubt she'd escaped and taken her daughter with her. "There was a fire *and* an explosion?"

Kayla shuddered. "Once the flames reached the gas lines...boom. It was a mess. They finally came in with a bulldozer and demolished the entire estate. I think it belongs to some developer now, who built a new golf course there."

"So the theory was that Liam set the fire and somehow got stuck in the house?"

"Most people assumed that he killed his wife and stepdaughter and hid them in the basement while he poured gasoline around the house and set it on fire." She shrugged. "No one knows exactly what happened after that, but he was overcome with the smoke and heat before he could get out."

Or he was knocked unconscious and placed there while the true arsonist managed to slip away, Jesse silently acknowledged. But surely the cops would have considered that theory because there were no bodies found?

"Why did the police suspect Liam Tanner killed his wife and stepdaughter?"

"He'd taken out million-dollar life insurance policies on both of them just weeks before the fire," Kayla said. "Plus, there was money missing from his auto business. Like he was planning to leave town once he got the insurance."

"Interesting," Jesse murmured.

It wouldn't have been hard for Victoria to have taken out the life insurance policies to frame her dead husband. And even if she couldn't get the money from the policies, she would have the embezzled cash to fund her disappearing act.

"It was a huge story around here for years," Kayla murmured, glancing at the picture. "I just missed my friend."

There was no mistaking the sincerity in her voice, and Jesse was once again struck by the notion that the two girls were genuine friends. How odd.

Before she could respond, the snotty Carol stepped into the office. "Ms. Burlington is here."

It sounded like a royal announcement, and Kayla shrugged. "I'm sorry, but I can't keep my client waiting."

"No worries." Jesse reached out and gently pulled the picture from the younger woman's tight grasp. "Thank you so much for answering my questions."

"I hoped I helped."

"More than you can imagine."

Jesse crossed the parking lot and climbed into her truck, her thoughts churning. Kayla had given her more information than she expected. Not only had she confirmed the fact that Victoria was lying about her name, about her dearly departed husband who she'd claimed was a surgeon along with being Tegan's father, but she'd given Jesse even more reason to believe the woman was out there somewhere, conning yet another man. Perhaps even plotting his murder.

The question now was what she did with the information. She had zero hope that Sheriff Adam Tillman would search for the missing woman. Even if he was willing to believe that Victoria was still alive, he had the investigative skills of a turnip. And she didn't have the money to hire a private investigator. At least not one that might have the skills needed to track down and expose Victoria.

So what did she do next?

Switching on the engine, Jesse slowly drove across the parking lot. She'd accomplished what she came to do, but she was oddly reluctant to make the journey back to Canton as she watched the traffic rush past with no interest in who she was or where she was headed.

There was an unexpected freedom in being just another anonymous motorist cruising through the city. No one was staring, no one was waving or trying to attract her attention. And she felt no fear that she was being watched by her unknown stalker.

Giving into a sudden impulse, Jesse pulled into the traffic, heading toward St. Louis instead of home. Why not spend a few hours enjoying some mindless activity, surrounded by complete strangers?

Dark had fallen by the time she left the large mall where she'd wandered in and out of stores before eating questionable sushi and enjoying the crush of shoppers who whizzed past her without a second glance. Once in her truck, she headed north, the radio blasting to keep her from thinking about the empty building that was waiting for her.

It was only for a few more days. And then...

She didn't know. And that was the honest truth.

She could return to Chicago to buy a nightclub she didn't want with a man she wasn't sure she loved. She could stay in Canton and battle the ghosts that felt dangerously real.

Or she could keep driving and see where she landed.

Like Victoria.

A shiver crawled down her spine, and Jesse instinctively glanced in the rearview mirror. As if she expected to see her stepmother appear in the back of the truck.

She wasn't there, of course, but there were headlights that were closer than they should be, considering the highway was nearly empty. With a frown, Jesse slowed her speed, waiting for the car to pass her.

It didn't. Instead, it remained stubbornly on her bumper, the headlights nearly blinding her as they reflected in the rearview mirror.

Her heart thundered in her chest. It could be nothing more than one of those annoying drivers who enjoyed tailgating. Some people got a kick out of pushing other drivers into road rage. Then again, it could be someone who was following her for a reason.

A terrible reason.

Doing her best not to panic, Jesse reached over to grab her phone from her purse. She didn't want to call 911; not when it would more than likely be Adam Tillman who showed up. But if she was being followed, she needed someone to know where she was and what was happening.

Her thumb was hovering over the emergency number when there was the sound of an engine revving and the car darted into the passing lane, the horn blaring, as if they were pissed off they had to go around her.

Jesse breathed a sigh of relief. She'd overreacted. Thank God.

Waiting for the car to race past her, Jesse tossed her phone onto the passenger seat. A second later, a scream was ripped from her throat when the vehicle swerved directly toward her. What the hell? Were they trying to run her off the road? Or were they drunk?

Reacting on instinct, Jesse pressed on the gas pedal and yanked the steering wheel to the side. Clenching her teeth, she rattled along the shoulder until she could veer off the highway onto an access road. Even then, she urged the old truck to its maximum speed, ignoring the suspension that squeaked in loud protest.

It wasn't until the car behind her sped past the exit ramp—either unable to get turned in time or tired of the game—that she slowed her speed and switched off her headlights.

She continued down the road before turning onto a dirt lane. Canton was a couple of miles north, but she zigzagged through the countryside, her fingers clutching the steering wheel in a death grip. She didn't need to see the street signs; she knew these roads like the back of her hand. She should. How many years had she spent riding her bike through the maze of fields and pastures?

Right now, her concentration was focused on making sure she'd lost whoever had run her off the road. She didn't know if it'd been an accident or on purpose, but she was going to assume they wanted to hurt her.

Or worse.

She needed to get back to the bar, where she could lock and barricade the doors. Once she was safe she could decide whether she wanted to involve the sheriff. Or maybe pack her bags and head back to Chicago. The past could stay in the past and she would move on, as Parker wanted.

Reaching the edge of Canton, Jesse crawled through the quiet streets, backtracking and circling blocks to make sure that no one had followed her. Only when she was certain she wasn't being tailed did she turn onto Main Street and park her truck in front of the Tap Room.

She grabbed her purse and darted across the sidewalk, hurriedly unlocking the front door. Once inside, she slammed it shut and rammed home the bolt. A part of her felt like a fool. She couldn't count how many times she'd had an idiot driver weave across the center line, nearly causing a wreck. Hell, there'd been a few times she'd cut off a car when she wasn't paying attention.

But tonight, she wasn't going to take any risks.

Dropping her purse on a nearby table, she grabbed one of the wooden chairs and carried it across the floor to wedge it under the knob. Even if someone did have a key, they wouldn't be able to push the door open. Then, returning to get another chair, she dragged it through the main bar and into the back foyer. She wasn't going to be like one of those idiots in the movies who hid under the bed, hoping the monster wouldn't find her. She was going to make damned sure that she took every precaution.

Wrangling the chair down the narrow hallway, Jesse had her back turned to the foyer. Which meant that she didn't notice the dark form that was hovering near the back door. Not until the sound of a footstep had her jerking around to see it lurch forward.

Her lips parted to scream, but they were smothered by a wet rag that was shoved over her face. She stumbled backward, her feet tangled in the chair. She would have fallen if it wasn't for an arm that wrapped around her waist, keeping her upright, as the rag was shoved so tight she couldn't breathe.

Oh shit.

Was she going to die?

The thought was oddly shocking. Despite being stalked, and tormented, and even locked in the cellar, deep in her heart she hadn't believed they intended to kill her. Drive her out of town? Sure. Force her to stop her investigations into the past? Absolutely.

But not this.

And she didn't know what was worse.

Dying without knowing who wanted her dead. Or without discovering what happened to her dad.

The world started to shrink, her thoughts condensing and narrowing until all she could see was a tunnel of light that slanted through the open door. Whoever was attacking her had obviously been waiting for her to return to the bar.

She tried to lift her hands to push away the smothering cloth, but they refused to obey. Instead, they hung limply as the tunnel slowly disappeared and everything went dark. A moment later, her knees buckled and she dropped to the floor with a painful thud.

She was on the edge of unconsciousness when a voice whispered in her ear.

"This is your last warning, bitch. Leave now or everything you love will be destroyed."

Chapter 17

"Jesse. Jesse!"

The sound of her name sliced through the blessed silence, forcing her back to a reality that included a sluggish brain fog and a nasty coating on her tongue. With an effort, she managed to lift her lashes, which felt as if they'd been glued together, trying to focus on the face that hovered just above her.

She'd had a few hangovers in her day, but none of them had ever been this bad. Certainly she'd never awakened with no memory of what she'd been doing or even where she was.

Taking a minute, she carefully glanced around, relieved to discover she was in the foyer of the Tap Room, and that there was a flood of sunshine pouring through the door, which was hanging at a weird angle. At least she was home. Which meant she hadn't been making a fool of herself in some strange bar.

Next, she focused on the face that was disturbingly close.

It took her a little longer to dredge through the fog to call up a name.

"Noah," she at last croaked, struggling to sit up.

"No, don't move."

She ignored his command, trying to recall why the words sounded familiar. Oh yeah. She'd said them to Bea in this precise spot just a couple of nights ago.

Jesse shook her head, as if she could shake away the fog. "Is this a nightmare?"

Noah leaned back on his knees, an unreadable emotion tightening his features. "You see me and assume you're having a nightmare? You're brutal on a man's ego, Jesse Hudson."

"No, it's just . . ." She let her words trail away, the thought lost in the mist. It didn't matter. At least not now. "What happened?" she demanded instead.

"I was going to ask you that question," Noah said. "I texted you this morning to say that I was coming over to start the repairs at eight. When you didn't get back to me I was worried, so I drove over to make sure everything was okay. I was about to knock when I saw you through the back window." He glanced over his shoulder. "I kicked in the door to get in. I'll have it replaced."

Well, at least that explained why the door was hanging at a weird angle. And why Noah was at the bar.

"What time is it?"

"Eight thirty." Noah scowled as Jesse grimly shoved herself upright. He straightened, grabbing her upper arm. "Careful. You might have a concussion."

She shook her head. It was sluggish, but it didn't hurt like it'd been smacked. "I don't think so."

His brows arched. "Now you're a doctor?"

There was another sense of déjà vu as he repeated the words she'd said to Bea, only this time the sensation was overshadowed by another memory that hovered on the edge of the fog.

"My head is fine," she muttered.

"Are you sure? It looks like you fell down the stairs."

"No, I don't think so."

"Then what happened?"

"I'm trying to remember." She scowled, annoyed as the memories began to form only to slip away. Like figments of a dream.

Noah brushed a gentle finger over her cheek. "Maybe if you start from the beginning? What happened after I saw you at the storage locker?"

Jesse took a deep breath, forcing her tense muscles to relax. It seemed an eternity since she'd been standing in front of her dad's unit with Noah next to her. But his words did jolt the memory of finding the picture of Tegan in Victoria's wrecked car, and tracking down Kayla Murphy.

"I remember going to St. Louis and—"

"St. Louis?" Noah interrupted. "Why?"

Jesse flinched at his sharp tone. He sounded almost angry. Was it because she'd gone without telling him? Or because he didn't want her to continue to dig into the past?

"I did some shopping and ate dinner," she said, deliberately avoiding any mention of her conversation with Kayla. "I just needed to get away for a while."

"Okay. You went to St. Louis. And then?"

Jesse had a fuzzy vision of leaving the shopping mall and driving back to Canton. She'd been fiercely satisfied to have her suspicions that Victoria was a fraud confirmed. And that there was every likelihood that she was out there somewhere, conning yet another man.

The problem was, she hadn't had the first clue how to expose the woman. Or how to track her down to get answers about what had happened to her dad. That was why she lingered in St. Louis. There was no need to rush home when she was just going to pace the floor in frustration. And why it was dark when she'd been driving back to Canton.

"Oh."

"Jesse?"

An icy chill spread through her body. The looming sense of danger that she'd felt since opening her eyes wasn't caused by her trip to St. Louis. It was the near-death experience on the highway.

"I was on my way home when I realized someone was following me," she murmured.

"Who?"

"I don't know. I didn't recognize the car."

"Can you describe it?"

Jesse reluctantly forced herself to recall the horrifying moment when the vehicle swerved into her lane. It'd been dark, but the glow from the headlights had allowed her to make out a few details.

"It was light. Maybe silver."

"Midsize? An SUV?"

"Midsize." She hesitated. She was certain of the size, but the lines of the vehicle hadn't been the usual boring style. "But not like a cheap car."

"What do you mean?"

"It was fancy."

"A sports car?"

Jesse hesitated again, struggling to describe what she'd seen. It had happened so fast, and she was more intent on avoiding a crash than taking notes on the car trying to run her off the road.

"More like a BMW or Mercedes sedan," she at last decided.

Noah's expression never changed, but Jesse sensed his body tense, as if he was bothered by her description.

"You're sure they were following you?" he demanded. "St. Louis has a lot of traffic."

"Of course I'm sure." Jesse frowned at the implication that she was overreacting. "I didn't notice them until I was almost to Canton. And then . . ." She shuddered at the memory.

"And then what?"

She licked her lips. Why were they so dry? Her mouth felt like the Sahara Desert.

"They started to pass, but when they were right next to me, they suddenly swerved into my lane. If there hadn't been an access road there, I would have been forced into the ditch."

"Damn." His jaw clenched. "I don't suppose you called the sheriff to report them?"

"No." Her tone let him know it was a stupid question. "The car didn't follow me after I was off the highway. I thought I'd managed to lose them, so I drove here to lock myself in and barricade the door, just to be sure no one could get in."

He stared down at her. "But they did get in."

"Yes." Her gaze drifted toward the wonky door. She'd been standing in this spot last night. And she'd seen the moonlight through the opening, right? "They must have come through the back door. I don't know how. I'm sure it was locked, but someone was waiting in the shadows. They put a gag over my mouth." She had to stop to clear the lump from her throat. "I thought they were going to suffocate me. The next thing I knew, you were calling my name."

"You must have been drugged."

His words hit her like a slap in the face. Of course. She'd thought that she'd passed out because of lack of oxygen. A stupid theory, but in her defense, her mind was still fuzzy.

"Yes, that makes sense. They must have put something on the rag they shoved over my face."

"Did you notice anything about them? Man or woman? Was there more than one?"

Jesse considered his question. After the form had leaped out at her, her mind had gone blank. She'd been locked in a primal battle of fight or flight. All she knew for certain was that there was at least one person. Oh . . . and they whispered in her ear before leaving her on the floor.

"Victoria."

"Wait. Did you say Victoria?" Noah demanded in confusion. "Your stepmother?"

Jesse pressed a hand to her stomach. The memory of the soft voice made her feel nauseous.

"She told me to leave or she would destroy everything I love."

"You're sure it was Victoria? I mean . . ."

She met his concerned gaze, her lips parting to insist that it'd been Victoria in the foyer with her last night. Hadn't she just discovered that the woman made a habit of pretending to be dead before she disappeared? But the words died on her lips. The truth was that she was nearly unconscious when she heard the whisper. And there was no way she could swear that it was Victoria.

"No. No, my brain was already fuzzy. I thought it was her," she admitted.

"But the voice belonged to a woman?" he pressed.

Again she forced herself to concentrate on what she'd actually heard, not what she wanted to believe.

"I'm not sure."

"Okay."

As if sensing she'd revealed everything she could remember from the terrifying night, Noah lay a comforting hand on her shoulder.

"Stay here. I'm going to check the building. I doubt if anyone was stupid enough to hang around, but I don't want to take any chances."

Panic spiked through Jesse as he dropped his hand and stepped back.

"I'm coming with you," she announced, her voice too loud.

"Jesse—"

"I don't want to be alone."

His features hardened, obviously battling between the urge to keep her safe and the realization that she was still recovering from being drugged.

"Okay," he conceded at last, turning to glance down the shadowed hallway. "We'll start at the bottom and work our way up."

Allowing Noah to take the lead, Jesse concentrated on placing one foot in front of the other. Her body felt oddly lethargic, as if it wasn't fully connected to her brain.

Noah halted as they reached the door to the cellar, pulling it open and flipping on the light. He glanced over his shoulder.

"You're sure you wouldn't rather wait up here?"

She shivered. "Absolutely."

"Okay. Careful," Noah grabbed her hand as they slowly climbed down the stairs. They reached the bottom step when he abruptly blocked her way. "Wait. Do you hear that?"

Jesse leaned forward, straining to hear what had captured Noah's attention. At first there was nothing. Then her foggy brain realized that the gushing noise wasn't coming from the outside gutters.

"Water. Crap," she ground out. A flooded cellar was the last thing she needed. "A pipe must have burst."

"Where's the shutoff valve?" Noah demanded.

"Behind the water heater." Jesse pointed toward the corner under the staircase. "Watch your head."

Noah dashed to the side, bending low to avoid knocking himself senseless on one of the floor beams. Jesse headed in the opposite direction, following the sound of money draining onto the dirt floor.

She'd nearly reached the far wall when she felt her foot sink into the spreading mud pit. With a grimace, she stopped and glanced up, not surprised to discover a pipe hanging down, spilling out water at an alarming rate.

"It didn't burst. It came loose," she called out, her heart sinking.

She had no idea how long the water had been running, but she suspected her bill was going to give her a heart attack.

"Not on its own." Noah's grim voice was closer than she expected. Jerking her head to the side, she discovered him heading toward her. On cue, the water stopped gushing, although a stubborn drip remained. "Someone did it on purpose."

"What?"

"Look." Noah turned on his phone flashlight and aimed it toward something stuck in the mud. Jesse hissed as she realized it was a wrench. Probably stolen from her dad's toolbox. She started to lean down, but before she could reach for the tool, Noah placed his hand on her arm. "No, don't touch it, Jesse. It might be evidence."

She sucked in a sharp breath, her teeth snapping together as anger seared away the clinging cobwebs.

"You're right. Whoever knocked me out must have come down here and separated the pipes before they took off."

"That's the most likely scenario," he agreed. "But why?"

"To drive me out of town." Jesse furrowed her brow, a voice in the back of her mind whispering that there was more than one reason someone might have caused the damage. What was the point in attacking her only to leave her alive? And why sabotage her home? They had to be warnings. "Or to stop me from looking into the past."

Noah held her worried gaze before his jaw tightened, and he turned his attention to the mess the water had made. As if searching for some clue that would reveal who'd messed with the pipes. Walking along the edge of the muddy pit, he at last made a sound of disgust as he bent down to shine the light from his phone toward the wall.

"Unfortunately, I was also right about the damage a leak would cause," he said. "The soft ground has collapsed part of your foundation."

"Oh no."

Ignoring the sodden dirt that clung to her shoes, Jesse moved to squat next to the pile of bricks that had crumbled to expose a large hole. They would obviously have to be replaced once the pipes were repaired, she acknowledged with a burst of anger. But right now she was more concerned about any damage that might have been caused to her neighbor. Bracing her hand against the bricks that remained intact, Jesse leaned forward, peering into the hole. Relief raced through her at the sight of the second wall, which remained solidly intact.

"At least it hasn't hurt Bea's side. At least I don't think so."

She leaned closer, trying to get a better view inside the hole. There was something sticking out of the mud. It was white and rounded on the top. Like a large stone, only it was too smooth to be natural. She inched forward. No, not a stone, she decided. In fact, it looked like a . . .

A scream of horror was wrenched from the depths of her soul as Jesse fell backward.

"What?" Noah demanded, swinging his phone to light up the hole. "Oh shit."

Jesse screamed again as the soft glow surrounded the skull, as if bringing it back to gruesome life. Crabwalking backward, Jesse battled through the mud, desperate to get away. She thought she caught a glimpse of more bones before Noah was thankfully blocking her view.

He bent down, scooping her trembling body off the ground and racing toward the nearby stairs.

The next hour was a blur for Jesse. She had a vague memory of being carried out of the Tap Room and bundled into Noah's truck. She shivered as she sank into the leather seat, not caring where they were headed as long as it was far away.

At last he stopped in front of the walk-in health clinic, demanding that she get checked out as he called 911 to report what had been revealed behind the crumbling foundation.

Enduring the checkup, which included blood work and an X-ray of her head to make sure she hadn't banged it on the floor when she passed out, Jesse was at last released into the wild. Or at least she was allowed to step out of the clinic without being fussed over by Noah and the medical staff.

She blinked as she stepped through the open door and onto the sidewalk. The late morning sunlight was blinding. She stopped to wait for her vision to clear, as well as for Noah to pull around and pick her up. He'd insisted on staying with her while she had her checkup, only leaving to get the truck he'd parked around the corner.

Jesse didn't like being treated like she was an invalid, but she was too tired to argue. Now she waited for the noise of his old engine to warn he was approaching.

"You need to come to the office with me."

Jesse screeched, jumping a full inch off the ground as the words were spoken directly into her ear. Then, stumbling to the side, she turned her head to discover Sheriff Tillman standing beside her, as if he'd appeared out of thin air.

Or, more likely, he'd crawled out of the gutter, she told herself, glaring at him as a toxic combination of anger and fear churned through her.

"Adam. What's wrong with you?" she snapped. "You nearly gave me a heart attack, sneaking up on me like a creeper."

His round face flushed at her angry words, his hand reaching out as if he intended to grab her. "Let's go."

"Go?" She instinctively slapped away his hand. "No way."

"Excuse me?" His face darkened to a deeper shade of red. "That wasn't an invitation."

"I'm not going anywhere with you. Not without my lawyer."

His lips snapped together, his eyes bulging. She didn't have to read his mind to know he was struggling to leash his urge to manhandle her to the courthouse. It was just a couple of blocks away and there was no one around to stop him.

Then, perhaps sensing a charge for police brutality looming in his future, he dropped his outstretched hand and contented himself with an evil glower.

"Why would you need a lawyer?" he snarled. "Only guilty people hide behind the slimy bastards."

"Because I don't trust you."

He jerked, as if caught off guard by her accusation. "I'm the sheriff."

"All the more reason for a lawyer," she retorted. "I watched you break laws when you were just a deputy. God knows what you're willing to do now."

"Christ, you're a pain in the ass."

"Me? Are you serious? I just got out of the doctor's office after being stalked, drugged, and traumatized by a skeleton in my cellar and you're harassing me as if I'm some sort of criminal instead of the victim." She met him glare for glare. "I'm not in the mood to deal with you."

"I need you to make a statement," he stubbornly insisted.

"Fine. I'll contact my lawyer and he'll call you with a convenient time for us to chat. Until then—" Jesse started to turn away, intending to discover what was keeping Noah.

"Do you recognize this?"

Moving with surprising speed considering his bulk, Adam was

blocking her path, holding out a brown wallet wrapped in a plastic bag.

"It's not mine, if that's what you're asking," she snapped.

"I'm asking if you recognize it."

On the point of stepping around the idiot to end the unwelcome encounter, Jesse abruptly froze, her gaze locked on the wallet. There was nothing special about it. Just worn brown leather. But as he tilted it toward her, the sun glinted off the small initials stitched in gold at the corner.

M.H.

A solid blow slammed into her heart, bringing it to a painful halt.

"Where did you get that?" she rasped.

"Did this belong to Mac?" Adam demanded.

"Yes." She trembled, the image of wrapping the wallet in bright Christmas paper before sneaking it under the tree searing through her mind. It was a running joke for her to buy him a new wallet and bottle of his favorite cologne for Christmas, and for him to pretend to be completely shocked when he opened them. The tradition started when she was a child and stayed even after he married Victoria. "Where did you find it?"

"In your cellar."

Jesse's mouth was still dry, making it hard to form the words. "He could have lost it last time he was down there. Honestly, he was always saying he'd lose his head if it wasn't attached—"

"It was found behind the bricks," Adam interrupted. "With the skeleton."

Jesse was shaking her head before he finished, as if she could somehow deflect the agonizing pain his words were inflicting.

"Are you . . . are you saying that it's my dad down there?" she finally managed to gasp. "You're sure?"

Something that might have been regret rippled over Adam's round face, as if realizing he'd allowed his delight in tormenting her to overcome his pretense of professionalism.

"No, nothing's confirmed," he admitted, lowering his arm. "The

DNA has to be sent off to the lab. You'll need to give a sample for them to use."

"But the wallet was with..." She couldn't force the word "skeleton" past her stiff lips. "Him?"

Adam nodded. "It was."

Jesse reeled beneath the avalanche of horror, her back slamming against the brick wall of the clinic. It was the only thing that kept her from collapsing.

Her dad. Her joyous, larger-than-life, devoted father was gone. Not disappeared. But vanished from this earth. Forever.

A kaleidoscope of memories flickered through her mind.

Her dad kneeling next to her as he braided her hair into pigtails. The two of them at the county fair, eating corn dogs and drinking lemonade. Sneaking down the stairs late at night to peer into the bar, where her dad was serving drinks and telling jokes to keep the customers entertained.

And at last... the sight of him kneeling on the floor as Victoria flounced away, his head in his hands.

"He's dead," she breathed. "Oh my God. All these years of wondering. Of telling myself he was out there somewhere. He was trapped in that awful cellar, just beneath my feet." Nausea rolled through her as she struggled to squash the knowledge she'd been sleeping in a bed just above her dad's corpse. "I'm going to be sick."

Shoving away from the wall, Jesse stumbled around the corner to where a narrow alley separated the clinic from a flower shop. She dropped to her knees, bending over in an effort to fight back the waves of sickness.

She heard the approaching footsteps but, assuming it was Adam, ignored the form that bent down next to her.

"Jesse, what's going on?" Noah's warm hand stroked down her back, his touch soothing. "What the hell did you do to her?" he snarled, obviously speaking to the sheriff.

With a sharp movement, Jesse shoved herself upright. As much as she appreciated Noah's attempt to protect her, she couldn't bear to talk about her dad. Or the fact that his skeleton was no doubt being dug out of the cellar by some clueless deputy who had no idea who Mac Hudson was, or how much he'd meant to this town.

"Please, Noah. I need to get away," she whispered, refusing to glance toward Adam, who was looming next to them like a vulture.

Noah studied her with a worried expression. "I'll take you."

"No, I want to be alone." She flinched. She hadn't meant to sound so sharp. "I'm sorry. I have to think."

"Okay." Noah's expression was impossible to read as he reached into his pocket and pulled out a set of keys. He pulled one off and handed it to her. "Go to my house. I'm going to be busy taking care of something for a few hours. Lock the doors and don't let anyone in."

She released a shaky sigh of relief. The last thing she wanted was to go back to the Tap Room. She wasn't sure she could ever step foot inside the building again.

"Thanks."

She turned to leave, a shudder racing through her body when Adam grabbed her shoulder.

"Call your lawyer, Jesse. We need to talk," he warned. "Soon."

Chapter 18

Jesse shook off Adam's pudgy hand, refusing to acknowledge his threat as she walked to the corner and turned onto the side street. She wouldn't give him the satisfaction of seeing the anxiety that bubbled through her.

Instead, she concentrated on placing one foot in front of the other, scanning her surroundings in search of danger. It didn't matter that the stalker had had plenty of opportunities to kill her when she was alone in the bar. And that it made no sense to wait until she was on a public street in broad daylight to do the deed. She wasn't going to let down her guard.

Not as long as she was in Canton.

Entering the quiet neighborhood at the edge of town, Jesse turned the corner and made her way to the white farmhouse at the end of the block. She climbed onto the wraparound porch and used the key Noah had given her. Once inside, she carefully locked and bolted the door.

That should have made her feel safe, but after last night, she wasn't taking anything for granted. Hadn't she just told herself she wasn't going to let down her guard?

Telling herself it only made sense to make sure she was alone, Jesse dropped her purse on the low coffee table before she began her search through the surprisingly tidy house, peering into closets and under beds. Probably there wasn't any need to examine the medicine cabinets or to check through the kitchen drawers, but she was already looking around, so it was impossible not to pry.

She didn't find much. She now knew that Noah was a neat freak, and that he didn't take any prescriptions. She also knew that he'd scrubbed the place of any hint of his former wife and their life together. Even the sturdy furniture was shrouded in dust covers, as if being condemned to the past.

Beyond that . . . he remained a mystery.

With her search done, Jesse headed into the kitchen. Her mouth was still annoyingly dry from whatever drug had been used to knock her out. She was in desperate need of water. At the same time, she pulled her phone out of her back pocket and hit a familiar number.

The sound of a female voice floated through the air as she grabbed a bottle of water out of the fridge.

"Hi, Sam, its Jesse Hudson. I don't suppose I can talk to Eric?"

"Actually, he told me to put you right through if you called," the receptionist assured her. "Hold on."

Jesse shuddered. She shouldn't be shocked that word had already gotten around town that she'd discovered a skeleton in her cellar. And probably the fact that her dad's wallet was found with it. But the thought that the people she'd known all her life were gathered at the coffee shop savoring the latest gossip made her stomach cramp.

"Jesse." Eric's sharp voice sliced through her misery. "Where are you?"

With an effort, she forced herself to concentrate. Later, she could wallow in all the self-pity she wanted.

"At Noah's house."

"Good. Have you talked to anyone?"

She took a drink of water. His crisp, professional tone wasn't doing anything for her dry mouth. He sounded like a lawyer who was worried about his client.

"No. I was waiting until you could go with me to the sheriff's office. Adam is demanding I give him a statement."

"Okay. I'll call and tell him that we'll be there in an hour. I'll come by and get you. That way we can go over what you're going to say before we go in."

A portion of the fear squeezing her heart began to ease. At least she didn't have to face the sheriff on her own.

"Thanks, Eric."

"In the meantime, stay put and don't talk to anyone," he commanded. "Do you hear me?"

"Yeah," she breathed, a shiver racing through her. "I'm not going anywhere."

The call disconnected, and Jesse shoved the phone back in her pocket as she emptied the bottle of water and paced the floor. She was reassured by the fact that Eric was going with her to confront Adam Tillman, but that didn't help with her other worries. Worries that threatened to crush her.

That was why she kept moving.

If she ever sat down and genuinely considered what had happened over the past few days, she might start screaming and never stop.

She was on lap—actually she'd lost count after one hundred—when there was a knock on the front door.

Assuming that Eric had arrived earlier than expected, Jesse scurried into the front room. She headed directly for the large picture window, cautiously checking the porch. She was done taking risks, right?

Her caution was rewarded as she discovered that it wasn't Eric who'd knocked, although she still hurried to yank open the door. A second later, Bea Hartman stepped over the threshold and pulled her into a comforting hug.

"Oh Jesse. Noah just told me what happened." Bea squeezed tighter, threatening to cut off Jesse's air supply. "You poor thing."

Jesse returned the hug, although she couldn't share the woman's obvious grief. She was thankfully numb.

"I can't cry," she muttered.

Bea released her hold and stepped back, her own face blotchy from tears. "Of course not; you must be in shock."

Jesse managed a jerky nod. "I suppose I must be. I mean, I just can't wrap my brain around the fact that he was there . . . all this time."

"Oh, my dear." Bea clicked her tongue. "Don't think about it."

A humorless laugh was wrenched from Jesse's throat. Not think about it? From the moment Adam had waved the wallet in her face, she'd been obsessing over the gruesome fact that his skeleton had been hidden at the bar. God knew it was easier to fixate on the details of death than the overwhelming sadness waiting to crush her.

Whatever the reason, she couldn't stop the questions from churning through her mind, like a hamster on a wheel.

"I don't understand," she said, her words coming out like a plea from her soul.

"There are some things we're not meant to understand, sweet Jesse. Death is one of those things. It's the great mystery."

It was the same thing she'd said when Jesse had asked why her mother was taken when she was just a baby. And it offered the same lack of comfort.

"I don't mean I don't understand why he died, although I don't," she retorted, her voice harsh. "It's obscene that he was taken in the prime of his life. I meant that I don't understand how his body got into the foundation of the Tap Room."

Bea made a sound of distress, clearly unwilling to discuss the gruesome details. "Please don't do this to yourself," she pleaded, her plump hands twisting together. "Now is the time to mourn, not to dwell on such morbid thoughts."

"Don't you see? I have to know," Jesse insisted. "Not only is it going to drive me crazy until I figure out what happened, I'm going to be in danger."

"Danger? From what?"

"Whoever's been stalking me."

"Wait. Are you suggesting the person pestering you is connected to your dad's death?" Bea demanded, as if surprised by the suggestion.

"That's the point, I don't know. But it seems a little coincidental that someone would be doing their best to frighten me out of the place my dad's body was discovered. Why else were they trying to get rid of me?"

Bea clicked her tongue. "I wish you would leave the investigation to the law officials, Jesse."

"Adam Tillman?" Jesse shuddered. "Are you kidding me?"

"I get that you don't like him—"

"I loathe him with every fiber of my being."

Bea continued as if Jesse hadn't interrupted. "But he is the sheriff. He'll have to investigate whether he wants to or not."

"That doesn't mean his investigation will be anything more than a sham. Just like the pretend investigation he did when my dad first disappeared. I don't trust him."

"Who do you trust?"

"No one." The words burst from her lips before she could halt them. Probably because they were true. Her past had destroyed any faith in her fellow human beings. It wasn't until Bea flinched that she realized she'd been too blunt. "Except you, of course," she lamely tagged on.

Bea reached up to cup her cheek in her hand, as if to prove she wasn't offended by Jesse's fierce words.

"You can't do this alone, Jesse. Let the professionals do their job."

Jesse stepped back. It wasn't that she didn't appreciate Bea's attempt to talk some sense into her, but she'd walked away nine years ago. This time she was staying until she knew exactly what happened.

"Adam's not going to do a damned thing to find out the truth. Not unless he can somehow pin the blame on me. You said yourself that he hated my dad. As far as he's concerned, Mac Hudson got exactly what he deserved."

Bea parted her lips, as if she intended to argue; then, perhaps sensing that Jesse was never going to trust Adam, she heaved a resigned sigh.

"I hate to say this because I'm not sure that he deserves you, but maybe it's time for you to go back to Chicago and start a new life with that man of yours."

Jesse grunted, the words hitting her like a blow. It was hard to believe that just a week ago she'd been in Chicago, wandering through an empty nightclub she was planning on opening with the love of her life. She'd been focused on the future, never dreaming her past was about to destroy everything.

Including her relationship with Parker.

"He's not mine," she said, a surprising hint of sadness in her voice. As if she was ready to mourn the loss of her lover, even if she couldn't face the grief of her father. "I don't think he ever was."

"But I thought the two of you were getting married and starting a business together?"

Jesse shrugged. "That was the plan, but plans change. I've learned that the hard way."

"Then find a new future," Bea insisted. "I'm terrified that staying stuck in the past is going to kill you."

"I can't."

"Jesse—"

"How did he get there?" Jesse interrupted the older woman's protest, turning to pace across the living room. The words tumbled out of her like water gushing out of a broken dam. "It couldn't have been an accident. Someone must have put him down there after they killed him."

"I suppose," Bea grudgingly agreed.

Jesse closed her eyes, forcing herself back to the afternoon her dad disappeared.

"But how? My dad was still at the courthouse with his lawyer when I returned to the bar. There's no way he could have been attacked on his way home and carried down to the cellar without me hearing them. Unless..."

"What?"

Jesse pictured herself grabbing her purse and charging out the front door to retrace her steps back to the courthouse. "I left to go search for him. I wasn't gone that long, but if someone had already killed him and was waiting for an opportunity to hide his body, they might have had time to carry him downstairs."

Bea studied her with a confused expression. "But I thought he was found behind the wall of the foundation?"

"True. They could have taken Dad down to the cellar, but there wouldn't have been time to remove the bricks and replace them that quickly." She tried to calculate how long it would take to accomplish the gruesome task. It seemed impossible, but then again, the foundation was in bad shape even back then. Her dad was always complaining the building needed to be refurbished from roof to cellar, and she hadn't gone back down there. Not until days later. "They could have carried him into the cellar while I was gone, and then taken the entire night to hide the body before creeping out while I was asleep," she decided at last.

Bea shook her head. "But why? Why take the risk of being caught when they could have taken him anywhere?"

She was right. It didn't make sense. Still, Jesse wasn't ready to give up. This theory was as reasonable as any other.

"Maybe he came home shortly after I left to search for him."

"Wouldn't you have seen him?"

"Not if he had to run a couple of errands," Jesse insisted. "Or went to visit my mother's grave. He usually visited the cemetery at least once a week. He would have missed going there while he was in jail. That would mean that he was coming from the opposite direction of the courthouse when I left the bar."

"I suppose," Bea grudgingly conceded. "That doesn't explain what happened to him."

Jesse took time to envision her dad walking back from the graveyard. He would have been distracted. Not only by his release from jail, but from his conversation with his dead wife. Sometimes he would be preoccupied with his faded memories for hours after he'd been to her grave.

Plus, this was Canton. People never considered walking down the street might be dangerous.

"Someone must have been waiting for him. He always used the alleyway, so they could have stayed hidden until he was stepping into the building and then attacked him from behind. From there, it would have been easy to drag him down to the cellar."

"Hardly easy. Mac was a big man."

"Not after his time in jail. He'd lost a ton of weight. Besides, there might have been more than one person involved."

Bea studied her with a worried expression. She seemed more concerned with Jesse's obsession with solving the mystery of the past than with what happened to Mac Hudson. Probably a good thing. One of them needed to keep a firm tether to reality.

"You were gone for years, Jesse. Isn't it possible he wasn't . . . you know . . ." The older woman struggled to say the words. "Put there until later?"

"You mean someone moved his body there after I left town?"

"Or he wasn't killed until later," Bea suggested. "Maybe he came back to Canton after you moved out and—"

No." The denial came out with a fierce anger that made the older woman blink in shock. "I'm sorry, Bea, but I knew."

"Knew what?"

"That he was dead." Jesse pressed her hands against her churning stomach. As horrifying as it was to think her dad was trapped in the cellar for all those years, there was also a sense of peace. As if one ghost that was haunting her had been laid to rest. "Deep in my heart, I've always known. I might have clung to the futile hope he was out there somewhere. And made up a dozen reasons why he might be hiding from me. But they'd never felt right. He would never have abandoned me."

"He might have if he feared he might put you in danger. Maybe Victoria got him in debt and there were bad people chasing him."

"No, not for any reason," Jesse adamantly insisted, beginning to understand her aching emptiness and inability to settle down.

Mac Hudson was a huge part of her life. His death left her floating in a sea of uncertainty.

Bea continued to look concerned. "Even if you're right, it doesn't change anything, does it? He's gone. Time for you to move on."

Jesse clenched her jaw. She might have solace in knowing her father could finally be laid to rest, but the acceptance that he was dead only made her more determined to discover exactly what had happened.

"I'm not moving on until whoever killed him is rotting in jail."

"What choice do you have? If you're right, then his death happened almost a decade ago. There's no way to discover what really happened."

"There's someone in town who knows." Jesse paused. It was more dramatic than she intended, but she knew she was going to sound like she'd lost her mind. "Victoria."

"Victoria?" Bea blinked. "Are you talking about your stepmother?"

"Yes."

"Jesse, I think you're in shock." Bea grabbed her hand, trying to pull her toward the covered sofa. "Sit down and I'll pour you a drink."

"This isn't shock." Jesse pulled out of her friend's firm grip. "I've suspected that Victoria is still alive for days. And yesterday I found the proof."

"You have proof that Victoria is alive?" Bea sounded unconvinced.

"Yes."

"You saw her? I mean, with your own eyes?"

"Not her face, but I heard her voice last night."

"I don't understand. She called you?"

Jesse made a sound of frustration. She didn't know why Bea was acting so confused. Okay, wait. She did know. She just didn't want to admit that she might be grasping at straws. If only she had something tangible to show her.

Wait. She did have something. Well, it wasn't proof that Victoria was in town, but that there was a very real chance that she was still alive.

Stepping toward the coffee table, she grabbed her purse, which she'd tossed there earlier, and dug through the junk that'd managed to accumulate since she'd last bothered to clean it out. Tissues and ChapSticks and a dozen pens cluttered the bottom, but not the picture.

Someone had stolen the photo of Tegan, probably when she'd been knocked out. But who the hell knew that she had it? Had they been watching her while she searched the storage unit? The thought made her skin crawl.

"It's gone," she muttered, dropping her purse in disgust.

"What's gone?"

"The picture I found." Jesse shook her head. "Look, it doesn't matter. I don't have everything worked out," she admitted, "but I'm certain that Victoria was once Sylvia Fulton, from Little Rock, Arkansas, who married a slumlord named Larry Maitland and had his baby. Tegan. My stepsister."

"I thought she was married to a surgeon—"

"No," Jesse interrupted, abruptly turning to pace through the narrow space. "Her husband was in to drugs and money laundering before he conveniently died from a bullet in his brain."

Bea sucked in a sharp breath. "Murder?"

"They labeled it a suicide, but I have my doubts. Just as I have my doubts about the death of her second husband." Jesse continued her story, knowing her nerves were making her babble but unable to stop the flow of words. "Or at least the next husband that I know about. He died in a fire while Victoria and Tegan's bodies were never found. Then, a few years later, she's in a car crash outside of Canton, and once again there are no bodies. Oh yeah, and her husband is dead."

Bea held up a hand, as if needing a second to absorb the full extent of Jesse's accusations.

"She killed her husbands?" The older woman shivered. "That sounds like something on one of those true crime shows. What do they call them?"

"A black widow?" Jesse waited for Bea's hesitant nod. "You're right. That's exactly what Victoria is. She sucks men dry and then disposes of them before moving on to her next victim."

"Could she really have been that evil? I mean, she lived here for what... three years or more without us suspecting anything."

Jesse clicked her tongue. "Don't pretend you liked her, Bea."

"No, no, I didn't like her," Bea readily admitted. "Or, more specifically, I didn't like how she treated your father. She broke his heart. And then she broke his spirit."

Those were the perfect words to capture what had happened to Mac Hudson.

She broke his heart and then she broke his spirit.

"And then she killed him," Jesse added in a sad voice.

They shared a moment of regret that the woman had ever stepped foot in Canton before Bea was lifting her hands in confusion.

"Why? I mean, if you're timeline is right, then she'd already disappeared with Tegan months before Mac died. Why come back to Canton?"

"My guess is that Dad figured out the truth about her past and intended to expose it. He'd been doing a lot of research, and I know for a fact that he'd discovered she'd lied to him both before and during their marriage." She shrugged. "Or maybe he managed to track her down and demanded she reveal that she was still alive. If she had a new husband lined up, she wouldn't appreciate being exposed as a liar."

Bea pursed her lips. "It does make sense."

"Yes." Jesse tried to sound confident despite the worry that niggled on the edge of her mind.

A worry that whispered she was missing something.

"Of course that still doesn't explain why she came back to Canton all these years later."

"At first I assumed it was someone trying to stop me from poking into the past. But now—"

"Jesse?"

Jesse stopped in the center of the floor, struck by a sudden realization.

"Now I think Victoria was trying to frighten me out of town because she was worried my repairs on the bar would expose my dad's body."

"Why would she care after so long?"

Another question without an easy answer.

"Maybe because my dad would no longer be a missing person. He would be a murder case, with no statute of limitations. If someone actually started investigating what happened." She stopped with a frown. "I mean, someone who wasn't Adam Tillman. Then her secrets would be revealed, and people would start asking uncomfortable questions. I hate her, but she's not stupid. She would have to know once his body was found I would do whatever was necessary to uncover the truth."

Bea shook her head, her fingers once again twisting together. "I can't believe she's alive."

"I can," Jesse said dryly. "She's like a cockroach. She'd probably survive a nuclear explosion, crawling out of the rubble without a scratch." A low vibration shimmied up her lower back, interrupting her grim memories of her stepmother. She reached around to pull her cell phone from her pocket, swiftly skimming the text. "It's from Eric Walker. He's on his way to pick me up."

Bea widened her eyes. "Why do you need a lawyer?"

"Sheriff Tillman is demanding that I give him a statement." Jesse felt a wave of sickness at the thought of being trapped in a small room while Adam forced her to recall every horrifying detail about finding her dad's skeleton. "I'm not talking to him without a lawyer."

"Oh my dear." Bea bit her lower lip, as if battling back tears. "I hate this, I really do."

"Yeah, I hate it too."

Bea sniffed. "I wish I could bring him back."

Jesse impulsively moved to wrap her arms around the older woman. Who else besides Bea had truly loved Mac Hudson? Who else could share her grief?

"There's nothing I wouldn't give to have him here with us."

Bea patted her back. "Do you want me to go with you?"

Jesse reluctantly stepped away, her gaze moving to the lump that was still visible on Bea's forehead. She'd forgotten the poor woman was recovering. Yet another of Victoria's victims.

"No, you go home and rest. I'll be fine."

Bea furrowed her brow. "You're sure?"

Nope. Not at all. The words whispered through her mind even as Jesse firmly moved to pull open the front door.

"Absolutely. I'll call you when I'm done."

Bea reluctantly nodded, walking slowly out of the house and down the front porch steps. Jesse watched until she'd disappeared behind a hedge before closing and locking the door.

Her conversation with Bea was a warning. Her theories might make perfect sense in her head, but when she spoke the words out loud it sounded more like a bunch of wild guesses strung together by desperation. And while she didn't expect Adam Tillman to believe anything she said, she had to convince him that she had enough evidence to go to the state officials who had the skill and technology to investigate a cold case.

That was the only way he would get off his ass and try to find out what happened.

She needed to collect her thoughts so she could lay them out in a concise, logical manner.

Closing her eyes, she forced herself to take in deep, calming breaths, trying to clear the clutter from her mind. She had no doubt she would eventually crash and burn from an overload of emotions. But her nervous breakdown would have to wait.

She was focused on easing the knots from her stomach when she heard the soft purr of an engine. Eric. Or at least she assumed it was Eric. She'd been wrong before.

Once again taking the proper precautions, Jesse moved to the front window to peer out. As she'd expected, a car had pulled into the driveway, and even from a distance she could make out Eric's silhouette. On the point of turning to grab her purse and head out the door, Jesse found herself frozen in place.

There was a warning bell clamoring in the back of her mind. As if trying to warn her of approaching danger.

What was wrong?

She remained frozen in place as Eric impatiently honked the horn, and then at last climbed out of the car, wearing his usual tailored suit.

Car. That was it. That was what was wrong. A silver BMW.

Jesse's mouth was dry as she stepped away from the window. She had no way of knowing if it was the same vehicle that tried to run her off the road the night before, but it was close enough to make her heart thunder in fear.

A knock shattered the thick silence, followed by the rattle of the doorknob.

"Jesse?" More rattling. "Are you in there? Jesse!"

The rattling stopped, and Jesse cautiously tilted to the side, peering out of the window. A part of her told herself she was acting like an idiot. There were lots of silver cars in Canton. That didn't make their drivers demented stalkers. Besides, she'd already decided that Victoria was guilty.

A larger part of her, however, whispered that there was no use in taking any chances. Once Eric drove away she would send him a text to meet her at the courthouse. If he was somehow involved, then there was no way he could do anything when he was in the sheriff's office, right?

It felt like a good plan. At least until Eric didn't turn around and head back to his car. Instead, he reached up to skim his fingers along the top of the doorframe. He was looking for the spare key. And, intimately familiar with how most people treated security in Canton, she didn't doubt he was going to find one.

"Jesse, are you okay?" he called out before she heard the scrape of the key in the lock.

Panic jolted through her. Without giving herself time to leash the impulsive urge to flee, she was racing through the house and out the back door. More than likely she was overreacting. Eric was probably just worried when she didn't answer the door. Of course he wanted to check on her. But her nerves were too raw to take even the slightest chance there might be another reason he was breaking and entering Noah's home.

Bending low, she was swiftly across the back veranda and down the stairs, nearly tripping over her own feet. She'd never been coordinated, and right now her knees were trembling so badly, she could barely stay upright. Veering toward the side of the house, Jesse abruptly changed her mind and darted down the tree-lined path toward the back of the property. She would call Noah to come pick her up from the access road he had mentioned that went along the back of the lake.

He was the only one she trusted right now.

Trying to ignore the tingling sensation that she was being watched by unseen eyes, Jesse rounded the long curve in the pathway, at last slowing her hectic pace. Her heart was thundering so hard it hurt, and her breath was coming in short, painful gasps. Obviously she needed to find a good cardio workout when she got back to Chicago. It was embarrassing to be huffing and puffing after a few minutes of running.

Of course, in her defense, the fear she was about to be murdered didn't help.

Near the end of the pathway, Jesse stopped in the shadows of the trees, sucking air into her tight lungs as she pulled her phone from her pocket. She'd left behind her purse, but that didn't matter. It wasn't like she needed money for an Uber or to catch the bus. Either Noah came to get her or she was walking.

Pressing Noah's number, Jesse's gaze skimmed her surroundings, and she wondered how it could be such a bright, beautiful day. It should be dark and gloomy, with lightning streaking across the sky.

Instead, the sunlight glittered off the nearby lake, nearly blinding her.

Blinking against the glare, Jesse impatiently waited for Noah to answer. Nothing. She cursed as the call was dropped into voicemail. Then she was distracted by a shadow flickering on the distant side of the lake.

Was someone there?

Hoping it was Noah, Jesse shaded her eyes, trying to make out details. Immediately, any hope that it might be her friend was crushed. The form was not only too short and slender, it was obviously female. And, weirdly, it was dressed in black, with a veil over the mystery woman's face.

Jesse shoved the phone back into her pocket, watching the woman lean forward to toss a handful of flowers into the water, as if performing some sort of religious rite.

What the hell?

Abruptly deciding that she couldn't wait for Noah to come to rescue her, Jesse turned to the side, intending to head to the courthouse. In that same moment, there was the loud crack of a branch being snapped off a nearby tree.

The sound pierced her heart with terror, and Jesse braced herself. She already knew that whoever had snuck up behind her was going to use the branch to knock her unconscious.

She was right.

Chapter 19

This time when Jesse managed to crawl her way out of the painful darkness, she wasn't confused about why her head ached. She had a vivid memory of the branch connecting with the back of her skull and fireworks exploding behind her eyes.

The knowledge that she'd been attacked . . . again . . . meant she had enough sense in her throbbing brain to avoid revealing she was awake. Instead, she held herself as still as possible while she cracked open her eyes.

Everything was fuzzy, like she was underwater, but she could determine the fact that she was in a shadowy room with bare wooden walls. And that she was lying on a narrow cot that smelled like mold. Overhead, she could see open beams with a bare light bulb dangling from a wire.

The place looked oddly familiar. As if she'd been here a very long time ago. It was at last the soft lap of the water from outside that jolted a specific memory of loud music, laughter, and the joy of being young and carefree.

Of course. The old boathouse next to the dock.

The realization brought a mixture of relief and sheer terror.

Relief that she hadn't been kidnapped and taken miles away from Canton. And terror that she was in a remote shack where no one could hear her scream.

"I should have known you would be a pain in the ass," a female voice drawled, shattering Jesse's pretense of sleep. "It doesn't matter that I spent years going over each detail of my plan in order to make it run smoothly. You just had to interrupt me paying my respects instead of patiently waiting for me at Noah's house. I shouldn't be surprised, of course, that you ruined the moment. You ruin everything."

"Victoria?" Jesse struggled to focus her blurry eyes as a face appeared above her. She frowned. No. The delicate features with bright blue eyes and bleached-blond hair didn't belong to her stepmother. "Reese?" she at last croaked in confusion.

"Keep trying," the woman taunted. "I'm sure it will come to you."

Jesse continued to stare in confusion. Why would her real estate agent be in the boathouse? Was she involved in kidnapping her? Then something about the petulant twist of Reese's lips struck a chord of memory. She'd seen that petulance before. "Oh my God. Tegan."

"Give the girl a gold star," Tegan mocked, abruptly straightening.

Cautiously, Jesse pushed herself into a seated position. Not only was she worried that there might be someone lurking in the shadows ready to give her another whack on the head, but there was a sickening throb behind her right eye. Any quick movement was going to stab shards of pain through her brain.

"You don't look the same," Jesse said.

"I was a child when I left Canton, I was destined to grow up."

She had a point. Anytime Jesse thought about her stepsister, she always pictured her as a little girl. Still, she should have been able to recognize her. "It's not that. Your nose is different. And your cheeks."

"Fine." Tegan clicked her tongue. "I've had some work done.

Didn't anyone tell you it's rude to discuss a woman's little nips, tucks, and fillers?"

Jesse leaned her aching head against the wall behind her, the initial shock of Reese's true identity beginning to wear off.

"I knew you survived."

"Survived?" The blue eyes that had to be the result of contact lenses slowly narrowed. Tegan had brown eyes when she was young. "I suppose you could call it that. Although there were lots of times I wished I hadn't."

Jesse felt a stab of anger at the bitterness in the younger woman's voice. As if she'd been the one to suffer instead of Jesse, who'd been forced to live with the aching horror of her father's disappearance.

"Where's Victoria?" she sharply demanded.

"Dead."

Jesse snorted. "I don't believe you. The bitch is a master of vanishing into thin air."

Tegan's taunting expression never faltered. "You know nothing."

"Oh yeah? I know that Victoria started off as Sylvia Fulton. And that she did her first vanishing act after she killed your father, Larry Maitland, in Little Rock, Arkansas. And then vanished again after she killed Liam Tanner in St. Louis and started the fire to distract the authorities. Unfortunately, that brought her to Canton to marry my dad."

This time the words came out with a bold confidence. The fact that Tegan was standing there, like a vision from her nightmares, proved she wasn't grasping at straws.

"Yes, her decision to come to Canton was unfortunate," Tegan readily agreed. "For all of us."

"She arranged the crash outside of town to disappear before returning to kill my father," Jesse continued, not so much to show off how much she'd discovered, but in an effort to figure out why she was currently trapped in the boathouse with Tegan smirking at her with that too white smile. "I assume she didn't kill him before leaving town because he wasn't worth more than the cash she'd already stolen from the safe. So what happened? Why did she come back? Did my dad threaten to reveal she was a psychopath?"

Tegan chuckled, unfazed by the fact that Jesse had just accused her mother of being a serial killer. Did that mean she'd followed in Victoria's footsteps? The thought sent a chill through Jesse, emphasizing the musty isolation of their surroundings.

If Tegan decided to kill her, how long would it take for someone to find her body? Would she end up like her dad? A forgotten skeleton?

Jesse shoved away the stomach-churning image. She had no idea why Tegan was in the boathouse or what plans she was so upset about Jesse ruining, but she did know that the only way she was going to survive was if she could be smarter than her stepsister. And that meant she couldn't give into the rising panic.

"So close and yet so far away," Tegan was drawling when Jesse managed to regain command of her nerves.

"Far away about what?"

"Victoria's villain origin story. To start with, Larry Maitland wasn't my father."

"Then who . . ." Jesse's words trailed away as she considered what she'd missed. Finally, the truth hit her. She couldn't believe she'd been blind to the obvious explanation. "Of course. Buzz from the trailer park was your dad."

For the first time since Tegan had revealed her true identity, she looked surprised. "My, my. You have been a busy bee."

"How did she end up married to Larry Maitland?"

Tegan shrugged. "They'd hooked up a couple of times. A purely casual exchange of sex for drugs. But when my mom discovered she was pregnant she knew it was her golden ticket out of the trailer park."

Jesse nodded, then wished she hadn't, as a stab of pain made her eye twitch. For a poor woman living in squalor, the fancy house in the suburbs must have seemed like the pearly gates were swinging open to enter heaven.

"It obviously wasn't a golden ticket for long."

"No. Maitland was a violent brute who cheated, lied, and threatened to kill both of us more than once. She did what she had to do."

Tegan was eerily nonchalant discussing her mother putting a bullet in Larry Maitland's head. Just another day.

"Including stealing his money?" Jesse demanded, shifting on the cot as if getting more comfortable while she tried to feel for the phone she'd tucked into her pocket before being knocked unconscious.

Hope flared through her heart. It was there. Either Tegan hadn't noticed it *or didn't care*, the worrisome thought whispered through the back of her mind.

"Trust me, she earned every penny," Tegan was continuing to defend her mother.

"Did she earn Liam Tanner's money as well?"

"He wasn't as physically violent, but he had a habit of trading in his wives for younger models."

Jesse slowly inched her hand toward her hip. "Had he already picked out the next Mrs. Tanner?"

"Yes. A stripper from Chicago who passed herself off as an interior designer. The only thing she designed was her way into Liam's bed. It was only a matter of time before we were going to be tossed out with nothing."

"Instead, she embezzled from his company before killing him."

"Trust me, the world is a better place without Liam Tanner."

"I can't believe you're that callous." Jesse shook her head, as if she was troubled by her stepsister's lack of empathy. In truth, she wasn't remotely surprised. There'd been a strange lack of emotion in Tegan even as a child. All she wanted was to keep her talking long enough to reach her phone and call for help. "You know that Kayla still grieves for her best friend who died in a terrible fire?"

"Kayla?" Tegan said the name without surprise. She'd known that Jesse had gone to see the younger woman. "You know, I genuinely liked her. She was the only real friend I ever had." She paused, as if enjoying a distant memory. "That's why I chose the name Tegan.

Kayla used to say when she got married and had a baby girl she would name her Tegan Reese."

"Tegan," Jesse breathed. "Reese Skylar."

"Yes. I missed her for a long time."

Jesse didn't bother to ask how Victoria had managed to change their identities so easily. Money and a connection to criminals could make anything possible.

"And my dad? He loved you. Did you ever miss him?"

The slap came without warning. One second Tegan was regarding her with a faint smile and the next she was smacking her palm against Jesse's cheek with enough force to rattle her teeth. Jesse hissed in pain as she was knocked sideways, nearly falling off the cot.

"Don't ever say that," Tegan commanded.

Still groggy from the earlier blow to the head, Jesse took a moment to clear the new cobwebs from her mind. At least the slap gave her the opportunity to place her hand behind her back as she shoved herself upright, she tried to reassure herself. She had to keep fighting.

"Don't say what?" she asked, her voice hoarse.

"That your father loved me."

"He did."

"No. If he loved me, he would have fought for me."

"Fought for you?" Jesse was confused. "I don't understand."

A hint of color touched Tegan's pale cheeks. A genuine emotion?

"Of course you don't, you stupid cow. How could you?" The blue eyes flicked over Jesse's rumpled form with an icy hatred. "You're the princess, right? The precious daughter who could do no wrong."

Jesse's heart missed a beat. She'd been wrong. So very, very wrong.

Tegan wasn't lacking emotions. It was that she kept them so tightly suppressed that they boiled deep inside her, like the lava in a sleeping volcano, just waiting for the opportunity to spew out her toxic fury. Jesse deliberately tilted her chin, knowing her only hope of getting out of the boathouse was to continue to provoke the younger woman.

"That's not true," she insisted. "My dad adored you."

This time Jesse was braced for the blow to her face, ignoring the pain as her head was jerked to the side to concentrate on pulling the phone from her pocket. She kept her hand behind her back, knowing she had to keep Tegan distracted as she pressed the buttons on the side and swiped her thumb over the screen.

She had no way to know if she'd activated the emergency call to 911, but she would try again in a couple minutes.

"I'll tell you what's true," Tegan snapped, leaning over Jesse like a vulture. "Do you know why my mother married Mac Hudson?"

Jesse tilted back her head to meet the smoldering blue gaze. It was a question that had haunted her for years.

"Honestly, I don't have a clue."

"Because of me."

"Why?"

"When we first came to Canton my mom did her usual routine. First she tried to land some gross rich dude who would give her the social standing she wanted," she said, reminding Jesse that Victoria had dated the local banker before turning her attention to her dad. "When that didn't happen she started playing the field, dating every man around in the hopes of finding a sucker who had a ton of money and was willing to share it with a single mother and her darling daughter. Eventually, she decided that the town was too small to attract the sort of mid-level criminals she usually ended up with, so she decided we were going to move on. I was the one who said I wanted to stay. And that I wanted Mac to be my dad."

The story fit with what Jesse had uncovered over the past week. "Why Mac?"

Tegan snorted. "Every man wanted my mother. I don't know what witchcraft she used, but the minute they met her, they turned into mindless idiots desperate to get between her legs. It was disgusting. Like dogs in heat."

Jesse blinked at the venom in Tegan's voice. She clearly hated Victoria as much as Jesse. Maybe more.

"I remember," she murmured.

"Most of them wanted me to disappear, of course. Who wants a brat hanging around when you're trying to get a woman naked? Some gave me money to stay in my room, and others threatened to beat me. Only Mac actually made the effort to treat me like I was something more than a nuisance." Tegan's icy features melted at the memory of Jesse's father. "He talked to me like I was a real person, and he listened to what I had to say. Or at least he pretended to."

"No. He listened." Jesse held her stepsister's gaze. "Because he genuinely cared."

A hint of vulnerability softened the blue eyes before Tegan was abruptly stepping back, her lips pinching together.

"My mother thought he was a local yokel who smelled like beer and had the charm of a turnip."

Jesse flinched. "Then why did she marry him?"

"We'd run out of money and she was getting desperate. Mac Hudson was better than nothing."

"So you got what you wanted."

Jesse ground her teeth. How many wounds had Victoria inflicted on Mac with her constant bickering and icy disdain? It was just like Bea said. The woman had broken his spirit before she broke his heart. And why? Because she couldn't bother to love her petulant daughter. If Tegan hadn't been desperate for a little affection, Victoria would have moved on from Canton and none of this would have happened.

"I would have if it hadn't been for you," Tegan snapped. "You ruined everything."

"Me? What did I do?"

Tegan lifted her hand, but with a visible effort she resisted the urge to hit Jesse again. Instead, she stiffened her spine, as if regretting her display of temper. Jesse sensed that Tegan liked to pretend she was always in perfect control. In control of her temper, of her situation, of her future.

"Don't treat me like an idiot," she warned, her voice coated in ice. "We both know you squealed and bleated like a stuck pig if Mac gave me the slightest amount of attention."

Jesse shrugged. She couldn't deny she acted like a prima donna. "I was a child too. Of course I was jealous of having to share my dad."

"You'd had him your whole life. You couldn't give me a measly couple of years?"

Jesse wasn't going to squabble over who'd been the bigger brat. If she had to be knocked over the head and held hostage by Tegan, at least she could get some answers.

"So you killed him." It was an accusation, not a question.

Tegan's lips parted, but before she could respond, the door to the boathouse was abruptly shoved open to reveal a form that was silhouetted by the late afternoon sunlight.

Jesse narrowed her eyes against the golden rays that flooded the cramped darkness.

Her first thought was that it wasn't nearly as late as she'd first assumed. The thick dust that coated the windows of the boathouse made her think it was at least dusk. Instead, she'd only been unconscious a couple of hours. Her second thought was that there was something intimately familiar about the slender body as it stepped over the threshold.

"He's tied up in the boat—" Parker bit off his words as his gaze moved to discover Jesse sitting on the cot, staring at him with her mouth wide open. "Shit, she's awake. What the hell? I told you to hit her with the chloroform if she started to wake up."

Tegan shrugged. "Plans change."

"Parker." His name came out like a croak as Jesse struggled to accept what she was seeing. "What are you doing here?"

Parker rolled his eyes, as if he couldn't believe how dense she was. Honestly, Jesse couldn't believe how dense she was, either.

"Do I really have to spell it out?"

No. No, he didn't. Her gaze moved from Parker to her smugly smiling stepsister.

"Oh my God. You and Tegan. You planned this together."

Tegan's laughter was filled with pure joy. "Very good, Jesse. You just earned another gold star."

Chapter 20

Jesse stared at Parker Moreau with his halo of honey brown curls and painfully beautiful face, telling herself she should be ravaged by his betrayal.

This was the man who'd shared her bed for months. The man she had once thought was the love of her life. The man she'd been prepared to trust with her father's worldly possessions.

But oddly, there was more a sense of resignation. As if she'd already accepted that he wasn't the person he pretended to be. What was the old saying? *A wolf in lamb's clothing*.

Still, she struggled to connect Parker to what had been happening in Canton. Maybe because in the past twenty-four hours, she'd been drugged and then smacked with a branch. Her brain felt sluggish.

"It wasn't destiny that brought you to the same nightclub where I was working," she finally managed to mutter. "Or for us to fall in love."

Parker shuddered, as if horrified at the mere thought. "Not hardly. Actually, I can't believe you swallowed that bullshit so easily." He deliberately paused, his head tilted back and his shoulders squared, as if he were striking a pose in front of a mirror. "Well, maybe I can believe it. I *am* a professional actor, and you were so pathetically desperate to be swept off your feet by a Prince Charming."

Jesse shook her head. The creep had obviously practiced that speech. Gross. How the hell had she ever been fooled by him?

Maybe he was right. Maybe she was desperate to be swept off her feet. But was that so awful? Wasn't it better to long for love than to cut herself off from the world?

Squashing the bitter anger at the knowledge she'd been so easily manipulated, Jesse forced herself to meet Parker's mocking gaze. She wasn't going to give him the satisfaction of knowing she'd been hurt.

"You know what? I'm not embarrassed to be a regular human being with regular human needs. At least I'm not such a failure I have to lie and cheat to get what I want." She flicked a dismissive glance over her ex-lover before turning her attention to Tegan. "You hired this second-rate actor to what . . . seduce me?"

Tegan narrowed her eyes, clearly disappointed by Jesse's reaction to Parker's betrayal. No doubt she'd hoped Jesse would be devastated. With a hint of the petulance that Jesse remembered from her childhood, she moved to thread her arm through Parker's, as if claiming him.

Good, Jesse bitterly acknowledged. She could have the worthless jackass.

"I didn't hire him," Tegan purred. "Unlike you, Parker tumbled madly in love with me."

Jesse shrugged. "If you say so."

"I do."

"If you're so much in love, then why was he in my bed?"

"Because I sent him there."

Jesse grimaced. "Quite the fairy-tale romance. You're just like your mom."

"I'm nothing like her," Tegan snapped, the anger that smoldered inside her glowing in the blue eyes. "I will never put myself in a position where I have to depend on a man."

"No?" Jesse arched a brow. "Then what is Parker?"

"A useful tool."

Despite the gnawing fear and sickening sense of disillusionment, Jesse felt a burst of satisfaction as Parker sent Tegan a glare of annoyance. They were both selfish narcissists who would eventually destroy each other. The knowledge helped to ease a portion of her resentment.

"Agreed. He's definitely a tool," Jesse drawled. "I'll have to take your word he's in any way useful."

Tegan ignored Parker's hiss of outrage at the insult. "He was the easiest means to get what should have been mine from the beginning."

"What's that?"

"My inheritance."

"What inheritance?"

"The one Mac would have given me if you hadn't been such a bitch."

Jesse stared at the younger woman in confusion. "You were his stepdaughter for what? Less than two years? You can't possibly think that gives you a claim to his inheritance."

"It would have been longer. He would have fought for me to stay with him if you'd given us a chance to get to know each other. But no. You had to make him feel guilty every time we spent a few moments together."

Jesse refused to feel guilty. She wasn't the bad guy. She hadn't lied, and tormented, and kidnapped someone because they were a sulky child who didn't get enough love.

"You talk about my dad like he threw you out of our house. It was Victoria's decision to leave."

"Not by choice."

"I was there, remember?" Jesse clenched her hands as the image of her father on his knees with his head bowed in pain seared through her mind. "I saw her pack her bags and storm out of the bar." She abruptly laughed, nearly forgetting Victoria's final act of treachery before leaving. "Oh wait, first she stole my college fund and then she drove away."

"Because she was running from my father."

Just for a second, Jesse thought she was talking about Mac, and she parted her lips in outrage. Then, she abruptly recalled that Tegan had revealed the truth about her father.

"You mean Buzz?"

Tegan's jaw hardened, as if she was clenching her teeth. "Why do you think she kept changing our identities each time we moved?"

"Because she was a serial killer?"

"My father was a total loser. He drank, he did drugs, and he slept with any sleazy whore who happened to be around."

"Your mom had strange taste in men," Jesse pointed out dryly.

Tegan wasn't amused. In fact, she looked like she was barely resisting the urge to give Jesse another slap.

"She was an idiot, but at least she had enough brains to get away from Buzz," she instead retorted in cold tones. "Unfortunately, he wasn't the kind of guy who appreciated being abandoned by his pregnant wife. Especially when he knew my mom had upgraded to a more prosperous lifestyle, leaving him to wallow in his squalor."

"What did he do?" Jesse asked, determined to keep Tegan talking.

Not only because she was genuinely curious, but she was clinging to the hope that she'd managed to contact emergency services and someone was on the way to save her.

Tegan shrugged. "At first he was content to be paid off for keeping my paternity a secret. Eventually, however, he wanted to have his cake and eat it too."

Jesse tried to imagine how a low-level druggie named Buzz could have any cake, let alone some left over to eat. He sounded like the sort of dude who was always scrambling for money. Then she recalled exactly what had happened to Victoria's husband.

"He was the one who shot Maitland in the head, not your mother," she breathed.

"Yes. I assume he thought it would scare my mom into going back with him to the trailer park. Along with the money she'd embezzled from his company."

Jesse snorted. The man obviously had fried every brain cell if he thought he could force Victoria to return to the trailer park.

"Instead, she took the cash and disappeared."

"Exactly. That's why we never settled down in one place."

Jesse had briefly considered the possibility that Victoria had hidden her identity to escape an abusive ex, but once she'd concluded that her stepmother was some sort of black widow, she'd dismissed the theory. A stark reminder that things weren't always as black-and-white as she wanted to believe.

Her father wasn't perfect. Victoria fought tooth and nail to crawl out of poverty. Even Tegan had battled a few demons. That didn't erase their sins, but it did give an insight into their motivations. Probably even Parker had some sort of sob story.

"Did Buzz kill Liam Tanner?" she asked, once again keeping Tegan talking.

"No, my mom drugged him and staged the fire along with the explosion after she overheard Liam telling his stripper that he was getting rid of us so she could move into his mansion."

It was said without emotion. Clearly, Tegan wasn't grieving that particular stepfather.

"That's when you came to Canton?"

"Eventually. When the money started to run low." Tegan curled her lips. "It was a cheaper place to live. Unfortunately, it didn't have the easy meal ticket my mom was hoping for. In the end, she was forced to marry Mac."

Jesse blinked, glaring at the woman who'd been the driving force in creating the tragedies in Jesse's life.

"*You* forced her. You were the one who wanted Mac as your stepfather. If you'd let her leave town, none of this would have happened."

"Shut up." Tegan looked annoyed. Jesse didn't know whether it was because Jesse had interrupted her story or because she didn't want to take the blame. "My mom was willing to endure the marriage for a few years, just to get back on her feet and start looking for her next husband. Unfortunately, she waited too long. Dear ol' Dad showed up."

"In Canton?"

Tegan nodded. "The day before we tried to leave town. He cornered her in the park, insisting that she leave with him."

So it hadn't been Adam Tillman threatening Victoria. Yet another mistake that Jesse had made. No wonder she ended up kidnapped in a decrepit boathouse. She'd been so stupid.

Her bout of self-pity was interrupted as she was struck by a sudden thought. "How did he find her? Canton isn't exactly the first place you would look for a missing wife."

"I have no idea. She was always careful to stay off the radar. No social media or large public gatherings where a picture might end up in the newspaper."

The mention of a picture jogged Jesse's memory. "It must have been Dix."

"Who?"

"A college kid who worked for Bea. He recognized Victoria from her days in the trailer park, when she was still Sylvie Fulton."

Tegan waved away the explanation, clearly not interested. "She didn't say anything about him. All I know is that she convinced my dad that she could get her hands on a large chunk of cash if he'd wait twenty-four hours."

"Yeah, *my* large chunk of cash."

Another dismissive wave of her hand. "Whatever. Mom had no intention of becoming a hostage to her ex, so we snuck off early."

"Snuck off?" Jesse rolled her eyes. "She staged a raging fight with my dad before storming off with my money."

"She didn't want Mac looking for us. Better to make a clean break so she could disappear and become someone new."

Jesse was confused. "She *did* disappear and become someone new."

"Is that what you think?" Tegan's hard laugh echoed eerily through the cramped space. "My dad might have been a loser, but he knew every dirty trick Victoria ever pulled. He was watching the bar when we drove away and followed us out of town. It was the first time I'd ever seen my mom panic."

Jesse stilled, realizing that she'd once again jumped to conclusions. A nasty habit that might literally be the death of her. With an effort, she tried to imagine Victoria in her pretty sports car, suddenly realizing her plan hadn't worked. No wonder she'd been on that gravel road. She'd been trying to avoid her demented ex.

"That's when she crashed her car?"

"Yes." Tegan's expression hardened, a sure sign she was battling intense emotions. "She hit her head on the steering wheel. I think it must have made her groggy, because she didn't even try to struggle when my dad opened the door and strangled her."

The words were said with such cold indifference it took Jesse a second to realize what she was saying.

"Wait. He killed her?"

"Yes."

"In front of you?"

Tegan glared at Jesse, as if infuriated by her appalled shock. "Don't act like you care. You hated both of us."

"Oh my God. That's awful." Jesse struggled to accept Victoria's brutal end. Tegan was right. She'd hated her stepmother. And now she hated Tegan. But that didn't mean she couldn't be horrified to think that a woman was strangled to death just because she wanted to leave her marriage. And a young girl had been forced to witness her mother's death. "I can't believe she's really gone."

"Ding dong the witch is dead," Tegan taunted.

With an effort, Jesse shoved aside her sympathy. Tegan intended to murder her. Who cared how she turned into a sociopath?

"What happened to Victoria after she was dead?"

"My dad loaded her body into the back of his truck and drove to a nearby lake. He let me say goodbye before he tossed her in, and then we were headed back to Arkansas, as if nothing had happened."

Jesse felt a pang of frustration. Clint Frazer was so close to witnessing what had happened that morning. What would have changed if he'd gone down to check on the crash? Victoria would probably still be alive and Tegan would never have been taken by her father. The futile wish that things had been different abruptly evaporated as Jesse realized exactly what Tegan had said.

He dumped her body in a nearby lake...

"Do you mean the lake behind Noah's house?"

"That's the one."

Jesse grunted, as if she'd taken a blow to the chest. She'd been more than blind. She'd been unforgivably dense.

"God, that was why you were putting flowers there when I saw you this morning," she rasped. "And why you were so desperate to buy Noah's house."

"Very good." Tegan's words were a mocking pat on the head. The bitch. "I didn't really love my mom. In fact, most of the time I hated her, but that lake is her final resting place. I didn't want someone draining the water and disturbing her. Not only because it would stir up unpleasant questions, but she'd earned some peace. Unfortunately, the stubborn bastard wouldn't sell. Now, thanks to Parker, I can at last have what I want."

Jesse leashed her anger. If she survived, she could hash through all the clues that had been staring her in the face, including the ruthless motivation of Reese Skylar to buy an aging farmhouse with mediocre value.

Right now, she was just trying to stay alive.

"My father's inheritance?"

"That's first. Next is Noah's house."

Jesse frowned. "You just said he'd never sell. Not for any amount of money."

"No, but his dad will." Tegan was back to purring, as if she recalled she was trying to act complacently in control of this encounter. "He's up to his ears in debt. Plus, with his son dead, he won't have any need for the ratty old house."

The world stopped. Just like that. One minute it was spinning out of control and the next she was floating in a fog of numb disbelief. It was like her brain couldn't process the mere thought that the big, tenderhearted man who carried the weight of everyone's troubles on his shoulders was gone.

Fate couldn't be that cruel.

"Dead." The word came out as a croak. "What did you do to him?"

"He came to the office this morning, babbling about my silver Mercedes. He accused me of trying to run you off the road and demanded that he look at the vehicle to see if there were any dents."

"It was you," Jesse snapped, a shard of pain piercing her numbness at the knowledge that it was entirely her fault that Noah had gone to confront Tegan.

If she hadn't told him about being run off the road, he would never have gone to confront her.

"Of course it was me. You shouldn't have been prying into my past," she chided. "Thankfully, I convinced him that I left the car at my house and he'd have to meet me there if he wanted to see it. He didn't know Parker was there. It was easy to knock him out and bring him here."

Knock him out? A portion of anguish started to ease. Maybe it wasn't too late. Maybe if the sheriff finally bothered to show up, they could save him, regardless of whether she made it.

"Where is he?" she demanded, glancing around the cramped space, as if she might have overlooked his large form tucked in a corner.

"He's outside in a boat, waiting for you to join him."

"He's still alive?" She desperately needed confirmation.

"For now," Tegan admitted. "We need to make the authorities believe the two of you drowned in a tragic accident. I don't want any questions asked when I demand my inheritance."

About to return her attention to her stepsister, Jesse's gaze was snagged by the tip of something sticking out from the bottom edge of the cot. It was nearly hidden by a pile of rotting netting, which was no doubt why Tegan or Parker hadn't noticed it. Jesse, however, had spent enough time in the boathouse to recognize the knob of an oar.

If she could get her hands on it, she had no doubt her years playing softball would come in handy. One whack with that oar would knock out at least one of her captors.

It was a start.

"Then let's get on with it," Parker abruptly intruded into the conversation. "We take any longer and the lumberjack is going to wake up. It was hard enough to get him in that boat. Not to mention this place is giving me the creeps."

Tegan turned her head to glare at her lover, as if she'd forgotten he was even there.

"Don't hurry me. I've waited a long time to have a reunion with my sister."

Parker scowled. "This wasn't the plan."

Jesse's mouth was dry as she tried to inch way down on the cot. Was it possible to provoke the annoyance brewing between them? All she needed was a moment or two of distraction to make a grab for the oar.

"Then what was the plan?" Jesse asked, scooting another inch.

Parker turned to send her a taunting smile. "You were supposed to hand over your inheritance. After that, I was going to have the pleasure of killing you."

Chapter 21

There was a nasty pleasure in Parker's voice, but Jesse could tell it was nothing more than shallow bravado. When push came to shove he would chicken out. Tegan was both the brains and the brawn of the operation. Parker was deadweight.

Hopefully, she could use it to stir Tegan's annoyance with him.

Jesse rolled her eyes. "You really thought you could seduce me and I would blindly hand over all my money to buy your seedy nightclub?"

"That's exactly what you were prepared to do." A taunting smile curved his lips. "Do you know how hard I was laughing when I convinced you that I wanted that trash fire of a nightclub? Not that I'm surprised you were ready to pour everything into it. I'm very persuasive." He blew her a kiss. "Especially in bed."

Jesse didn't have to pretend her shudder of disgust. "Not really. I'd already decided to dump you, along with our business partnership."

"Doubtful. I could have convinced you to come back like that." He snapped his fingers. "Have you forgotten? You adore me."

"You're a shallow prick who caught me in a moment of weakness and the mere thought of you touching me is repulsive. I'd rather crawl into bed with a snake."

"Oh yeah?" Parker flushed as he took a step forward. He didn't like the thought that he wasn't irresistible. "You came scurrying back to this hillbilly backwater to please me, didn't you?"

Jesse shook her head, as if he was too stupid to live. Then she deliberately turned her attention back to Tegan. "Parker is obviously a clueless pawn in your game. What was your real plan?"

"Hey ..." Parker started to protest, only to be waved into silence by Tegan.

The younger woman looked pleased to be acknowledged the mastermind of the operation.

"In the beginning my plan was simple," she informed Jesse, adding her own dramatic flair as she lifted a hand to smooth back her bleached hair. "After I was kidnapped by my father I spent the next four years being dragged from one crack house to another. My dad didn't want me, but he knew he could get handouts from the local charities if he had a kid. When I was sixteen he had the decency to overdose and I was free. I went to Hollywood to make my fortune." She turned to send her companion a glance that wasn't entirely affectionate. More ... long-suffering. "That's where I met Parker."

Jesse didn't allow herself to imagine what it must have been like for a young girl to be in the care of a violent drug user who'd strangled her mother in front of her. Tegan was the enemy. When it came time to swing the oar, she couldn't hesitate for a second.

"If you were in Hollywood making your fortune, why come back here?"

She clicked her tongue. "It turned out a lot of people have the same plan. I started to wonder if there was an easier way. That's when I began investigating what'd happened to my dear, sweet stepsister, Jesse Hudson."

"Why me?"

"Because you've been handed everything on a silver platter."

Jesse blinked. "You can't be serious. I was born in this small rural town you call a hillbilly backwater and raised by a single father because my mom died when I was just a baby. On top of that, I lived in an apartment above a crumbling bar that barely generated enough money to keep a roof over our heads. We never had a vacation, or fancy clothes. Hell, we barely went out to dinner unless it was a burger at Bea's Diner. Hardly a glamorous existence."

"You think any of that stuff matters?" Tegan was genuinely angry as she lifted her hand to tick off a list of grievances. "You had a devoted dad. A place you could call home. Friends and an entire town that treated you like you were something special just because your mom died when you were a baby." She made a sound of disgust. "Yes, you really suffered. Boo-hoo."

The world did that weird halting thing again. This time, however, it wasn't fear or grief that was squeezing her heart in a vise. It was the explosive realization that Tegan was right. Her scheming, selfish, vain stepsister had seen Jesse's life with a clarity that was shocking.

"It's true," she breathed, shaking her head in disbelief. "I was blessed."

Tegan's brows snapped together. She didn't want her moment in the spotlight interrupted. "I discovered you were working as a bartender. I also discovered that your dad was still missing, and that you owned the bar."

"My dad wasn't missing. They just hadn't found his body yet," Jesse deliberately interrupted again, scooting to the side. She was getting closer to the oar.

"I started to realize that you were sitting on a gold mine," Tegan continued, her features hard as she deliberately tried to punish Jesse. Obviously she didn't think her stepsister was properly appreciative of her cunning plans. "Well, not a gold mine. Mac Hudson was a nobody bartender in the middle of nowhere. He was never going to be worth much," she mocked. "But at least it would be enough money to get us a decent apartment and pay the bills until we got our big break."

Jesse refused to be provoked. "So you sent Parker to Chicago?"

"Yes, and I moved to Canton to set up my disguise as Reese Skylar."

"Do you really have a real estate license?"

"Of course. How do you think I made a living in between acting gigs?" Tegan shrugged. "It should have gone smoothly. You would put the bar up for sale and cash in your dad's life insurance policy. A few weeks later, you would write Parker a big fat check to buy the nightclub, and we could get rid of you. Easy-peasy." The atmosphere in the boathouse seemed to thicken. As if Tegan's hold on her volcanic emotions was slipping. Jesse sensed it was only a matter of time before she exploded and bad things happened. "Only you wouldn't follow the script. Not only did you drag your feet about selling the bar, but you started poking your nose where it didn't belong."

Jesse licked her lips, daring another scootch toward the end of the cot. "You were the one who tried to drive me out of town."

"A few pokes to hurry you along," Tegan admitted.

"The blow to the back of Bea's head was more than a poke."

"She shouldn't have followed me into the bar." Tegan sounded more annoyed than repentant for bashing the poor old lady. "I wanted to scrawl another message for you to leave or else, but she interrupted me."

"And last night you drugged me and flooded the cellar."

Surprisingly, Tegan sent her partner in crime a fierce glare. "That was Parker. A mistake, in the end."

For a second, Jesse was confused. Why would Tegan care that she'd been drugged? Oh wait. She was mad about the water that had allowed the foundation to crumble.

"Because it exposed my dad's body."

"Exactly. We can't sell the bar now." Tegan continued to glare at Parker. Her patience for the dim-witted boy toy was wearing thin. A bonus for Jesse. At last she leashed her annoyance to continue her gloating. "So I devised a new plan. One that was a lot easier after Noah conveniently walked into my trap and you were patiently waiting at his house." Her glare shifted to Jesse. "Of course you had to screw it up."

Jesse wondered what would have happened if Eric hadn't shown up and frightened her into running out of the back door of Noah's house. She'd probably be unconscious and tied up in a sinking boat.

Instead, Tegan had chosen to use the opportunity to prove how much smarter and more desirable she was, giving Jesse at least a small chance.

"So you keep telling me," she drawled. "Now what? You'll never get your money if anything happens to me."

"She's right," Parker dared to say, flinching as if he expected a blow.

Maybe he wasn't completely clueless.

"No, she's not right," Tegan snarled, not bothering to glance in his direction. Instead, she pointed a finger in Jesse's face. "I realized after they found Mac's bones that I don't need you. In fact, you're just in the way. Again. Once you're dead, the inheritance comes to me. Mac Hudson's daughter."

Jesse used the opportunity to lean to the side. She was close. Another inch and she could reach out and grab the oar. All she needed was a distraction.

"You're not in his will; his inheritance wouldn't go to you," she pointed out.

"Doesn't matter if I'm in the will or not," Tegan insisted. "He was married to my mother and they never divorced. Once I make the grand revelation that Reese Skylar is indeed the long-missing Tegan. Mac's beloved stepdaughter, they won't have any choice but to give me my money."

Jesse stared at her in confusion. "But they weren't married, were they?"

Tegan froze, as if genuinely shocked by Jesse's accusation. "What are you talking about? They went to Vegas for a quickie wedding, you dumbass. And don't act like you've forgotten. You pouted and stormed around the apartment for weeks after they got back."

Jesse refused to be distracted. "They might have gone to Vegas, but they weren't married. At least not legally. My dad checked after you and Victoria disappeared. He has legal proof it was a sham."

Tegan licked her lips. She'd no doubt known her mother had arranged a faux wedding, but she hadn't expected Jesse to discover the truth. Now she had to wonder if another plan was about to go to hell.

"It doesn't matter," she finally muttered. "Everyone believed they were married. I can easily get a fake marriage license. Who would question it?"

"Eric Walker, my dad's lawyer, would question it," Jesse assured her. "He knows the truth."

Tegan was shaking her head before Jesse finished speaking. "No."

"I showed him the letter from the Clark County Vital Records Office saying there was no marriage certificate. He'll never let you get your hands on my dad's inheritance."

The tension in the room amped up, sending a rash of goose bumps crawling over Jesse's skin. It felt like lightning about to strike. Or the seconds before an earthquake.

"What have you done?" Tegan growled, her eyes shining with a hectic fury.

Parker cautiously reached out. "Babe."

"What have you done?" Tegan screeched.

With an unholy scream, Tegan released the fury that had no doubt been boiling and churning inside her for years. She leaped toward Jesse, wildly swinging her fists. Thankfully, she was too angry to notice that Jesse wasn't trying to fight back. Instead, she rolled to the side, her fingers closing around the wooden knob.

Sending up a silent prayer that the oar wasn't broken or so rotten it would crumble at her touch, Jesse jerked it up, managing to connect with Tegan's vicious punch. There was a loud crack as the wooden board hit Tegan's upper arm with shocking force, followed by Tegan's shrill cry of pain. The sound was deafening in the cramped space, but the blow did nothing to faze the woman.

In fact, it just seemed to piss her off.

Aiming a kick at Jesse's knee, she continued to throw wild punches, apparently unaware of the blood that was flowing from a cut on her arm, where a splinter had sliced open her skin. Honestly, Jesse didn't doubt she could stab her stepsister in the heart and the demented fool wouldn't notice. She looked like a rabid dog, with her eyes wide and her lips pulled back in a snarl. She was even foaming at the mouth as she lost control.

Jesse struggled to get to her feet, unable to get a full swing while she was trapped on the cot. Unfortunately, Parker had followed Tegan forward, whether to calm her crazed attack or to help maul Jesse was impossible to guess, but his presence kept her trapped in place.

Twisting to the side, Jesse managed to stab the oar in Tegan's direction, catching her in the gut even as her stepsister's fist slammed against the side of her face. Her ears rang, but with a shake of her head, she managed to give another jab. She was managing to keep Tegan at bay, but she wasn't gaining any ground.

A dangerous position, as Parker finally decided to tag team with his partner. Reaching out, he wrapped his fingers around Jesse's throat. She pulled back as he tried to squeeze, but she was trapped by the cot behind her and Tegan in front of her.

Cursing at the irony of Parker Moreau discovering he had a spine at the worst possible moment, Jesse released a low growl. She might die, but she was getting in a few good whacks first.

With a surge of desperation, Jesse pretended to jab the oar at Tegan, only to twirl it downward and shove it between her legs. Then, with a sharp jerk, she thrust it to the side, knocking the younger woman off-balance. At the same time, she turned her head, meeting Parker's terrified gaze before she headbutted him with enough force to send him stumbling backward.

She hadn't really gained much advantage as her two attackers swiftly regained their balance, but she could at least breathe again. And she could finally lift the oar high enough for a good solid swing.

Spreading her feet and clenching her muscles as she prepared for a last moment of glory, Jesse barely noticed a shadow pass by the dusty window. It wasn't until the door silently slid open that she realized she was no longer alone.

Noah stepped into the room, his face grim as he moved to grab Parker by the back of his shirt and casually threw him against the wall, with enough force to bust the window and send up a cloud of dust.

Parker squealed as he flew through the air, his arms windmilling. Then there was blessed silence as his skull connected with the window frame and his eyes rolled back in his head as he crumpled to the ground.

Jesse took a second to appreciate the sight of her former lover sprawled on the filthy floor, blood running from his nose, which she'd busted, before she turned back to her stepsister, who was backtracking as she belatedly came to her senses.

She'd been in complete control of the encounter; now she was trapped in a corner. But like any rat, she was scrambling for a way to escape.

"Jesse. We can work this out—"

"Shut up, bitch."

Stepping toward the woman who'd gleefully plotted her murder, Jesse swung the oar with a practiced ease. It'd been years since she played softball, but she still had the skill to modify her angle as Tegan hastily ducked to the side.

With a sickening thud, the oar smashed against the woman's cheek, the old wood once again cracking from the force of the blow. Tegan immediately dropped like a sack of potatoes, her face swelling from the force of the impact.

Did that mean she was still alive?

Jesse shrugged, dropping the oar as she walked straight into Noah's waiting arms. Who cared what happened to her stepsister or her worthless ex-lover?

She'd survived.

Nothing else mattered.

Chapter 22

Despite Jesse's protest that she was fine, the sheriff and EMTs that belatedly arrived at the boathouse insisted that she take the ambulance, along with Noah, to the local hospital. Once there, she was poked and prodded and X-rayed once again before a doctor arrived to inform her that she was badly bruised and there were traces of drugs left in her system, but she would recover.

He reluctantly released her, along with Noah, with the promise they would be together in case either of them passed out or became dizzy.

It'd been late by the time they returned to Canton, and neither was in the mood to discuss what had happened. Especially not after Adam Tillman displayed his usual lack of empathy by arriving just minutes after they'd pulled into the driveway, demanding that they give a statement.

Jesse didn't fight. What was the point? She was no longer worried about Sheriff Tillman, or whether he thought she was somehow involved. Especially not after he'd grudgingly revealed that he was being forced to turn over the case to the FBI.

Missing persons was one thing. Dead bodies popping up around town was something else. The state authorities had decided to send in the bigwigs.

Too late, as far as Jesse was concerned, but better late than never.

They would be the ones to prosecute Tegan and Parker, who were currently lodged in the jail.

After a restless night, Jesse woke early to discover that Noah was already up and out of the house. A quick glance out of the kitchen window revealed he was at the edge of the lake, where a large group of people were standing around a tarp spread on the bank.

Jesse whirled around, refusing to watch. She already knew that Victoria's remains were down there. She didn't need to witness them being wrapped up and hauled away.

Not when she had something more important to do.

Drinking a cup of coffee in the hopes of clearing the lingering cobwebs from her mind, Jesse headed out of the front door. It was another beautiful morning, with plenty of sunshine and a nice breeze that was laced with the scent of roses.

Jesse shuddered. For some reason, the roses made her think about death and funerals.

Or maybe it was just her dark mood.

Zigzagging her way through town, she at last entered the alley behind the Tap Room. The police tape had been removed, although Adam warned her that the FBI would be wanting to do their own investigation. That was fine with her. She wasn't planning to stay there. Probably never again. Instead, she walked past the dumpster and knocked on the back door of the diner.

It took a few minutes, but at last Bea appeared, still wearing her dressing gown, with her hair pulled back in a headband. She looked like she'd just gotten out of bed. Odd, considering she was usually up by four in the morning to bake her pastry goodies. Of course, the diner was still closed, and it was possible she was taking advantage of the opportunity to sleep in.

Or it could be something else. Maybe she'd shared Jesse's restless night.

"Come in, come in." Bea waved her into the kitchen, a smile of pleasure spreading across her face. "I've been so worried about you."

Fluttering toward the center of the room, she pulled out a seat at the table. "Sit down. Are you sure you should be out of the hospital?"

Jesse hid a wince as she entered the gleaming white and stainless-steel kitchen. The brightness stabbed into the dull ache that lingered in her brain.

"I'm fine," she insisted, taking a seat. "A bump on the head, but my skull is too thick to fracture. That's the doctor's diagnosis, not mine."

"I'm just glad you're okay." Bea grabbed a basket of muffins from the counter before taking her own seat. "I couldn't believe when I heard that Reese Skylar was actually Tegan. All those years she was missing..."

"I can't believe I didn't recognize her," Jesse said dryly.

"How could you? She didn't look anything like the girl we knew."

"No," Jesse agreed, still annoyed that she'd been so gullible. She'd assumed she was too jaded to be easily fooled, and then she'd fallen hook, line, and sinker for every lie that Tegan and Parker had fed her. "But she hadn't really changed. She was still a selfish, petty brat who always wanted what she couldn't have."

"Such a shame." Bea pinched her lips. "I blame that mother of hers. Terrible woman. I heard rumors that the authorities found her body in the lake behind Noah's house early this morning."

Jesse arched a brow. She wasn't surprised that the rumors of Victoria being dumped in Noah's lake were running rampant, but she was astonished that they already knew that she'd been pulled out. There must be someone with binoculars keeping tabs on the FBI.

"I know they were there working when I left," Jesse confirmed the gossip, watching Bea's reaction. "Tegan confessed that her mother never made it out of Canton alive. Her ex-husband tracked her down and strangled her after she crashed her car. He was obviously a monster."

Bea clicked her tongue. "I know it's not nice to blame the victim, but Victoria had it coming. I mean, when you choose to lie and cheat and manipulate innocent people, bad things are bound to happen, right? I'm just relieved that he didn't hurt you."

Jesse wasn't shocked by the older woman's reaction. Just... sad.

"I think I was safe enough. His only interest was in Victoria and his daughter."

"Well, thankfully it's all over now." Bea grabbed one of the muffins. "The past can finally rest."

"Not quite yet."

"No?"

Jesse reached up to rub the aching muscles at the back of her neck. "I didn't sleep much last night."

"Oh my dear. Are you in pain?"

"It wasn't that. I was puzzling over something Tegan told me."

Bea arched her brows, taking a bite of her muffin. "I wouldn't trust anything she said."

"She intended to kill me," Jesse pointed out. "She had no reason to lie at that point."

"What did she say?"

"That she didn't know how Buzz managed to track them down."

"Buzz?" Bea furrowed her brow in confusion. "Was that her father's name?"

"It think it was a nickname. It's still stupid, but I don't think he was overly burdened with brains."

"Probably not."

Jesse studied the woman she'd known her entire life. "Which makes me wonder how he found them after Victoria managed to stay hidden for a dozen years."

"Who knows?"

"My first thought was that it might have been Dix. He recognized Victoria as Sylvie Fulton from Little Rock during a birthday party for Sam and Tegan," Jesse admitted. "It was easy to assume that he was responsible for Buzz's presence in Canton."

Bea abruptly set aside her half-eaten muffin before rising to her feet. "We should have some tea. I brewed it fresh this morning."

Jesse watched the older woman pull out the pitcher of tea and grab two tall glasses.

"But I'd already talked to Dix, and he truly believed it was a case of mistaken identity. More importantly, he didn't care. I doubt he cares about anything unless he can drink it, smoke it, or get it in his bed."

Bea poured out the tea before returning to the table and placing a glass in front of Jesse. She settled back in her chair, lifting her glass to take a sip.

"Does it matter?" she asked at last.

Jesse's heart felt as if it had an anchor tied to it, trying to drag it down to her toes. She should walk out of the diner and keep walking. It would be a lot less painful in the end.

But she couldn't.

She'd come too far.

"You know it matters, Bea," she said gently. "Did you overhear Dix call Victoria by her real name?"

Bea hesitated before stiffening her spine and tilting her chin to a defiant angle. "Yes. Not that I was surprised. I knew Victoria was a liar from the minute she arrived in Canton."

"What did you do?"

"I asked one of my college workers to do a search for Sylvie Fulton on the internet. I told her that Sylvie was my niece, and that I'd lost contact with her. She found a Facebook page that listed her as a missing person, along with a phone number to contact." Bea took another gulp of tea, as if her mouth was dry. "I didn't know it was her husband. I just wanted her gone."

Jesse was confused. She hadn't seen the Facebook page pop up. Then realization hit with a sickening blow. It had obviously been removed by Buzz after he'd tracked down and strangled his wife.

"Why not tell my dad what you found?" she asked.

"Do you think he would have listened? And even if he had, Victoria would have found some way to make him forgive her lies. He was blinded by his lust."

Jesse couldn't argue. Her dad was obsessed with his beautiful young wife. He would have forgiven everything if she'd revealed the truth.

Well, maybe not everything. He might have been disturbed by the fact that she'd killed her former husband and burned his corpse.

Not that the what ifs mattered. She was more concerned with what actually *did* happen.

"You let Dad be arrested."

"I knew it would never go to trial. It was a charade performed to pacify that ridiculous deputy."

Jesse made a sound of horror. "He spent months in jail. He was devastated by the time they let him out."

Bea flushed at Jesse's sharp tone, but her defiance remained firmly intact. "It gave him time to forget about Victoria. He was dangerously obsessed with his need to find her. I did it for him."

With an effort, Jesse forced herself to temper her seething frustration. She wasn't going to get answers by accusing the older woman. She had to convince her to tell the truth.

"Bea." She reached across the table to pat her arm in a comforting gesture. "What did you do?"

Bea's gaze lowered to her fingers, which were clutched around the glass. "He wouldn't listen."

"Listen to what?"

"To what I had to say when he came to see me after he left the courthouse—"

"He came here?" Jesse interrupted, the breath squeezing from her lungs as she at last understood.

Of course. She'd never been able to understand how something could have happened to her father between the courthouse and the bar. There was the possibility that someone had picked him up in a vehicle, or forced him into a building when he was passing by, but it made no sense that no one had noticed anything.

This was a town who kept a close watch on their neighbors.

Now it made sense. He'd strolled into the diner like he did every other day. There was nothing to catch anyone's attention.

"Yes," Bea continued. "He wanted to thank me for all I'd done over the years. And to tell me goodbye."

"That's what he said? Goodbye?"

"He was planning to pack up and leave." Bea lifted her glass and drained the last of the tea. "He said he couldn't stay in Canton. Not after everything that had happened."

Jesse wasn't entirely surprised. Her dad had hinted in the courthouse that he needed a break from Canton. Who could blame him?

Obviously Bea Hartman.

"But you didn't want him to leave," Jesse said. It wasn't a question.

A sudden fury twisted Bea's features. "After all I'd done for him! All the years of being his friend and confidante?" she rasped, smacking her hand on the table. "I was always here when he needed a shoulder to cry on, or someone to take care of you, or to loan him money to keep his lights on. It was me. And I did it without asking for anything in return. All I wanted was for us to be together. A family, even if it wasn't a traditional one. And he was going to abandon me."

Jesse's stomach twisted. Last night she'd paced the floor, deciphering each word that Tegan had spewed during their confrontation. Her stepsister had filled in most of the blanks that had haunted Jesse, but not the biggest one.

What had happened to her dad?

Victoria was dead and Tegan was already in Little Rock with her drug-dealing dad. They obviously weren't responsible.

It wasn't until she was wondering if it was Dix who'd contacted Buzz that she realized there might have been someone who'd overheard Dix call Victoria by her real name. The most obvious choice would be his employer. The woman who claimed she had no memory of him despite the fact that Dix worked in her diner as a dishwasher.

Oddly, from there it'd been painfully easy to imagine Bea as the killer. At least after she considered the fact that her dad hadn't been murdered out of hate. But out of love.

"What did you do?"

"I told him there was a leak in the cellar. I asked him to go down there and see if he could fix it."

"And then?"

"I shot him in the back of the head."

A pained gasp was wrenched from her throat. "Oh God."

Bea never glanced up, her shoulders hunched. "Once I was sure he was dead, I put him in an old walk-in freezer I have down there."

Jesse blinked back her tears. Her poor dad. He would never have dreamed this woman could be so evil. He'd walked into that cellar without once suspecting he was walking into his grave.

"And then you brought me muffins, as if nothing was wrong," Jesse accused.

"What choice did I have? I needed him to stay. Don't you see? He belonged to me."

Jesse shook her head. There was no point in arguing. This woman was obviously unhinged, no matter how well she might be able to hide her madness.

"How did he get in the foundation?"

"I needed repairs done. I asked Noah to come to replace the old bricks. Once he finished, I pulled them out before they dried and..." Her words trailed away, and she reached up to wipe a layer of sweat that had bloomed on her forehead. "And I put your dad's body between our two walls. Then I replaced the bricks and put in new mortar. It was sloppy, but no one goes down there."

Jesse swallowed the lump in her throat. She had her answers as to what had happened. But that didn't ease her confusion.

"Why?" she demanded. "Why move his body after he was dead?"

"I couldn't let him stay with her, could I?" Bea muttered. "He deserved better, even if he disappointed me. Besides, I wanted him to rest in the home he loved so much."

Jesse parted her lips to point out that her dad was beyond caring where his remains were buried when the older woman's words sank in.

"Wait. What do you mean, you didn't want him with *her*?"

Bea managed to hunch even lower. "That's another story."

Dread rolled through Jesse, but she forced herself to demand answers. "Tell me, Bea. It's time for the truth. The whole truth."

There was a tense silence before Bea heaved a deep sigh. "I suppose you're right."

"What happened?"

"Kelly showed up late one night a couple of years ago. Just out of the blue."

It took a second for Jesse to realize who Bea meant. "Noah's ex?"

"Horrible girl. A sneaky, selfish bitch," Bea snapped.

"What did she want?"

Bea visibly shuddered as she recalled the visit. "She sat here at this table and told me that she'd come to the diner on the day your father was released from jail. She said that her mother was in the hospital and was begging for one of my peach pies. The woman was already losing her mind, and Kelly was willing to do anything to please her." Bea licked her lips, as if they were dry. "When she found I'd closed the restaurant for the day to go to Mac's hearing, she went to the back door to see if it was unlocked. I suppose she intended to break in and see if she could find some pie." Bea sniffed. "Like I said, sneaky."

"Did she get in?"

"No, but she was peeking through the window and saw me urging your dad to go down the stairs. Then she heard the gunshot."

Jesse flinched. Bea said the words with a callous indifference. As if she wasn't talking about killing the man she claimed to love.

"Why didn't she say anything?"

"She told me she was scared." Bea made a sound of disgust. "Just another lie. She was simply waiting for the right time to use the information."

"That's why she came here?"

"Yes. After Joe dumped her and moved in with another woman she decided she didn't want to stay in Des Moines."

"Did she want to come back here?"

"Good lord, no. She thought she was too good for Canton. She wanted to go to Florida. She said she intended to buy a condo on the beach, but she needed money. *My* money."

Jesse arched a brow. Kelly had obviously been a victim, but her willingness to profit from Mac Hudson's murder made Jesse less than sympathetic. If Kelly had gone to the sheriff the moment she heard the gunshot, she could have prevented so much heartache.

"What did you do?"

"I told her I'd give her what cash I had in the safe and then offered her a piece of the peach pie that her mother had wanted all those years ago. It seemed fitting. She sat where you're sitting now and cleaned her plate. By the time I returned with the cash, I didn't have to worry about her anymore."

Ice crawled down Jesse's spine. She didn't have to ask how Kelly had died. Bea obviously had sprinkled some sort of poison into the pie.

"She's still in the freezer downstairs?"

Bea nodded. "Her old car is in the shed across the alley. I occasionally put out a rumor that she'd been seen by someone in Des Moines, but honestly, it's never been necessary. No one ever missed her."

A sharp, bitter regret sliced through Jesse. So much pain. So much loss.

"Oh Bea."

Bea at last looked up, a strange glitter in her eyes as she reached out to push the glass in front of Jesse an inch closer.

"Drink your tea, Jesse."

Something in the older woman's expression had Jesse slowly rising to her feet, a new sense of horror swelling in her heart. There was something in the tea. Just as there had been something in the peach pie.

That was why Bea was dripping in sweat and a line of blue was visible around her lips.

"I don't think so." Jesse pulled out her phone to dial 911. It was becoming a habit.

"Please drink, Jesse," the older woman pleaded, her voice faltering. "Come with me. We can all be together again. A real family."

"No, Bea." Jesse headed for the door to wait for the ambulance without looking back. "You were never my family."

Epilogue

Two Weeks Later

Jesse stood at the end of the pathway that led to the lake behind Noah's house. The past days had gone by in a blur. Dealing with the FBI, who continued to question her about Tegan and Parker, along with Bea's confession. The older woman was whisked to the hospital quick enough to save her life, but she remained unconscious. Jesse privately thought she was trying to will herself to die. It was the only way she could be with the man she'd loved to the point of madness.

And then there'd been the small ceremony she'd arranged to lay her father's bones to rest in a grave next to his beloved wife.

Now, she stood staring at the lake, not sure what had brought her to this spot. Her bags were packed and stowed in her pickup, and she'd already dropped off the keys to the Tap Room with her lawyer to hold on to until she decided what she intended to do with the place.

There was nothing keeping her here.

But even as she headed out of Noah's house, she'd found her footsteps leading her to this spot.

Maybe she needed a few minutes to gather her courage. Or maybe she was waiting.

The sound of approaching footsteps brought a smile to her lips. Yes, she'd been waiting.

Slowly turning, she watched Noah appear around the curve of the pathway, wearing the T-shirt with the lumberyard logo that was stretched deliciously tight over his chest and faded jeans. His hair was wet from a shower and he smelled of warm cedar.

Her heart fluttered, her hands itching to smooth over his rippling muscles. Only the knowledge she wasn't ready for what a man like Noah would demand kept her from doing something silly.

And of course, there was the fact that he was dealing with his own grief. Kelly might have been his ex-wife, but he'd loved her. It would take time for him to come to terms with her death.

"I heard you packing your bags when I was in the shower." He reached out to run a finger along the tattoos on her bare arm, sending a delicious shiver through her. "Running again?"

"Not running," she denied. "This time I'm searching."

"Searching for what?"

"Me." She sighed. "She's been lost a long time."

He studied her with an expression of sadness. As if he was disappointed by her answer.

"Do you think you're going to find her in Chicago?"

Jesse shuddered. That was the last place on her list. "No, although that's another past I'm going to have to clean up eventually." She shrugged. "Right now I just want to drive with no destination in mind."

"It sounds like a dream."

She chuckled. "It would be your nightmare."

"True." He shook his head. "I'm an old stick-in-the-mud who can't imagine living anywhere but Canton. Will you ever return?"

"Eventually. I have stuff I'll have to deal with, and people I want to visit again." Giving in to her impulse, Jesse stepped forward and placed her palms flat on his chest. Then, going up onto her tiptoes, she swept a soft kiss over his lips. "You know, there's no reason you couldn't come find me. If you ever get the urge. A few weeks away from Canton wouldn't hurt."

"Maybe." He deepened the kiss, searing her with the promise of an explosive passion before reluctantly stepping back. "Until then, take care of yourself."

"I'm going to." She glanced over her shoulder toward the tree that marked the spot where Victoria's body was discovered. "I didn't find the closure I was hoping for, but I did remind myself that you can never take life for granted. The past can wait, along with the future." She turned back to Noah, brushing her fingers down his cheek. "I'm off to enjoy the right here, right now, and hopefully meet the real Jesse Hudson along the way." With a smile, she headed up the pathway. "See ya later, Noah Allen."

"That's a promise."

Visit our website at
KensingtonBooks.com
to sign up for our newsletters, read more from your favorite authors, see books by series, view reading group guides, and more!

BOOK CLUB
BETWEEN THE CHAPTERS

Become a Part of Our
Between the Chapters Book Club
Community and Join the Conversation

Betweenthechapters.net

Submit your book review for a chance to win exclusive Between the Chapters swag you can't get anywhere else!
https://www.kensingtonbooks.com/pages/review/